The Hybrid King
Prophecy

by Sharlina Honeycutt

RoseDog 🐾 Books
PITTSBURGH, PENNSYLVANIA 15238

RoseDog Books
585 Alpha Drive
Suite 103
Pittsburgh, PA 15238
Visit our website at www.rosedogbookstore.com

ISBN: 978-1-6480-4199-0
eISBN: 978-1-6480-4215-7

Prologue

She had seen the future of Atlantis. She received many visions in the past that she had prophesized to the council, but this one was different, more significant. Even though she did not understand it completely, she comprehended its importance. What to do with this vision was her dilemma. She had kept its secret for over twenty annutides. Looking around at the cave's smooth walls had given her the idea. Writing it down before she proclaimed it to the Atlantic Council preserved it in the event that her prophecy was dismissed. She did not deceive herself into thinking that this prophecy would be wholeheartedly embraced by the council. There were already divisions surfacing throughout Atlantis.

Instinctively, she clutched the large pearl that rested above her heart. Its history was as old as the Atlantis Kingdom, passed down through the royal line for thousands of tides. This eventide, she would give Marius the pearl, and then read him the prophecy. She would tell it like a story. Marius did love a good story. Being so young, would he understand the significance of the prophecy and the value of the pearl? Somehow she had to help him realize it was more than just a story, that it was the future. Possibly Atlantis and the Mer Kingdom's very existence rested upon his young shoulders. No one else had to know about this cave, the pearl, or Marius' involvement just yet. She still had a few tides to set the plans in motion; however, she felt urgency for its inception. She didn't know how or when these events would unfold, but she knew they would, and that Marius was wrapped in every layer. Dark tides were coming to Atlantis and the Mer Kingdom.

Book One

A mountain is composed of tiny grains of earth. The ocean is made up of tiny drops of water. Even so, life is but an endless series of little details, actions, speeches, and thoughts. And the consequences whether good or bad of even the least of them are far-reaching.

—Sivananda

Chapter One

The water off the Mid-Atlantic coast of the United States is often referred to as the Graveyard of the Atlantic. Here the Gulf Stream drifting up from the south merges with the Labrador Current flowing down from the north. For centuries, this union that caused the formation of shifting shoals, which helped form barrier islands, has brought about the untimely demise of many ships and schooners. Every year thousands of treasure hunters comb these waters hoping to discover a fortune hidden on the ocean floor, buried by centuries of sand. The treasure part of the story never really interested Michael Moses. Instead, what Michael found intriguing were the stories of the people—the victims these murky waters claimed and the survivors who battled the salty brine and emerged victorious over it. Discovering their stories was what led him here almost every morning as far back as he could remember.

Michael had never ventured far beyond the waters of his childhood. He and generations of his family had lived by the ocean as far back as he could trace his ancestry. His heritage was what his mother had called a "mixed bag." He never really understood what that meant until he was old enough to do the research himself. Heritage had always been important to his family, especially through his maternal line. It was through her side that his empathetic abilities had come. This ability set Michael apart from others in his circle of friends and even in his immediate family. Only his mother understood. Both her mother and her grandfather had been Empaths. She recognized the ability in Michael almost from his birth and knew the joyful burden he would carry his entire life. She had nurtured this gift and helped Michael refine it. He still didn't understand its powers or its origin completely, but using it now was as natural for him as reading, writing, and speaking. This gift was not something Michael shared about himself. Few would understand it. Most people would consider him abnormal. So during his adolescence and young adulthood, he masked it, hiding his ability to read and understand people's emotions from even his closest friends. That is until he met Thad Destin, his best friend. What a difference moving thirty miles had made in the course of Michael's life.

When the job offer had come from the university, Michael knew this was the job for him. Taking the job meant taking a cut in pay, but that ranked way down the list of his priorities. The Anthropology position had been custom-made for him. Without a second thought, he immediately accepted the position and moved thirty miles to the university town that had been his home ever since. Here he met Thad and eventually his beautiful wife Charise. Yes, life had been good to Michael Moses.

This morning a nor'easter that had cut a wide path of destruction had blown out and moved on. Restlessness had awakened him before the sun had risen and prompted him to take a solitary walk on the shore. The beach was deserted. Locals still slept, exhausted from waiting out the storm and relieved the storm had ended. Tourists had long since departed for the season. Michael had the beach to himself apart from the birds that floated on the water and the occasional fiddler crab that scurried across the sand.

Overnight, tons of sand had disappeared from the beach and ocean-front houses whose pylons once stood on sandy dunes a good distance from the surf now waded in the water. Michael walked toward a few of the remaining dunes that somehow managed to escape the maw of the hungry tide. As he approached them, something shiny caught his eye. By this time, the sun had peeked above the horizon slowly casting an orange glow across the water and its shore. Sometimes a storm roiled the waters enough to bring long-lost relics to the shore from the floor of the ocean. Usually though, the items it deposited ashore were worthless pieces of human garbage and debris. His curiosity piqued, he headed toward the area where he had seen the reflection.

Picking his way carefully through the flattened sea oats, Michael kept his eyes focused on the area. As he closed the distance, some unseen force pulled at him, urging him closer. The corner of a very large shell jutted out of the sand. He knelt down in front of it, unsure if his eyes were really seeing what appeared right in front of him—a huge, dark shell spanning a width of over three feet with some kind of strange etchings. Michael, who had lived at the beach his entire life, had never seen anything like it. From his study of sociology and language, Michael realized he had never seen this writing and that this find, at least from an archeological standpoint, could be significant. Nestled in the corner of the shell and partially buried in the sand was the top of a large pearl attached to a thick golden chain with the same strange writing on its links. That was what had glimmered in the sunlight. With shaking fingers, he reached down with both hands and scooped up the huge milky white orb out of the sand. He cupped it in his hands while the sand sifted through his fingers. The pearl, larger than a robin's egg, had to be priceless. Many questions swirled through Michael's racing mind: *How did the shell get here? From where had it come? Why was this necklace buried in the sand with this strange shell? And what about the strange writing on the shell? What did it mean and who had written it?*

He realized time was of the essence. He nervously glanced over his shoulder. Before long, more and more people would make their way to the beach. This shell could be valuable, so he had to do something to protect it from the curious on-lookers who might venture close to where he was and alert the news media about it just so they could be on television. Michael struggled with the next step. What should he do? He sat holding the pearl, not wanting to make this decision hastily.

Keep it safe. Keep it secret.

Michael jumped up startled at the words. He looked around at the deserted beach. There was no one there. He was still completely alone.

Keep it safe. Keep it secret.

The voice he heard was barely a whisper, distinctively female. The hairs prickled along the nape of his neck. This kind of encounter was nothing new to Michael. Being an Empath, he had connected with people and even spirits before. But still, it never failed to catch him by surprise. He felt the desperation in her plea. Even though he could not see her, he felt her presence and her fear. He knew she was referring to the pearl. The power of her emotion poured through him, almost drowning him with its urgency. Without a second thought, Michael knew what he was supposed to do. He put the pearl in his coat pocket, determined to keep it safe and keep it a secret, at least for now. As soon as he made that decision, he knew it was the right one. He felt her fear turn to relief, and the wind around him turn warm, caressing him like a friendly good-bye kiss. Suddenly, like the tide shifting, Michael felt her spirit ebbing away as she whispered her final breath.

Keep it safe. Keep it secret.

His hand rested over the pearl now hidden inside the pocket of this thick windbreaker. He would honor her request. No one would know about this discovery. Michael pulled out his cell phone and called the university research center. He would not leave this site until it was secured. The shell would become the property of the university; the pearl, however, would remain with him.

Chapter Two

Thad had always heard the sea does not reward those who are too anxious, too greedy, or too impatient. He recognized the irony. Those were the qualities that epitomized the ocean. He had been nothing but patient for the past fifteen months, coming daily to this same stretch of ocean. But was there any reward? *Not yet*, his mind whispered.

He swam to the ocean floor and surveyed the "laboratory" where he had been conducting his research. Thad Destin considered himself an expert on the ocean, if there was such a thing. He had spent his childhood on the coast, had studied in its tide pools to earn his bachelor's, master's, and Ph.D. in marine biology, and now worked daily in its depths researching the marine life whose very existence was threatened by commercial development.

Thad had spent his entire childhood around the ocean. He loved its waters, but he also realized its danger; its lulling, murderous melody could hypnotize even the most seasoned mariner into believing the waters were benevolent. Thad knew better. He had lost countless friends, colleagues, and family to the hungry depths. His uncle had succumbed to its smothering arms. The ocean followed no human laws or limits. It simply gave and took, not necessarily in equal measure, on its own terms and conditions. That alone demanded respect.

He came again, day after day to this section of ocean about two miles off the coast to determine the long-term effects of the oil spill several years prior. He had placed a camera on the ocean floor to track the migration of marine life and had set up equipment to monitor the health of the food supply. The oil companies boasted about their renewed efforts to clean up their mistake quickly, promising to monitor and offset immediately any lasting negative effects on the marine life. Like it was that simple. People's memories were short and their grace of forgiveness was extensive when the prospect of jobs was involved. Data, however, didn't lie. Thad had been here every day collecting samples. On the surface, the ocean looked healthy, but its deeper layers revealed a lurking, slow-growing illness waiting to be diagnosed. It was just a matter of time, when and not if, before the terminal symptoms would begin to reveal themselves. Then it would be too late. Thad retrieved the material from the recorder and hastily made his way to the surface.

Selale hid among the seaweed watching him. She recognized him on sight. Many tides had passed since his arrival. He had consistently come to this same place for a long time. Time moved differently in Atlantis, her underwater world. No sun measured a day, a night, or an hour. In the human world, time was as important as it was unimportant in the Mer Kingdom. Selale knew the danger of encountering a human, yet this one she perceived posed no threat to her or her world. From her observation, she deducted he was some kind of scientist—again, a human word. She wondered what compelled him to come to this spot every day, wondered what he discovered about her world. She longed to ask him, so she could explain what she knew. She discovered him purely by chance. This was her domain, her world. The Merman restrictions and limitations did not exist this far away from land. Initially, she had been outraged that her freedom in her world had been curtailed. Until his arrival here, she moved freely below and up to the surface. This area was her haven, her escape from the confines of the kingdom. Few of the SCEROH sentries ventured this far from the Center City. Now she had to exercise caution. Seeing him for the first time shocked her, shattering the idyllic sanctuary she loved. Because she was so surprised by his presence, he almost saw her, so she had to conceal herself. She found a perfect hiding place, one far enough away where she could see him, but he could not see her. Now, watching him had become a frequent occurrence. Luckily for her, he always came alone. *What was he doing here?* Selale wondered as she watched him work with his equipment, and then pull something out from one of the pieces, and hastily swim back to the surface. Yestertide, she had boldly swum to the area where he had set up his work after she made sure he had left and would not come back. She wanted to understand his work, understand him, and gain some insight as to his purpose for coming here. After so many tides, she knew his comings and goings, and secretly, anticipated his next visit.

The Atlantic Council's warning roared in her ears. *Intentional contact between humans and mermen is strictly forbidden.* She understood the rule. She knew why: the prophecy. From the earliest childhood lessons taught by her parents, she had heard the prophecy, knew the story of her great-great-grandmere's vision by heart. The prophecy permeated through all of the rules, rituals, and routines of the Mer Kingdom of Atlantis. What should have been a source of anticipation that unified all mermen had ironically caused a division many tides ago. The Mer Kingdom now had split into two factions with two entirely different ideologies regarding humans: education versus eradication. Sadly, Selale's own father and his twin brother, her only uncle, represented the starkly different sides.

When she thought about her uncle, a cold current engulfed her from head to tail. She tried not to think about Uncle Calder. Marius, her father, was the antithesis of his brother. He brought warmth and joy to the domain he ruled. He was the heir apparent, a king loved by his subjects. The throne should have been passed down to him, but before his father, King Nero, Selale's grandfather, had died, the struggle for power had already begun. To salvage any vestiges of family harmony, King Nero divided the duties and the boundaries of the Mer Kingdom between his two sons. His own grandmere, the prophetess, had warned of the consequences of the division. Even though Nero knew the prophecy, he split control of Atlantis. Selale often wondered if it was because of the prophecy or in spite of it that led to his decision.

Now thinking about this human and his presence here, she realized she had to consider the implications. Every contact with a human, regardless how innocuous, stirred the murky waters of the prophecy causing it to swirl the question of *What if?* Unlike her great-great-grandmere, she was not blessed with the gift of prophecy. Perhaps it was just a lack of faith in what she could not see. Her studies in history, linguistics, and literature were to blame. She loved a good story—stories of the past from different worlds above on land and below in the sea. She enjoyed their vivid characters, their twisting plots, and their timeless themes. But she understood they were merely that—works of fiction or embellishment of the truth. Deep down inside a corner of her heart, she harbored a thread of doubt. She kept it moored tightly, afraid that once it sailed to her lips giving voice to thought, it would become only a story. Entire Mer generations had come and gone since that vision so long ago. Yet another larger part of her believed the prophecy with every fiber of her being. Even though there were minor problems in the kingdom, no real danger presented itself to demand a savior just yet. When, not if, that situation came, Selale hoped she would recognize it for what it was—the tide that desperately needed the prophecy's fulfillment: a king both human and merman who would unite the worlds of land and sea and save Atlantis from destruction.

Chapter Three

Marius adjourned the Atlantic Council meeting and slowly swam back to his dwelling. His watery kingdom floated by as he swam, his mind too preoccupied to enjoy the ancient pathways engineers from generations before him had constructed or the recent Benthic passages he himself had designed. He needed solitude and several currents to think. To say he was worried about the affairs of Atlantis was an understatement. Mermen lived in peace with the fish and all marine life, so why couldn't it be the same with humans? In the back of his mind he knew that with every tide that ebbed and flowed, more and more mermen were abandoning his philosophy and aligning theirs with that of Calder's and the SCEROH. The Atlantic Council meeting evidenced it. Rahwah, one of the youngest councilmen, had questioned the prophecy's legitimacy aloud. Aloud. *Did he really call it a fictional story for children?* Marius sighed. He just didn't understand this youthful generation of mermen. He knew better than anyone else the prophecy's details and how important its preservation was to the future of Atlantis. He remembered the tide vividly when his great-grandmother had led him to the cave and told him the vision she had seen. Marius surfaced in the cave and let the memory envelop him.

"*Great-Grandmere, where are we going?*"

"*Somewhere special. Somewhere secret. Can you keep a secret, Marius?*" she asked. He looked hurt, like she should already know the answer to that question. Still, he remembered nodding his head to affirm the answer. "*Good, because I am sharing this only with you. No one else will know. It will be our own secret.*" She smiled, but he recollected there had been a sadness that had tinged the corners of her mouth, as if her smile didn't quite reach her eyes.

"*Keep swimming, Marius. It is just a little further on,*" she said, looking over her shoulder constantly.

"*What are you looking for, Great-Grandmere? You keep looking back. Are you looking for Calder or Papa?*" he asked her.

"*No, I just want to make sure no one else shares this secret with us. No one else can know what I am going to tell you this tide. Understand? Not Calder or your Papa.*" She tried to make her voice sound light, but still there was tension that even then he had recognized. He understood that this was important.

He had never been to this stretch of ocean before, its unfamiliar structures made him uneasy, but Great-Grandmere held tightly to his hand, gently guiding him to their destination. They had passed the education chamber leagues ago where Marius spent each tide learning different languages, some from the Atlantis, but just as importantly, from the human world as well. Few mermen his age were chosen for this educational opportunity. Great-Grandmere was especially proud of his studies there. She herself had studied there many tides ago. He knew she held more knowledge of the past and present than any merman in all the oceans. She possessed the Mystical Gifts of Prophecy and Healing. He knew her importance to Atlantis. She was the first Healer in over a centennitide to embody both Mystical Gifts.

They approached a towering mountain of stone and coral loom-ing in the waters ahead. Debris littered its base. Marius shivered, unsure if it was from fear or anticipation. Perhaps it was a little of both. Darkness made it difficult to see where they were going, but it would soon be light. This tide had come and gone quickly. He clung more tightly to his great-grandmere's hand and let her lead him. He wasn't going to miss out on this secret no matter how far or how deep they had to swim. Because he trusted her implicitly, the tension slowly left him and his swimming became more relaxed. They en-tered from the side of the mountain through a small, narrow cave obscured by seaweed. Upwards they swam through a series of caves and winding tunnels, the waters becoming brighter and brighter. Suddenly they surfaced, and Marius found himself basking in golden light. His great-grandmere laughed at his expression.

"What do you think of my secret place, Marius? No one knows about this place apart from me and now you. Amazing, isn't it? I call this place Beulah Cave. From your studies, you know what it means I take it."

"It means beautiful. Oh, what a perfect name for a perfect place. How did you find it, Great-Grandmere? Why is there so much light? What is all that writing on the wall?" He swam around the perimeter of the waters that pooled at the top of the vast cavern, his eyes scanning the golden circumference of wall. He pulled himself out of the water up on a shelf of rock and sat there ready to hear about their secret cave. She slowly pulled herself out of the water as well and smiled at him.

"Slow down! One thing at time, tadpole! First, I found this cave purely by accident. When I was about your age, I foolishly thought I wanted an eel for a pet, so I followed him to this moun-tain. He swam through that same hole we entered, and being the nosy mermaid I was and still am, I explored every inch of this

mountain. I forgot about that silly eel. On the fourth tide of my exploration, I found this cave. I have been coming here ever since, almost one hundred twenty annutides. It's where I receive most of my visions. As for the light, we are close to the surface of the ocean. We did swim up quite a way. Through the side tunnels, light reflects off the gold that is embedded in the walls, illuminating it like the sun." She paused and becoming more serious, she took a deep breath. "Marius, I have something for you and much more to tell you, but we don't have many tides."

Marius jerked his head suddenly to look at her. "What do you mean we don't have many tides? Fear caused his heart to race. "Are you sick, Great-Grandmere?"

She took his hand and turned it over, palm up. "I'm old and tired. It's just I have so much that I want to tell you. That's all." In his hand, she gently placed a large milky white pearl that dangled at the end of a golden chain. Random words were engraved into each link. She then closed her hand around his causing him to hold the pearl in his small fist. "That pearl was given to me by my grandmere over one hundred annutides ago. It is as old as the kingdom of Atlantis itself. It holds great power. This tide I am giving it to you. There is greatness in you, Marius. You are a light in these dark waters."

"But Great-Grandmere, what does it do? What do the words mean? Tell me how it works." Holding it up to the light, he rolled the pearl between his two fingers trying to peer into its opaqueness.

"The power lies not in the pearl, but in its possessor. We will talk about the pearl later. Right now, you need to hear the details of a vision I had many annutides ago. No one has heard this prophecy in its entirety yet, so listen to the story as I tell it to you. I have written the prophecy on these walls to ensure its permanence, and so you won't forget a single detail. And Marius, the details are important."

Now all these tides later, no one else had seen their secret place. Before she had passed, his great-grandmere had written the prophecy down to preserve its history for all of Atlantis and the entire Mer Kingdom. Only Marius knew that some details had been omitted—details that directly related to him. With her death, Prophecy and Healing had died as well. His hand touched the pearl hanging around his neck. His eyes scanned the complete script that decorated the golden walls of Beulah Cave. *Oh, Great-Grandmere, you had more faith in me than I have in myself.* He could feel the darkness closing in on his kingdom, and the weight of self-doubt pressed down on his shoulders. Some of his own Atlantic Council didn't believe in the prophecy; some claimed they believed, but only half-heartedly. If his own council wavered so in their convictions, whom could he trust and how could he prevent this deep division from tearing Atlantis apart?

Chapter Four

Calder brooded in his chamber. The SCEROH's officers had just left with some interesting news. There had been some tension and disagreement at last night's Atlantic Council meeting between Marius and some of the council. This morntide, Rahwah, one of the young councilmen, had resigned his position and then brazenly contacted the SCEROH, vowing to align his allegiance with them. Calder smiled. Defection to his camp seemed to increase with every annutide, but it was slow, too slow.

Impatience surged through him. He wanted the throne and complete control, but now was not the tide. *Just a little while longer.* As those words echoed in his mind, he thrashed his tail hard against the base of the chair where he sat. Marius and his idealistic foolishness blocked the path to gaining complete control of the ocean. He had never liked to share. Calder scoffed at the notion. If anyone should have known that, it was his father. What Nero was thinking by dividing the kingdom instead of just naming the heir to the throne he would never know or begin to understand.

From the genesis of the Mer Kingdom of Atlantis, its control had never been divided between two members of the royal line. Because the kingdom had been so vast, the original founders created smaller, more manageable regions to help the king govern the tide-to-tide affairs that arose. Each of the five regions appointed the charter members as a governor, and even until this present tide, one of his descendants still governed each of the five regions of the underwater kingdom of Atlantis. This group of mermen was the beginning of the Atlantic Council. Several generations ago, each of the five regions added another representative. Now there were twelve members, ten from the five regions and two at-large positions appointed by the king. The royal line descended from the scientist who created their species. The other men unanimously elected him to singularly lead and rule their new species and its underwater kingdom. It set a precedent that up until King Nero's rule had been strictly followed—one king who ruled Atlantis. To say the division of power between Nero's two sons was scandalous was an understatement. It created quite the stir, especially with the older generation of Merpeople. Eventually, the decision was accepted. Now, twenty-five annutides later, it still remained divided; Calder still shared control with Marius. But change was coming.

Already he had started the process. A plan was taking shape. He just needed to exercise patience. The kingdom would eventually be his, but it was still several annutides away. Every tide, more and more mermen and women from every region of Atlantis were coming around to his way of thinking— humankind was the enemy. Out of this philosophy, SCEROH had been born. The Society for Complete Eradication and Removal of Humankind was his baby. This was the realm he ruled and he brooked no rivalry for control of it. Everyone understood who was in charge. He had coercion, manipulation, and yes, brute force at his disposal. Humans had no part in the waters of Atlantis. Their meddling had caused great problems. Ridding these waters of their presence was his mission, his duty to preserve their way of life.

He had seen the handiwork of humans and watched as their ideas of progress destroyed everything in its path. Mankind had taken the only mermaid he had ever unconditionally loved. He knew her death had made him bitter, but it had also made him more equipped to lead the Mer Kingdom. He was no longer that idealistic young boy who had loved deeply, lived freely, and viewed humans positively. He had a responsibility to protect his people from humans, no matter what had been foretold.

As for the prophecy, what a wave of nonsense! How Marius had been so gullible to believe that fairy tale was beyond his comprehension. Calder even wondered if he was mentally stable. Sure, Great-Grandmere had believed it, had seen it in one of her visions, but not all of her visions had come true. He could understand why she would believe so wholeheartedly. Why did Marius believe this story of a mermaid falling in love with a human? The idea was preposterous. It was like falling in love with an octopus! To his way of thinking, it didn't matter if contact between humans and mermen happened merely by chance or if it was intentional. It could not be ignored; it would not be tolerated. Humans must continue to live in ignorance of Merman existence. This protected the entire Merman race. By eliminating any human who had contact with the Mer Kingdom, he and the SCEROH prevented the prophecy from ever becoming reality.

Chapter Five

He was tired, and it was only 10:00 A.M. He had already taught two classes and met with the dean of academics. Thad left his university office with a stack of papers in his hand. Sometime before the next two days, he had to read each paper, make suggestions for improvement, and return them to his students. That work was in addition to his own research materials he had to review and record. Right now he was headed to a faculty board meeting regarding all research projects being conducted and next year's budget. He had to swing by his house and retrieve some of the data he had recorded. There had been no time to view the latest recording. He would do that later today.

"Good morning, Professor Destin," chorused a group of students sitting on the lawn of the university.

"That it is! See you all in class on Thursday. And Rob, I do mean all," Thad emphasized his point by staring right at the football star sitting in the circle of young ladies. He had missed at least three of Thad's classes since the football season had ended two weeks ago.

"Yes sir, Professor Destin. You can count on me to be there," Rob said a little too brightly.

Thad walked past the student union building. His house sat on the edge of the next street over, just off campus, so he could swing by quickly to get his documents. As the science chairman, he had gathered reports from each member conducting a research project. At the moment, there was only one other. The botany professor had just begun working on a project in the last month, so his data was very lean. His project, however, had been going on for months. He knew he had to account for data he had collected in his research in order for funding from an anonymous donor to continue. He had spent hours over the last week compiling the readings and preparing documents to outline his findings. The results disturbed him. Whether the donor would find his data sufficient to continue its funding was the real issue. Thad knew that with a little more time, which translated to a little more money, he would be able to formulate a theory as to what the long-term effects of this contamination would be.

As he crossed his yard and climbed the front steps, he wondered if this donor was tied to the petroleum giant responsible for the mess in the first place. He dismissed the thought. No need worrying about that at the moment. He entered the front door and grabbed the folder sitting on the foyer table. Thad took a cleansing breath and slowly exhaled. He glanced at the recording sitting on the desk in the next room. *Tonight*, he thought. *I will watch it tonight.* Turning, he hastily locked the door and jogged back to the campus.

The meeting had not started when Thad walked into the room. He had told his colleague and best friend Michael Moses to save him a seat. Was it wise to sit beside Michael? No, he knew both of them would wind up laughing at something and once again get called down like students. Michael was already raising and lowering his eyebrows. Thad knew mischief was already a-brewing. Without a second thought, he slid into the empty chair.

Two friends could not have been any different. Michael was married; Thad was single. Michael was black with curly, shortly cropped hair; Thad was white with a blond mane that needed a good trim. Michael was an anthropologist who loved studying and getting to know people on a very personal level; Thad was a marine biologist who would rather get to know fish. Yet the two had been drawn to each other right from the beginning of their introduction. They had come to the university the same year, and since then, the two had become best friends. Michael's wife Charise was pregnant, expecting their first child in less than four months. He couldn't stop smiling. Even now Michael sat there with a silly grin on his face.

"Ladies and Gentlemen, let's get started. I have called this meeting for several reasons. If you will look at the agenda each of you received at your seat, you will see there is much to discuss. First let's hear updates on various research projects being conducted in each department. Then we will discuss next school year's budget which involves the rest of the items on the agenda. We will begin with the arts department. Lester?"

There had been talk of a financial budget crisis facing the university. Rumors had been swirling through every major, every department. This was especially worrisome for the sciences. It was the university's largest department, almost double the size of many others. Over one-fourth of the current students had declared a science as a major. Thad knew many of the other departments resented their numbers and the funding the science department received. He was prepared to fight tooth and nail to keep it that way.

Michael and the history department reported next. Michael's department had several research projects being conducted, but one large project had just started that involved the chief anthropology, sociology, and archeology professors working together. Michael had instigated the dig after finding the shell. Now the scope of the project would involve many departments. Some of the findings could be interesting considering they were working at the coast. The project was in its infancy, but a few artifacts from an apparent ancient civilization they had uncovered were promising, especially one gigantic shell with interesting markings that resembled hieroglyphics or an ancient language. These findings grabbed Thad's attention. He leaned forward trying to concentrate on every detail. Michael saw the machinery of Thad's mind turning. Addressing the rest of the faculty members, Michael concluded, "That's all I have." He made his way back to his seat next to his curious friend.

Immediately Thad whispered, "Could I come down and examine this shell, Michael? I would be able to tell about the type of marine life. It's not much, but it may offer more insight."

Michael was already nodding his head. "Our department had already discussed it. I will talk to you a little more after the meeting is over."

Only the science department's report remained. Thad described the progress that the botany research project had made and discussed its goals. Then he elaborated on the research he had been conducting for the last fifteen months. He handed each board member a copy of the data he had collected along with a graph detailing the increased toxin levels of the ocean. His voice conveyed his concern as he finished up the report.

"According to the data, this stretch of ocean is just a microcosm of the larger problem facing our ocean. My research will continue for about six more months at this location, and then I will collect more data from an entirely different location. By cross-referencing the data, I expect to see a similar pattern of toxin levels from the Gulf to the Carolinas. Are there any questions? If not, that concludes the science department's report." Thad sat down as the dean stood up.

"Finally," he said, "I come to the matter of the upcoming year's budget. I know the rumor mill has been churning. To be honest, it is as bad as the rumors indicate. We will be facing some deep cuts if the revenue levels remain where they are projected. Right now I don't have specifics, but I can tell you that every department will be affected. As the department chairs, it is your job to start trimming the excess and even some of the essentials. We will reconvene in two months for the final budget numbers. Prepare a report detailing the cuts you can make and the cuts you may have to make. Are there any questions?" He faced a silent assembly. They seemed too stunned to speak. After a long silence, Michael asked a question.

"How will these cuts affect our student population? They are the reason we do what we do," he finished.

Classic Michael, thought Thad. *He is thinking of the students while every other person here is thinking of himself.* It made Thad happy that he was his best friend. He knew that Michael's concern for others was genuine. He had a special gift of understanding difficult circumstances from many different perspectives. Some more discussion about increased tuition ensued, and the dean reassured the board that tuition increase was minimal. As the meeting adjourned, the two best friends lingered in the board room.

"So, you found a strange, giant shell, did you? When were you going to spring this on me? Over a couple of beers or better yet, a board meeting? What other secrets are you keeping from your best friend?" Even though there was lightheartedness to his banter, Michael could tell Thad's feelings were hurt.

"I am a man of mystery, my friend. Seriously, I just unearthed it completely yesterday morning and sent it to be cleaned. I didn't examine it closely until this morning when the entire team got a closer look. We discussed bringing you on board due to your knowledge of marine life. Could you come by my office tomorrow some time? We'll go examine it together. I'm gonna have to take a rain check on the beer. I've got a hot date with Charise. Get this, she called this morning and wants me to bring her some chocolate chip cookies and dill pickles home today. Man, talk about a mystery! This pregnancy thing is crazy. I mean really—pickles and cookies? See you tomorrow, buddy." Shaking his head and mumbling about weird food combinations, Michael left the board room. Thad laughed at the bemused expression on his best friend's face.

He gathered his materials and headed out the door toward his house. He too had a hot date with the recording he had retrieved yesterday. Yeah, he was strange, but the thought of viewing the recording excited him much more than any date he had been on in the last two years. He would watch it and evaluate the migration of marine life to see if anything interesting was recorded. *Who knows,* he thought. *I may discover a new species of fish.* He laughed at the ridiculous notion as he walked up his front steps.

Chapter Six

Michael knew something was wrong the minute he pulled into the driveway. He felt it before he turned in. His fear was confirmed when Charise didn't meet him at the door. He called her name as he entered the house. A low moan came from the nursery.

"Charise? Where are you? What's wrong?" Alarm pitched his voice higher than normal. He came to the nursery and stopped at the door. In the darkness, Charise sat in the rocking chair in the corner. He ran to her side. "What is it? Are you in labor? What's going on? Talk to me, please, Charise," Michael pleaded.

"It's the baby. He hasn't moved. I even ate some chocolate to stir him up, but nothing. I thought if I sat really still, he would move. Michael, he hasn't moved in several days. My baby, my baby," she wailed. Tears ran down her cheeks as she started to sob.

He bent down and scooped her up in his arms. "We are going to see the doctor. You'll see; everything's gonna be all right. Just wrap your arms around my neck and hold on tight. I'm here for you and always will be. Shhh, don't cry, honey." Fear clutched his heart, but he tamped it down. He had to be strong. He gently loaded Charise into the car and drove fast. The hospital was only six miles away.

He pulled into the emergency entrance and jumped out of the car. A nurse met him at the door. He quickly explained the situation as he unloaded his wife from the car. He placed her in a wheelchair and followed the nurse into the emergency room.

After several rounds of tests and hours of waiting, the obstetrician on call came into the room. His grim expression caused Charise to start crying again. "There is no easy way to give you this news. I'm sorry, but the baby is dead. Charise, it is nothing you did. There seemed to be some genetic defect in his heart. Please accept my condolences. I know this is devastating. We are going to admit you. We have decided to bring in a specialist tomorrow to do a genetic profile. He will elaborate on the test and why we need to do it. Right now, let me explain what will happen over the course of the next day or two." Both Charise and Michael were deaf to his explanation. They only knew that the baby they so wanted would never arrive.

After the doctor left, Michael took Charise in his arms. They sat locked in each other's embrace, too overwhelmed with emotion, too numb to speak. Michael knew he needed to call Thad, but he couldn't make himself let go of his grieving wife. The life they had dreamed of and planned for their child had now shifted into some dark nightmare. Michael closed his eyes and prayed once again to wake up from the black sleep that threatened to smother him, but when he opened his eyes, he realized it was no dream. His child was gone. The joy of all the other families celebrating the births of their newborn sons or daughters in the nearby rooms sliced through Michael's entire being. How ironic that he could feel their joy when he felt so much pain and loss. Michael let his mind close off their feelings. He needed time to focus on Charise and to allow himself to grieve. He would not become bitter because of others' joy and his loss. He realized this would be the toughest week of their marriage. Healing would be slow.

When a nurse came in to examine Charise, Michael left the room to call Thad.

Thad set up the recording so he could view it. He had already analyzed the water samples and recorded the data. There had been little change in the last week. That data was promising. With that finished, his full attention could be focused on the marine life and the migration patterns he had been tracking.

Sharks, rays, dolphin, and other smaller species came within view of the camera. The numbers seemed slightly down according to his calculations. He noted this on the spreadsheet on his computer. Out of the corner of his eye, he saw something swim by in the background of the waterscape. He stood staring hard at the screen, waiting for the creature to come closer to the camera's lens. *What is that?*

The phone rang suddenly startling Thad. Reaching for the phone, his hand groped for it without his eyes leaving the screen. Sighing, he paused the recording and looked at the number on the screen. A smile spread across his face.

"What's up, bud? Your hot date not work out? Don't tell me you forgot the pickles," Thad chuckled. The silence on the other end let him know something was wrong. "What is it, Michael?"

"Thad, I'm at the hospital. There have been complications," he choked up, unable to finish his sentence. After several seconds ticked by, he finally said, "We lost him."

"I'm coming there now. I'll be there in fifteen minutes." Without a glance back, Thad rushed out of the house to be with his best friend.

Chapter Seven

Selale studied her father from across the chamber. He was unaware of her scrutiny. She enjoyed watching him work, loved his passion for the Merpeople whom he ruled. He was embroiled in a discussion with one of the Atlantic councilmen. Tension filled the waters.

"I am not going to be swayed with this guilt you seem to think I should feel," Marius snapped. He flicked his tail in frustration then lowered his head to collect himself. "Rahwah's defection hurts, but I refuse to be bullied into changing my position regarding the value of life, even that of humans. I will never, and I repeat, never agree with Calder on this issue. Humans are tied to our past, and especially to our future. We share a kindred connection with them. Harming them equates to harming ourselves. Let's not discuss this anymore." With that, he dismissed the councilman. He turned and caught Selale watching him. A smile spread across his face. It changed his demeanor completely.

"Selale, my favorite daughter, come sit down here beside me. What brings you here so early this tide? Didn't your mother and I teach you not to stare at others? Ah, it seems we failed in so many ways," he chuckled.

"Well, I won't mention that I am your only daughter; I will just focus on the favorite part. What was all that about?" she asked referring to the dismissed councilman. "It appeared he was as frustrated as you. What's going on here, Papa?" She looked into his eyes and studied his expression. Her concern was genuine.

Marius sighed. He just didn't know where to start. He didn't want to burden her with his problems, but he knew he could confide in her. This tide, he needed a confidante and an ally. "Tell me what you know about the prophecy, Selale. Tell it to me as a story like I used to tell you when you were a child." Sadness filled his voice that pierced Selale's heart. She hugged him tightly, her love for him overwhelming her like a wave.

"Is that what all the disagreement was about—the prophecy? Oh, Papa, I just don't know what some mermen are thinking. It's like—it's like they have forgotten who they are. How can that happen? I know the prophecy. I believe it to be true, and you are exactly right in what you said. We are tied to man in the past and future. I believe it, but I wish I shared your unadulterated certainty that it will all come to pass as the story I have been told predicts. When, Papa, will it happen? We have waited so long." Selale smiled. "Sorry. I know that wasn't the story." Suddenly Marius felt a burning sensation beneath the robe he wore around his shoulders, its source originating from the pearl. He had a strange, faraway expression on his face. His eyes glanced down to the large pearl, and then they focused on something only seen by him. He was here, but not here. The Atlantis Pearl had a way of getting his attention. It took him to the cave. "Papa, where are you? Talk about a short attention span," Selale laughed.

The pearl had caused the idea to surface in his mind. *Why had he not thought of this before?* It made such logical sense that Marius couldn't believe it had taken the pearl's burning to give him this revelation. "Come with me." He grabbed Selale's tiny hand and led her through the passageway. "Don't ask me any questions. Just trust me, all right? Do you trust me, Selale?" He stopped abruptly and looked her in the eyes.

She nodded even though she was confused with the turn of events, "Completely and with all my heart, Papa."

"All right, come with me and don't let go," said Marius. He moved a stone in the floor and suddenly a portal opened revealing a hidden tunnel. With a wry smile, he turned to Selale and raised his eyebrows but said nothing. Still retaining a tight grip, he led her through the dark, murky waters. The tunnel stretched many leagues. Selale marveled that her father had a concealed passageway. Where it led, she had no idea. She knew this tunnel served an important purpose because of its hidden, deceptive nature. The smooth walls appeared to stretch endlessly ahead of them. Finally, they swam toward lighter waters and suddenly emerged out into the open ocean.

Light floated through the waters, its depths brightened by the surface's increasing light. Every corner, every nook was somehow transformed. Marius followed the familiar route. He knew it by heart, even without the light. The further they swam, the more secure Marius became with this decision. Levity filled his heart—a feeling that had somehow become foreign to him. He welcomed it as they approached their destination.

Selale had no idea where they were going. Once they emerged from the tunnel, the surroundings were unfamiliar. These were waters she did not recognize. She had only read about this area in school. Annutides before, right after he came to power, Marius had declared this area off-limits due to its toxic waters. She didn't understand why they were here, but she followed without question. They swam straight toward a mountain wavering in the distance, its height impressive against the backdrop of ocean.

Marius led Selale around the base of the mound to an opening hidden by seaweed and other flora. They disappeared into the narrow crevice. She was unable to orient herself in the darkness that pervaded the mountain's interior, so she kept a tight grip on her father's hand. She knew they were swimming up, but she was clueless as to where up was. Obviously, this too was another of her father's secrets.

The higher they swam, the brighter the waters became. Marius increased his speed. Selale thought she would burst from the anticipation of getting there. Suddenly as they broke through the surface of the water, she gasped in amazement. Wonder at the cave's intense beauty and light rendered her speechless. Her eyes scanned the complete circumference of the cave before she tore them away to look at her father.

"What is this place?" she whispered in reverence. Even as she asked the question, her eyes spotted writing engraved on the wall. She turned to face her father. "Now it is your turn to tell me the story of the tunnel and this cave. I feel there's magic here because it has me under its spell. I want to know everything starting from the beginning." She settled on a smooth bank of rock around the edge of the pond of water. Marius pulled himself up beside her. He smiled with understanding.

"I had a similar to reaction the first time I was brought here by my great-grandmere. I was only ten annutides, but is seems like last tide. Great-Grand-mere wrote the prophecy on the cave walls before she proclaimed it to the Atlantic Council. She told me the details omitted from the version she told the council. That same tide she also gave me the Atlantis pearl that I wear around my neck. This pearl and the golden chain can be traced back to Atlan-tis, the lost island where our ancestors lived like humans. It is from those sur-vivors that our race, our species evolved. This pearl is one of the few relics that remain from that civilization." Here Marius paused his story to pull the pearl from beneath his robe. He lifted the chain over his head and placed it in Selale's hand. She ran her fingers over the large orb's smooth surface. It was about the size of an eye. She returned it to her father. He placed it back around his neck.

"Are there any other remnants from that society? I remember studying about the genesis of the merman race in history class, but how do I know those facts are true?" Selale questioned.

"Legend has it that near the beginning of our society, there were actually two pearls, identical in every way. Over the tides, one has been lost. There are, of course, the tomes that contain the details of our history penned by the orig-inal survivors from the island, but those volumes are housed in the Records Chamber. No one has access to them except the curator. Unfortunately, one of those volumes is also missing. Even though there is written proof, I believe it has a great deal more to do with faith. So it is with the prophecy. That is the reason I have brought you here. Come with me." Marius slid back into the water followed by Selale. He swam to the wall covered with writing.

"This is the prophecy of the Hybrid King. I know we don't have enough of the tide left for you to read it in its entirety, but I do want you to read it, study it, and absorb all the details later. For some reason, you and I are en-twined in the tentacles of its details. I don't know how, but we are. The pearl prompted me to bring you here. No one has seen this cave except for my great-grandmere, you, and me. Not even Ettore has seen this cave. Important parts of the prophecy were omitted from the one she proclaimed to the Atlantic Council. For some reason, she didn't trust them with all the details even back then. Perhaps she realized they wouldn't embrace it as truth." He turned to Selale with an expression of determination. "Once you read it, you will understand why I believe in the prophecy and know that it reveals truth about the future of Atlantis and our entire race. It predicts events that have already occurred, events that only I understand as significant.

"As for the tunnel, that was constructed solely by me. Remember, I did study engineering along with language. While Interpretation is one of the Mystical Gifts passed down through the royal line, engineering and construction were my loves as a student. It took me an entire annutide to design it and three more to complete it. Even back then when I first inherited the leadership of Atlantis, I knew I had to keep this place a secret. It had to be protected. So, I built the tunnel to conceal my comings and goings to and from the cave, and then I condemned the area around this mountain. Because everyone believes it is toxic, no one ventures here." He shrugged. "It has worked. Could you get back here without me leading you? The tunnel is at your disposal."

Selale smiled. "I definitely can get here, but I don't want to leave yet. I want to read it all, this tide, right now. Just the thought of leaving this cave without knowing every detail causes panic to well up inside me. It's like I must read it or explode! Oh, Papa," she exclaimed as she leaped in his arms and threw hers around his neck, "You don't know how much it means that you trusted me with this. I love you so much." She hugged him fiercely. "Can't we stay just a little more of the tide?"

"I don't want my absence to raise suspicion. Come back later after the tide has shifted. Then you can stay as long as you like. This place is named Beulah Cave. It is now as much yours as it is mine, just one more thing you have inherited from me. It belongs to both of us. Come, let's get back." Reluctantly, she took his hand, and they swam back the way they had come.

As they swam, he wondered about her work in the Translation Chamber. Selale had inherited the Mystical Gift of Interpretation. There were six gifts passed down through the royal line. Marius himself possessed three of the

Mystical Gifts: Interpretation, Water-Bending, and Sand-Stirring. While Ettore had inherited the Water-Bending Gift, Selale had delighted Marius by possessing the Gift of Interpretation. From a young age, she had shown an advanced aptitude for it. Nothing could have pleased Marius more. He inquired, "Have you finished your translation of the documents the Council sent you? They did seem to contain some information from the human world about these waters."

"I finished my translation, but I sent it over to the Ecological Chamber for them to analyze the impact of the information on the waters, marine life, plant life, and our people. I'm sure they will send their report soon," she assured him.

They entered the tunnel and swam back to chamber they had left earlier. Selale smiled as she watched the tunnel's entrance vanish right before her eyes. "Impressive, Papa, impressive."

He laughed and said, "You act surprised. I'm a merman of many talents, of many gifts. But now, I must head to the council chambers. More discussion is needed on the SCEROH's proposal presented a few tides ago." He kissed her on the forehead. He ran his finger down her cheek, winked and then swam away.

Selale watched him leave. Pride welled up inside her that he was her father. How she had been granted such good fortune, she would never understand. They had always been close, shared a special connection. Now, Beulah Cave and its secret bonded them even more closely.

Chapter Eight

Thad spent the night sitting at the hospital with Michael. He had listened to, cried with, and ached for Michael and Charise. About sunrise, he left to get them coffee. He was devastated. He could not imagine how they felt. Stopping in a deserted hall, he leaned against a wall and let the tears flow. He cried until he was spent. Finally, composing himself, he entered the coffee shop and ordered two coffees.

Thad returned to the lobby. Michael stood looking out the window at the sunrise. Today would be another tough day for him and Charise, one of many more to come Thad feared. He walked over to Michael and offered him a cup of coffee. Michael took the steaming cup of coffee and turned to face his friend.

"Thanks, man. This night has been less miserable because you were here for us. You've done enough for now, so go on home. Please let the department know where I am. I will leave it up to you as to what you want to tell them. My classes are supposed to meet at the site today, so you may need to meet them there. I don't know when I will be back." Here he paused and stared down an empty hall. He continued, "Charise and I are supposed to meet with the geneticist later this morning. I'll know more after that," his voice trailed off. Clearing his throat, he placed his free arm around Thad's shoulder and said, "You're a great friend. I'm gonna get back to Charise. I'll call you later."

Overcome with emotion again, Thad could only nod as Michael squeezed him in a hug. Both turned and went their separate ways, each knowing that they would not be far from the other's thoughts.

Thad was numb as he drove mindlessly home and parked in his driveway. He glanced at his watch. It was only three A.M. He walked in his front door, threw his keys in the tray, and headed straight to his bed. In his periphery, he saw the computer screen still frozen with the recording he had just started watching when he got Michael's phone call. He needed rest right now. The recording would have to wait. Removing his shoes, he crawled into bed and exhaustion overtook him in a matter of minutes.

When he awoke, the sun was varnishing the sky, its rays trying to dispel the darkness. The night's events replayed in his mind. Thad moaned, wishing it had only been a nightmare, but reality suddenly weighed him down. As Michael's friend, he knew the responsibility of notifying the university rested with him, alleviating one burden from Michael and Charise. Being friends with Michael had taught Thad so much about putting others first. Without Michael, Thad knew he would still be the young, arrogant, selfish science geek who came to the university years ago. Through Michael's friendship, Thad had learned trust and true acceptance. Slowly he lifted himself out of bed and headed to the shower.

After showering, he headed to the university. He stopped by the history department and informed them of Michael and Charise's loss. Thad had no classes scheduled for today, which allowed him time to drive to the beach and notify the research project's site manager. He arrived in less than fifteen minutes and walked to the site. From the number of tents and amount of equipment, it seemed the entire history department was involved. People worked with deliberation and precision, completely focused on their individual task. Thad spotted the site manager standing in the midst of eager students. He recognized Thad. He finished talking with the students and made his way over to Thad, his hand extended with a smile.

"Welcome, Dr. Destin. We are so excited that you came. Obviously, you have talked with Michael. Where is he this morning?" He looked over Thad's shoulder hoping to spy the history department chairman.

Pausing, Thad cleared his throat and quietly said, "Michael and Charise lost their baby this morning. He is at the hospital with his wife. I don't know when he'll return. I can try to cover some of his duties here today, but you may need to make other arrangements for the rest of the week. They will know more today after they run more tests and meet with the doctors. I'm sorry to be the bearer of such terrible news today." Trying to regain his composure, he stopped talking and gazed out at the ocean. The blue waters never failed to comfort him. He turned back to the manager and said, "Please put me to work so I can get my mind off this for a while."

As they walked to the largest tent, the manager said, "Michael found some type of large shell with a foreign manuscript etched into it. It is like nothing any of us here have ever seen. It is a huge shell, spanning a diameter of about forty-five inches. It's amazing! We don't recognize the writing or the type of shell. While I know shell identification is out of my department's league, ancient manuscripts are not." They arrived at the tent and the manager walked inside a pressurized vault and where the shell was housed. "We thought that if perhaps the shell was identified, then it could give us more insight as to where this manuscript might have originated. We have not used radiocarbon dating yet, but the shell looks ancient. The writing is quite sophisticated, but not a language that anyone in our department has ever seen." He presented the large shell for Thad's inspection.

Thad gawked at the shell. He walked all the way around the shell unable to believe he was really seeing what was in front of him. Could this really be a giant fossilized oyster shell? He had only read about them in magazines. Hundreds of these same types of shells had been discovered in the Andes Mountains in Peru and in a mountainous area of California. There were many theories as to how they got there, miles above sea level. That part did not interest Thad. What fascinated him were the shells themselves—their size, their composition, their age. "I can't believe what I am seeing, but this is a giant fossilized oyster shell. This is an amazing find. May I look at the writing on the other side?" The manager nodded and with the help of two other interns, they gently turned over the shell to reveal the writing etched into its interior.

"You know, when I first saw this writing, I thought it resembled writings from the ancient Greek and Minoan civilizations, but there are only a few similarities. Otherwise, the letters are entirely different. Michael is the most knowledgeable of ancient languages and cultures." Here he stopped. Thad could tell how much Michael's loss affected the manager. Everyone who knew Michael loved him.

"I will send him your condolences when I see him later today. May I take some photographs of the shell? I have my camera in the car. I want to do my own research when I return home. I will share my findings with you. There are a few colleagues with whom I often consult. Do I have your permission to share the pictures and discuss this with them?" The manager agreed completely. Thad jogged to his car to retrieve his camera. He spent the rest of the day at the site, taking pictures and touring the areas being excavated. He had brought a notebook to jot down ideas and questions he might pursue later.

When he returned home later that evening, guilt hit Thad like a ton of bricks. He realized that Michael and Charise had been far from his mind while he had been at the site. He dialed Michael's number. Michael answered with, "Thad, I'm so glad it's you. I'm not ready to talk to anybody else yet. The news just keeps getting worse. I need to talk to you. I'm...." He was unable to continue.

"Michael, I will be there in less than fifteen minutes. Have you eaten?"

"No, I have been with Charise all afternoon. I don't know if I can leave her. She seems so lost. I will meet you in the lobby."

"Let's go get something to eat and drink when I get there. I won't take no for an answer." When Thad hung up, he put his face in his hands. He knew he couldn't offer any words that would comfort Michael. He just knew that he would be there. That was all that he could offer at a time like this.

Michael was waiting in the lobby when Thad came in. Silently they walked together to Thad's car. They drove to a familiar restaurant that sat on the water a few miles down the street from the hospital. They ordered, and as they sat sipping their drinks, Thad waited until Michael was ready to talk, understanding he was struggling to control his emotions. Finally, Michael choked out, "The genetic counselor did some more tests today. It's more bad news. This defect wasn't just a fluke or an isolated problem. It will kill any child we try to have. Translation: no children. Why, Thad? Why us? What did we ever do to deserve this? Why?" He lifted red-rimmed eyes that brimmed with tears. Michael closed his eyes and then looked up at the ceiling. He blew out a long audible, cleansing breath. "Whew, I'm sorry. I didn't know I had any tears left. I've gone from crying and sobbing to yelling and praying. I'm a mess."

"How's Charise? I mean, I know, well, I don't know," Thad trailed off.

"She's taking this much better than I am, seemingly handling it with acceptance, not bitterness. She's cried a lot today, but I really don't know if it has all sunk in, you know. Charise often keeps her emotions inside. I worry about that with this kind of devastating news. I want her to scream, yell, rant, rave, something, but she seems to lack the anger that I feel." He paused to sip his drink. "So, did you let everyone know kind of what is going on?"

"Yeah, I went to the site today and talked to the manager. He and everyone send their condolences. They truly are sorry. He said for you not to worry about things for a while. You know, I agree. You definitely need to take some time off."

"Did you see the shell? Even though I'm drowning in grief, I still am excited about it. Tell me what you think it is."

"I can't be sure, but I feel certain it is a fossilized oyster shell. I read about it in a journal. And the writing on the inside, well, all I can say is, wow! What a find! I spent the entire day at the site. I walked around with your classes and learned as they learned. To be honest, I was blown away. Michael, I think this discovery is something significant. I walked away today with many more questions than I did answers. Hey, I know you've got a lot going on right now. This will be waiting for you when you return. Take some time off, for not only Charise's sake, but for your own."

They spent the rest of the afternoon talking about important things and trivial matters. Thad hoped that it helped begin the process of healing for Michael. They rode back to the hospital and walked up to Charise's room.

She was sitting up drinking a cup of water when they walked in. "Thad!" she smiled with obvious sadness. "Thank you so much for being here for Michael, for me." She opened her arms to give him a hug. He walked into them without hesitation. "What a special friend you are," she murmured. "We love you so much." Thad stood up as Charise wiped her eyes on the corner of her gown.

"I love you too. I'm so sorry, Charise. That sounds so empty, but I'm grieving with you both," Thad whispered.

"We're both numb from everything—from losing the baby and hearing the news we won't ever have a baby. It's just…too much to take in at one time. Having friends like you makes it more bearable. I read a saying by Willa Cather once that read, 'Where there is great love, there are always miracles.' I see the love all around me; I just don't know if there are any miracles left." Michael reached over and wiped away the tears that ran down Charise's cheek.

She took a deep, shaky breath and whispered, "Well, I've always been a believer in miracles. I don't know when, where, or how a miracle can come from this, but hope for that miracle will somehow sustain me. I just gotta believe that or I will go crazy thinking of the alternative." She squeezed Michael's and Thad's hands.

As Thad left the room, he marveled that Charise was the one encouraging him. Even though his heart ached for them, he felt so blessed to have their friendship.

He arrived back home around nine that evening. He realized that he had not finished viewing the recording from four days ago. He remembered the image he had seen right before Michael called. Curiosity quickened his steps. There was plenty of time left tonight to watch it. He looked across the room at the computer screen as he shut the door. The screen was still frozen in the exact spot where he had paused it two days ago. He hurriedly changed clothes and grabbed a beer. He sat down at the computer and pressed the play button. He watched for a few seconds and then hit rewind. Maybe he had just imagined it. Again, he pressed play.

There it was. The same creature he had seen before entered in the camera's view, its image fuzzy in the background of the lens' scope. Thad paused the recording again and grabbed his magnifying glass out of the desk drawer. He studied the image on the screen until his eyes could no longer focus. He pressed the play button.

With his utmost attention, he kept watching the recording, hoping somehow that whatever the creature was, it would come closer. When it appeared again, it slowly made a straight line for the camera, its image gradually coming into focus. Thad found himself holding his breath. Suddenly it was there right in focus, right before his eyes. Thad shook his head, unable to believe what his eyes saw. The creature was not a fish; it was not any type of marine life he had ever encountered or seen either live or in a magazine. He paused the recording and stared into the beautiful eyes of a mermaid.

Chapter Nine

Selale knew she needed to focus, but with the events of this early tide, that was a tall order. Her work at the Language Chamber demanded complete concentration. She found that impossible because her mind kept wandering to the cave. She knew she had to finish deciphering the document the director had given her before she left her post. This particular document was written in Spanish from a country above named Mexico. Deciphering it took little effort, but it did require a little concentration. She looked over her shoulder. Sighing, she realized the director would stay as long as it took. Regaining her focus, she double checked the translation, made a notation in a file, and then signaled the waiting director to come over to her station. She read the translation aloud to the director as her job required. Seemingly satisfied, the director dismissed her. The rest of the tide belonged to her. Elated, Selale decided to go to the site the human had been visiting. He had not come for three full tides. She hoped he would show up this tide, so she could watch him work. As wrong as it sounded, she had missed him.

She had decided to inspect the equipment closely and investigate the site to see if she could figure out the nature of his work. Perhaps there was something written down that she could translate. That would give her more insight as to where he lived and what his purpose was for his presence there. Selale had the Mystical Gift of Interpretation. From the time she was very young, she had been able to decode and speak many languages with very little exposure to it. Her father had called it that—a Gift. She could read and speak the Mer language long before other merchildren her age. By her second annutide, she could speak two other languages. Because he too had this same gift, her father encouraged her talent, often speaking to her in different languages. Selale knew how happy her having this Gift made him. Naturally, her work at the Language Chamber followed her schooling. Marius wanted her placed there immediately following her graduation. The Chamber's translations played a crucial part of what drove policies and regulations made by the Atlantic Council. It also served in an advisory role for the administrators in charge of school curriculum. She was proud of her work because of its importance—it was one of the few connections the Merpeople had with the human world.

She arrived a little later than usual. She feared he had already come. Using caution, Selale swam slowly to her hiding place where she could scope out the area. This spot insured she could not be seen but enabled her to view his comings and goings clearly. For many currents, she hovered there watching the site. When she was certain no one was around, she made her way to the equipment.

The piece of equipment she examined a few tides ago no longer had a flashing red light. She identified names she assumed were companies. Selale remembered studying about the human "business" world. Her entire class had found that word funny. It so aptly described humans—busy. Aside from those labels, she saw no other writing from which she could glean any information. She swam over to inspect another device. She reached down to touch the metal, and studied its construction. It appeared to filter the water out, collecting the plankton and other tiny particles within. As she released the bag-like filter, she turned to leave.

Before she could turn around, she found herself unable to move, her arms pinned to the sides of her body. Suddenly she found herself being swiftly dragged to the surface. She struggled to free herself, but her actions proved futile. As the bottom of the ocean rapidly disappeared from Selale's line of vision, startled fish darting frantically away from the path of the terrified, captured mermaid streaked through the water. As she thrashed her body in a desperate attempt to escape, her mind raced with wild thoughts—the fear of discovery, of imprisonment, of death, or of never seeing her family again. She was bound by some type of strong chain or cord. As she broke the water's surface and breathed in the warm air above, she found herself face to face with the human.

Thad gasped as he threw off his diving equipment into his waiting boat. He didn't realize he had been holding his breath even with his breathing equipment. Panting with anticipation, he let out a yell as she surfaced. A gaping smile covered his face as the creature stared angrily at him. She continued to struggle to free herself from the cord. Pity and something like guilt pierced his heart; unfortunately, curiosity won the war of his conflicting emotions. He reached out his hand toward her and gently said, "Calm down. I swear I'm not here to hurt you. My god, I'm still trying to convince myself I'm not crazy, that you are real." He continued to smile and shake his head with disbelief at this treasure he had pulled from the ocean. His hand touched her hair. She flinched at the contact. Its tenderness startled her.

That gesture defused some of her anger. Still, Selale felt something very close to panic. She knew she had to calm down and think rationally about how to escape. She stopped her struggling and slowly took several loud, audible breaths. Maybe she could reason with him. He was as surprised by her presence as she was by his. From the many tides that she had observed him, she believed he meant her no harm. She recognized the language he was speaking as English. Familiarity with the language helped soothe her nerves somewhat. It was one of the first languages she had learned as a child. Over two-thirds of the documents she translated were written in English. She decided to shock him and answer in his own language. "If you're not going to hurt me, then why am I bound by this chain? Why force me so violently to leave my home, human?" Her brilliant blue eyes challenged him. Her sudden ferocity surprised him and even herself.

"O my God!" Thad babbled. Almost to himself he said, "She is speaking English. She's a mermaid and speaking English. O my God!! Okay, is this a prank? Is this some kind of bad joke?" he stopped his babbling and looked around just to make sure he was alone here with her. Was this really happening? Again, he gazed at her and she glared at him, both intensely scrutinizing the other. She answered his question.

"I can assure you this is no joke. Well, we are at an impasse, eh, human? Until you grasp the seriousness of this situation and until I am released, neither of us can do anything. I want you to release me. Tell me, what are your intentions? Why have you imprisoned me? I demand an answer." Her voice revealed none of the fear she felt. Bravado spurred her on.

"Well, first, uh, my name is Thad, Thad Destin. Second, I really don't mean you harm." Selale looked skeptically at the chain that bound her. "All right, I'm going to remove this cable. You're right. That does seem a little aggressive. Hold on." Thad reached over and removed the cable over the top of her head. In the blink of an eye, as soon as the cable cleared her body, his mermaid disappeared below the surface. One second she was there; the next it was like she never existed. Frustrated, Thad's eyes scanned the endless expanse of blue looking for the most beautiful creature he had ever seen. She was gone, and he realized he would probably never see her again. He knew he should kick himself for releasing her from the cable, but deep down, capturing this creature had somehow felt wrong. Knowing he might never see her again grieved him, yet ironically he was relieved that she was no longer imprisoned even though he had been her captor. That fact made no sense to him, but nonetheless, it was true. Somehow, someway, he had to see her again. She needed to understand he meant her no harm. He just wanted to find out who and what she was. With the cable still in his hand, Thad knew the chances of her seeking him out were next to impossible. How could she ever trust him?

Selale swam as fast and as far as she could. Her heart continued to beat hard. She needed some distance from this human before she could begin to think about the situation. The realization of what had just happened flooded her mind and caused her skin to prickle and her hands to shake. A contradiction of emotions warred inside her. Palpable fear gripped her heart, but exhilaration lurked there as well. She felt relief that she escaped, yet she also experienced guilt that she had deceived the human into thinking she wouldn't. If he had meant to harm her, he would have never freed her. That thought only made her feel even guiltier. *Thad Destin*. What a funny name. Only when she had put many leagues between them did she pause to really consider the implications of the encounter. She rested against a smooth stone lodged against a ridge of rock on the ocean floor and let the scene replay over and over in her mind.

If he meant me no harm, why did he capture me and force me to the surface? A spark of anger flared up inside her as Selale rubbed her arms where the cable had pinned them to her side. Was she just another part of his experiment? But then, remembering how he had gently touched her hair and carefully removed the cable from her arms dismantled the fuse of anger. Thoughts of what could have been filled her mind. He could have dragged her all the way back to shore or worse, he could have put her in a cage, but he didn't. He could have drugged her, knocked her out, or killed her. Now, instead of feeling anger or even fear over the encounter, she realized she empathized with him. Strangely, she no longer felt anger toward him. He was simply curious about her like she was about him. Perhaps she would sleep on it before she made the decision whether or not to ever see him again. He knew she existed, so she doubted he would just give up searching for her. Selale ascertained Thad Destin would not just disappear. Would he risk telling someone about her? Without any proof, other humans would think he was crazy. She wondered if he would bring someone else with him on his next visit. Revealing the news of his "discovery" could lead to other humans searching for and eventually discovering the Mer World. Fear coursed through her veins. Would this Thad Destin keep his discovery a secret? After all he had released her. *Why not be proactive about the situation?* She asked herself. If she controlled when and where they met again, she would be in less danger. As she swam back toward her chamber, her captor's face swam through her mind. Without realizing it, she had already made her decision.

Chapter Ten

Thad spent the rest of the week strategizing how to see her again. He had to or else he would go stark raving mad. Isn't that what mermaids did to those ancient mariners—sing away their minds? He could understand how it could happen. His beautiful mermaid had put a spell on him. She controlled his mind by dominating every thought. A clear plan of how to see her, meet her again, or communicate his intentions eluded him. Why had he tried to kidnap her? In retrospect, he realized that binding her and forcing her to the surface had not only been the wrong course of action, it had been sheer stupidity. He didn't know how, but he had to make it up to her by proving to her he meant her no harm. How he could accomplish this, he had no idea.

He had stayed away from the ocean to give both of them time to process the encounter. By the end of the week, however, his research had suffered. He could stay away no longer. Returning to his research site, Thad decided to check the site, collect the samples, and leave. He needed more time to devise a plan that could repair the damage done by his reckless and impetuous decision to capture her.

He submerged himself under the water and steadily made his way to the ocean floor. The water, clear and calm, enabled him to see the research site long before he arrived. Schools of small fish darted in synchronized harmony away from the music of bubbling waters created by his breathing. The brown sandy ocean floor contrasted with the bright colors of the marine life. His equipment seemed strangely out of place, its man-made shininess paled in comparison to the natural loveliness of the ocean expanse. He gathered the samples and checked the recording, exchanging the disc with a new one. As he turned to grab his bag, he saw her watching him. He stood there mesmerized at the sight of her. She made no move to come nearer or to move away. Their eyes locked and both remained motionless.

Thad realized this moment could be the turning point in their relationship. He held up both hands and slowly backed away. He had to make her understand he meant her no harm. His oxygen tank made it impossible for him to speak to her, so waving his arm, he motioned her to follow him. Never taking his eyes off her, he slowly made his way to the surface. Reluctantly, she followed at a moderate distance.

Selale made a conscious decision to follow him to the surface. Leaving enough space between them to ensure escape if it became necessary, she gracefully ascended to the surface. Even as she followed him, she realized between their last encounter and now she had chosen to trust him. Why, she didn't really know, but some mysterious force seemed to draw her to him. She couldn't explain it, but he didn't seem to be a threat. Instead, he intrigued her. She wanted him to be her friend. She broke the surface of the water and breathed in the salty air. Never taking her eyes off him, she watched as he removed his equipment. A smile spread across his face as he turned to speak to her.

"I'm so glad to see you again. Can we start over? Will you ever forgive me for scaring you and dragging you to the surface? I'm sorry and want to make it up to you." Thad stopped and waited for her answer. He didn't realize he held his breath.

Hesitantly, Selale nodded. "I forgive you. I'm going to pretend this is our first meeting." Her eyes twinkled with mischief.

Thad smiled, relieved that she didn't swim away. "Can we get out of the water and sit in the boat? I want to talk to you. I've got so many questions. Please forgive me for my rambling. I—I just can't believe you are real. Will you promise to answer my questions if I promise to answer yours? We both have to trust the other's honor." That somehow spoke more loudly than anything else he had said. Selale realized this human acted differently from how humans were characterized in the stories she had read as a child. Her father's message about faith and trust rang in her ears. She decided this human, Thad Destin, could be trusted to keep his word. Intuition told her he was a man of honor. She was rarely wrong about her first impressions of others. Hopefully that included humans.

Reluctantly she agreed, "So you agree to just talk to me if I talk to you? No capturing me or tying me up?"

Thad put his hand over his heart and said, "I promise."

"All right, so you will know I won't swim away, I will get in your boat. However, I don't want you to bind me or hinder me from getting out if and when I want. If I trust you, you must also trust me. I will answer your questions, and you can answer some that I have as well. Perhaps we can learn from each other. My name is Selale." The smile she flashed him transformed her face. He recognized the guileless sincerity of her offer. Her beauty stunned him. Thad couldn't believe she could be any more beautiful, but the smile made her just that. She seemed to be as curious about him as he was about her. He pulled himself, then Selale into the boat. He gently lifted her by the arms and placed her on a seat near the bow.

A thousand questions swirled in his mind, but all Thad could do was stare. He sat mute just looking at her. She folded her arms and said saucily, "Do you like what you see? If you are not going to ask me any questions, let me ask you some. I don't have all tide. First, tell me about yourself and your work here in these waters, Thad Destin. That should be something easy to start our conversation." Selale couldn't believe it, but she was trying to make him feel at ease. The thought registered in her mind that humans knew nothing about the Mer Kingdom's existence, but the Mer Kingdom knew a great deal about humans. She realized he must be in a state of shock.

"Sorry again. Uh, well, I'm a marine biologist at a university. My research involves the effects of commercial development on the marine life in these waters. I've been in and around the ocean my entire life. It's my one real passion. To find you here, well, it's just completely unexpected. How could I not know your species lives in these waters? Everything I ever thought I knew has just been turned upside down." He stopped, stunned with this realization. After a long pause, he continued, "I know I must sound like a babbling idiot. I consider myself fairly intelligent. You probably find that hard to believe. There are so many things I want to ask you, but I just don't know where to begin. You are just so...beautiful, so unexpected, so... unreal! How long have you lived in here in these waters? Do you call it the Atlantic Ocean?"

Selale laughed at his admission. "We're the best kept secret in the waters. We have been here for thousands of your years in the so-called Atlantic Ocean. In our world, this is Atlantis. Its waters stretch from North to South, although most live within the area of your Americas. As ignorant as humans are of our existence, we are as knowledgeable of yours. Entire realms of our society are devoted to studying aspects of human affairs. My studies cover languages. I am fluent in all major human languages. That is why I comprehend English. Tell me about your job at the university and what your research here has revealed." Here, Selale turned the conversation back over to Thad.

"Well, I teach students about the marine life that inhabits the ocean, their habitats, their food sources, their migration patterns. I help them focus on how our habits impact, all too often negatively, everything that lives here. My research really highlights this. From the data that I have collected over the past several months, the plankton has been significantly reduced. That will have far-reaching effects for years to come. Unfortunately, right now there's no solution in sight for this problem. Far too few people are concerned about the ocean's health." That this could be detrimental to her species crossed Thad's mind immediately. A play of emotions crossed Thad's face. Selale studied him, relieved to know that his passion for these waters was real.

"Tell me more about your world, Selale. Did you say it was Atlantis? Oh my gosh! Start there. I'm your hostage for as long as you wish. You're free to go whenever you are ready, but please, before you leave, tell me some details, anything, everything, seeing as I know nothing." Thad leaned forward like a child watching a movie thriller. It reminded Selale of how she used to listen with rapt attention to her father's stories when she was a merchild.

"All right, where to start? Atlantis comes from the island where our species originated. My father is the ruler of this domain. His name is Marius. We evolved from humans, so you and I share a common ancestry tides far back in time. We eat, sleep, learn, and love much like your society. We just do it all under the water. As you can see, we can survive out of the water, but not for long periods of time. Water is a life essential for the merman species as it is for humans. In many ways, our species are similar. People whether human or merman are people. Some embody good; others embody evil." Here she paused. She met his steady gaze with her own, "I've decided there's good in you, Thad Destin. But now, I must return to the waters. I believe we will meet again," she said with a smile, "but in the future, I would prefer not to be jerked to the surface. I will find you. Don't come looking for me." She climbed over the side of the boat and gracefully slid into the water. Staring straight into his eyes which pierced straight into his heart, Selale murmured, "Until we meet again, take care of yourself. As for our meeting this tide and again in the tides to come, let's keep it a secret just between ourselves." She reached her finger over and put it to his lips. "While I know this discovery intrigues you, it represents a real danger to me and the entire Mer Kingdom. Promise me, you will keep our meeting a secret."

How could he refuse? She had him under her spell. "I promise," Thad said nodding. His lips tingled with her touch.

Selale whispered softly, "I promise I will too. You see, I don't want to share you with anyone else." With those words, she disappeared into the ocean depths.

Chapter Eleven

Marius arrived at the council meeting early. He entered the chamber to find Calder sitting in the executive seat. Marius gave him a sardonic smile and asked, "Comfortable?"

Startled, Calder recovered smoothly, "Oh, good tide, brother. Sorry for taking your chair." Rising, he swam to another chair at the end of the table. "Please forgive me for exceeding my boundaries. By all means, take your rightful place here at the head of the table. I merely sat here to rest up and meditate until everyone arrived. As you know, it's going to be a long meeting. There is much to discuss and decide regarding Proposition PAPT. I already know where you stand. Unfortunately, once again we represent opposite sides."

Marius regarded his brother warily. "Why does it seem more and more like that lately? This proposal is nothing more than an attempt to harm the very humans you and I descended from. The only group that will benefit from this so-called 'protection' is the SCEROH. It gives that group the license to harm the human race even without proof of provocation. I can't support that kind of detrimental legislation. Humans are not the enemy, Calder. We just need to keep learning more about them so we can understand them better." Marius' voice was filled with sorrow.

Calder mistook it for pity. "Ah, yes, good, idealistic Marius, who sees himself as the savior of Mer traditions steeped in human loyalty. My advice to you, brother, is to swim into this centennitide. You are so mired in the past with fairy tales of what supposedly is to come that you can't or won't see the present. Humans can no longer be ignored. They are destroying our way of life! Wake up! They are the enemy. That is all I need to know about them."

Marius softly said, "Don't you remember one of the first tenets we were taught by Grandmere and Grandpere: 'Ignorance results in fear and fear in hate, but knowledge results in understanding and understanding in love.' I have lived by that ideal my entire life, and I refuse to abandon it now. It is what has sustained our kingdom for so long. Doing harm to humans will only do harm to the entire merman race."

Calder spat out with anger and bitterness, "Talk to me about love when the human race destroys the one you love. You wouldn't be spouting out this nonsense then. This legislation will enact exactly what it proposes—Protection Against Potential Threats. Humans by their very nature are threats to our kingdom. My role is to protect this kingdom. I thought it was yours as well, but sometimes, Marius, I just don't know. I just don't know...." His voice trailed off as others began entering the council room, but his eyes remained deadlocked with his brother's. The council members could feel the tension in the water. Even when his son Ettore and friend Sandoval entered the room to tread by his side, Marius refused to break the stare he cast at his brother.

Finally, Calder submitted and turned to greet the members. Marius may have won this skirmish, but the war was just starting. *It will be a long one*, Calder decided, but he had already strategically planned for this eventide's battle. Smiling, he knew this tide would conclude with a victory for him and the SCE-ROH. Proposition PAPT would be better than any weapon at ridding the waters of intruding humans: for the first time, it would put the merman race on the offensive, not the defensive, against the human race.

Marius called the meeting to order and quickly covered all the mundane business before the last item on the agenda. Everyone on the Atlantic Council knew PAPT was the only reason this meeting had been called. The rest of the business was just formality. To introduce the final reading of the legislation,

Marius called on his senior advisor and childhood friend, Sandoval. This too was a formality. The members of the council knew every detail of the radical proposition, its name alone controversial. The council had spent many tides reading, studying, and discussing the pros and cons of the legislation. Marius and Calder both had spent one cyclotide preparing for their arguments against and for the proposition. Marius began the debate.

"For countless generations of merman who came before us up until the present tide in which we live, our species and humans have lived in harmony. The roots of both species share a common ancestry. In other words, we are brothers. Throughout the history of Atlantis, peace has reigned. To abolish this peace goes against who we are and what our ancestors represented. This proposition does just that—abolishes the peaceful co-existence between human and merman. Furthermore, the prophecy of the Hybrid King describes unity among all living things in the water, the Mer Kingdom, and humans. To enact this legis—"

"What is this? A history lesson?" Calder interrupted. "We had the same instructors as you, King Marius. Make a point unless you want us all to die of boredom before we ever get to vote. The next generation will be birthed and grown if we continue at this rate." He smiled smugly at his brother as good-natured laughter filled the chamber.

"Yes, Calder, this is a history lesson. It is imperative that we remember who we are and where we came from so we can understand where we are going. The future is at stake. In order for the prophecy to come true, peace with humans must be maintained. This proposition eliminates the future hope of peace and the way of life we have cherished for generations. I urge you, do the right thing. Vote against this proposition this tide." Marius' impassioned plea was met with murmurs of assent. He sat down in the executive chair and relinquished the floor to his brother.

"Yes, it seems to always come back to the prophecy. Listen to me, every-one! This proposition is not about protecting the past; it is about ensuring our future, a future which is becoming more and more threatened every passing tide due to human interference in the waters of Atlantis. This must stop; our very existence is at stake. I'm a realist. I see the effects their race is having. I don't have to rely on some fairy tale king to save our people in the murky future. This proposition gives real mermen the power to do that right here, right now. It's time we turn the destiny of our race toward the future, not the past. Pass the PAPT Proposition without delay. By doing so, you are protecting our future." He looked each member in the eye before taking his seat.

A lengthy discussion among the Atlantic Council ensued. Several voiced concern over innocent victims getting hurt. Others questioned the motivation of the SCEROH and the threat of them exceeding their limits of control and becoming power-hungry. Still others pointed to the polluted waters and dangers yet to be discovered lurking in the chemicals the humans poured into Atlantis. Finally, Marius interjected, "Let's put this to a vote. All in favor of the PAPT Proposition, raise your hand now." Six hands, some confidently, others tentatively, lifted into the water. "Those opposed?" Six opposed the proposition. Marius cast the decisive vote and PAPT was defeated. Calder was enraged.

Leaving the room, he simply threatened, "This is far from over."

Marius knew truer words had never been spoken. Hurt from the fact that half the council disagreed with his philosophy, Marius realized this was just the beginning.

Chapter Twelve

For three tides, Selale forgot about exploring the cave. Her handsome kidnapper dominated her every thought. She replayed the scene in the boat over and over again in her mind and even imagined the next scene in her mind. She purposely stayed away from the research site. She needed to put some distance between her emotions and this human until she could sort them out and think through the consequences of where this friendship might lead. Just saying his name *Thad Destin* made her smile, and she knew that kind of emotion could only bring trouble.

She remembered the cave only when her father told her about the vote at the council meeting. She swam to his office chamber and opened the portal to the tunnel. Selale didn't hesitate to swim into the secret passageway that led to Beulah Cave. She hoped that spending the tide in the cave could somehow help her focus on making the decision to see or not see him again and put the entire situation with Thad Destin into perspective. The emotion she felt just thinking of him sent warning alarms sounding in her head, but the pounding of her heart drowned it out. She knew the relationship was forbidden; she knew it was wrong. But like a fish drawn toward the baited hook, she couldn't stop her thoughts or this inexorable yearning for more.

She surfaced in the cave, again amazed by its beauty. She treaded in the middle of the pool of water surrounded by the cave. Turning a full circle, Selale felt a wave of serenity pour over her. It was like the cave had been waiting for her, like she had finally come back home. She pulled herself out of the water and perched on the smooth rock that sat perpendicular with the prophecy on the wall. Touching the delicate etching, she only could imagine how long it had taken her great-great-grandmere to write it. That alone echoed its importance. Although it would take several tides, she knew she must read the prophecy in its entirety. She took a deep breath and began reading the prophecy:

> *"Atlantis has always been an island of unity since the physical island itself was destroyed. Peace reigns among the species in these waters and those who inhabit the land above. We share not only the waters, but also the air above with everything that lives in this world. As long as peace remains between human and merman, the Mer species shall be sustained. But dark shall be the days if peace is broken, for not only shall war ensue between humans and mermen, but between merman and merman. Atlantis' destruction shall come from both the inside out and the outside in. There is but one savior of our nation, one who embodies both human and merman qualities: the Hybrid King. He alone can save Atlantis. His birth will be conceived from undeniable love of Mer royalty and a human descendant of the Lost Ones. Look for the signs on the tide of his birth: the earth shall quake both land and water and showers of light shall explode. Though born of royal lineage, this king shall live as an exiled orphan, his true identity obscured, unknown by him and all men below and above the waters. This rare pearl shall live the life of a human…."*

Selale stopped there. She shivered with the knowledge that the Hybrid King would come from the royal family. That part had not been included in the prophecy proclaimed to the inhabitants of Atlantis. She recognized the danger of this information. No wonder her great-great-grandmere and her father had concealed this information. That one line left everyone in her family now and in the future vulnerable and at risk.

Great sadness filled her heart when she thought about the Hybrid King being raised by humans instead of the Mer people. How could a mermaid give up her child to a human mother? It was inconceivable. Selale doubted she could ever relinquish a child she birthed to anyone, merman or human. She knew how much her father and her mother loved her and her brother. Nothing would make them give up their children. Their love bonded the family together so strongly that no force could tear it apart.

For some reason, Thad crossed her mind. Maybe he would visit the site again today. Her heart suddenly beat harder at the thought. Right or wrong, all she knew was she had to see him again. She couldn't get him out of her thoughts or out of her system. Like some kind of fever, thoughts of him raced through her body leaving her weak with desire and anticipation. She left the cave determined to find the cure.

Chapter Thirteen

Thad docked his boat still uncertain that the entire encounter had ever happened. *Selale*. Just saying that name left him breathless. Was he going crazy? Was he delusional? Maybe. But one thing he knew for certain, he couldn't get her name or her face out of his mind. That fact alone scared him. He had never felt this way about any woman before, let alone a half-human one. Just saying those words sounded insane! Keeping this knowledge to himself shouldn't be too difficult considering telling someone would mean he would be deemed mentally deranged. He smiled all the way back to his house.

Women had never been a problem for Thad. He was good-looking by most people's standards, so attractive women were naturally drawn to him. The problem was they either lacked depth or were too caught up in advancing up the career ladder. He had never been in a relationship that lasted over a few months. He liked women, but he had not found one that he wanted to keep around. Some might call him cynical about love, but he had never found a woman whom he loved more than his work. So naturally, he poured himself into his work instead of investing it in a relationship that would lead nowhere.

He entered his house and plopped down on the sofa. He sat there trying to figure out what his next step should be. Rising, he went over to look at the recording again. For the rest of the evening, he watched it, rewinding it over and over again. He went to bed dreaming of a half-human beauty that had completely bewitched him.

He visited the research site the next two days, but Selale was nowhere to be seen. By the third day, he had almost convinced himself he had imagined the whole episode. His mood continued to worsen with each day that passed without seeing her. Michael had come back to work that week and noticed Thad's surly mood.

"Who licked the red off your lollipop, bro? What's up with the mood? You act like someone stole your best girl," Michael joked. Deep down, he sensed some deep emotion stirring inside his best friend.

"It's nothing. I'm just tired I guess," Thad tried to shrug it off, but Michael wasn't having any part of it.

"No way am I buying 'just tired.' I've known you for a long time. This is not a just tired Thad Destin." He studied his best friend. "If I didn't know any better, I'd say it was a woman. But wait, this is Thad we are discussing. What gives?" Michael knew. It was a woman. He recognized that feeling and wondered why Thad was being so secretive.

Thad so wanted to confide in Michael. He needed someone to reassure him he was not crazy, but what could he say? *Yes, it is a woman, but she's a mermaid.* Even to his own ears, it made him sound like a lunatic. Unknowingly, he smiled. He turned to look at Michael and said mysteriously, "All right, maybe it is a woman, but I just met her. I will let you know." And with that, Thad left the office with his flabbergasted best friend standing in the empty room.

Chuckling, he made his way to his car. The trip to the docks only took about ten minutes. That was the beauty of living in a university city at the beach. It was only ten minutes to anything. Sometimes traffic could be a nightmare, but it was always short lived because of the close proximity of the university to the beach.

Thad parked and walked the short distance to his boat. He never got tired of looking at the *Sea Science.* It wasn't much to look at, but the boat was his. He had saved every penny for a year to buy it from a retiring professor who decided to move inland to be with his family. Thad had owned her for over three years and never once had he regretted his purchase. He tried to take her out every day because he loved being on the water. There everything made sense, even lovely mermaids who spoke English. Again, his thoughts headed straight to Selale.

He made quick work readying the boat for the ocean. Anticipation had him racing through the mundane tasks, and Thad had to purposefully slow himself down so he wouldn't make a careless mistake. Finally, he pulled down on the throttle as he navigated the boat through the Intracoastal Waterway and into the open waters of the Atlantic Ocean.

On the short ride to the research site, his mind revisited some of the conversation he and Selale had shared. He still had so many questions about her, about the merman species, and about the history of Atlantis. He didn't know if a lifetime was enough time for her to tell him everything he wanted to know. What he did know was that he needed to see Selale again, if for no other reason than to prove to himself that she was real.

He stopped the boat and lowered the anchor. He had arrived at the site. Hastily pulling on his wet suit and equipment, he dove into the warm water of the ocean and descended to the site. He checked on the equipment, gathered the water samples, and exchanged the recorded disc with a new one. His eyes scanned the murky waters around the site, hoping to catch a glimpse of Selale. Several types of marine life swam around the area and off in the nearby waters, but not his mermaid. He busied himself, finding any excuse to delay his leaving. After about an hour below, he surrendered to the fact that she would not be making an appearance today. Frustrated, he kicked hard all the way up to the surface.

Where was she? he wondered. He jerked off the mask and tossed it into the boat. Grabbing the side of the ladder, he hoisted himself over and landed squarely in Selale's lap.

Chapter Fourteen

Charise sat in the kitchen drinking a cup of hot tea. She stared out the window at the yellow sunshine reflecting off the water in the distance. Had it only been a week since her whole world caved in? It seemed like a lifetime ago. The doctors reassured her that this sadness was a normal part of the healing and grieving process, but nothing seemed normal to Charise anymore. She realized she could do one of two things: sit here and drown in self-pity or keep busy and survive one more day. With resolve, she pushed the chair back and rose to her feet. She needed to call her grandmother. She knew she should have called her before now. If anyone could put things in perspective it was Gramma Winans. She had never failed to be there for Charise.

Charise grew up in the foothills of the Smoky Mountains. Family and faith were the cornerstones of her life. All her aunts, uncles, and cousins lived within five miles of each other and attended the same small white clapboard church every Sunday, come rain or shine, hail or high water. Her parents instilled hard work and toughness in their only child. So when Charise lost her parents less than a year apart when she was in college, first her mother in a car accident, then her father of a heart attack, Gramma Winans was her rock even though she herself was drowning in grief. She encouraged Charise to finish college and make her parents proud of the young woman they had raised. She threw herself into her studies and graduated *summa cum laude* at the top of her class.

Job offers poured in from all over the country. Charise decided to stay close enough to home to keep an eye on Gramma, but far enough away to establish her independence. She needed a new start, so she chose a job at a coastal university teaching African American literature while she finished her PhD. because the drive to the foothills was only about a seven-hour drive. She could get there in a day if necessary. That had been five years ago.

In between, she had met and married Michael Moses, the love of her life. She still marveled that he was her husband. The thought that he would never be a father threatened to send her over the edge into the darkness yet again. Somehow this possibility seemed so unfair. She could handle being handed the short end of the stick when it came to good things. Practice made perfect. But for Michael, it just made no sense. He was so good, so kind, so loving—the perfect qualities needed in a wonderful father. *Why?* The question kept reverberating in her head.

She dialed the familiar number. Her grandmother answered on the third ring. "Hello?"

"Hey, Gramma Winans, it's Charise. How are you? I miss you so much," Charise broke off before the tears overwhelmed her. Her grandmother instantly knew something was wrong.

"What is it, honey? Talk to me. I miss you too. What's wrong, Charise?" The tenderness in her grandmother's voice opened the floodgate of tears. Charise cried into the receiver without reservation.

"It's the baby, Gramma. I lost him. Michael and I lost him. He's gone. Gone, Gramma, and I can't have any more children. Everything, everything has been taken from me, my baby, my whole world," Charise wailed into the phone. "Why, Gramma, why? What have I ever done to lose so much when some people never lose anything? Why?" Charise sobbed uncontrollably.

Charlotte Winans let her tears fall silently as she listened to her granddaughter cry. She was so young, and yet she had experienced so much loss. She whispered a silent prayer for guidance. What could she say to console a broken heart? "Oh, honey, I'm so sorry. I don't know why. I don't know what to say. I just don't know why. Baby, why don't you come home for a few days? I want to see you, and you need time to heal. Let me take care of you for a little while. Let me take care of you. Please come home, Charise, just for a few days," her grandmother pleaded.

Charise knew she couldn't outrun the reality of the situation, but she needed the healing touch that only Gramma Winans could give. Michael may not want her to go, but he would tell her to go anyway. That was how he was. He always understood perfectly how people felt. He always put others' needs first. She agreed to come home if it was all right with Michael. They hung up, both knowing she would be there tomorrow before nightfall.

Michael smiled as Charise once again met him at the door. He knew how much she was trying to gain some normalcy to their overturned lives. He took her in his arms and said, "Hello, beautiful." She let his strong arms hold her as she wrapped hers around his waist.

She replied, "Hello, handsome." This was and had been their after-work routine for almost five years. She smiled up at him as she led him through the door.

"Have I got some earth-shattering news for you," Michael paused dramatically. "Wait for it—Thad Destin is in love." He nodded to his disbelieving wife. "I know, I know, it sounds crazy, but it's true. The crazy part of it all is that he doesn't even know he's in love with her. He supposedly just met her. What do you think about that?" Michael laughed.

"Well, I don't believe it. Why do you think he's in love?" Charise asked dubiously, even though she knew Michael was never wrong about his observations when it came to his best friend.

"Are you really questioning my ability to know what my best friend is feeling? Well, here's proof for you. For the past two days he had been in a foul mood, so unlike our even-tempered Thad. Today he just about bit a student's head off for submitting a paper in the wrong font. Again, not my buddy Thad. So I questioned him. At first he said he was just tired. I called that for what it was—a load of horse manure. Finally, he said maybe it was a girl, but he had just met her and he'd let me know. Can you believe that?" Michael still couldn't get over it.

Charise's eyes had gone soft and misty. "I hope he finds true love just like I did. There's nothing like it in the whole wide world." A ghost of a smile played upon her lips. Then she added suddenly. "Whoa, let's not get too ahead of ourselves. This is Thad we're talking about. We've seen this kind of thing happen a couple of times before. Remember, it lasted all of about a month. Time will tell if Thad has found love. True love lasts." Here she put her arms around Michael's neck. "But I still want you to find out all the details. If he is in love, he won't be able to keep her a secret long."

The conversation turned to Gramma Winans. Like Charise knew he would, Michael encouraged her to go home for a few days. He knew she needed her grandmother as much as her grandmother needed Charise. Their spending time together would help begin the healing process Charise so badly needed. In the meantime, he would keep prodding Thad for all the juicy details so he could share them with Charise when she returned home. Michael couldn't wait to find out more about this mystery woman.

Chapter Fifteen

Selale laughed at the shocked expression on Thad's face. She had decided at the last second to climb aboard his boat and wait for him. Deep down she wanted to surprise him, to see if he had wanted to see her as badly as she wanted to see him. He had stayed underwater for so long that she actually contemplated swimming down to check on him. He had some type of equipment that allowed him to stay underwater for quite awhile.

Catching his breath and scrambling off her, he smiled and said, "Hello, Selale. You know, I almost convinced myself that you were a dream when you didn't show up for two entire days. I'm glad you're real because I missed you. You're all I have thought about for three days." That kind of mushy admission normally would have embarrassed Thad, but because it was so true, it was easy to confide his feelings to her. He had never felt this way before. Overwhelmed and confused by this powerful emotion, he understood one thing: meeting her had already changed his life forever. "Have I crossed your mind at all, Selale?" He reached for her hand and looked quizzically into her piercing eyes.

Selale was frightened by the emotions churning in her, but when he touched her hand, she felt her heart melt. She whispered with fervent honesty, "You've been anchored there since we said good-bye." She looked down at their clasped hands and then gazed out across the water at the horizon. "I tried to sort out my feelings and gain some perspective on this situation, but inevitably I couldn't stay away." Here she turned and stared straight into his eyes. "I don't know where this relationship will lead, but I've decided I'm willing to risk finding out." Her candor made Thad smile. "So, where do we go from here? Where can we go is the real question."

He had already considered the question in his mind. "I just want to know you, to spend time with you. That's all, Selale. And not like a science experiment either. I've never met anyone like you, and I don't mean the mermaid part. You are so genuine, so intelligent, so…different from any woman I know. I've been waiting to meet you my entire life. It's like I was destined to meet you. Does that sound crazy? I've always been a fish out of water my whole life when it comes to relationships." Thad smiled at the unintended pun. "Maybe I was merely waiting to meet you. I don't know, but it seems more than just coincidence or chance." He released her hand and impatiently ran it through his hair.

Selale found the gesture charming. "In Atlantis, intentional contact between humans and mermen is forbidden. By my continuing this relationship, I am purposefully breaking one of our strictest laws. It frightens me that I'm breaking that law even as we speak, but it terrifies me to think I will never talk to you again. Does that make me bad? Maybe, but I have to be honest with you. For me, if seeing you is wrong, I don't want to be right. We must be careful. Not only can your world not know about me, but my world must also not know about you." She stopped here and drew a deep breath. "I want to know everything about you, so let's get started." Dramatically throwing her arms open wide, she laughed and said, "Tell me everything."

Thad laughed at her refreshing honesty. "All right, I'm going to start at the beginning, but you've got to do the same. Okay, I'm thirty-three years old. I was born here on the coast. My parents had me, their only child, late in life. Mom was forty-four and Dad was fifty. They have both passed away, Mom just a little over a year ago. I miss them." He paused and looked at her. "They were great parents because they encouraged me to do more than I thought I ever could, especially when it came to the ocean. Dad brought me here almost every day. It was like he knew I couldn't stay away. Mom and Dad loved the ocean almost as much as I do. Dad worked at an aquarium his entire life. He loved it. Mom taught biology at a university, much like me. She was passionate about her work and her students. I was quite a handful when I was young. I played sports like soccer and golf, but my real love was swimming. Mom and Dad couldn't get me out of the water. I loved the ocean, so I decided to pursue a career where I could spend as much time in the water as out. That led me to marine biology where I study everything that lives in the ocean. I just never imagined mermaids lived there." He laughed and asked, "Is there anything else you want to know?"

"What do you do for fun? What are soccer and golf? I know you work, but apart from that, what do you enjoy?" she asked smiling.

"Soccer and golf are definitely human pastimes. They are played on grass. They have nothing to do with water. I gave them up when I was a teenager, but I still like to swim and surf. I don't think I will ever outgrow those. My best friend is Michael Moses. He's fun to be around. We always manage to get into trouble when we hang around each other. I spend a lot of time with him and his wife Charise. They have just been through a terrible ordeal. Charise was pregnant, but lost the baby. Doctors told them they can't have any more children. Needless to say, they are devastated. So am I." Pausing, he looked at Selale. She had tears in her eyes. "Hey, I didn't know mermaids could cry." He reached over and wiped the tears from her cheeks. The gesture endeared him to her.

She reached her hand up and placed it over his, pressing it closer to her cheek. "You must be a wonderful friend. You love them very much, I can tell."

Thad leaned over and kissed her tenderly on the lips. Desire shot through him. He consciously had to stop himself from losing control. He broke off the kiss suddenly, breathless from the experience. He looked into Selale's confused eyes. He said hoarsely, "God, I'm sorry, Selale. I—I don't know what I'm doing."

"What do you call that embrace? Oh, please tell me you really aren't sorry because I can't say that. I—I …" Thad took her in his arms and this time, deepened the kiss. He couldn't stop himself. He had to kiss her again or explode into a million pieces. He lowered their bodies down to the deck of the boat, his mouth never breaking contact with hers. Finally, he rested his forehead on hers and tried to gain some semblance of control of his emotions.

"A kiss," he croaked. "It's called a kiss." He breathed deeply hoping to slow his racing heart.

She stifled a giggle. "It was amazing, that kiss." To lighten the mood, she smiled impishly at him. "We've got a lot to learn about each other's world."

Thad helped Selale back onto the seat of the boat. He slid himself onto the seat beside her, putting a little distance between them. Thad understood she wanted to slow down. He didn't know what had come over him. He had never felt like that. Thad also knew Selale was affected just as strongly as he was. Her flushed cheeks and shallow breaths indicated he was having the same effect on her as she was having on him. They sat in silence smiling at each other.

Thad broke the spell. "It's my turn to ask questions. Are you ready?" Selale nodded. "Tell me everything," Thad mimicked, extending his arms just as she did.

Musical laughter rang through the air. "I can't say I understand completely in terms of years, but I am twenty-six annutides, which are similar to your years. My father is Marius, king of Atlantis. I am not an only child. I have a brother named Ettore. He is a little older than I am. My mother died when we were young. Papa has done a great job raising us both. He also encouraged my gifts. Language is my talent. From the time I was able to speak the Mer language, I started learning other languages. English was the second language Papa taught me. From there I continued my formal and informal schooling. I now can speak and translate many important human languages: English, Spanish, Japanese, Chinese, French, Russian, and even some Arabic. My job involves translation of your documents into our language, so we can gain insight into your world to understand how it could potentially impact ours. I also enjoy reading and studying history. Really, my life is quite boring compared to yours. What else do you want to know?"

"Do you have a boyfriend, a merman you are involved with?" Thad wondered where that had come from.

Selale shook her head. "No, and I never have. Much to my father's dismay, the male counterpart of our species has never interested me much. Anything else you want to know?"

"Do you sleep? What do you eat? Where do you live?" The barrage of questions Thad rattled off had Selale laughing again. "Sorry, but I could stay here all night with you and still have a million more questions. Tell me more."

"All right, you want the mundane, tide-to-tide workings of merman life. Yes, to your first question. We sleep. We have an underwater world complete with pathways, avenues, and waterways we travel, and abodes much like your caves that I've read about. My father's engineers have constructed a well-organized, efficient infrastructure that makes traveling and commuting very efficient. We eat types of kelp, fish, and shellfish. Our highly developed society runs almost seamlessly. For hundreds of tides, we have been a people at peace with the marine life, with humans, and with each other. Hopefully that will always remain, but with some recent events, I just don't know, I just don't know." Her eyes took on a faraway look, her face filled with concern.

Shaking herself out of her musings, she continued, "Our population has grown very slowly, but it has steadily increased in number. Our species started with a handful and now has grown to thousands. It is very difficult for merwomen to conceive. They can only get pregnant about once every three years. I'm not sure if it's a problem with the women or with the men," she chuckled. "Anyway, every birth is a miracle. It is rare for families to have more than one child. Two is definitely counted as a blessing. We go to school, we play, we dance, we sing, we love, much like you humans. After all, the merman ancestry traces its genesis back to humans. Is there anything else you want to know this tide?" she asked him teasingly.

"Yes, there is. When can I see you again, Selale?" Thad asked with a grin on his face. "I can't go three more days or I will be out of my mind. Say we can meet tomorrow. Please, say yes," he begged.

"Yes, I will see you tomorrow. Come to your research site, and I'll find you. The tide is changing. I must go before I'm missed. Will you miss me as much as I'll miss you? Tomorrow seems so far away." Thad helped her into the water. He leaned over the side, almost eye level with Selale. They stared, neither making a move to leave.

Finally, Thad leaned over and kissed her on the cheek. "Go. Dream about tomorrow. Dream about us. I know I will." With that, Selale reluctantly dove under the darkening ocean.

Chapter Sixteen

Calder had spent several tides planning his next step. His idea for putting the merman world on the offensive instead of the defensive was not abolished; it was only somewhat delayed. Marius was the real problem. His benevolence toward the human race was not only baffling, but downright revolting. Anger surged through Calder. The human race continued to destroy Atlantis. They had to be stopped.

He looked over the offensive strategy he and the SCEROH had devised. His specially trained youth army was now in its seventh annutide, its members selected from the most agile, most skilled young mermen ranging in ages from twelve to seventeen. Most had already become blindingly loyal and followed his every command. Some of them were now battle ready in their skill set. And now, even more important to the strategy was this new ray weapon that had real potential. Its volts of energy could incapacitate human intruders. He smiled. Being properly equipped changed the game completely. No more were the mermen race gullible fish waiting to be snagged by human nets. The tide was turning in favor of the Mer kingdom. The tide for playing nice was over. Soon human trespassing would cease and their destruction of Atlantis and its waters would end.

First, though, a change in leadership and direction must take place. Calder knew there was no easy way this could take place. Marius would be hard to dethrone. Though they were twins, two brothers couldn't be any different. In the Mer world, a multiple birth resulted in celebration. So when King Nero and his wife birthed twins, the entire kingdom had launched a forttide-long celebration. It had been a tide of great joy and great promise. Whereas most twins shared a special connection, with Calder and Marius there was only competition. From the first current of their birth and throughout their entire lives, he and Marius had been in competition over something: first, the battle over who would be born first; then, over who would receive their papa's blessing; finally, over who would be king of Atlantis. In each of these battles, Marius had won. But, the war was far from over. As a matter of fact, it had just begun.

Calder understood favoritism from a very young age. Papa and Great-Grandmere had treated Marius differently. Both of their twin sons had been endowed with some of the Mystical Gifts. Marius had three of the six: Interpretation, Water-Bending, and Sand-Swirling. He could learn languages with ease and could communicate with various species. In addition to the Mystical Gifts, he had been born with incomparable wisdom. He was given special access to the inside workings of the kingdom and was often sought by their father for his counsel; all of these privileges were denied Calder. Marius had not only inherited the title of king, he gained the fortune and palace that came with that title. He also received the Blessing of the Water, an ancient ritual that bestowed special protection and honor to the recipient. It gave the recipient a magical control of the waters around him. Sure, Marius was born with the Mystical Gifts to bend the waters around him and swirl the sand. This blessing only added to that power by enabling Marius to control currents, waves, and the tide itself. This power came through possession of the pearl. By Great-Grandmere giving Marius the Atlantis pearl, she single-handedly had put him in line for the blessing. Calder never had a chance. True, there was inherent goodness in Marius, but, in Calder's opinion, not enough ambition, edginess or cunning to rule Atlantis. Those qualities were why Papa had put Calder in charge of security and safety.

The ability to communicate and control the marine life in the waters of Atlantis was Calder's only Mystical Gift. In the Mer world, it was one of the rare and special Gifts. It came along once every generation. With both twins having some form of this Mystical Gift, Nero had recognized both the value and danger of this ability and its importance in protecting the Mer kingdom. To be able to control the large animals and fish in the waters ensured their obedience and compliance with the Mer people and offered some protection to humans who ventured beneath the ocean depths. Unfortunately, Calder's power of communication did not affect the ocean mammals, and Marius' influence on the large fish was quite limited as well. Mammals were immune from Calder's influence. But when it came to the large fish, especially the sharks, Calder wielded almost complete control. If his power to control the marine life were left unchecked and unbridled, Nero understood this ability could turn the marine life into an army more destructive than a hurricane to not only the Merpeople of Atlantis below, but to the entire human population above.

So when his father Nero divided the kingdom, all in Atlantis were shocked and stunned. To suggest that one king couldn't rule the kingdom alone spoke volumes about Nero's confidence, or the lack thereof, in Marius. The decision immensely pleased Calder, but had troubled the entire Atlantic Council as well as Marius. Nero's own Grandmere even tried to compel him to revoke the decision saying this would only divide the kingdom more, but Nero had remained firm. His decision was immutable. For over twenty-five annutides this two-man system of rule had remained. Marius was king and made all decisions concerning the government and domestic policy. Calder controlled the safety of the water and security of anonymity from human interference. By no means was the power evenly distributed. Calder had far too little power and virtually no influence in policy. Marius constantly thwarted any attempt to build an army to protect their world. In his blinded view, Atlantis needed to continue providing protection for the humans, not from the humans.

Wresting control would take planning and careful manipulation of the Atlantic Council. Already many had been lured to Calder's side. They were witnessing the adverse effects of playing nice with the human race. Nicety was antiquated and dangerous. With every tide, more and more pollution floated through these once pristine waters. Atlantis needed more than a defensive front. What had humans done to deserve protection and peace? Absolutely nothing.

Just the thought of how his world had been destroyed by them sent fury surging through him. Had it only been ten annutides? It seemed like only yestertide. Just saying her name brought pain, raw and undiminished, to Calder. He could still see her face, still hear her laugh, still feel her embrace. His beautiful, innocent Leila was never far from his thoughts. They had been so young and so in love. Leila, his wife, had brought joy and love to everyone she touched. The world had been clear, pure, bright, and good. Somehow back then everything made sense. But in one half tide, all that changed.

Leila had worked in the Water Purification Chamber. Her job entailed monitoring the pollutants and chemicals floating through the waters of Atlantis. She had been working on creating a machine that could filter the water in every chamber of Atlantis. She was on the verge of a breakthrough that never came. It had died along with her at the hands of the humans. Four tides before her death, someone had discovered some old barrels dumped carelessly in the waters many leagues from the depths of the Center City of Atlantis. She had received information about these barrels by some of the Calder's border patrols who happened to see them from a distance purely by chance when they pursued a potential threat of a newly sunken ship in the area. The storm that had sunk the ship had stirred the waters, causing the sand that hid the barrels to shift, bringing them into view. Upon hearing the report, she asked her immediate supervisor if she and a team could swim to the site and inspect the contents. Her supervisor had authorized the request, but would approve only Leila leaving for the tide to explore it. So she had gone alone. Calder didn't give her trip a second thought. He knew she would be safe from human discovery and from the marine life in the nearby waters. His influence and control stretched far beyond the area.

What should have been a half-tide, exploratory trip had turned into her death sentence. It wasn't the dangerous sharks or whales that attacked her and ultimately led to her death. Poisonous chemicals found in the barrels that she opened and inspected proved toxic to Leila's system. With her remaining strength, she had made it back even as sick and close to death as she was to warn the others in her work chamber. That epitomized who she had been—someone who always put others in front of herself. She had been one of the few Merpeople to have the Mystical Gift of Empathy. This Gift was one of those that had almost become extinct. It surfaced only once every few generations. Those Merpeople who had the Empathy Gift were the descendants of one of the Lost Ones. Leila's Empathy was one of the many things he had loved about her. Had his Great-Grandmere not died six annutides before, Leila could have been saved. With his Great-Grandmere's passing died the last of the Merhealers. No merman in the royal family or in any of the other founding families since that tide embodied the Mystical Gift of Healing. Leila died in Calder's arms the next eventide. He had never recovered. Bitterness took the place of love and antipathy toward the human race remained. How his own twin brother who loved Leila could protect any species that had so recklessly destroyed the one good thing in his life, Calder would never understand.

Marius controlled the tide-to-tide decisions of Atlantis right now, but Calder planned to control everything, every aspect of the kingdom in the future. Atlantis' destiny would not lie in the hands of humans, his idealistic brother, or some Hybrid King. No, the future of his home would eventually rest solely in his hands, and he alone would increase Atlantis' power and dominance. No amount of human bloodshed or restitution could atone for Leila's death or bring her back. But when he gained complete control of Atlantis, humans would not intrude in his domain, or they would be destroyed. It would be a war he was ready, willing, and with these types of weapons, able to wage. He couldn't wait to get started.

Chapter Seventeen

Thad had seen Selale every day for over two weeks. He couldn't stay away. He was finding it increasingly difficult to focus on his job, his research, and his day to day routine. When he was not with her physically, she remained with him, dominating his every thought. Michael noticed how distracted Thad had become. With Charise at her grandmother's, Thad had spent almost every evening with Michael. He wanted to tell Michael about Selale, but what could he tell him? That he was in love with a mermaid? It saddened him to think that his best friend couldn't meet the girl who had stolen his heart. He could tell Michael was hurt and confused by his reluctance to talk about his new girlfriend, but Thad didn't know how to even begin the conversation without Michael carting him away to the psychiatric ward. Instead, he asked Michael about the shell and how the team's research had progressed.

"We are at a dead end. Nobody can decipher the language. We have had different types of experts in from all over the world: language, history, archeology, and sociology. All agreed that the language resembled ancient Greek, but it is much more sophisticated and too complex to decipher. Just when they think a letter is decoded, it leads them nowhere. It is frustrating. The one thing all of them found complete agreement on was the fact that the shell predated ancient Greece. That fact alone makes this discovery one of a kind. Everyone wants to translate what is written on it. I believe its complexity has concealed something earth-shattering, a kind of Rosetta Stone from the waters." He stopped and looked over at Thad who had a faraway look on his face. "Do you think I'm crazy or are you thinking about your mystery woman again?" Michael met Thad's startled eyes. "I guess it's okay to keep a brother in the dark about this girl who has taken over your mind," Michael finished. Thad realized he had to tell Michael something. He decided he would start with some truth. It was as good a place as any because Michael would know if it was something untrue.

"I told her I wouldn't tell anyone about us and our meeting. It's complicated," Thad floundered for something else to say.

"If it involves a woman, it's always complicated," Michael chuckled. "Look, the last thing I would ever ask you to do is break someone's confidence, but you've really got it bad, buddy. She's got some kind of hold on you. Why can't you tell anyone? Wait, she's not black, is she?" Michael howled laughing at his own joke. For years and after many failed, short-lived relationships, Michael and Charise had kidded Thad about finding a good black woman. He could never tell if they were serious, but in reality, he had not been totally opposed to the idea. It's just he never made the time to find one, and they had never found anyone to introduce him to. "Tell me something about her, anything, just one thing, please?"

"Well, she's not black," Thad smiled, stalling the conversation.

"Now that's a just a tease. C'mon, buddy, don't stop there. You're killing me!" Michael was going to get the lowdown or die trying. "Why can't you tell anyone? That sounds very strange and, if I must say so, alarming. Please tell me you haven't got mixed up with a married woman. Why all the mystery?" Michael's brow furrowed with concern. He could feel there was something significant to this relationship, he just hoped it wasn't that.

Thad shook his head, "No, she's not married. Again, it's complicated. I can't tell you more about the situation other than that. I will tell you about her. She is beautiful, jaw-dropping beautiful. Her name is Selale. Just listen to that name: Selale. There's something so different, so honest about her. She specializes in—oh my God! Michael! The shell! The shell!" Thad bolted up suddenly from his chair and then speaking almost to himself he said, "Why did I just now think about it? Of course, yes, of course!" The turn in the conversation totally mystified Michael. He looked at Thad like he had completely lost his mind.

"What are you talking about? What does this girl have to do with the shell?" Michael grabbed Thad by the shoulder. "Are you all right, Thad? What has gotten into you?"

Thad took a deep breath to control himself. Michael already thought he was crazy. If he knew the entire truth about Thad's last several days, he would think he had gone stark raving mad. "Selale specializes in language. She can speak at least every major language in the world, not to mention her own. I wonder if she could decipher the shell. It's worth a try, don't you think?" He turned toward Michael. "I would like to see the shell again and take some more pictures of it to see if she could actually read what it says."

Michael had a better idea, "Why don't you bring her with you and let her see it firsthand? Then I could meet her too." He saw Thad already shaking his head. "Why not?" Michael asked, frustrated with all the secrecy surrounding this woman.

"I'm sorry, but I can't tell you." Thad pursed his lips together forcing them to remain silent. Michael could visibly see how upset this made Thad, so he backed off. He knew the importance of keeping a secret.

Trying to lighten the mood, Michael responded, "Hey, really, it's okay. I know you will let me know what you can when you are ready. My gut instinct tells me that this relationship is something good, not something bad, so I trust you'll tell me in good time." Michael threw his arm around the shoulder of his best friend. "Hey, I've got an idea. Let's go to the research center and look at our mystery shell. We moved it to the research center last week. So many people have now heard about our discovery that its security is in jeopardy. But, I've got a key." Here Michael pulled a silver key ring from his pocket and twirled it on his finger. "Take your pictures and see if your Selale can crack the code. Who knows? Your mystery woman may just be the one to solve this shell's language mystery." Thad smiled and grabbed his keys. Michael laughed again at Thad's enthusiasm as they both headed out the door.

Chapter Eighteen

Charise had spent two weeks basking in the love and care of Gramma Winans and her extended family. Healing had come from the loving arms of her family. They had almost smothered her with their love. She hadn't meant to stay this long, but every day, someone found something else that required her assistance. Somehow coming home always helped her put things in perspective. She no longer felt lost. Her grandmother would not allow her time to start feeling sorry for herself or to get sidetracked to despair. She always found something else for Charise to do. That busyness had been therapeutic. Through the day to day routine, she found comfort in the fact that life would go on for her as it does for anyone facing loss. But that didn't mean it would be an easy road back. Like most detours on life's road, it would be a long, arduous trip to get back to where she was supposed to be. The problem was she still didn't know where that was or how to get back to that place. Getting back was difficult when the entire road had disappeared.

The day she was scheduled to return home, she rose early just as the sky began turning a light gray in the eastern corner of the horizon. As a child, she had loved getting up early to watch the sunrise. It always seemed to hold such promise for the day. Now wrapped in an old patchwork quilt, she sat on the front steps waiting for the sun to peek above the inky mountains in the distance. Her eyes scanned the vast ceiling of stars. She so wanted to find that promise for her future. Even though she no longer felt lost, she desperately needed direction. She found herself holding her breath, hoping for some sign.

Charlotte Winans stood behind the screen door looking at the silhouette of her beautiful granddaughter. She held two mugs of steaming coffee in her hands as she covertly studied Charise. She was better. Whether she had completely healed was another story. She had been at the edge of despair when she arrived. It saddened Charlotte when she thought of all the tragedy Charise had already faced and at such a young age. Charlotte herself was no stranger to loss. With those tragic experiences came the wisdom to understand that those trials and tribulation had made her who she was. It had given her Charise and what a blessing she had been. Charlotte knew that Charise saw her grandmother as a tower of strength, but in truth, it was Charise who had given Charlotte the will to go on after the loss of her daughter in a car wreck and her son-in-law shortly thereafter. Charise had been a gift from God. Looking back now, Charise had saved her life and helped her realize that there was some bigger plan and that it ultimately worked for good even in spite of tragedy. Charlotte opened the door and walked over to sit on the steps beside Charise.

Handing Charise a cup of coffee, Charlotte put her arm around her shoulder and whispered, "Good morning, Sunshine." Charise smiled at the familiar routine. Those words greeted Charise every morning when she was a child. "Are you sure you won't stay a little longer, honey?" Charlotte pulled her granddaughter closer to her side.

Charise shook her head, "I've got to get back to my life, Gramma. I can't hide here from the real world, no matter how dark and ugly it is, any longer. Everything seems so much clearer here. I've found peace with the situation, but I keep waiting for some sign that it's all going to get better, that perhaps one day I may understand why, but I just don't know. Does that sound rational or completely crazy?" She laid her head on her grandmother's shoulder.

"It sounds perfectly rational, even logical. We in our limited understanding want all the lines to connect, for everything to fill beautiful colors in the picture we think we see. But God in his infinite wisdom knows we can only see our own little corner of the bigger picture. We get angry when whites, blacks, browns, and grays paint the canvas because we can't see how those add beauty and definition to the overall picture. We only know the whites, blacks, browns and grays aren't pretty. That is when we have to put our brush down and let the master paint the masterpiece. We have to trust because he is greater than we are, and he sees the finished picture."

Charise smiled at the lovely analogy her Gramma had painted. Drinking their coffee, they sat in silence watching the orange sunrise light the eastern sky. Its rays spilled over the mountains pouring its warmth over the entire landscape. Charise was ready to go home. She had healed as much as anyone could in two weeks' time. Rising, she and her grandmother went in to get her bags. After loading them in the car, Charise hugged her grandmother and promised she would come home again soon. She got in her car and started the long trek back to the ocean.

Charise had driven for over two hours when she stopped at a rest stop just off the interstate to stretch her legs. By now, the sun had risen high in the sky, dispelling the last remnants of the night. She made her way to the grassy area where several towering sycamore trees shaded a grove of picnic tables. Sitting down at one of the tables, she extended her legs and leaned back against the top. Suddenly a sparrow lit on the table top beside her. Charise didn't move. She stared at the small bird and held her breath so she wouldn't move even an inch. Tears welled in her eyes as she remembered Gramma Winan's stories from her childhood concerning sparrows. The sparrow, according to legend, symbolizes birth and the resurrection of life. Its presence represents eternal hope and the love that God has for even the least of his people. The sparrow looked at her and then flew up toward the blue sky. Charise raised her tear-stained face to heaven and smiled. She felt a sense of peace. Somehow she knew in that moment that everything would be all right. She didn't know how, but better times were ahead. With a new-found confidence and a spring in her step, Charise walked back to her car to finish the journey back to her life at the coast with Michael.

Chapter Nineteen

Thad and Michael arrived at the university's research center after everyone had left for the day. The only other person in the center was Tillman, the night security guard. He had worked for the university for over twenty years, so he was well acquainted with the comings and goings of the science and history professors and knew them all on a first-name basis. He threw up his hand as he walked in the opposite direction of Thad and Michael. The two men turned down a series of long corridors and staircases until they finally arrived in the basement of the building. Here a research complex covered the entire floor of the massive university building.

Michael unlocked the door to his office using his identification badge and thumbprint. Two years before, someone had breached the security of every department in the complex by stealing a professor's badge and burglarizing the artifacts from several research projects being conducted. The history department had experienced the biggest loss. The intruder had taken a box of rare coins on loan from a prominent museum valued at over a half million dollars. The coins had never been recovered. Since then and by learning the hard way, the university had invested in state of the art security. Each department head had the only pass to their department and only his or her full thumbprint would open the door.

"Ah, such is the cloak and dagger life of a history professor," chuckled Michael.

Even after using the technology himself for two years, it still amazed Thad completely. He put his index finger to his cheek. "I forgot. Is James Bond's office next door or right down the hall?" Both men laughed at themselves.

Michael opened the door and automatically the lights illuminated the entire room. Rows of neatly lined tables held a vast array of artifacts—shells, coins, pottery, weapons, jewelry, and other items that had once been every day, common things used by people just like Thad and Michael. What made them valuable now was their age. These items offered glimpses into bygone lives and gave insight to the people who had long since died. This was Michael's specialty.

Walking over to another door on the opposite wall, Michael said, "We put the shell into the pressurized chamber. I'm not sure that was necessary, but it couldn't hurt it. I would rather err on the side of caution. Even though it's not fragile, it is ancient." Thad followed him as he once again went through a series of security measures to open the door. Slowly, the door opened with a hiss as the chamber depressurized. Both men walked in silently with something akin to reverence. The chamber's small, dim space created an almost mystical atmosphere, as though the men stood in the presence of something truly remarkable.

Michael and Thad stood shoulder to shoulder looking at the magnificent oyster shell, its complex etchings barely visible in the wan light. Neither spoke. Michael reached down and unlocked the wheels on the cart that held the mammoth shell. He wheeled it slowly out into the bright lights of the research chamber. In the glaring light, the shell's mysterious language lined the shell edge to edge, top to bottom. Every inch of the shell had been used by the ancient author. Thad thought this certainly pointed to the message's significance. This was not some story or trivial event. Its elaborate and lengthy etchings pointed to something far greater.

His fingers itched to touch the symbols. A thousand theories floated through his mind. He looked at Michael's expression. Thad whispered, "It's so amazing. I can only imagine what it says. I just know it's something important. You feel it too, don't you? I know this sounds hokey, but it feels like destiny, like we were supposed to find it in this time, in this place. It has some inexorable pull on me that I just can't explain. Can I touch it?"

Michael nodded. "The history documented here definitely meant something to the person who wrote it. There's a mystical, unearthly quality to the work. Why would anyone take the time to write something this elaborate and time-consuming if it wasn't life-changing? It must have taken years to finish. What patience and persistence it must have taken the author! I would love to know his story just about as much as what this story says here." Michael reached out his hand and gently ran it around the outside of the shell.

Taking a cue from Michael, Thad stretched out his hand and started to trace one of the ancient letters, but his hand stopped in mid-air. He turned to Michael and suddenly blurted, "I know I've been secretive about Selale, Michael, but something tells me she is the key to translating this shell. Could it be merely coincidence that I met her right after you discovered this shell and she translates languages? She can speak almost every language in our world."

"What do you mean 'our' world? She's not an alien, is she?" Michael laughed.

Thad realized he had to proceed carefully. He laughed, "Yes, she is. She has a penchant for young scientists. She's just waiting to beam me up to her spaceship and have her way with me." Michael snorted. He hoped this comment had deflected Michael and the conversation away from his inadvertent mistake. Thad turned his attention back to the shell and once again grew serious. After several silent seconds, he asked, "Don't you wonder where this shell came from? It definitely did not originate here. Someone brought it from somewhere else. That adds to its mystery. How did it get here? Why did they write it on a shell and bring it here? What does it say? Who wrote on it? All these questions, and we may never find the answers. Just standing here, it feels so other-worldly, so...I don't know...it's almost like it has me under a spell. I know, that sounds absolutely crazy." He pulled out his camera and began taking pictures so he could avoid Michael's bemused expression. He wanted to be sure he captured all the writing, so in case Selale could translate the language, she could read it all.

Michael stood regarding Thad closely. He sensed something was a little off kilter with Thad and his relationship with this girl Selale who had him so completely enamored. Michael couldn't quite put his finger on it, but he knew there was something important Thad was not telling him. He was torn whether to pry for Thad to tell him more or to ignore his strange comment and wait patiently for Thad to confide in him. He had always prided himself on being open-minded. He couldn't imagine anything that Thad could tell him that would change his feelings toward his best friend in the whole world. He just wished Thad would trust him. He remembered Thad told him he had given his word not to talk about her, but why? What was the mystery surrounding this Selale? Obviously, she was educated. Naturally that would attract Thad. Superficial beauties never held his attention long. Michael realized this girl must be different, special. He would be patient for a little while longer. He could never ask Thad to betray a confidence. Sooner or later, Michael would meet Thad's mystery woman.

After taking pictures from every angle, Thad decided he had all of the shell's language for Selale to translate. He was eager to see if his gut instinct proved true. Somehow the key to this shell mystery led straight to Selale.

Snapping one last picture, he smiled at Michael. "Thanks for allowing me to see the shell again and letting me take these pictures to Selale. To me, it's worth a shot. Don't you agree? I don't know if she can translate this language, but you have tried everyone else whom you know. What do we have to lose?" Thad didn't wait for Michael's answer. "I'm not sure when I will see her again. She is quite unpredictable. I'll need to get these pictures developed and en-larged so she can see each symbol." Thad stared again at the shell, awestruck not only by its delicate etchings, but also by its sheer width. The shell was enormous. He knelt down and lightly stroked the outside of the shell. Sud-denly, a bright light blinded him. It physically knocked him off his feet. In the light Thad clearly saw a vision of himself, Selale, and a baby boy in her arms. Their heads and shoulders bobbed above the water. The baby reached for him, and wriggling out of Selale's arms, swam to Thad. The vision left him with a strange sense of calmness that flooded his entire body, so palpable that it made him audibly draw in a sharp breath. Michael stooped down beside him, and placed a large brown hand on Thad's back. With a look of alarm, he fixed his eyes on his friend who had gone pale and was breathing raggedly.

"What's wrong? Are you all right?" Michael waited for Thad to respond, unsure whether to help him stand up or make him sit down.

Thad's head was spinning. He dropped back to sit on the cold marble floor. *What had just happened?* Still breathing heavy and feeling very shaky, he realized Michael had felt nothing. As he sat down on the floor beside his best friend, he was certain of two things—that baby was his son and he had never felt that kind of river of contentment before this moment. Thad wondered what was going on. Was he going crazy or what? Looking at Michael, he realized verbalizing what just happened would make him sound just that—crazy. He shook his head and trying to lighten the mood, said, "If I tell you, you're going to commit me tonight. I can't explain what just happened except to say this shell spoke to me, not audibly, but with a flood of serenity and a vision so real, so tangible it took my breath away. As crazy as that sounds, it is exactly what just happened to me when I touched this shell. I know I should be scared to death, but I feel perfectly…perfect." Michael, rendered utterly speechless, sat there gaping at Thad. This person speaking was not the self-centered, data-driven Thad Destin Michael had known for the past three years. He didn't know how to respond.

The two sat there in silence for several minutes until Thad could reign in his breath and his pounding heart. Finally, Thad punched Michael on the shoulder and said, "Say something! Don't look at me like I'm a babbling idiot! Have you ever known me to act like this or say something completely ridiculous like this?" To Michael's smirk Thad interjected, "Ok, don't answer that, but really, I'm telling you it was like that scene in *Phenomenon* when John Travolta is hit with that light. I felt something, saw something crazy, and it came from this shell. I don't know what it means or how it happened. All I know is that it did and this definitely involves Selale. I just don't know where all this is leading." Thad trailed off, shaking his head. He knew it was futile to understand everything that had just happened.

When Michael didn't respond, Thad rose to his feet. He reached out his hand to help pull Michael to his feet. Michael grabbed Thad's hand and said, "I don't know what is going on with you, but something is. No, I don't believe you are crazy crazy, but I do believe this girl has got some kind of spell on you. I don't know whether to be jealous or alarmed. And what just happened to you, well, all I can say is, I know this shell is special, even mystical. I feel it too. If you say it spoke to you, who am I to say otherwise? Something happened to you just now. You weren't here for a few seconds. And yes, I agree with you. There's a greater power at work here with a bigger picture than our human minds can see. Who knows, maybe your Selale is connected to this shell. Only time will tell how all of these pieces fit together. So, are you going to tell me about what you saw or not? I can't take not knowing," Michael pleaded.

Thad had no trouble remembering the vision; it was imprinted on his brain. Describing it to Michael, however, required a little adjustment of everything he had seen. Thad took a deep breath, "We were in the ocean, swimming, Selale and I, and…she was holding a baby that was my son. He reached his tiny arms out to me and then this amazing feeling poured over me. Then just like that, the vision vanished." Thad stopped and looked Michael right in the eye. "Why did I see that vision when I touched this shell? Help me make some sense of it all, Michael."

If Thad had said he sprouted wings and flew, Michael would have been less surprised. He realized Thad's relationship with this girl was much more serious, almost marriage serious if this vision was any indication. Michael looked at Thad and bluntly said, "How is it that you had a vision of a baby and your best friend hasn't even met your future wife? Thad, to say this relationship is sudden is an understatement. Do you love this girl? You've only known her a couple weeks." To Thad's startled look, Michael figured out quickly that this thought hadn't even dawned on Thad. Michael chuckled. "You just now realized you love her, huh?"

Thad nodded. "I think about her every waking minute. I can't wait to see her, to hear her voice, to touch her hair. She's amazing. Yeah, I love her. She's such a mystery. I don't know for sure, but I know she feels something for me. I'm scared to death. I've never loved any woman like this. I don't know myself this way, but I like it." Thad stopped and smiled at Michael.

Michael quipped, "Now I know you are crazy—crazy over a woman. Mark this day down in the annals of history: Thad Destin is in love. I never thought

I would see the day. Charise won't believe me. I want to meet this girl, Thad. Tell me I will soon or else I will think she is some alien. Charise will pester you until she meets her. You know that, right? She is very protective of you. Charise and I agree that Selale must be someone special if you love her."

Michael turned and pulled the shell back into the chamber. He and Thad worked in companionable silence to secure the shell and re-pressurize the chamber. As they closed the door to the laboratory, Thad threw his arm around Michael's shoulder and simply said, "Thanks."

As they walked down the long corridor toward the stairs, Michael replied, "No problem, buddy. Hey, you wanna grab a beer and watch the game? Charise went back to work today. She told me she would be late getting home. That way I can interrogate you more about Selale. What do you say? Hot wings are on me if you say yes."

"Are you asking me on a date and bribing me with hot wings? Oh, you naughty boy. How do I know you won't ruin my reputation?" Thad joked.

"Believe me, your reputation was in ruins long before I met you. Maybe Selale will make an honest man of you after all," Michael observed.

"I'll buy the beer if you'll buy the wings, but don't think I'm going to reveal all my secrets on our first date. I'm not that fast," Thad batted his eyes, flirting with his friend.

"I consider myself an excellent interrogator. I will get some info out of you tonight even if I have to get you drunk." The two got in the car and headed to Chaney's Bar.

Chapter Twenty

Calder covertly hovered across the room regarding his nephew Ettore. The saying he is just like his father was the truth. He was Marius' clone. He not only looked like Marius and acted like him, but he also spouted the same antiquated doctrine. He could potentially be a bigger problem than his father because he was so young, enthusiastic, and blindingly loyal to Marius. Then there was Sandoval. With him around, Marius might as well have a bodyguard. He was fiercely protective of his king. Yes, before he made his bold move and swept in a desperately needed change of leadership, what to do with those two had to be carefully considered. The Mer people not only loved Marius, but also his two closest confidants and advisors. They viewed Ettore as the heir apparent. That thought made Calder cringe.

The council room itself circled the members. Its convex ceiling domed above their heads. Iridescent shell lined the walls giving the chamber a sacred glow which bathed it with a calming atmosphere. Its architect must have somehow sensed the future tension that would emanate from its floor and proactively tried to quell its impact. Calder was able to conceal his presence by treading at the corner of one of the many huge columns that ran floor to ceiling. The council table sat in the middle of the room, its size taking up most of the room. The ornately carved stone chairs rose above the massive table, surrounding it like gray sentries. The chairs remained empty as the council members mingled in small clusters around the table's perimeter discussing banal topics far removed from the heated debate of the last meeting. He smirked at the chamber's cordial atmosphere. Even though almost a cyclotide had passed since the last council meeting, the bitter memory of the defeat of the PAPT Proposition drowned out the cheerfulness of the members' conversation.

Smoothing away his animosity, he situated a beaming smile on his face and entered the council room with a flourish. "Ah, Ettore, my fair-haired nephew! Hello, all! Marius, you are looking well. And Sandoval, how are you?" Calder threw a casual arm around his shoulders as if they had been the best of friends for a lifetime. Immediately, Sandoval grew suspicious. Mistrust surfaced in his mind, and it immediately raised a warning flag. He knew Calder's intentions were never honorable. They were often selfish and always filled with deceit. Sandoval didn't trust Calder. Sandoval considered himself an excellent judge of character; it was his gift. As much good as there was in Marius, an equal amount of evil filled Calder. How twins could be so different, Sandoval would never understand. He and Marius had been friends as far back as either could remember. Both had been drawn to each other and now each trusted the other with his life. Even with all the tides that had come and gone, his mistrust of Marius' twin had failed to ebb. Calder realized Sandoval could read his often harmful intentions toward Marius from an early age and therefore had steered clear of Sandoval's intuitive scrutiny. Even now as his arm lay draped over Sandoval's shoulders, Calder sensed the other's intense suspicion and slowly withdrew his arm.

Calder strategically planned where he would sit. His main objective was to woo a couple more members of the council to accept his ideology of what Atlantis needed to be. He knew that two of the twelve members would never betray Marius. He already had five members who had voted with him on the PAPT Proposition. That meant he only needed two more to have a majority. When, and not if, that happened, he could set the rest of his plan into motion. Calder seated himself beside Gaillard, a pompous merman in charge of distributing information to the public concerning the council meetings. He ultimately decided what information to disseminate to the Mer people and what information remained classified. Calder understood Gaillard would be an asset to his cause. Luring him over to Calder's camp would take little work if Gaillard thought it would benefit him. Gaillard considered only one thing when he made a decision—himself. The self-proclaimed bachelor owned the Olympus Complex, a structure which housed much of the competitive games held in Atlantis. Many Merpeople reviled him because of his selfish ambition; others loved him because of the entertainment that his intensely competitive nature had provided. Gaillard was a gambler who won often and lost rarely. With this thought uppermost in his mind, Calder engaged him in trivial conversation right before the meeting started, inquiring about his health, his complex, and his latest love interest, anything to have him think his little world was important to Calder. He would have Gaillard in the palm of his hand by the time the tide had turned.

The meeting's agenda included none of the controversy of the previous meeting. The volatile waters had settled and now a friendly camaraderie filled the chamber. A series of reports ensued and little discussion resulted. The highlight of the meeting in Calder's estimation was Gaillard's report on the human vessels that frequented the waters of Atlantis. One ship had sunk during a fierce storm, and its debris had destroyed one of the buildings in Gaillard's Mertropolis of Chambers. Calder recognized instantly that this incident could shift Gaillard to his side. He knew exactly how to use it to his advantage.

As the meeting adjourned and the council members exited the chamber, Calder and Gaillard remained seated at the table. With a solicitous shake of his head, Calder inquired about the state of Gaillard's investments. "Tell me what happened and what I can do to help. You know how important your position here on the council is to me." Those words had the effect Calder intended. Gaillard needed little more than to feel that he mattered more to Calder than the other members to make him open up about how Marius' nonchalant attitude about his loss disappointed him. Calder nodded sympathetically, "Your investments and your position are vital to the Mer people. How my brother can dismiss them confuses me too. Sometimes I wonder what Marius is thinking, if he even is thinking. Can't he see how important you and your investments are to Atlantis, not just now, but also to the future? Marius needs to step into this tide and wake up to what really matters."

Gaillard eyed Calder shrewdly, "Perhaps Atlantis could use a new direction. I like your style, Calder. Atlantis seems steeped in the past so much that we can't move forward. You have a forward vision. You see Atlantis' potential; its future is more important that its past. I like that. Tell me what I can do to move us there. I'm your man."

Calder smiled as he confided his plans to his newest ally.

Chapter Twenty-one

Selale waited while Thad finished his work. She watched him. Something stirred in her as she watched him. It started in the pit of her stomach and fluttered up to her heart. She loved him, and it scared her to death. Could it be possible to love someone so soon, after only a matter of one cyclotide? She knew he felt something too. But where could this possibly lead? Selale couldn't envision a positive scenario. Still, she couldn't stay away from him even though she knew she should. A force far stronger than good intentions pulled them together.

Thad looked over at Selale. Her ethereal beauty stunned him. He hurried to finish his work, so he could spend the rest of the afternoon with her. She followed him to the surface, and both floated there as Thad removed his scuba gear. He tossed it into the boat then hoisted Selale over the side. He climbed in after her. He couldn't wait to show her the pictures.

Thad grabbed her hands, "I've missed you! Have you missed me?" His teasing grin made her laugh.

"Perhaps I have. Where have you been? I haven't seen you in two tides. I thought you had forgotten all about me. Yes, I have missed you." Selale squeezed his hand that was joined to hers.

Without hesitation, Thad leaned over and kissed her. He had thought of little else since she met him at the research site. She left him breathless, his head spinning. He leaned his forehead against hers trying to reel in his emotions. Breathing hard, he said, "I can't get you off my mind. You are all I think about, Selale. I have never felt this way about anyone. Does that admission scare you like it scares me? I'm just trying to be honest with you. This is so sudden, but I have never been more certain of anything in my life. I just want to be with you." To Selale's silence, he said, "Say something, please."

Selale responded by gently kissing his lips again. She whispered, "I'm scared too. There's so much more to our meeting that you don't know that makes this relationship so dangerous. Even though I know the danger, I still can't resist being with you. I can't stop. This pull you have on me is too strong. What are we going to do, Thad? Where can this lead?" She allowed him to pull her into his arms. They held one another, each desperate for the other's comforting touch.

Thad broke the silence. "I don't care where it leads or how dangerous it is. We belong together. I'm going to tell you something that I have never told anyone other than my parents: I love you, Selale." When she started to speak, Thad put his finger over her lips. "No, don't say anything yet. Just listen to me. I know this is sudden. We've only known each other for about four weeks, but I can't deny it any longer. I had to tell you. Destiny appointed us to meet. Of that I am convinced. I don't understand it, but we belong together. I want you, want to be with you all the time. How I don't know, but we can find a way. Tell me you feel the same way, please, Selale."

Selale pointed to her tail. "What about our differences, Thad? How can we be together when my world is the water and your world is the land? I feel this pull too. I love you, but to be honest, I have to ask myself, will it be enough? For me, danger lurks above the water; for you, it lurks below. Will it be enough just to meet occasionally in your boat? Is that all we have to look forward to? A secret tryst every few tides? Thad, I want so much more than that for you, for me." Tears filled Selale's eyes. "It just seems impossible."

Charise's words echoed in Thad's ears: *Where there is great love, there are always miracles.* The memory made him smile. Though he didn't understand it all, he knew the vision the shell had given him played an important part in his confidence of their future and that a miracle was possible. They belonged together, and things would work out for them. The vision confirmed that for him. He remembered the pictures he had taken. "I want to show you something and tell you about what happened yesterday. My friend Charise once told me that where there is great love, there are always miracles. I didn't understand that quote until just now. Hold on and let me get those pictures." He quickly descended into the cabin below to retrieve the pictures he had developed late last night.

Selale considered the words Thad had just said. She marveled at their implication. Could they somehow be together? She looked across the vast blue waters as she waited for him to return. Why he felt so sure things would work out, she couldn't imagine. That he loved her in spite of their differences left her baffled. Thad Destin was definitely special. Smiling, Selale wrapped her arms around her shoulders.

Thad emerged from the cabin and slid beside Selale holding some photographs. She knew the word from her work translating documents. "Before I show you these, I want to tell you about them and about something that happened to me yesterday. All right, about six weeks ago, the week I first saw you, my friend Michael found this enormous shell with strange etchings on the inside. He and his research team called me to come inspect it because they had never seen a shell like it before. It was during this time that Michael and Charise lost their baby. I went down to the research site on the beach to help them identify what kind of shell it was. To say I was blown away is putting it mildly. It was a huge fossilized oyster shell. I had only seen them in pictures. Michael and the best linguists from all over the world have tried to decipher the language written on the shell, but they haven't been able to crack the code of this language. It doesn't exist in our world. Yesterday, Michael and I discussed the shell, and suddenly, I realized perhaps you could decipher it because you know so many languages. So, we drove to the university, so I could take some pictures of the etchings on the shell. Now this is the strange part. Please keep an open mind about what I am about to tell you." Here Thad paused.

He took a deep breath and exhaled slowly. By telling Selale, Thad knew he was taking an enormous risk. One of two things was sure to happen: she would accept the implications of this vision or they would completely drive her away from him. He continued slowly, "Okay, after I finished taking photographs of the entire shell, something compelled me to touch it. I reached out to touch it when bam! Suddenly I saw a bright light and this vision of us together with a baby. That baby looked like me, and he reached his little arms out for me to hold him. Just as suddenly, the vision disappeared and a feeling that everything was going to be all right poured over me, head to toe. It felt tangible, like warm water. Selale, I don't know what it all means, but I know the vision and the feeling were as real as our sitting here together right now." Thad paused his story to hand Selale the pictures, but he stopped when he realized she was pale and shaking. He dropped the photos, and reached over and gathered her into his arms. "Selale, what's wrong?"

A loud roaring filled her ears. Selale felt herself swaying, slipping away, utterly powerless to stop the panic that enveloped her. The description of Thad's vision threatened to overwhelm her grip on consciousness. She could hear the alarm in Thad's voice, but she was unable to respond before she succumbed to the darkness.

Chapter Twenty-two

Thad held Selale's limp body in his arms. *Was it his vision that caused her to faint?* Now regretting his decision to reveal the vision, he realized he should have waited. Obviously, this kind of talk of babies and love came too soon, too suddenly for her. He didn't know how to help her, so he simply held her as he waited for her to gain consciousness. He inspected her eyes, her skin, her tail, her torso. She was amazing. Her skin felt and looked different from human skin. Thad caressed her arm and shoulders. It wasn't scaly, but it was smoother, thicker, and with fewer pores than his skin. Instead of a pink undertone, hers had an olive color. The shape of her tail resembled that of a dolphin; the texture, however, resembled a fish crossed with human skin. Translucent, visible scales started just below her hipbones and extended in symmetrical rows down to the tail. Thad ran his hand down her tail surprised at how it felt. The scales were thick and flexible, not brittle. Her hair, by now dry, hung well below her shoulders, the strands a shiny cascade of dark, thick, limp curls. He rubbed a curl between his thumb and forefinger to feel its texture. Selale stirred, trying to awake. Slowly, like waking from a long, deep sleep, she opened her eyes and tried to refocus them on Thad. He helped her up and sat her on the boat's padded bench. A faint smile lifted the corners of her mouth as she realized what happened. She closed her eyes and shook her head.

"Well, this is embarrassing. I'm sorry, Thad. I don't know what came over me. Usually I am not this weak-minded. Let me sit here for a little while and compose myself." She looked out at the ocean instead of looking at Thad. He sat beside her giving her time to collect herself and her thoughts.

Her mind was swirling. Fear and foreboding weighed upon her as she pondered the vision Thad shared with her. What should she do? What could she do? Fate seemed to be stronger than her will to end their relationship. Should she tell him about the prophecy? Could it possibly involve her and Thad Destin? Selale turned and looked at Thad. She finally broke the silence.

"I'm scared." When he started to say something, Selale put her finger over Thad's lips. "No, I must say everything before I lose my nerve. There is something I must tell you about our meeting. There is a prophecy made over a hundred annutides ago. It is the prophecy of a Hybrid King. The Merpeople believe this king will unite the water and land worlds. He will be both human and merman. According to the prophecy, he will save the Merpeople. I don't understand it all, but I understand one thing. I recognize the hand of fate in our meeting and your vision. It scares me to death. For a centennitide, my people have tried to thwart this prophecy by preventing contact with the human world. Our leaders have believed that as long as humans live in ignorance of our existence, we are safe from harm. This belief has perpetuated the myth that if the Merpeople aren't in trouble, they don't need saving. Thad, this is important. Was the baby in your vision human or merman?"

Thad closed his eyes as if seeing the vision in a dream. He smiled at the memory of it. He could see himself and Selale in the ocean and with arms outreached and legs kicking through the water, the baby swam toward Thad. "Human. He had legs." A frown furrowed Thad's brow. He looked at Selale. "Why is that important?"

Selale closed her eyes, understanding that the crucial part of Thad's vision was the baby's being human. She whispered, "According to the legend of the Hybrid King, the baby is human." She opened her eyes and looked at Thad. How could he understand this vision since he didn't know the prophecy of the Hybrid King? Perhaps if she showed him Beulah Cave and read him the entire story, he would comprehend the significance of the vision he had seen. "How long can you stay underwater with one of those tanks? I want to show you something, but it will require being under the water for a long time." Getting her barrens on their current location in proximity to the cave, Selale realized they could move the boat and swim there much faster. "Can we move the boat to another location? If we can move closer to where I want to take you, we will stay underwater for much less time. What I want to show you will help me explain the significance of what you saw."

"Sure, I can move the boat. Let me check the tanks first, and then we can go where you want to go. You navigate, and I'll drive." Thad got up and readied the boat. Selale glanced down and saw the photographs on the bench. The glossy film reflected the afternoon sun. She reached over and took them in her hand. The first glance at the images on the pictures caused her to gasp. Again, she felt as if she could not breathe. Just then the boat's engine roared to life, and almost immediately the boat started gliding through the water. Fear gripped her heart just like Selale's hand clutched the pictures. Her eyes scanned their contents and translated the shell's writing. Without realizing it, she sat there, her mouth agape. She raised her eyes and instantly they locked with Thad's. He had watched her look at the pictures and understood just from her reaction that she read the inscription on the shell. He cut the engine and walked over to her side. Once again, Selale sat there pale and trembling. He took the seat next to her and put his hand over her smaller one that tightly gripped the pictures. She closed her eyes, unable to stop the tears from spilling over onto her cheeks or the roaring in her ears. Slowly she opened her eyes and looked at Thad.

"You know what it says, don't you? I knew it. I knew you would be able to," Thad said. "The university has called in linguists and other scientists from all over the world, but still no one could decipher the writing. Last night I took these pictures and when I touched the shell, that's when I had that vision. Selale, what does it say? Read it to me. This shell, it's important, isn't it?"

Selale stared mutely once again at the image of the shell, unable to anything but nod. She took a deep breath, trying to collect her thoughts before she said anything else. The connection of all the events of the past cyclotide— her meeting Thad, the cave and its prophecy, Thad's vision, and now the shell—seemed to drown her in uncertainty. This was more than coincidence. Something much bigger was at work here, and it scared her to death. How could she explain all this to Thad? How could he ever understand? As the emotions warred inside her, she tried to make sense of it all. Thad drew her to him and held her gently. Her love for him rose up like a tidal wave above all the other emotions and washed them away leaving only a flood of trust in the reality of what they both felt for each other. She wrapped her arms around his waist and let him hold her.

Selale withdrew from Thad's embrace and put her hand on his cheek. "Before I translate this, I must show you something. I must begin somewhere to make sense out of everything that has happened. Put these pictures aside for right now; we'll get around to them later. First, continue moving east until I signal you to stop. We will need something that can shine light underwater. I know from the equipment in your research you have something like that. We will need it where we are going. Do you trust me, Thad?" With her fingertips, she brushed back the hair off his forehead and searched his beautiful eyes for an answer.

Thad stared intently into her eyes and fervently said, "More than anyone or anything." He kissed her softly on the cheek and stood. "Wave your arm when you want me to stop. I won't take my eyes off you." Smiling, he walked over and once again, the engine roared to life. They set off moving at a moderate pace toward the east. After a few miles, Selale signaled for Thad to stop. He secured the boat and from his equipment bag, he grabbed two powerful flashlights, turning both on to ensure they worked. He quickly put on his scuba gear and hooked the flashlights onto his side. The tank's gauge indicated he had almost three hours of oxygen. Walking over to Selale, Thad swept her into his arms and together, they jumped in the water.

Under water, Selale grabbed Thad's hand and slowly they descended into the ocean depths. If she had judged the distance correctly, the boat floated near the cave and arriving at its entrance would not take long. Anticipation led her steadily on. By herself, she could span the distance quickly, but Thad, even with his equipment, would be unable to keep up. She stopped and secured his hands around her shoulders and mouthed for him to hold on tightly. He nodded, and suddenly he found himself gliding effortlessly through the waters propelled by his lovely mermaid. It felt as if a boat pulled a skier. After several minutes they arrived at a mound of what appeared to be debris. Selale led him down to its base and entered a dark, narrow chasm. He held tightly to her hand, letting her navigate the way. He had no idea where or to what this journey led, only that Selale wanted to show him something important. The dark, murky waters limited his vision to mere inches, so he had to trust her. Thad closed his eyes and blindingly trusted his beautiful guide. As they made their way through a series of twists and turns, Thad opened his eyes and noticed the waters had lightened considerably. Up, up they swam to brighter waters. Suddenly they surfaced and Selale pushed Thad up onto a ledge of rock. He sat in what appeared to be a sea grotto.

"Turn on your magic light, Thad, so you can see Beulah Cave. Prepare to be amazed!" He could barely make out Selale's silhouette in the dim light. He reached for the most powerful flashlight and turned it on. Golden light suddenly revealed the beauty of the place. Selale's musical laughter filled the cave. "Isn't it the most fantastic place you have ever seen? It still takes my breath away! Papa shared this place with me only two cyclotides ago. I'm still exploring it. But, look behind you. Does that writing look familiar?" A smile could be heard in her question.

Thad turned around, and spanning the entire wall of the cave was the same complex language that he had photographed on the giant oyster shell. He sat gawking at the writing, his eyes scanning the entire wall. He spun around and said, "Tell me what it says. All of it. I can turn off the oxygen tank to save it for the ride back. I don't care if it takes all night, I must know what it says. Will you read it to me? Don't leave out anything; don't paraphrase it or change its story. Read it verbatim, word for word."

Selale hesitated. She knew this would change everything. By Thad knowing the prophecy of the Hybrid King, he would understand all the implications, good and bad, of their relationship. She swam over to his side and took the light from his hand. "I will read it to you, but you must promise me that you will listen to it in its entirety before you ask me any questions. After you hear the prophecy, you will understand the danger of our relationship and its implications. That shell your friend found contains the genesis of my species. It has been missing for many centennitides. While I only read the first picture, if that information fell into the wrong hands...." Here Selale's voice trailed off. "Well, do you promise to let me read it all, no interruptions?"

Thad raised his hand and placed it over his heart. "Cross my heart." To Selale's questioning glance, he murmured, "That means I promise."

"Here goes." Selale moved closer to the cave wall and as she read, her voice reverberated through the cavern:

> *"Atlantis has always been an island of unity since the physical island itself was destroyed. Peace reigns between the species in these waters and those who inhabit the land above. We share not only the waters, but also the air above with everything that lives in this world. As long as peace remains between human and merman, the Mer species shall be sustained. But dark shall be the days if peace is broken, for not only shall war ensue between humans and mermen, but between merman and merman. Atlantis' destruction shall come from both the inside out and the outside in. There is but one savior of our nation, one who embodies both human and merman qualities: the Hybrid King. He alone can save Atlantis. His birth will be conceived from undeniable love of Mer royalty and a human descendant of the Lost Ones. Look for the signs on the tide of his birth: the earth shall quake both land and water and orbs shall explode in showers of light. Though born of royal lineage, this king shall live as an exiled orphan, his true identity unknown by him and all men below and above the waters. This rare pearl shall live the life of a human. Though blessed with all the Mystical Gifts, his true value shall be concealed, understood only by those who love him best. Prosperity shall bless all who endeavor to help him for the sun shall always on his shoulder shine. The current to the human world will bring a streak of Darkness that will pierce the sun, a cloud that*

will scar its light, a reminder of the battle yet to come, the war of good versus evil ever-present in both worlds. The Hybrid King's absence in the waters will signal an end of the Light. Dark the waters shall be. Light extinguished; dark shall reign. For many annutides, in the hands of a Dark reflection, the kingdom's fate shall rest. Suffering shall come to those loyal to the Light, for mercy Darkness shows not. Despair not; hope for restoration will rise with the sun's entry into the waters. A great battle for the waters shall ensue, for Dark and Light cannot co-exist. Both reside and war within us all. If the Hybrid King discovers and unites with the Light, good shall triumph because only his knowledge can render the Dark powerless. The Mer Kingdom of Atlantis will shine once again. But woe if the Hybrid King fails to discover the Light! He will doom Atlantis and become a slave to the Dark! Victory shall come only if this Hybrid realizes that true power lies not in mankind's force or weapons wielded, but in love and the merciful redemption of mankind that comes only through sacrifice. All this shall come to pass just as foretold."

Selale's voice was tired. She turned toward Thad wanting to gauge his reaction to the prophecy. Utterly speechless, he sat on the rock ledge staring at Selale. She sat the light on the ledge and pulled herself out of the water to sit beside him and said, "That's it. Now, do you see why this relationship, your vision, and the shell's discovery, all frighten me? It leads to this—the Hybrid King Prophecy. I'm involved, you're involved, Papa is involved; it's all connected. Now that you know what is at stake, is loving me worth it?" She turned and gazed steadily into his eyes. "Will you leave me knowing that our love could ultimately lead here? I can't say that I blame you if you do. It's a heavy burden for both of us to carry."

Thad gently took Selale's small hand in his and brought it to his lips. "It is not as heavy as losing you forever. That is a burden I could never carry. Is loving you worth it? Absolutely. Loving you is priceless. Will I leave you?

Never. Selale, this scares me too, but I don't believe we can run from it. If this is destined to happen, it will happen, one way or the other. As long as we are together, we can make it through anything. I won't let anything happen to you or to anyone you love if I can help it. That is a promise I make to you."

"Cross your heart?" Selale mimicked his last promise.

"Cross my heart." He took her in his arms. How could he ever live without her? At this moment he couldn't even imagine spending one day without being in her presence. He suddenly had a brilliant idea. "In my culture, we have a marriage ceremony. We pledge our vows to be faithful and to love each other forever. Married couples are called husbands and wives. They are partners, together forever. Selale, will you marry me right now? Will you be my wife? Will you let me be your husband? I can't live without you."

Too emotional to speak, Selale could only nod.

Thad continued, "I'm going to say my words of promise to you, then you can say your promise to me. I learned these for Michael's wedding in case he forgot what to say." Here he pulled Selale out of his arms so that he could look her in the eye. He took her hand and said, "I, Thad, take you, Selale, to be my wife, to have and to hold, from today forward, for better or worse, for richer or poorer, in sickness and in health, to love and to cherish, till death do us part; and I pledge myself to you forever. Cross my heart," Thad smiled as he kissed the tears streaming down Selale's face. "Your turn."

Selale whispered, "I, Selale, take you, Thad, to be my husband. I will love you forever and stay by your side, through good times and through bad. I will cherish you and remain loyal to you and our love forever, even after death has separated us. You will be my only love. Cross my heart."

Thad took Selale in his arms. He had no idea if or how he could make love to his new bride, but for now, just knowing Selale was his was enough. He loved her so much.

Selale pulled back and with passion in her eyes said, "Let me show you what marriage means in my culture." Kissing him gently, she pushed his back onto the ledge and proceeded to show him how a mermaid makes love to a human.

Chapter Twenty-three

Marius marveled at Ettore's ability with a waterbow. Of course, it helped that Ettore had inherited his father's Mystical Gift of being able to control the waters around him. He was a Water-Bender just like Marius. Ettore could hit any target from any distance with his waterbow, his specially made arrows piercing through the waters with speed and accuracy unrivaled by any other merman. Pride for his son welled up inside him. As he watched his son compete in the annual games at the Olympus Complex, he felt a sense of accomplishment that he had raised not only successful children, but ones who had a true love for their fellow mermen. Both Ettore and Selale embodied goodness. Their mother would have been proud of them. A pang wrenched Marius' heart as he thought about his children's mother. Oh, how he missed Giada! It was events like this that he longed for her to share with him.

Ettore competed against some of the finest bowmen in the kingdom, including one of his closest childhood friends and Calder's newest ally, Rahwah. Rahwah's defection hurt. He and Ettore had been friends even in the womb. His mother and Giada had been childhood best friends and their friendship brought together Ettore and Rahwah because they were born nearly the same tide. The two boys had remained virtually inseparable friends even after Giada died. Until recent events at the council meeting, Marius thought they still were friends. Now, however, watching the annual games, it was obvious to even those unfamiliar with the two archers' history that their once amicable relationship had somehow turned hostile. An almost tangible animosity filled the waters. Rahwah had been a part of their family and secretly Marius thought Rahwah felt more than a brotherly love for Selale. Marius felt a sense of loss.

Speaking of Selale, he wondered why she was not here. Though the games held little interest for her, Marius felt sure she would come to see her brother. The two had always been close. Now as he thought about it, he had not seen his daughter in over two full tides. She seemed preoccupied, like something or someone was on her mind. Maybe the cave had fascinated her so that she was spending a great deal of the tides there. Whatever it was, something was going on with her, but Marius didn't know what. Women had always mystified him. He didn't pretend to understand them.

He watched as Ettore hit his final target with precision and accuracy no merman could rival. The entire auditorium resounded with applause as the announcer declared Ettore the winner. As Ettore raised his hand to acknowledge the applause, Rahwah's eyes flared with hatred.

Ettore swam to Rahwah's side to congratulate him on a good match. One important lesson he had learned from his father was to be gracious. He never wanted to seem haughty and arrogant to anyone, including a challenger. As he approached his longtime friend, Ettore received a frigid reception. Rahwah begrudgingly shook the hand Ettore extended. Ettore shrugged it off as Rahwah's competitive nature, but when he started to speak, Rahwah spat out, "One of these tides, golden boy, you will get what's coming to you. I hope I am there to witness the fall. You and your father are in for a rude awakening really soon." He turned his back and swam angrily away. Ettore was stunned. He didn't know what to make of this sudden and unprovoked hatred. Hurt and confused, Ettore made his way to Marius' box.

Marius knew words had been exchanged, but his son seemed reluctant to divulge the specifics of the conversation. He put his arm around his son. Before he had a current to console and congratulate him though, a group of lovely mermaids had lined up to congratulate the winner. Standing at the front of the line was the mermaid Ettore loved. Noting her smile and shining eyes, he realized his son's feelings were reciprocated. Marius withdrew from the box as the mob of Ettore's admirers began gushing praise for his performance. Ettore had eyes and ears only for his beautiful Julette. Shaking his head, Marius decided to make a quiet exit and swim back to his chamber.

As he approached the portals of the Olympus Complex, he spotted Rahwah having an animated and heated conversation with his brother Calder. He should have known Calder was responsible for poisoning Rahwah and Ettore's friendship. Recently, Calder appeared to be collecting more friends, including the young, impressionable Rahwah. A current of suspicion drifted through Marius' mind. He needed to watch this development carefully. With anyone else, Marius would have attributed it to coincidence. With Calder, there was always an ulterior purpose, a less than honorable one. Of that, Marius was certain. Making his way out of the chamber, several mermen, including Sandoval and the inner circle of councilmen, crowded around him congratulating him on Ettore's victory. Unbeknown to Marius, Calder's eyes followed his twin all the way out the portal and until he was no longer in sight. Mirroring his mentor, Rahwah watched Marius leave as well.

How he could have ever thought Marius was fit to be king Rahwah would never understand. Most of his childhood memories involved Marius and Ettore. In truth, Rahwah had considered Marius as much his papa as Ettore's. But that had been many tides ago, before Rahwah had faced one rejection after another in the line of promotions at the Engineering Chamber. Rahwah had turned to his father-figure for help, but Marius had refused to intervene, citing some tidal wash about Earning not Entitlement. It was then Rahwah realized how things in the Mer World really worked. It wasn't who you knew; it truly was who you were. He had never forgiven Marius or for that matter, Ettore, the merman who would inherit the throne. He turned toward Calder and muttered, "Soon, Calder, you will be king, and mermen will crowd around you. I'm your man. Just instruct me when, where, and how, and it will be done accordingly. Your rise to power can't come soon enough."

Calder firmly placed his hand on his eager, young follower's shoulder and whispered, "Patience. It won't be long. It won't be long." A slow smile spread over his face.

Chapter Twenty-four

Swimming slowly enough for him to hang on to her, Selale led Thad back to his boat. She dreaded being away from him even for one tide. She still had no idea how they could overcome the obstacles that prevented them from being together permanently. That was something she didn't want to dwell on right now. Thad's boat floated right where they had left it. So much had changed in less than one tide. Selale's cheeks burned as she thought of their time together in the cave. She loved him so much it left her weak.

Thad helped Selale into the boat, and then he pulled himself over the side. As he removed his scuba gear, his eyes never left hers. It was getting late, or he should say early. His eight o'clock class would start in less than four hours. As he finished putting away the last of his equipment, he realized that his world had completely changed in the last few hours. He knew he could never go back to the life he lived before he met Selale. That life no longer mattered. All that mattered was Selale and his future with her. He would do anything to make her happy and keep her safe. Those were his only priorities. He moved to her side and gathered her into his arms.

"So where do we go from here? Even though we have separate lives, our lives are now one. The entire ride back I kept thinking about how we can make this work. I have to be honest. I just don't know. I do know I have to be with you. You have a job; I have a job. We both have responsibilities. Until we can work it out, we can meet like we have been for the past six weeks, here in my boat or at the research site. I do know that after today, that won't be enough for me. I want to spend every waking and sleeping hour with you," Thad wiped a tear that slid down Selale's cheek. "Hey, we will work it out. Remember? Great love and miracles. I've never been a patient person; however, this is worth the wait. Go home, Selale. We will see each other tomorrow."

Selale looked into his eyes and wanted to believe in those miracles. She nodded, "I will see you then, before the tide changes. It will seem an eternity." She kissed Thad and slid back into the water. She bobbed in the same spot until her husband could no longer be seen, their eyes locked on each other.

She headed away from the cave toward her chamber, swimming mindlessly through the water, her mind consumed with thoughts of her husband. She didn't see Rahwah off in the distance at the edge of a multi-chamber complex, but he had seen her. He wondered where she had been at this current of the tide. Had she been with a merman? Jealousy sliced through him. He wanted her all for himself and the thought of her spending time in another merman's arms about sent him over the edge. He decided this situation deserved more investigation. This could prove interesting. He would consult with Calder. Something fishy was going on with the king's daughter and he intended to find out if this could be the leverage Calder and the SCEROH needed. Eliminating any competition for Selale's affection also motivated him. While he wanted Selale, he also wanted the power that Calder offered. Maybe he was overreacting; maybe not. The passing tides would tell. A scandal could be the impetus to set Calder's rise to power in motion. Rahwah continued to patrol around the multi-chamber complex eager for his shift to end so he could report his findings to Calder.

Chapter Twenty-five

Selale slept fitfully. Nightmares that seemed so real plagued her dreams and jerked her awake. Her heart pounded in her chest as fragments of the nightmare surfaced in her memory. Thad was at his research site. As she approached him though, she saw the SCEROH lined up right behind her with strange weapons aimed straight for him. Right before her eyes, they bound him and removed his breathing equipment. She too was bound and watched powerlessly as he drowned. Her screams reverberated through the waters, yet her husband's executioners appeared deaf to her pleading. Selale got up and moved around her chamber desperately trying to erase the dream. What could this mean? She wondered if this was some kind of warning of things to come. She shivered at the thought. At times like this, Selale wished for the Gift of Prophecy. No mermaid or merman from the royal family had possessed that gift since her Great-Great-Grandmere. If nothing else, the dream was a wake-up call for her to use more discretion when meeting Thad in the future. The SCEROH would not care if she was "married" to a human. In fact, that would only raise their ire. Her intentional contact with a human would not go unpunished.

Selale remembered the tunnel. Using the tunnel to the cave would ensure that no one would follow her. She had to be careful. Now that she had a plan, she felt more confidence seeing Thad, but this dream had warned her that they must not act carelessly. Their relationship presented real danger to both of them.

Selale decided to go to work early. She knew it would take much longer to translate and complete her job this tide with her mind fixated on one thing: seeing her husband. She smiled at the memory of their marriage ceremony and the subsequent consummation of their marriage as she readied herself to leave her chamber for work. With her mind a thousand leagues away, she swam squarely into her father. He had stationed himself near the doorway of her chamber to watch his daughter. He had heard her rise early and wanted to ask where she had been hiding the last couple of tides. He assumed she had been in the cave. He hoped that perhaps she had wanted to read and study the entire prophecy. However, after studying her, he realized there was more going on with her. He recognized the faraway look to her eyes. She was in love.

"Papa! I'm sorry," Selale stammered as she laughed at herself. "I really didn't see you. My mind was far away. Are you all right?" Selale put her arms around Marius' shoulder, still laughing with good-natured mirth.

"Yes, I'm fine. Where are you going so early this morntide? I heard you moving around. Could you not sleep?" Marius' brow creased with concern. "I've missed you the past several tides. Where have you been hiding?"

Selale hesitated just a moment too long. She knew her father would know if she wasn't completely honest. She sighed and whispered, "It's complicated. That's all I can say right now. I have been to the cave and have read the entire prophecy. Oh, Papa, it scares me to death to think that this prophecy somehow involves you and me. Does it not terrify you? It's just, I don't know, such an enormous responsibility." Selale lifted her eyes to meet her father's steady gaze.

"You forget. We know how the story ends. That in and of itself should give you some hope, some comfort, no?" Marius pulled his daughter into his arms. He knew she wasn't telling him everything, but he figured she was just apprehensive about voicing her fears if it involved the merman she loved. "You know you can tell me anything, right, Selale? You never have anything to fear by being honest. I am here and always will be." With that, Marius kissed her on the top of her head and then swam out of her chamber.

Selale sat back down on her couch. How did he always know when she had a secret? Guilt welled up inside her, threatening to drown the sweetness of the past two tides. With resolve, Selale rose from her couch, refusing to give in to her guilt for not confiding in her father. How could she explain what she felt when she couldn't even completely understand it herself? Too much had happened in the last two tides to trivialize it to just love. She would not change anything that had happened with Thad. She would tell her father if or when the occasion presented itself. She had no idea how he would react, but Selale knew one thing for certain. She loved Thad and nothing would ever change that, regardless of the consequences.

Selale swam out of the chamber more determined than ever to keep their love a secret and protect Thad at all costs, even if it meant being less than honest with her father.

The swim to the Chamber of Records which also housed the Language Chamber where she worked took only a matter of currents. Selale wanted to go see the other shells that contained the history of Atlantis to put the information found on the shell in Thad's picture in perspective. She needed to read the entire shell to be certain it contained what she thought: the metamorphosis from human to merman of the six original founders—the scientist from whom the royal family descended and the five other educated men he had recruited to join him—and their families.

If that information fell into the wrong hands, it could present a real danger to not only the entire Mer race, but also to humans. Selale knew about the conflicts and violent acts between different races of humans. She had read about the tumultuous history of human governments that waged wars on land and in the very waters of Atlantis. The information on the shell may give the specific process along with the chemical ingredients about how humans transformed into mermen. Having the knowledge to mutate a species could shift the balance of power for or against one race of humans. No doubt that if someone with malevolent intentions acquired this information, a catastrophe of epic proportions could result. Fortunately, humans could not translate the complex language of her species written on the shell. The Mer language of her people dated back to Atlantis itself long before its eventual destruction.

It was the only language spoken and written for several centennitides in the waters of Atlantis.

Selale realized how dangerous this information could be to the Mer people if it fell into the hands of Calder and the SCEROH. That could definitely cause a shift in power. Her father would not stand a chance. Perhaps this was the very reason the shell had been "lost" from the other tomes of history. Maybe someone many centennitides ago concluded the same thing Selale herself just did: the information had the capacity to cause great suffering and hurt if misused. Selale wanted to see the other shells to obtain some context of the history of Atlantis, so when she translated what was written on the lost shell, she could understand it in the context of the remaining history. Perhaps then it would make sense like a story.

She arrived at the Chamber of Records early and swam to the back chamber that housed all the important artifacts and records. To get clearance to enter required a special permit granted by the chamber curator. Without his consent and approval, access to the chamber was denied. A sophisticated security system surrounded the chamber making unauthorized entry an almost impossible task to fulfill. Selale debated what to tell the curator. She trusted him and believed him to be a man of integrity. His name spoke volumes of his character: Stedman. The truth had always served her well, and she decided he could be trusted to keep this visit confidential. Swimming over to the desk, she rang the call button and waited for the curator to arrive from his personal office chamber. She didn't have to wait long. Very few visitors came to the chamber this early in the tide, so the curator arrived quickly, his interest piqued as to who needed his assistance. Stedman's pleasant smile greeted Selale. He had always liked her because they both shared a mutual interest in language. Even though he was more than ten annutides older, Stedman had watched with interest as Marius and his twin brother grew up. While he was not a confidant of Marius, he did consider him a friend and an ally of the chamber. Marius valued the history of their species and that quality alone earned him Stedman's respect. Because he knew of her work here at the chamber, he also admired Selale's sharp mind and was impressed with her Gift of Interpretation.

"Good tide, Selale. It's been almost an annutide since we've spoken. How are you and what brings you here so early?" Stedman's questions voiced his curiosity about her early arrival.

"Good tide to you too, Sir. It has been quite a while since I saw you last. I have been well and hope you are. I'm sorry for this unusually early visit, but I was here in the building anyway and decided to see you before I went to the translation chamber. First, I want to ask that you keep what I am going to tell you confidential until I learn more information. Will you promise me?" Selale flashed him her most winning smile.

Rendered almost speechless from her charm, Stedman nodded mutely.

"Great! I told myself you were a man of integrity and that I should stick with the truth. All right, here goes. About two cyclotides ago, a human walking on a beach discovered a large, ancient shell with strange etchings on its interior side. It was uncovered after a storm. So far, no human can translate the language on the shell, even though experts from all over the human world have tried." Selale observed the curator's look of alarm. She nodded and continued, "Only yestertide did I learn of this information. No one else knows this. You are the first whom I have told. I know this news is very disturbing, but I don't want to alarm our people unnecessarily until I am sure that this is the missing shell that contains the Merpeople's genesis. What I desperately need to do is read the other eleven shells to see if this shell's information fits in the context of the history detailed in the other tomes. With my knowledge of the language, I should be able to determine this rather quickly and with certainty. Then, with your counsel, we together can decide how to proceed." Selale met Stedman's stunned gaze. She waited for him to regain his composure.

Finally, he cleared his throat and said softly, "If this discovery is the missing shell, then you comprehend the danger and the magnitude of its information. Thank you for confiding in me. How can I assist you?"

Selale continued, "Could you help me read them and catalog a brief synopsis of what each contains? I know this will take most of the morntide, but this is of the utmost urgency. It terrifies me to think of the 'What if's?' You with your knowledge of the past, present, and the future understand the implications more than any other merman I know."

Stedman solemnly nodded. "Let's get started. We may not have a moment to lose. I'm going to send a message with my assistant to the translation chamber that you will be helping me this tide." Here he paused the conversation to swim into a smaller chamber. He returned shortly. "Now that we have that minor detail taken care of, let me get some tablets and etchers to record our summaries. You will want to take this information with you, right?" Without waiting for her answer, he went to a drawer and withdrew two tablets and two etchers. He turned and, with Selale following him, swam down a long narrow corridor. From a cord that hung like a belt around his hipbones he took an ancient key. He asked Selale to please turn her back while he entered the sequence to accessing the chamber housing the shells. Without hesitation, she turned, not wanting to compromise his integrity or the security of the ancient artifacts. She only had to wait briefly. A moment later, he tapped her on the shoulder, so they could continue to the tome of shells.

As they swam into the Chamber of History, a reverence flowed through the room. Selale stared in awe seeing all eleven shells lined up along the chamber wall. "Impressive, isn't it? Stedman asked. Selale nodded her agreement for fear her voice might desecrate this special place. They swam to the shell on the far left wall. The curator ran his hand around the outside.

He turned to Selale and whispered, "You start with the first two shells, volumes two and three. I will start with the seventh one. He handed her a tablet and etcher, and in silence, they began the tedious process.

Almost half the tide passed, both exhausted, yet relieved that it was finished. Selale realized she had made the right decision to trust the old curator. He, better than any other merman, understood the importance of her request. It would have taken her at least two full tides to complete the summary and recording. They had managed to get the entire history recorded on two tablets. Stedman had transcribed six tomes; Selale, five. Together they swam back to the main atrium of the chamber. Gratitude overwhelmed Selale. She became emotional and began to cry. She hugged Stedman's neck and he, confused over her sudden emotion, hugged her gently like he did when he saw his grandchildren.

He pulled her back and studied her. "Selale, I'm putting these tablets in a bag. Take them to your chamber and don't let anyone read them until you figure out this dilemma. Be careful in whom you put your trust. These are strange tides, and mermen's loyalties can shift like the currents. As for me, I trust that you will make the right decisions. Our future may very well rest in your hands. Now, go. You know where I am if you need my assistance again. I will not speak of this to anyone. You have my word." He handed her the tablets and with a final squeeze of her hand, she left him. She quickly swam out of the chamber of records and headed straight home.

With her mind on getting the tablets home safely, she almost swam right into Rahwah. He laughed at her distracted face as he halted her progress by swimming right in her path. "Whoa! I didn't know we had freight trains running through Atlantis! I swear you about ran over me. Where are you going in such a hurry? You were swimming like a shark was chasing you."

Selale tried to smooth away the irritated frown that creased her forehead. The last thing she wanted to do was to raise the suspicion of Rahwah. Her father had told her of his defection. While she considered him more her brother's friend than her own, he had recently given signs that he was interested in her more than just as her brother's friend. That thought disturbed her. He was someone whom she would never find romantically appealing. They had absolutely nothing in common. She tried not to shudder as his hand caressed her neck. Pasting on an overly bright smile, Selale played along with him. She dipped away from his possessive touch. "Rahwah, I'm so sorry I ran into you. I've been at work and it has been exhausting to say the least. I've been buried in history with the ancient curator Stedman all tide, so yes, I was distracted." She decided to stick to the truth as much as she could.

"I'm not sorry you ran into me." Again, his hand ran up Selale's arm. She jerked it back as if he had stung her like a ray. "Do I make you nervous, Selale?" He laughed at her discomfort. "You make me feel many things, but nervous is not one of them." Flashing an insinuating smile, he acted like he had all tide to swim there.

"Rahwah, I'm tired and I'm not interested in your games or insinuations. Please let me go. I want to go home." Selale tried to swim around him, but again, he blocked her path.

"Let me guess, you're tired from your all-eventide rendezvous." To Selale's startled look, Rahwah let out a sarcastic laugh. "Oh, yes, I saw you coming back right before the tide was over." He grabbed her arm tightly. "Where had you been? Who had you spent the tide with?" Jealousy made his eyes blaze.

Selale jerked her arm from his painful grasp. "Let me go. Who are you to ask me where I had been? My father? My brother? My lover? You are none of those and never will be, so you have no right to ask and no claim on what I do during any tide. I owe you no explanation, so get out of my way." Again, she tried to swim away, but he jerked her around to face him. He pulled her into an embrace. As she struggled to free herself, he became even more empowered. He clutched her jaw with his hand and angrily made her stare into his eyes.

Through clenched teeth he said, "Don't fight me, lovely Selale. You will belong to me. One of these tides you will bow to me, bow to my wishes. You will be mine. Mark my word."

Selale broke free and swam as fast as she could away from him. She turned to see that he had not pursued her, but she was aware his eyes watched her until she swam into her chamber. Shaken and frightened, she swam to her bedchamber and sat on her couch clutching the bag holding the two tablets. For the first tide in her life, she no longer felt safe in the waters of Atlantis.

Chapter Twenty-six

After the most wonderful night of his life, Thad arrived home and crashed for three hours. Even with a lack of sleep, he awoke infused with a new vigor, a new purpose to his life. He had Selale. Right at this moment in his life, everything was perfect. Showering and then dressing quickly, he rushed out the door with just enough time to stop and grab a cup of coffee from the university coffee shop. Today he had three morning classes. That meant he had the rest of the afternoon free to spend with Selale. The morning classes went well. There were only four weeks left in the semester including exams. Excitement welled up inside of Thad as he thought about the month he would have free from his duties at the university. The winter holiday break afforded him the luxury of a month to spend focusing on Selale. He smiled at the thought of spending Christmas with her.

Thad didn't go home even to change clothes. He headed straight to the dock where he had moored his boat. An almost desperate yearning to see Selale and find out about her day propelled his steps even faster. There were still four hours of daylight left. As he boarded the boat, he spotted the pictures he had taken of the shell still stacked on the cushion where he and Selale had left them. He reached down and picked them up in his hand. Studying the images carefully, he knew Selale could read the inscription. The language inscribed on the shell had been etched on the cave wall—the language of Atlantis. He would again ask Selale to translate it for him. He put them in a small compartment next to the steering wheel. Without another thought about the pictures, he started the engine and headed for the open waters of the ocean.

The waters were calm today, making the ride to his research site an easy one. The sun streamed down on the sparkling water casting a diamond-like gleam across the expanse of blue. Today the Atlantic Ocean looked more beautiful than ever. Anticipation raced through Thad as he changed into his diving gear. First, he would check the data, collect the samples and recording, and then he would wait on Selale to join him. He secured the boat and plunged into the glittering depths.

Thad spent over an hour checking his equipment and gathering the week's samples. The data continued to show a deterioration of the minute marine life many larger sea animals relied on as their source of food. He would continue to track this decline and come up with possible scenarios that pinpointed the cause and ultimately, the effects of the loss of this food source. This shift in the ecological balance of an important food source could theoretically impact the Mer species. He would need to question Selale again about their diet. Eyeing the camera, he realized it too posed a potential danger to Selale, so he decided to pack it up and take it to the surface. He made a mental note to destroy the recording of Selale. Keeping it could threaten her and her entire species if the wrong person saw the film. While he was distracted, Selale made her way up behind him. She wrapped her arms around his waist and breathed the water with contentment. With the equipment in one arm and his wife in the other, they returned to the surface wrapped in an unbreakable embrace.

Selale had used the tunnel, so she had come from the opposite direction to the research site. With the nightmare and the encounter with Rahwah still fresh on her mind, she didn't want to take any chance, regardless how remote, of being discovered with Thad. The nightmare reminded her that her interaction with a human would not go unpunished. Both she and possibly Thad would pay a heavy price if their relationship was discovered.

After sitting paralyzed with fear on her couch for a while, Selale finally quelled the panic building up inside her. She took the two tablets and hid them in her chamber. Finally, she composed herself and forced her mind to function and devise a plan. She realized a strategy must be formulated. It was her responsibility to protect Thad from the SCEROH. Now that Rahwah had suspicions of her liaison with someone, jealousy would propel him to find out who his competition was and destroy him. Selale would not let that happen. She could not continue meeting Thad here at this site because they were too exposed. The SCEROH had spies everywhere, and it was impossible to know where loyalties lay. Because she had a plan, Selale felt more in control. Thad would need to take his boat to the waters over the cave. There, because the waters were condemned, they were safe from the suspicious eyes of the SCEROH.

"I missed you. I didn't think the morning would ever end. How was your day, Selale?" Thad kissed her without waiting for her response.

"Let's get in the boat. There is so much that I have to tell you. Put your equipment away so we can spend the rest of the tide together." Selale touched Thad's face with her hand. Thad took it and kissed her palm. Selale smiled. Without another word, they climbed into the boat. Thad removed his scuba gear and put away his research equipment. He could tell something had happened to upset Selale, but he would wait and not jump to conclusions. When he had finished unloading everything, he sat down on the bench beside his lovely wife. He took her in his arms and just held her.

The boat bobbed in the water as the sun sank lower on the horizon. The calm water slapped the boat gently and a cool breeze blew their hair slightly. In spite of the beauty of their surroundings, Thad could feel Selale's restlessness.

"Tell me what's wrong. It's written all over your face that you've had a terrible day. Talk to me and let me make it better." He stroked her hair and waited for her to begin.

"It's better now that I'm with you. Just hold me for a while because it has been an awful tide. I'll tell you everything, but first, let me draw some strength from your love." They held each other, and Thad shifted Selale so that he could see her face. He kissed her closed eyes, her cheeks, and her nose. Last, he kissed her lips gently.

She smiled and opened her eyes. She sat up and turned to face him. "This tide has been one of the worst of my life. I don't know how that happened since yestertide was the most beautiful. Let me start at the beginning. So much has happened since I left you." She took his hand and clasped it in her own.

"When I arrived at my chamber before the tide turned, I immediately fell asleep; however, all night I was plagued by nightmares, one right after the other. The last one involved you. The SCEROH discovered our relationship, and they killed you. I woke up and couldn't go back to sleep. I decided we had to use more discretion when we meet. The SCEROH spies are everywhere. If we are discovered, the punishment will be swift and brutal. Thad, we must change where we meet. This site is too exposed. Do you remember the cave?"

He met her steady gaze. "How could I ever forget it?" A smile stretched across his face. Selale's face turned red as she remembered their lovemaking.

She leaned over and kissed him again before she continued. "The waters surrounding the cave have been condemned, deemed unsafe by my father. They really aren't contaminated, but no one knows that. This ensured protection for the cave. I have a secret tunnel to get there. If you come to the waters above the cave, no one will see you. You will be safe. Will you promise to meet me there from this point on? That way I don't have to worry about our relationship being discovered. I have to know that you won't be harmed. Promise?" Selale waited for his answer.

Thad raised her hand to his lips, kissed it, and then placed it over his heart. "I promise. Cross my heart."

Selale smiled at the phrase. Then she turned serious once again. "Let's go to the cave, and I will tell you the rest." Selale looked up when Thad rose.

"Hold on. Let me get the pictures before we set out. We definitely need to discuss these when we get to the cave." Thad opened the compartment and withdrew the photographs. He held them in his hand as once again he took his seat beside Selale.

She took the photos from him, but she did not look at them. Her sultry eyes stared into his. "We have the entire tide to spend together. What better place to spend it than at the cave!" Her eyes twinkled with the flirtatious reminder of the last tide they spent together there. He embraced her and felt desire well up inside him. They really needed to get to the cave before he made love to her right there. He kissed her passionately, and then he wisely disengaged himself before he burst into flames.

"All right, captain. I will ready the ship for our destination." Thad stood and with a mock salute, he set their course for the cave. Selale smiled at his silliness. Watching him ready the boat and start the engine, she realized he had a way about him that made her happy regardless of the lousy, stressful circumstances of the tide she had had. She loved him, plain and simple.

As the boat skimmed through the water, Selale decided to examine the photos of the shell. Slowly piecing the pictures together, she read the delicate writing etched by her ancestors many centennitides ago. She held her breath as she read the story of the transformation the men and their families made as they readied themselves for the impending demise of Atlantis. A catastrophic natural disaster was coming, and with just days to spare, they finished the metamorphosis that saved their lives. Because the king and his council would not listen to the pleas of Immanuel the scientist to evacuate the island, everyone else living on the island perished. Twenty-two people survived the destruction of Atlantis. After watching its destruction from the water, they swam due west for three days unable to ever return to the land of their birth.

Tears rolled down Selale's cheeks as she thought of the massive loss of life caused by the disaster and her ancestors having to watch helplessly as their home was destroyed. She breathed a sigh of relief because nowhere in the writing was the formula or the ingredients the men used to make the change from human to merman. Once again, she pored over the writing, just to reassure herself that the information was not there. So engrossed was Selale on reading the shell that she didn't realize they had come to the waters over the cave. Like coming out of a trance, she adjusted her eyes to focus on Thad as he moved to sit beside her. He reached his hand up to her cheek, and gently with his thumb, wiped away the tears.

"What does it say, Selale? It must be sad since it has brought you to tears." Selale merely nodded, unable to speak. He enfolded her in his arms and let her cry. She did not know why this tide she had become so sentimental, emotional, and weepy. This was not her usual nature. She had always prided herself on being strong and immune to the shifting tides of emotion so many merwomen her age drowned themselves in. Composing herself, she wiped away the remaining tears.

Selale reached for Thad's hand and held it in her lap. "Let's swim to the cave before I tell you about this tide or the photos. Everything makes sense there, especially when I'm with you. It will be easier to talk about the things that happened this tide and what is written on the shell when I am bathed in the soothing golden light of Beulah Cave.

Thad nodded. He quickly put on his scuba gear. Taking a water-tight container from a nearby compartment, he put in the photos, along with two lights. Securing the equipment to his suit, they jumped in the water and swam to the cave. Because they were right over the cave, it took only a matter of minutes for Selale to lead him there.

As they surfaced in the cave, Selale took a deep breath. Already the tension and anxiety of the past tide had ebbed and now a sense of equanimity soothed her spirit. Thad pulled himself and Selale up on the bench of rock that jutted out from the golden walls. He reached into the container and pulled out the pictures and one of the lights. Turning it on, golden light filled the entire chamber.

He stood on the ledge of rock and surveyed the entire cave. "This place is incredible." He walked over to the writing engraved into the cave wall. His hand traced the delicate symbols. "There's a serenity that this place emanates. When you are ready, tell me about the rest of your day, your tide, as you call it and the writing on the shell. As you so aptly reminded me, we have all tide." He sat down beside Selale and leaning against the wall of the cave, pulled her into his arms.

She relaxed and listened to the steady beat of his heart as it pounded in her ear that rested on his chest. The rhythmical beat set a soothing contrast to the tension-filled waters of the morntide. Selale took a deep breath. "All right, I'm going to finish telling you about what happened before I met you at the research site. I went to the Chamber of Records early this morntide. I couldn't go back to sleep after the nightmare I told you about. The Chamber houses the shells with our species' history. There are eleven shells just like the one in your picture. The curator is an acquaintance of mine. After today, I would say he is more of a friend. Together we spent the entire morntide etching a synopsis of each shell so I could put the information found on the shell in these photographs into context. I had to confide in him about your friend discovering the missing tome of Atlantis. He and I agreed that the information etched on it could be catastrophic if it fell into the wrong hands. We believed it may contain the metamorphic genesis of our species. After examining and reading the manuscript on the shell closely, I am somewhat relieved by what is not on it. The exact formula and the chemicals the men used are not mentioned on the shell. That information was what I was worried about that could be misused if someone had the capability to replicate the formula. So that is one disaster that has been averted. However, that's not the end of it."

"All right, let me hear the rest of the details."

"It gets worse. As I was leaving the Chamber, Stedman—that's the curator's name—had put the two tablets in a bag. In my haste to get home so I could review what the shells contained, I swam right into one of my brother's friends. Just recently he has been interested in me romantically I believe." To Thad's questioning look, Selale said, "Don't worry. The feeling is absolutely not reciprocated. You are my only love, remember?" She kissed Thad before she continued. "This next part is what ruined my tide completely. Rahwah implied that he had seen me coming back in the middle of the eventide and from my shocked reaction, he knows I was with someone. Jealousy will drive him to keep track of my every movement. His fixation on me scares me to death. That's why we must meet at the cave. I can get there undetected and meet you safely. No one below will see your boat in these waters. In the cave you won't have to use your breathing equipment, so we can stay for the entire tide together. I cherish that more than anything, Thad. A chance just to be with you." Selale wrapped her arms around his waist and pulled herself closer to him. "Nothing can stop me from loving you. It's my responsibility to protect you from the SCEROH. They won't tolerate your interference in our world."

"Tell me about the SCEROH. Why do they care about someone as insignificant as a scientist in these waters? I mean, for centuries men have been exploring these waters. Why are they suddenly intent on harming humans now?" Thad's confusion mirrored Selale's own bewilderment.

"The SCEROH stands for the Society for the Complete Eradication and Removal of Humans. Scary, isn't it? My uncle is the creator and leader of this group, much to my father's dismay. Its creation has created a rift between the two of them and choosing loyalties to one side or the other has divided our people. Uncle Calder is bitter. He blames your entire species for the death of his wife. Vengeance is what drives him, and the SCEROH's one motivation is to destroy humans who meddle in the affairs of our world. Don't you remember that part of the prophecy? The division? That and so many things that were foretold so many annutides ago have recently come to pass. To be perfectly candid, it's disturbing. Somehow this prophecy concerns you, and me, and my father. And now that the shell with the lost tome with our history surfaced, I can see this goes beyond coincidence. Everything's connected. Ultimately, I know where these signs lead," Selale's voice turned to a whisper as she sat up and gazed into Thad's serious face. She then turned her attention to the writing etched on the golden walls. "The fulfillment of the prophecy of the Hybrid King." Selale once again let Thad pull her in a strong embrace.

Stroking her hair with his hand, Thad said softly, "We can't fight destiny. The past several weeks have been the happiest of my life because I met you. I can't describe our love as a mistake. This kind of love comes around only one time in life, the kind of love that is eternal. Nothing will ever destroy what I feel for you. This body may pass away, but my love for you will live on forever. The SCEROH may try to stop us from being together, but they won't ever stop my love for you. Let's not spend our time together worried about what might happen and when. Let's spend every moment enjoying just being together." Thad took Selale in his arms and in the glow of the golden light, made love to her with an urgency and passion that drowned out everything beyond the walls of Beulah Cave.

Chapter Twenty-seven

As Thad came in his front door, he decided to check his voicemail first since he had been MIA for almost three days. The bright flashing number four indicated someone wanted to talk to him. The first three messages were from Michael. In the first message, he and Charise wanted Thad to come spend Thanksgiving with them. The next two were messages from Michael wanting Thad to call him ASAP and ending with some funny remark about Thad running around on him and then dumping him for a woman. Thad snickered. He knew he would have to tell Michael something more specific because Michael would already know something had changed in his relationship with Selale the minute he talked to him. Yes, Thad would have to tell him more about his beautiful wife.

The fourth recording was a terse message from the chancellor informing Thad that funding for his research had been revoked. That was the extent of the message, no explanation and no condolence over it. It stunned Thad. First, how could the chancellor inform him with a voicemail about the funding? Second, why had the funding been cut off so suddenly? There had been no warning, but there had to be a reason. Thad's initial response was one of anger. He deserved an answer. He stood in his living room staring at the equipment that covered every last bit of space on his desk without his eyes really seeing anything.

Shaking himself out of his musings, Thad reached for the phone to call Michael. It was not late. Thad had two classes to teach tomorrow morning. The semester was rapidly coming to a close, and with the impending holidays, he knew it would be a busy time for everyone at the university. He dialed the familiar number.

"Hello?" Charise's mellow voice greeted Thad.

"Hello, Charise. It's Thad. How are you? Are you keeping that troublemaker of a husband straight? You're a saint, honey. Yes, a saint," Thad chuckled.

"I know. I've already chosen my crown. It's shiny, golden, and studded with gems of every color. Speaking of golden, where have you been hiding yourself, golden boy? I haven't seen you around. I miss you, Thad. Are you coming over here for Thanksgiving? You know I won't take no for an answer."

"I wouldn't miss it for the world. Will you make me a pecan pie, one with toasted pecans? Please? You know it's my favorite," Thad pleaded in a syrupy sweet voice.

"Why, it wouldn't be Thanksgiving without it. I'll even have vanilla ice cream ready if you say you'll be here," Charise promised.

"I wouldn't miss it for the world. Is Michael around? I know he misses me because he called me three times. Talk about a stalker," Thad teased.

"He's here. Hold on. Michael? Thad's on the phone. Yeah, I'm not sure if I should be grateful for you dumping Michael, so I can have him back or if I should be angry because you dumped him. It's such a complicated love triangle." Charise laughed. "See you on Thanksgiving. Bye, Thad." Still smiling, Charise handed her husband the phone as she sauntered out of the room.

"Where have you been? I almost sent a search party out to rescue you from the clutches of this mysterious Selale. That is where you have been, right?" Michael waited for Thad's answer.

"Yes, Daddy, that's where I've been. If I didn't know any better, I would say you are jealous. Hey, seriously, could you come over? I know it's late, but I need somebody to talk to. The chancellor called, giving me the news that my research funding has been axed. I need someone to listen to me vent before I face him. He didn't give me any details, the smug scoundrel. Maybe together we can figure out what is going on, what my next step should be. Or maybe we'll just go kick the chancellor's butt. I don't know. I'm just so confused, so disappointed, so...angry." Thad paused. "I've got some beer, and I'll call in pizza. What do you say? Please?"

"Sure. I will be there in a few minutes. Don't break anything and don't break into the beer until I get there."

They hung up, and Michael, still holding the phone, stood considering the news of Thad's funding being revoked. He didn't understand the reason, but he did comprehend the implication of the withdrawn funding. It was not good. Obviously, Thad had done something or found something that displeased his benefactor. Charise came up behind Michael and wrapped her arms around his waist.

"Is everything all right with Thad? Where has he been the last few days?" Charise asked as she hugged Michael tightly.

"No, everything is not all right. The chancellor called Thad and told him his research funding has been revoked. He is angry and confused. I don't blame him. He wants me to come over. Is that okay with you?" Michael turned and faced her. He took her beautiful face in his hands and gently kissed her. "If you want me to stay, I will."

"No, Thad needs you. Go spend your man time together. I will see you when you get home. That's a promise. Oh, and Michael?" He looked at her quizzically. "Don't get too sloshed." Charise kissed him on the lips, withdrew from his embrace, and sashayed dramatically down the hall toward the kitchen.

Michael's eyes followed her. He whistled and said, "What a woman!"

Michael arrived at Thad's house and almost immediately, he knew Thad had more than the funding weighing on his mind. He wanted some answers tonight about Thad and Selale's relationship. He could feel the joy, the love, but also the worry and fear that surged through his best friend. This woman was much more than a mere girlfriend. This thought scared Michael. He didn't want Thad to get hurt. If Michael could just meet this girl, then he could get a "read" on her to see if these strong feelings were returned. Why was Thad so reluctant to introduce them to Selale? If he was honest, it hurt.

Thad extended a cold bottle of beer to Michael as he entered the living room. Taking a seat on the couch, Michael waited for Thad to start the conversation. He sensed Thad's apprehension and frustration but Michael was unsure if the news of the funding was the real source. Many conflicting emotions warred inside of Thad.

"You already know how I'm feeling, don't you?" Thad eyed Michael surreptitiously from across the room.

Michael nodded. "Thad, tell me what's going on with you. I'm not here to judge or to condemn you; I'm here to listen. Just talk to me." He took a slow swallow of his beer as he waited on Thad.

Thad ran an impatient hand through his too-long, blond hair. He sighed. "I am furious and frustrated. I just don't get it. Why now? What was in the data that could have possibly warranted this? What did I miss? If anything, the data shows more research is needed to determine the long-term effects and the extent of the oil polluting these waters. I just want some answers. This research is important, especially now." He stood there with his hands hanging limply at his side. Michael studied his best friend. There were no physical signs indicating distress emanating from Thad. The primary emotion Michael could detect was resignation, but something else other than just the revoked funding preoccupied his best friend's mind.

"There's more than just this funding that's on your mind. I understand that you are upset and angry, yet it doesn't extend deep down below the surface. There is a conflict of emotions here. Do you care about the funding or not? Confide in me. Tell me what is really going on. There seems to be much more here than what you are telling me." Michael waited for Thad to deny it, but Thad stood up abruptly and walked over to the window.

Thad didn't turn around, but stood looking out into the darkness across the yard toward the university. He took a swallow of his beer which gave him time as he considered how to proceed with this conversation. Slowly he turned and asked Michael, "Have you ever had something happen to you that you can't explain? Something so strange, so extraordinary that telling it would make people think you were crazy?" He cast a solemn stare at his friend. Michael met his steady gaze. The hairs on the back of his neck stood up. He knew exactly how that felt. Without breaking their connection, Michael nodded.

"I can't explain everything that's happening, buddy, but I can tell you there are some strange things going on right now in my life. Destiny has her hand in the waters of my life, and she is intent on stirring them. Everything seems so surreal, so beyond coincidence. It scares me to death, to be perfectly honest." Thad took another swallow of his beer. "How can I tell you what's going on if I don't understand it myself? Selale, the shell, the vision, and now this revoked funding —all these things that seem on the outside to be random incidences somehow are connected. Man, I just don't know anymore." Thad's voice trailed off as he turned and once again stared out the window.

Michael probed, "What can you tell me about Selale? Everything else revolves around her. She's the source of your happiness, your disappointment, your fear. Just tell me what you can and maybe together we can figure it out. Let me get another beer before we go any further."

Michael smiled and walked over to the refrigerator. "Do you need another one?" Thad nodded. Michael grabbed two beers, opened them, and walked over to hand one to Thad. He sat down on the couch and waited for Thad to gather his thoughts. Both sat drinking their beer.

After a long silence, Thad murmured, "Selale can decipher the language on the shell."

Startled with this admission, Michael jumped up to his feet and yelled, "What the- What?" He was suddenly rendered speechless. He stood staring agape at Thad as though he had morphed into an alien. "How long have you known this? What does it say?" He stood glaring at Thad and before he continued, he took a deep breath to calm himself. "You are going to explain this, right? Who is this girl Selale? I am all ears, Thad." There was a hint of frustration and hurt in Michael's eyes as he waited for Thad to continue.

The doorbell rang, breaking the palpable tension that now filled the room. Thad opened the door and paid the delivery boy for the pizza. He was grateful for the break in the conversation. It gave him an opportunity to gather his thoughts and allowed Michael to recover from the shock of Thad's admission. Thad knew the interruption was only temporarily delaying the inevitable barrage of questions that Michael would fire at him once the delivery boy left the premises. But no amount of time was sufficient enough for Thad to come up with answers that he couldn't or wouldn't be able to give. There was no easy way to proceed with the conversation.

Thad placed the box on the coffee table in the middle of the living room, opened it, and offered Michael the first slice. Michael reached over and took one from the box. He wouldn't pressure Thad to continue. Thad would tell him only what he wanted. He probably should get Thad sloppy drunk, so he would divulge his secrets. Michael smiled at the notion. If he didn't get some answers tonight, he may have to resort to that kind of trickery. It wouldn't be the first time both of them had gotten sloshed together.

"And what's so funny?" Thad asked.

"Oh, nothing. I was just thinking that I might have to get you drunk just so you will tell me something. You seem intent on keeping mum about every-thing and anything that involves this mysterious Selale. I'm beginning to wonder if she really exists. And now you drop this bombshell on me that she has translated the shell. Wow, she must really be something. I've had experts from all over the world who have tried to decipher the language. Not a single one even came close to figuring out this complex language, and yet, a girl you met less than six weeks ago, whom your best friend has not ever seen, can read the language. This sounds like something out of *The Twilight Zone*, Thad. What have you gotten yourself involved in?" Michael exhaled audibly before he continued. "I'm sorry, but I am really worried about you."

Thad sat poised with a slice of pizza in his hand. "I know. Michael, there's so much I want to tell you, but it's just…an impossible situation, one that is too complicated to explain. There are some things I can tell you about her. She has these amazing blue eyes that twinkle with mischief. And her hair cas-cades down her back like a river of curls. I love her more than I have ever loved anybody. I can't live without her. I will do anything to protect her and keep her safe from harm. She makes me happy, and if I can figure out a way, I want to spend the rest of my life with her." Overcome with emotion, Thad ceased his confessions and ate his pizza. Silence filled the room.

Michael regarded his best friend carefully. He had never felt this level of emotion from Thad as long as he had known him. His love for Selale was in-tense, deep, and very real. However, fear and uncertainty snaked their way through the current of emotion. So strong was the depth of the feelings that radiated from Thad that it almost moved Michael to tears. Overwhelmed with emotion, Michael cleared his throat. "If I can be completely honest with you, this whole relationship scares me to death, too. But, I know love when I see it. I won't pretend I understand anything that is going on, but there are forces at work here that I can't ignore. Fate, destiny or the hand of God—call it what you will, but some force has brought you two together and it's for real. So, what can I do to help you?" Michael's offer should not have surprised Thad after all they had been through, but it did. His simple offer of help spoke loudly about the kind of friend Thad had in Michael Moses.

"There's not much you can do except trust me. I know there is so much you don't understand and that frustrates you. But since we are being honest, I can't explain it because I don't have any answers or solutions to the problems that Selale and I face when it comes to our being together. For right now, I will have to be content with what we have. I wish you could meet her. You and Charise would love her. Before I tell you about what is on the shell, let me eat this piece of pizza and get another beer." Thad rose and walked to the fridge. Smiling as he came back in the room, he thought about Michael's plan to get him drunk.

"No, you're not still planning to get me drunk and take advantage of me, are you? I want you to respect me in the morning." Thad took a huge bite of his pizza and drank his beer.

Michael quipped, "Your reputation and your secrets are safe with me, pretty boy. Tell me about the shell before I throttle you." He leaned over and grabbed another slice before Thad started.

"Before I begin, I want you to remain open-minded about what I'm going to tell you. As fantastic as this is going to sound, it is the truth. I swear it on my life. All right." Thad took a deep breath, exhaled loudly and began. "It tells the story of the destruction of Atlantis, Michael. Only twenty-two people survived the cataclysmic disaster, and those survivors watched the island's fiery demise. The survivors included a scientist, five other educated men and their families. For almost a year, these men warned the king and his council of the impending disaster, but the king would not heed their warning. The families left the area together and started a new life far from the waters surrounding their destroyed island. With the few mementos they could carry, they created a new home, a new government, a new life from absolutely nothing. The author of the manuscript was named Immanuel, the chief scientist from Atlantis who came up with the strategy for the men and their families to survive. The shell chronicles their poignant story of loss, survival, and rebirth," Thad stopped and waited for Michael to say something.

Completely motionless and speechless, Michael sat on the couch like a statue, a half-eaten slice of pizza in one hand and a beer in the other, and his mouth slack with amazement. He could do nothing but stare at Thad.

Thad smiled at Michael's reaction. "I told you to keep an open mind, not an open mouth!" He motioned with his hand, demonstrating to Michael how to force his gaping mouth to close. "So? Say something. Call me a liar or a lunatic, or if you can wrap your mind around what I just told you, let's talk about it. My reaction was much the same when I heard the word *Atlantis*."

Michael cleared his throat and shook his head. "How would Selale have known how to translate this language? That is the first question I want answered. If what you have just told me is true, no one alive should be able to decipher this language. This history details events that happened thousands of years ago. This is a dead language, long extinct just like those survivors of Atlantis. So how can she read it? Every language expert in the world, the brightest and the best of them, could not decode even one line. Thad, I'm trying to be objective and open-minded, but in order for me to give credence to what you just told me about the shell, you have to answer that question." Michael stared intently at Thad, his brown eyes pinning his best friend for an answer.

Thad sighed and turned once again to stare out at the night that had by now enveloped the university grounds. Easy answers eluded him. The answers were as complex as the situation in which he now found himself. What to tell Michael that would be convincing had to be balanced with withholding information that absolutely could not be divulged. Thad knew Michael could be trusted, but Selale's safety could not be jeopardized. Secrets had a way of leaking out even when told in the strictest of confidence. Not telling anyone, even a best friend, insured secrets stayed that way.

Still staring out the window, Thad finally murmured, "I can tell you a little, but you're still not going to be satisfied. You must take what I tell you and leave the details alone. Can you promise you will do that, Michael?" He turned around and rested his weight against the windowsill. His hands gripped the edge as he waited for an answer.

Michael put his beer and slice of pizza on the coffee table then stood and faced Thad. "I'll promise I'll try. That's about all I can promise." He put his hands in his jeans pockets and waited for Thad's response.

"Fair enough, I guess. Let's sit down and eat our pizza and drink our beer. I think the answer will go down more easily that way." Thad made his way to the chair. Michael sat back down on the couch, and grabbing his beer, he chugged half of it. He picked up his pizza and waited for Thad to continue.

"Selale descended from those survivors of Atlantis. She knows and speaks that supposedly extinct language along with many others presently spoken. Her job involves translating language. I give you my word that what I just told you is the truth. As far as telling you anything beyond that, I can't. You must be satisfied with that for now."

"Where does Selale live? Where does she work? Why have I never met her if she is such a language expert? Will you answer any of those questions, Thad?" Michael voiced some of the questions he had been dying to ask since first hearing Selale's name, knowing that Thad would probably not answer any of them.

"She doesn't live here or work here in town. Her work is not research-based, so you would have never met her. Her line of translation and language relates more to government and security issues." Thad used deliberate deception to deflect the real truth. Though nothing he said was a flat-out lie, he had purposefully answered Michael's questions evasively.

Michael realized Thad was telling the truth, but now he had more questions than answers. Many more flooded his mind, but those were questions he knew Thad would not answer. He asked a question to which he already knew the answer. "Is Selale in danger? Is that why you can't tell me?" Michael perceived this was the real reason Thad couldn't confide in him completely. He handed Thad another piece of pizza as he continued, "I don't want to know anything more if telling me would endanger her safety. That is a concern, isn't it? I can tell you are worried about her safety and keeping her secret."

Thad nodded his head. "It's not that I don't trust you. It's more that I gave her my word and breaking it could be dangerous."

The words from months before echoed in Michael's mind: *Keep it safe. Keep it secret.* How ironic the words sounded to Michael, yet how very appropriate. Some secrets were never meant to be shared. He knew the burden he carried of keeping his secret from not only Thad, but also from Charise. "What you've told me is enough, at least for now. I do trust you, and Selale does too. However, I want to know more details about the story that is on the shell. Do you think she could write it down for me? I won't share it with anyone. I just want to know this scientist's story. Would you ask her if she would do that for me? You can tell her what a terrific friend I am." Michael flashed Thad a toothy smile.

"I will ask her. Maybe she will say yes. I'll tell her how much you like old stories and how desperate you are to hear this one. From one language expert to another, that will probably convince her more than anything else."

"She sounds like someone I would like. I just hope someday I get to meet this girl who has completely stolen your heart. You have got it bad, my friend."

"One day you will meet her. I can't promise when or how, but I hope sooner or later, we will work it out."

"I look forward to it. Someone needs to tell her the truth about you and fill her in on the juicy details from your past, and who better than your best friend to tell her?" Michael drank the rest of his beer and finished off the last piece of pizza.

"And here I thought all my secrets were safe with you, especially the bad ones," Thad contended.

Michael laughed out loud, "Oh, those are not secrets, buddy. Most of the details I was referring to are common knowledge! On second thought, I won't run Selale off by telling her about your sordid past. Your secrets are safe with me." Michael sobered as the words he had just spoken really sank in. He stood up. "I need to get home before Charise sends out a search party for me. I promised her I would come home sober, so I need to go home right now. I'll see you tomorrow at lunch." Thad rose and walked with Michael to the door.

Michael held out his hand and Thad clutched it with his. "Once again, your secrets are safe with me." He looked his best friend in the eye emphasizing his promise.

Thad nodded. He closed the door behind Michael, relieved that he had confided in the one person whom he trusted the most.

Chapter Twenty-eight

Rahwah waited for Calder to come into the chamber. Since his confrontation with Selale, jealousy consumed him, his mind incapable of shaking the thoughts of her in the arms of another merman. Over the last cycle, he had watched her every move inconspicuously. In those tides, she had never wavered in her daily routine: going to work, breaking for meals, swimming home. Aside from the occasional conversation with friends, no one or nothing else captivated her attention. Either there was no relationship or Selale was trying to shake off his suspicions. Somewhat mollified, Rahwah relaxed his surveillance of Selale.

This morntide he was meeting Calder to discuss the upcoming Atlantic Council meeting. Rahwah realized that he had acted rashly by relinquishing his position on the council. Calder had advised him on exerting patience and encouraged him to penitently approach Marius to ask for reinstatement, asserting how important it was to have Rahwah, an ally, on the council. The thought of being perceived as impulsive caused Rahwah embarrassment and shame. He didn't want Calder to view him as anything but an asset. If he wanted Rahwah to crawl back to Marius and ask forgiveness, then he gladly would. Someday, he would prove to Calder how valuable he was. He just needed the chance.

In Rahwah's estimation, Calder was a genius, the kind of leader Atlantis needed to sustain and increase the power of the merman population. His mentor had the vision and the toughness to do just that. Marius, on the other hand, was soft, too kind. While those qualities might be important to their people, those were the attributes that Rahwah had come to despise. Marius was weak; Calder was strong. How could there be any question as to who should lead Atlantis?

Rahwah remembered a scene from a few annutides on the tide of his father's death. It was during that difficult tide that Rahwah had decided to claim the Atlantic Council seat that had been held by his father who had died suddenly. Though he had never been close to his father, Rahwah understood that his mother needed him and the seat would give him a purpose and a reason to stay in the Center City. While Rahwah had not respected his father, he did respect his council position. It gave him elevated status and importance in the Kingdom. That importance was the only thing Rahwah had admired about his father. Marius had attended the memorial and had been by his mother's side continually the tide of the ceremony. Rahwah approached Marius after the memorial to discuss his claim to the position. He felt certain that Marius would embrace the idea and immediately name him as the successor. So stunned was Rahwah at Marius' refusal that he was rendered speechless. Marius dismissed Rahwah as too young and misinterpreted his motivation as grief. When Rahwah finally found his voice to object to Marius' concern, he reminded Marius that Ettore held a seat on the Council and they were born nearly the same tide. Marius had simply declared that their situations were different. Fortunately for Rahwah, Calder had intervened and recommended him for the seat. All but Marius had been in favor of his father's replacement. From that tide on, Rahwah had harbored animosity for Marius.

Calder then entered the room, his very presence exuding power. He smiled broadly when he spotted the young, eager Rahwah. Such blind loyalty and ambition would serve him well on his quest for sole leadership of Atlantis. Rahwah embodied enough of these attributes for Calder to consider him quite an asset as well as a potential threat if these were left unchecked. He saw a little of himself in this young merman: confident, arrogant, power-hungry, and a little mean. Calder liked Rahwah immensely.

Early this tide he had summoned several members of the council and a few other powerful mermen, those whom he considered like-minded friends, to discuss the legality of proposing changes in the constitution of Atlantis. Among these members were an expert in the law, Gaillard, Rahwah, and two other council members from distant regions of Atlantis. The three remaining members included an Atlantis messenger and two other young, somewhat ambitious mermen, one from the SCEROH and one from the Engineering Chamber. Rahwah's position on the council was crucial. By his impetuous decision to surrender his seat on the council, Calder realized he had one less ally. That had been the sole reason he had pushed for his election to the seat. If, however, Marius thought him to be truly remorseful over his actions, Calder knew that Rahwah would be allowed back on the council. In fact, he was counting on it. Rahwah had an appointment to meet Marius privately later this tide.

"Good morntide, my young friend. You are here very early in the tide. What's on your mind?" Calder swam next to Rahwah and took a seat on the bench.

That's what Rahwah liked about Calder. He was direct and straight to the point. Rahwah said with importance, "I wanted to discuss your niece Selale before anyone else arrived. Something interesting has recently happened that may need further investigating, and since you put me in charge of gathering evidence to discredit Marius, this warrants attention. About a cycle ago while doing my early patrols, I saw Selale stealthily coming home early in the tide. She had been out all eventide. When I questioned her, she seemed nervous and became defensive and very evasive about where she had been and why she was coming home at that current of the tide. Her job gives her no reason to be out that late, so naturally I assumed it had to be personal. I thought this could be the evidence we need to use against Marius and his lack of leadership. Why, if he can't control his own daughter, how can he control a kingdom as vast and important as Atlantis?"

Calder thought about this news. "If this was so important, why are you just now telling me this? Are you sure this is not motivated by jealousy on your part? You want her for yourself, isn't that right?"

Rahwah sputtered with embarrassment, "This is not just about my wanting Selale. If this was a legitimate relationship, why would she sneak home?

Why not just flaunt it in my face, so to speak. No, she is hiding something or someone from Marius, from everyone. As for my not telling you sooner, I have been watching her. It seems she has gone out of her way to make it appear there is no relationship. For the past cycle, she has gone nowhere other than work and home. She leaves for work; she takes a break for meals; she swims home. It's as if she knows she has raised suspicion and is purposefully trying to cast it off. I'm telling you, something is going on."

As the other members started making their way into the chamber, Calder reassured his young ally. "Perhaps you may be on to something. Continue to pursue this and keep me informed of any changes. This could be something insignificant, but let's not take any chances. Thank you for the information. You are proving to be more and more valuable every tide, Rahwah." With that, Calder dismissed his youthful follower.

Calder greeted each member personally. As soon as they all were assembled around the table, Calder began the conversation of implementing the process of if and how he could depose his brother as king of Atlantis. With authority he addressed the group, "Greetings, friends. You have been invited here this tide to ensure the future of Atlantis. United, we can lead this great kingdom in a new direction toward prosperity and power. United, we can sustain our kingdom for generations to come. United, we can usher in a new order: Ownership and control of the very waters we call Atlantis. For centennitides, we have lived in the shadowy depths in these waters, hidden from the very humans from whom we descended. There has been an unbalanced scale of power. For far too long, we have allowed humans to limit our comings, our goings, our very lives. United, we can end the imbalance of freedom this very tide. Protecting human life should not be the focus of our government. Far too many resources—our time, our wealth, and our energy—have been wasted on ungrateful humans who hold us hostage in our own kingdom. At this tide in history, we have a great opportunity to liberate our people from the limits of freedom imposed by the fear of human discovery. This freedom should be every merman's goal. What will it take for this to happen? Another one of our loved ones lost at the hands of these intruders? What can we do to make this a reality? We are bound by the laws of the Atlantis constitution."

Here Calder paused, turning to address a pale, slight merman seated at the end of the table. "Preslar, as an expert of the laws governing our kingdom, tell us, what are our options?"

Calder sat down and gave the floor to the frail-looking merman who swam forward to the head of the table to address the assembly. Although Calder had already discussed the matter thoroughly with the barrister, he waited patiently for Preslar to verbalize the rehearsed answer to the others present. In a surprisingly strong voice, he explained the details concerning the throne of Atlantis outlined in the ancient laws of the constitution. "The constitution gives absolute control of the government to the king of Atlantis. Our founding fathers ensured the lineage of the royal line would never change or transfer to anyone other than a direct descendant of the original king. This title cannot be stripped from the rightful heir by the Atlantic Council. Once the Blessing of the Waters has been bestowed upon him, his power is immutable; his position, permanent."

Rahwah, in frustration, blurted out, "Well, what is the point if Marius cannot be deposed?" Others joined in voicing the futility of the situation, until Calder rose and, with a commanding voice and fearsome look, quieted the discussion.

"Preslar, please continue. Forgive our interruption."

"There is, however, one obscure clause in the constitution that grants the council power to appoint someone other than his rightful heir to take over the king's position. If the king is deemed unfit, becomes incapacitated, or is otherwise unable to fulfill the duties of his title while still alive, then and only then can the council, pending approval of the Atlantic Arbitrator, appoint a replacement in his stead, someone other than the king's biological heir."

Silence filled the chamber as Preslar resumed his seat at the end of the table. The assembled mermen considered the implications of the clause while Calder swam back to the head of the table. Placing his hands on the table gently, he faced the mermen there. "So, my friends, what questions do you have?"

Gaillard spoke up first. "According to what was outlined here, Marius cannot be harmed; he must be alive. What about Ettore? He is the heir to the throne behind Marius. If Marius is unable to act as king, why then would Ettore not ascend to the throne?"

Calder had taken a seat at the head of the table. All eyes rested on him as he considered the question. He knitted his fingers together and rested his chin on them. "He would. He still presents a problem. So, what should we do about Ettore?" Though he said it without expecting an answer, Rahwah posed a solution.

"There is nothing in the constitution that says the heir to the king must remain unharmed. That is the solution." Hatred burned in his eyes as a malicious smile slithered across his face.

The council member from Cecilia, a region in Atlantis far to the south, became alarmed at the turn the discussion had taken. While he disagreed with some of the decisions Marius made concerning Atlantis, he admired his king and enjoyed Ettore's well-mannered personality. Tentatively, he interjected, "What are we doing here? This sudden turn in the discussion sounds treasonous. While I agree with you, Calder, politically on the direction of the country, I do not condone taking extreme measures, especially anything detrimental happening to Ettore. I'm sorry, but I feel compelled to leave this meeting." With that, he hastily swam from the room.

Calder remained seated. With a calm, steady voice he posed a question to the remaining mermen still gathered around the table. "Is there anyone else who wishes to leave? Either you are with us or you are against us. Now is not the tide for weak actions enacted by weak mermen. Desperate tides require desperate measures. These tides, my friends, are desperate. This tide, our campaign to discredit the king begins. I propose to the council members seated here that Marius is unfit to be King of Atlantis. Are you with me? If so, rise and join me. United, my friends, we shall triumph and restore our kingdom to its great past and power." Without hesitation, his remaining followers rose and treaded shoulder to shoulder beside their future king.

Chapter Twenty-nine

Ettore and Marius studied the map of Atlantis etched onto the thin stone sheet, its size covering almost the entire table. The cartographer had outlined every intricate detail of the kingdom including the significant features in each of the five regions and the extensive Benthic Passage System designed and built by Marius that branched throughout the Atlantis' expansive domain. This efficient system of travel made passage among the regions safe for merpeople, especially those whose duties required constant movement from region to region. Benthic passages connected exposed stretches of ocean through a series of underground tunnels that made merpeople traveling them less vulnerable to human discovery. Though constructing the entire system took more than five annutides to complete, it allowed greater protection and freedom to travel enabling communication and commerce to flow freely and effortlessly. It was Marius' crowning achievement.

Yestertide one of the tunnels in the southernmost region of Cecilia collapsed. This morntide, an emissary, who waited near the portal in case Marius chose to reply, had been sent by Cecilia's chief commerce director informing Marius of the situation. Not wanting to alarm the merpeople living in the area or in the adjacent regions, the director had shut down the entire southern Benthic tunnel citing scheduled maintenance as the reason for the closing. The disturbing truth was sabotage had actually caused the destruction. Sadly, Cecilia's council member had died in the catastrophe. As Marius and Ettore studied the area surrounding the southern Benthic tunnel, they discussed potential causes and the implications of the intentional disaster.

"How unfortunate it is that Cimon perished in the collapse! I can't believe it was just terrible timing or unlucky fate. Do you think he was the intended target or in the wrong place at the wrong time?" Ettore said as he shook his head sadly. "Why would any merman want to disable this area of the Benthic passages? What would any merman gain by doing this?" Ettore looked to Marius for an explanation.

"This, my son, was no accident, nor was Cimon's death. Someone wanted him off the council. Whom I don't know, nor do I understand the why. I don't believe in coincidence. Cimon often aligned himself with Calder. Although he and I frequently disagreed politically, we generally liked and respected each other. His death is tragic indeed." Marius turned to the emissary who had delivered the message and motioned him to the table. "What do you know about this situation? Do you know the reason why Cimon had traveled out of Cecilia? Where had he been and why had he been there?"

The young merman appeared reluctant to speak. He looked around the chamber nervously to assure himself he was truly alone with Marius and Ettore. Finally, he whispered, "He had been here, Sir. He left the capital after attending an important meeting two tides ago. He was summoned here by Rahwah at Calder's request. I know this because I delivered the message to Cimon. The meeting was by private invitation only. Cimon swore me to secrecy about the summons, intimating the confidential nature of the assembly. He requested that I travel with him here for that meeting, so I joined him in the assembly. I was allowed only to tread at the back of the chamber, well out of earshot of the discussion." Leaning closer to Marius, he continued, "He left the assembly abruptly; seemingly, he was very upset and confused. I immediately swam after him, but Cimon refused to discuss with me specifically why he left or what had disturbed him so. All he would say to me was 'Be careful in whom you place your trust, Perimicles.' He sent me to Cecilia a half tide ahead of him. I didn't find out about his death until the director summoned me to deliver the missive to you. Cimon saved my life by dispatching me to Cecilia ahead of him. He was a good merman, your Majesty." Perimicles saw Marius gaze at the square-cut ruby ring on his finger. He immediately knew the king recognized the sign.

Marius nodded. "He was very honorable." He turned toward Ettore. "Please send our condolences to his family. Thank you, Perimicles, for confiding in us. Cimon left you with sound advice. These are strange tides, my young friend. Cimon knew that all too well. He was right to admonish you to be careful in whom you put your trust. Unfortunately, it appears he realized too late that his trust was misguided. He shall be missed. Please keep us informed of any other developments from your end. Cimon trusted you, so, therefore, we can trust you too. Speak of this to no one. I will keep you informed on any developments from here." Marius extended his hand. "Godspeed, Perimicles."

Immediately, Perimicles made a determined decision. He placed his hand under the king's outstretched one, the square-cut ruby ring visibly evident on his finger, and bowed his head, touching his forehead to the king's fingers. It was the symbolic gesture of fealty. "My lord, my eternal allegiance I pledge to you." Marius offered his acceptance; then Perimicles lifted his head and swam hurriedly from the chamber.

Ettore swam beside his father and watched the messenger quickly and covertly leave the chamber. Concerned at the implication of Calder's meeting, Ettore voiced his thoughts aloud. "What do you make of this, Papa? Is it a coup? Surely Calder wouldn't do anything as rash and short-sighted as trying to overthrow you. That would be political suicide. If what Perimicles just told us is true, Calder already has blood on his hands. What will stop him from shedding more blood?"

Marius didn't answer. He grasped the severity of the situation. Calder wanted control. Nothing would deter him from obtaining it, not some minor Atlantic Council member, nor his twin brother. Marius was prepared for a fight, a battle, a war for control of Atlantis; he had no doubt that Calder would lose and he would triumph. As king, he realized a power struggle would ultimately cost the lives of innocent mermen and merwomen. How much was he willing to sacrifice to maintain control of the kingdom? Marius wanted no casualties, no loss of life, but realistically, he understood this would happen. To Calder, the merpeople were expendable, a means to an end. Marius knew the prophecy and comprehended its relevance to this situation. The events seen by his great-grandmere over a half centennitide ago were beginning. Altering the inevitable dark events to come would prove futile. They would come, and nothing he or anyone else did would stop them.

With a heavy heart, he turned to study his son. Finally he answered, "Nothing. Nothing will stop him or the bloodshed that will ensue as the fight for control begins. We must prepare now to battle the evil lurking in shadowy depths; its wave of destruction is cresting on the horizon. Good will prevail; however, control of Atlantis will not be easily or quickly won. I fear the tides of peace will soon cease to flow through our great kingdom. Once the war begins, many tides will pass before peace settles again upon Atlantis. War is coming, my son."

Ettore turned to tread face to face with his father. Marius extended his hand toward his son. Ettore clutched his father's hand and with a fervent bow proclaimed, "My eternal allegiance, my life, I pledge to you, my lord. I offer my life, all that I am, to protect you and our great kingdom of Atlantis."

Proudly, Marius commanded, "Rise, my son. We have much to do to prepare for the battle. Summon Sandoval. Until we know where their loyalties lay, none of the other members can be entrusted with our plans. Before you go, however, one thing more will I do. This tide, I pour the Protection of the Waters over you." Marius grasped the pearl hanging around his neck and raised his hand high above his head. Suddenly the water swirled in a whirlpool encasing Ettore in its center. Light from the Atlantis pearl infused the water funnel illuminating the prince in its glow. Marius chanted the blessing recited by generations of his royal ancestors:

Wrapped in water, wrapped in light, this blessed protection holds you tight. unshakable hold, impenetrable field, in its midst from harm will it shield.

Slowly, Marius lowered his hand, and the waters stilled. Ettore, overcome with wonder, couldn't speak. Awed by the display of power, he regarded his father with a newfound sense of respect. Marius smiled with understanding and simply said, "Go in peace." Without hesitation, Ettore hastened to find Sandoval.

Chapter Thirty

Thanksgiving arrived. Charise had spent the entire morning preparing food for tonight's Thanksgiving meal. She had enjoyed every minute of it from stuffing the turkey and peeling the potatoes to baking the pecan pie Thad had requested. In the middle of the busyness, she felt alive and happy. This evening she would be surrounded by the people whom she loved the most. Knowing that they loved her in return made all the work and preparations worth every minute. On this day especially, she realized she had so much to be thankful for.

They had invited several friends. If everyone who was invited came, there would be twelve of them. Some of the guests were married; others widowed or single. It would result in some interesting conversation and discussion. Charise smiled at that thought. She had placed Thad next to Michael, but Charise would be seated close enough where she could get some answers from Thad about his mystery woman. He had been seeing this woman for months, yet she and Michael had still not met her. Something was definitely strange about this relationship. Thad seemed happy though, happier than she had ever seen him about a woman. Maybe the trade-off would be the pecan pie for some answers. She nodded at her idea; it was a good one.

She finished setting the table and putting the last-minute touches on the decorations. The centerpiece candle still needed a little extra sparkle. She tried to remember where she had put the mirror that she had used last year. Going to the study, she opened the cabinet where she and Michael often stashed items in a rush. Filled from top to bottom, Charise shook her head at the clutter they had acquired over the span of their brief marriage. She wondered what it would look like in twenty years. She didn't want to think about it!

She opened the center drawer and inspected the contents. Surely the mirror was in here somewhere. As she pulled the drawer completely out of the cabinet, an old piece of cloth caught her eye. What was this cloth doing in the drawer? She carried the drawer to the large, beautiful mahogany desk that spanned half the back wall of the study. Michael had spotted the desk at an estate sale the summer after they had bought the house. Somehow he recognized its beauty and worth even in its neglected and dilapidated condition. They bought it for a fraction of what it would have cost, and then together they refinished it. Now it was the hallmark of their furniture. She sat the drawer down gently on the corner of the desk and picked up the cloth wedged inside the corner of the drawer. Surprised at its heaviness, Charise realized something was inside. She gasped as she uncovered a huge pearl dangling from the end of a thick gold chain. Confused at why it was hidden, she examined the priceless necklace. She stood lost in her musings as hundreds of questions swirled through her mind. So intent was her inspection and wonderings that she didn't hear Michael come into the room.

Michael abruptly stopped when he saw the pearl necklace in Charise's hand. Now was the right time to tell her the truth about the necklace. Deep down, he knew she would understand if he told her the truth. He said gently, "It's beautiful, isn't it?"

Charise jumped like she had been burned. She whipped around. Hurt and confusion filled her eyes. "Michael, what is this? Why had you hidden it from me?"

He motioned to the sofa in the corner. "Sit down, Charise. I have to tell you a fantastic story." He extended his hand. Still holding the necklace, she took Michael's hand in her other one as he led her to the couch.

"Do you remember the northeaster when I found the shell the week before we lost the baby?" Michael prompted. Charise bobbed her head without speaking. "This pearl was buried with the shell. As I stood on the deserted beach trying to decide what to do about the discovery, suddenly I felt this female presence there with me. She was there, but not physically there. You know what I mean. That's when I heard a woman's whispery voice tell me to keep it safe and keep it secret. She spoke with desperation, and though she never mentioned the pearl, I knew that was what she referred to. I know this sounds crazy, but it was like she had been waiting for me to find it. Once I made the decision to not turn it in to the university, I placed this pearl in my pocket, and instantly serenity replaced her desperation. Her spirit gently urged me as she left, '*Keep it safe. Keep it secret.*' Then, as quickly as she had come, she was gone." Michael paused lost in the memory of it. He shook his head to clear his musings before he continued. "This is not the first time I had experienced an encounter with a spirit, but it never ceases to catch me by surprise. With this spirit, it was different. It was as if she had been waiting on me, Michael Moses, to find the shell and the pearl." Michael rubbed his forehead. "I never meant to keep something like this hidden from you, but with the events of losing the baby and the weeks that followed, the time never seemed right. I believe you were meant to discover the pearl too, just like I did. I don't know where the pearl came from, what the writing says on the chain, why it is important or why it must be kept a secret, but I do know that it is important. Why us? I don't know. We are somehow intertwined in its future. Hopefully one day we will find out. Will you forgive me for keeping this secret from you?" Michael lifted Charise's hand that still clutched the necklace to his lips and kissed it tenderly.

Charise touched her husband's cheek. She leaned over and kissed him. "Of course, I forgive you. You were right. It is a fantastic story. Now we will share the secret. Put it back in the drawer. Something tells me we will discover the answers to these questions when the right time comes. Now come on. We've got guests coming in less than two hours and there's still so much to do." She handed the pearl to Michael and pulled him up off the sofa. He wrapped it in the cloth and placed it in its hiding place once again. He pushed the drawer back in the cabinet and closed the doors. Arm in arm, they went to finish the last-minute preparations for the party.

Chapter Thirty-one

Sleep had eluded her again last night. She had not felt well this morning from the moment she opened her eyes. She attributed it to fatigue. She had spent the past several tides with Thad. He had been on something he called holiday break from the university. They had fallen into a routine of seeing each other for almost half a cyclotide. Selale went to work, came home, then swam through the tunnel before her father returned. There in Beulah Cave, she and Thad spent the rest of the tide together. She constantly reminded herself to swim home from a different direction; she did not want to draw attention to her comings and goings. The suspicious eyes of the SCEROH could be watching.

Early this tide, both her father and Ettore commented on her paleness. "Really, Selale. You look as pale as the belly of a fish. What is wrong with you? Are you sick?" Ettore put his finger behind Selale's ear. She swatted his hand away playfully.

"Stop hovering and leave me alone, silly. I'm just tired. It's been an exhausting series of tides at the translation chamber. The next three tides I am free from work at the chamber, so I have an opportunity to rest and recuperate. It is just what I need." She dismissed Ettore's concern by turning the conversation to matters other than her health. "Where are you and Papa off to so early this tide?"

Selale felt her father's eyes on her as Ettore explained they were preparing to leave the capital for a meeting with the chief commerce director concerning the rebuilding process at the collapsed southern Benthic tunnel near Cecilia. She avoided looking at her father for fear he would ask more questions about her. He could always sense secrets she tried to keep hidden from him.

Ettore continued, "It will be a busy tide. Reconstruction has already begun on the south tunnel, but finding answers to why it collapsed in the first place will take some investigation. We won't be home for at least two tides, maybe even three. Are you sure you will be all right? Do I need to have someone come check on you? I have plenty of friends lined up waiting for the chance, Selale. How about Santo or Delinius?" Ettore smirked at his younger sister as he reminded her of his two quite unmotivated friends. This was a long-running inside joke between them.

"Those two blowfish—and I do mean blowfish!—don't stand a chance. Ettore, I am fine. Stop worrying over me. I feel all right, much better than I would if those two friends of yours were here. Blah!" Selale laughed good-naturedly with her brother.

"All right, Lale. I know they will be devastated by your refusal. See you in a few tides," Ettore winked at his sister and swam out of the chamber room. The old nickname softened her heart causing her tears to mix with the water. With her back to her father, she watched Ettore swim away.

Marius swam over behind his daughter and caressed her shoulders. "He loves you almost as much as I do. Take care of yourself, and get some rest. You do look exhausted." He pulled her in for a brief hug then said, "I will see you soon." Marius, still unconvinced by her insistence that she was well, departed without further comment or questions. As he left his home, he couldn't help but be concerned. Something was going on with Selale. Perhaps it was work; she looked tired and pale. Maybe she just needed some rest. Hopefully in the next three passing tides, she would feel rested and well. He and Ettore left the chamber together and swam toward Cecilia.

After they both left the chamber, dizziness and nausea hit her suddenly, without warning. Selale lay down on the chamber bed. Not this tide! She could not waste the opportunity to spend three entire tides with Thad just because she didn't feel well. She forced herself up, willing herself to feel better. Sitting there on the corner of her bed, a terrifying question raced through her mind: could she be pregnant? Suddenly she couldn't move. Panic welled up inside her. She tried to think of symptoms to indicate whether she was or was not. Frantically, she counted the tides since her hormonal cycle ended, but too many tides and events had elapsed since then. How could she be pregnant? Well, she knew how, but wasn't it supposed to be very difficult for merwomen to conceive? She tried to think of someone, anyone who could help her.

The realization hit her that she really had no one in whom to confide. Apart from Ettore, her father, and Thad, there was no mermaid or merwomen she could trust. Oh, how she missed her mother at times like these. Remembering her mother brought pain and a gaping emptiness. This home had once been flooded with the presence of merwomen, laughing and gossiping. Lost in the happy memory of those tides, Selale could still hear her mother's mellifluous laugh and visualize her silly mischievous smile. She had been so full of life. Everyone had loved Giada and mourned her deeply. The face of her mother's friend Monica came to Selale's mind.

Selale had not thought of Monica in several annutides. Monica had been a constant presence in their home before and after Giada had become ill. The two merwomen had known each other their entire lives, and Selale distinctly recalled her mother telling her that they had been inseparable as young mermaids. Up to the tide Giada passed, they were each other's confidante and advisor. The two had drifted apart in proximity after Giada married Marius, but their friendship and devotion to each other never wavered. Monica had never married and had moved to the edge of the capital. After Giada died, she became more and more reclusive, to the point that she became the target of rampant speculation and gossip. Rumor had it she practiced the Dark Arts of sorcery and magic. Selale vaguely remembered that scandal that had rocked the kingdom when one of the king's advisers had been convicted of practicing the Dark Arts. Semirah had been her name and ironically she was Monica's niece. For blatantly admitting that she used the Dark Arts, Semirah was permanently banished from the kingdom. The scandal had happened long after Monica had moved away from the hustle and bustle of the Center City. Selale dismissed the notion of one of her mother's best friend's involvement in the Dark Arts and surmised Monica just wanted to be left alone.

She decided a visit was in order; in fact, it was long overdue. Perhaps Monica could give her some advice or at least answer some of her female-related questions. Without another wave of hesitation, Selale opened the door and swam toward the edge of the capital.

Even as she made her way down the Benthic pass of the capital, she felt eyes watching her every move. She stopped and swam in a circle trying to spot the culprit. Few merpeople were out this early in the tide. Selale attributed her worry to lack of sleep. Perhaps she was being paranoid, but still, she favored caution over carelessness. Rahwah's threat remained uppermost in her mind. She couldn't be too careful with his suspicion already raised. She used feigned errands and meaningless stops as a means to discourage anyone who followed her. Finally, she spotted Monica's chamber in the distance at the edge of the capital's boundary.

The tide had begun for Monica like the hundreds that flowed before it— arise early, eat a little, do a few menial chores, and concoct balms and remedies she provided to the local market exchange. Very rarely did her routine change. There flowed through this early tide, however, a warm, fragrant current. Monica recognized the sign for what it was—an omen of something good to come. Anticipation bubbled inside her. So rarely did anything good happen during the tide. Monica swam to the small chamber gazing panel that overlooked the capital. Swimming up her chamber path was none other than Giada's beautiful daughter, Selale. She couldn't have asked for a better surprise. Opening her chamber portal, Monica welcomed Selale into her arms.

"Oh, my dear! What a sight for these old eyes you are! How are you? Please, come in, come in!" She ushered Selale into the small quaint chamber and nimbly closed the portal behind her. Selale sat on a delicately carved bench beside the simple table situated on the left side of the room. She was glad she had come if for no other reason that it had brought joy to Monica. Sitting down next to Selale, Monica grabbed the young mermaid's hand. She was too overcome with happiness to speak. Finally, she said, "Tell me. How are your father and brother? Are they well?"

Selale nodded, "They are well. Together they have gone to Cecilia to consult with the commerce director about the progress made on the reconstruction of the southern Benthic tunnel that collapsed. Their trip will keep them away from the capital for at least two to three tides. I have a break from my job at the translation chamber. My mother was on my mind this morntide. I sat alone in my chamber room reminiscing about her and the laughter that once filled our home. I miss those tides. I remember all the many merwomen, but especially you, who constantly swam in and out of the kitchen visiting my mother. Please forgive me for not coming to see you sooner. I still miss her. Do you?" Selale looked into Monica's hazel eyes and knew the answer even before she heard the answer.

Monica arose and moved slowly to the counter. She brought a plate with an array of pickled fish to the table and sat it in front of Selale. "Not a tide flows that I don't think of Giada. When she died, part of me died with her. Yes, Selale, I still miss her as much this tide as the one she passed." She lowered herself on the bench beside Selale. "Here, try this fish." Monica pointed to the ones she wanted her to try. In companionable silence and with both their minds on Giada, they ate.

"This is good. I remember how great a cook you are." Selale looked around the walls of the chamber Monica had called home for almost forty annutides. As a merchild, she had often visited here with Giada. The familiar waters in the chamber had changed very little since her last visit. Bottles and containers were stacked on the shelf on the opposite side of the wall. In her delicate handetching, Monica had labeled each one.

Rising off the bench, Selale swam to the shelf. "Monica, tell me about some of these elixirs and balms. How do you make them and what are they used for?" She reached to a neat stack of flat containers. Turning the lid, she inhaled the water's aroma of the balmy paste.

"That balm is one type of sea anemone paste. It heals cuts and abrasions, especially those on the scales of our tails. The fragrance is lovely and soothing as well." Selale inhaled deeply and shook her head in complete agreement. Monica dipped her fingers into the paste and then massaged it onto Selale's temple. Selale closed her eyes. "There are many others here that help numerous ailments. Those tablets in the brown jar are made from kelp harvested from the northernmost region of Argonia. They don't taste good but are a remedy for aches and pains. However, my favorite is this one." She reached for a clear bottle that contained a thick, blue-colored liquid. "This is an elixir made from a rare blue sea anemone found only in the southernmost region of Cecilia. I only have this one bottle left. Unfortunately, I haven't been able to restock my pantry in several annutides. It requires a great amount of energy to travel that distance. The older I get, the more my energy wanes. But nevertheless, this elixir is very special. It has powerful healing and restorative powers. Your mother and I created this recipe together. As I recall, she used it quite frequently when she was pregnant. She was convinced it made you and Ettore healthy and strong." Monica handed the bottle to Selale. "This is just what you need, my dear."

Selale's hand shook as she grasped the bottle. "Wh—What do you mean? I'm not ill." Selale looked quizzically at her mother's friend.

"You don't know, do you? Perhaps destiny led you here this tide for me to confirm your suspicion." Monica took Selale's smooth, young hands in her older, wizened ones. "Selale, come and sit down." Once again, she guided Selale to the bench. "You, my dear, are pregnant."

"How do you know this? You have not seen me in over ten annutides. You don't even know me that well." Selale barely got the words out. Her throat had tightened up, threatening to suffocate her. Dizziness swirled the room around her causing Selale to cling to the table to steady herself from falling over.

Monica's tinkling laughter bounced off the walls of her small chamber. "Doesn't that confirm my diagnosis?" Clasping her hands together, she rose from the bench and spun around in a circle flinging her hands open wide. "What a delightful, wonderful tide! Oh, this news is better than any elixir! Selale, you are blessed!" Reclaiming her seat beside Selale, Monica embraced her beautiful new friend. Selale's fear and uncertainty were evident. She understood it and hoped somehow in her wisdom she might advise her best friend's daughter well.

Selale shook her head vehemently, "No, how can you say I'm blessed? You must be mistaken. I—I can't be pregnant. What am I going to do? What will my father say or everyone, for that matter? This news will bring disgrace to our family. Monica, there are many things you do not know about my situation." Despair fountained up inside her. "However can this tide be wonderful? Darkness is all I see." Selale put her face in her hands and wept.

Monica placed her finger under Selale's chin and lifted it. Selale's blue eyes stared into Monica's hazel ones. "An extravagant fragrance flows through the waters this morntide. It brings healing and peace to my spirit. That sign alone represents a beautiful portent of things to come—good, light, and hope mingle in the current. Nothing else matters in this situation. Despair not, my friend. Together, we will devise a plan. Come visit me again in two tides. By then, clarity about the situation will have rested on you." Wrapping the bottle in a thick piece of cloth, she extended the concealed bottle of blue elixir in her wrinkled hand to Selale. "Drink one swallow in the morntide when you rise and one swallow before retiring at eventide. Now, go, my friend, and fear not. All will be well; yes, all will be well."

Selale swam out of the chamber holding the bottle tightly. She glanced back at her newfound friend and waved. Lifted from her slim shoulders was the weight of bearing this secret alone. Now, lightness propelled her quickly back to her chamber, so she could swim through the tunnel to Beulah Cave to meet her beloved Thad and share the news: the Hybrid King had been conceived.

Chapter Thirty-two

Marius and Ettore swam side by side away from the construction site to the Hospitality Chamber where they had lodged during the trip to Cecilia. Repair and reconstruction on the tunnel had progressed well. The new design improved the flow of movement for mermen and cargo and strengthened the tunnel walls to withstand any future catastrophes, either accidental or intentional.

Many unanswered questions still weighed on Marius' mind. Pensively he swam trying to work through the fragmented answers he did have. Piecing them together would take patience. Though the cause of the tunnel collapse had been declared as "accidental," evidence pointed to sabotage. After meeting with the commerce director and chief engineer, the last bit of hope died when they confirmed his suspicion: the destruction had been deliberate, and Cimon had been the intended target. While they knew the *what* and the *how*, they still did not know the *who* or the *why*. Marius had a theory, but at this present tide, he decided to delay voicing it until he had compiled more proof. Perhaps more would surface later this tide after he met with Barretto, an acquaintance from many tides gone by, who specialized in discreet investigation. Barretto had contacted Marius, and it was he who had requested the meeting.

The waters in this stretch of Cecilia resembled none of the four other regions or even the capital of Atlantis. Here the pristine clearness of the water enabled its inhabitants to see for many leagues. The brilliant color of the fish and marine life of Cecilia contrasted with the drab monotony found in the northernmost regions. Plants bursting with colors of red, blue, and yellow dotted the white sand on the ocean floor creating a tropical flower garden. Warmth flowed year-round through the crystal clear waters giving a relaxed feel to everything swimming through the calm blue expanse. Marius always enjoyed the tides spent here because he felt so alive when he swam through these particular waters of his kingdom. The thought crossed his mind that he should visit Cecilia more often.

Far off in the distance, Marius saw the shiver of four great white sharks long before Ettore became aware of them. The sleek sharks included Massau, one of the fiercest and most aggressive inhabitants of Atlantis. They swam in a swift, direct course toward Marius, so he communicated telepathically with them, identifying who he was and for them to retreat. Surprisingly, they ignored him and continued swimming straight toward Ettore, seemingly intent on their course.

Once more he communicated, "Greetings, Massau. It is I, Marius, your king. Divert your path immediately and allow my son and me safe passage back to Cecilia. Surely you mean us no harm as we mean you none, so turn back."

"I know who you are." The simple implication was his only response.

Not one to become alarmed easily, Marius looked around for an escape. Finding no refuge from the eminent attack, he sent a warning to Ettore, but he too by now had seen the fearsome Massau and his companions. With determination, Marius braced himself in the sand on the ocean floor. He pushed Ettore behind him. Suddenly he raised his arm and circled it over his head. Without delay, the ocean floor geysered up forming a maelstrom of white sand. Marius calmly lowered his arm and fanned his right hand back and forth two times. The waters bent with a swift-flowing current causing the four sharks to topple over like they had fallen asleep in mid-course. The waters tossed around the shiver of sharks like small shells rolled around in the surf. Separated from the other three sharks by the tornado of sand, Marius isolated Massau, holding him captive in the center of the swirling sand.

He commanded the other sharks, "Disperse. Leave this area now. I know who you are. Punishment will be harsh and swift if you disobey. All is forgiven if you retreat." Immediately and without a glance back, the trio swam north, the direction from which they had come.

After many desperate attempts at breaking through the walls, the great white shark realized escape was futile. Begrudgingly, he submitted to Marius. Massau was trapped in the white sandy funnel, imprisoned in its swirling center.

Marius stilled the waters, but allowed the sand to continue its circular prison around the great white. The king swam to the edge of the funnel and eyed his attacker. "Why, Massau? This assault was undeserved and unprovoked. We have known each other for thirty annutides and have always lived peacefully in these waters. Why now, Massau? What could you possibly have to gain by attacking us, by attacking my son?"

Furious that the sharks, especially Massau, had ignored his father's initial command to stop, Ettore jumped in front of his father and declared, "We should kill him for his treachery, Papa. He meant to kill you. The law is clear. Treason results in execution." Breathing hard, Ettore stared down the huge great white shark.

Marius pushed his son behind him. "Son, now is not the time to act rashly. We must find out who ordered this attack. It was not instigated by the sharks; it was only carried out by them. Let me handle this." Turning to Massau, he demanded, "Explain your actions."

"My liege, promise me protection first, protection from your punishment and protection from the one who issued this attack, then will I reveal all."

Marius quietly threatened, "Who are you to issue any demands? You are in no position to negotiate, my old friend. It is I who will outline my demands, not you. First, I demand your unequivocal allegiance from this tide forward. Do you accept the first ultimatum? Speak to me your pledge."

Massau assented to the demand. He espoused, "My eternal allegiance, I pledge to you, my lord. I offer my life to protect you and our great kingdom of Atlantis."

Marius nodded with satisfaction. "Second, I want full disclosure of what led to this attack. I will do everything within my power as king of Atlantis to protect you from the reprisals of divulging this information. Finally, I offer forgiveness and pardon for your actions in return for our renewed friendship. Do you accept these terms?"

Humbled by the king's display of mercy and grace, Massau could only bow. The gesture instilled a newfound sense of respect for Marius washing away and replacing the hostility poured into his mind by the instigator of the attack. Ettore too was awed by the power his father wielded not only with gifts he used to control the waters and sand, but also with how graciously he dealt with his subjects. Surely diplomacy was one of his father's most powerful weapons.

Marius again raised his hand instantly calming the spinning sand which released Massau. He lowering his hand and said gently, "Come, my friend. Join us as we swim back to Cecilia. We will converse as we travel." Together, the three set off for the southern province.

Chapter Thirty-three

The morning dawned bright and clear. Thad saw the world with completely different eyes; everything had changed. Christmas had come and gone with a flourish. He had spent Christmas Eve with Michael and Charise. Since he no longer had any family, they had adopted him as a member of theirs. He knew this had been a difficult time for them. Instead of a new baby to celebrate the holidays, the Moses family felt an aching emptiness as they were surrounded by the children of their numerous friends and colleagues. Thad realized life was often ugly. It just wasn't fair.

But this morning, life was beautiful. Thad had spent Christmas with Selale. Though it was completely a human holiday, he wanted to expose her to the wonder of what Christmas really meant—the act of giving a great gift. So, he had wrapped his mother's wedding ring in festive paper and then placed it in a plastic bag. He had waited for months to give it to her. After placing the ring on her slender finger, she gave him a gift worth far more than any diamond ring: she was pregnant with his baby. She had laughed at his expression. He had been completely dumbfounded by the news. They celebrated together and dreamed of a future as a family in spite of the differences that kept them apart. In the wee hours of the morning he left, and after arriving home, he fell into a dreamless sleep.

Because Selale had to work, he had the entire day to himself. He sifted through the mail and catalogued several files and folders of his research. Impulsively, he decided to go for a jog. The day was warm and much too nice to spend it working indoors, so he changed clothes, laced his running shoes, grabbed his sunglasses, and stepped into the sunlight.

The balmy, late-December weather of the coastal Mid-Atlantic greeted him as he started the familiar five-mile course. Though an occasional burst of cold sometimes blasted through the region, much of the year the area's temperature allowed the residents to don T-shirts and jeans. Thad tried to remember the last time he had worn a coat. As he ran by the quaint cottages that lined the western end of the campus, he saw driveways filled with children riding new bicycles, experimenting with toys and playing with balls representing every sport. Kids were everywhere. He waved his hand to several professors and acquaintances. When he turned north heading back to the university, the number of people dwindled. He had the campus grounds to himself now that the students had departed for the winter break. The silence gave him the opportunity to think deeply and without distraction.

His thoughts turned to Selale and the baby. There was so much to do to prepare for the future. If he was completely honest with himself, he was terrified. He had no idea how to be a father, nor really a clue as to what was involved. Two things he did know: First, he felt an overwhelming sense of protection. Everything he had once valued now had shifted. Selale and the baby had now become Thad's top priority. Second, he knew he faced a situation unlike most fathers-to-be—his wife was a mermaid. As his feet pounded the sidewalks that meandered through the campus, questions raced through his mind. How did mermaids give birth? How long were they pregnant? What would this child be like being both merman and human? Still other disturbing questions came. How would he know when Selale went into labor? Would he miss the birth of his baby? How could they ever be together as a family? Thad had no answers to these questions and nobody in whom he could confide his fears, concerns, hopes, and dreams other than Selale. In his world, he felt alone.

He continued jogging around the perimeter of the football field, empty now that the season was over. He circled around the field one time and turned back to retrace his steps. As he passed the field house, light glinted off the lens of an abandoned camera left inside the window of the recording room. The camera reminded Thad of his recordings. A terrible question forced its way into his mind: what if someone saw the recording of Selale?

He stopped abruptly and, breathing hard, thought about the danger the recorded image of Selale presented if anyone else saw it. He recognized the irony of the situation. What was created by him and had led him to find the love of his life now endangered her. Resuming his run, Thad decided the recording had to be hidden—he couldn't bring himself to destroy it—to protect the ones he loved, now not only Selale, but their baby was at risk. He would take care of it today. The local bank where he had an account housed safe-deposit boxes. As he turned toward his house, Thad felt relieved, assured that with the recording locked away, no one would ever discover his secret.

Chapter Thirty-four

Marius had a great deal to consider as he swam toward the designated site Barretto had chosen to meet. Massau's confession and subsequent explanation of what led to the attack still weighed heavily on Marius' mind. Although Massau did not know the name of the merman who had brainwashed him and the other sharks, Marius suspected the identity of the conspirator by process of elimination. Only a few mermen had ever or now possessed the Mystical Gift of Interpretation. He could count the number of merpeople possessing the gift and still living on one hand: Marius himself, Selale, and his brother. What was Calder up to?

Ettore wanted to join Marius as he met with Barretto, but after learning that his son was the target of the attack, Marius decided he would be safer in Cecilia. Ettore had never met the reclusive merman renowned for his ability to defuse the most hostile situation. Very few people had. When merpeople met him, however, they never forgot him. Marius definitely remembered his first encounter with Barretto. Though it had been more than twenty annutides ago, he pictured the scene as if it had happened just yestertide.

Marius had recently inherited the throne of Atlantis, and now he faced the first test of his authority. A conflict had erupted in the northeastern region of Francoso over representation on the Atlantic Council. The disputed seat had been vacated by the sudden death of their councilmember. Because he had left no heir, two mermen vied for the position. One was the councilman's brother who was respected for his integrity; the other was a distant cousin who wielded a great deal of influence in the region because of his connections in the kelp harvesting industry. The region was on the brink of civil war, the Francosian people split almost equally. On one side were the common mermen and merwomen. On the other side were the affluent and influential. According to the constitution, if a controversy concerning representation occurred, the official Atlantic Arbitrator, along with the king, then determined the representative.

Barretto had been appointed arbitrator only two cycles before Nero's death. This situation was the first test of his ability as well. The Atlantis Arbitrator was a lifetime position, vacated only upon death or voluntary forfeiture. With the title came great respect and prestige, though sometimes several annutides passed without his skill being needed. In other words, many mermen and merwomen forgot his position existed. Only when his skills were required did people remember the Atlantic Arbitrator.

Marius had thought Barretto was an excellent, insightful choice for the position by his father. The mammoth merman was quite impressive and extremely intimidating. He dwarfed most mermen with his size and muscle mass. Sometimes merely his arrival quelled the disagreement; he didn't need to utter a word. The other quality that enabled Barretto to excel at his position was his unnerving calm. Nothing rattled him or swayed him from performing his duties with integrity and fairness. He possessed an innate ability to quickly assess a situation with impartiality and wisdom. Marius considered him one of the kingdom's most important assets.

During this first meeting requiring both newly appointed mermen to exert their given duties, neither had met the other. Almost instantly, there was a mutual respect for the other. Amid the crackling hostility that filled the chamber, both mermen greeted each other cordially as they made their way to the front table where the proceedings would take place. Tensions were high. Anger, frustration, and scathing accusations from both sides of the Francosian assembly reverberated off the chamber walls. Contrasting the chaos was the calm, cool demeanor of Barretto. He motioned for Marius to take the seat of honor, patiently waiting until the king was seated. Then, he assumed his seat. Pounding the stone gavel, he silenced the room with its powerful sound. Order was restored, but only briefly.

Once the delegation representing the powerful cousin finished presenting their case, its supporters began chanting, intentionally trying to disrupt and prevent the other side from presenting theirs. Someone threw the first punch, and all hell broke loose. Fists, bodies, and furniture went flying through the waters. It was a chaotic scene, and in the midst of the melee sat Marius and Barretto placidly watching it all with an almost amused amazement. Suddenly complete darkness blanketed the chamber. Every illumining panel had gone completely black stilling the fighting and silencing the noise. When the first hushed whispers drifted tentatively through the assembly, light slowly returned to each illumining panel, brightening the chamber like the sun's rays spreading over the waters. Before the darkness descended, in the periphery of his vision, Marius saw Barretto's hand clench, and now the same hand slowly relaxed as light returned. Absolutely speechless, Marius couldn't believe what his eyes had just witnessed. Could it really be? He caught Barretto's eye. An unspoken understanding passed between the two mermen, which bound them in an unbreakable new friendship.

Banging his gavel, Barretto rose from his seat, towering over the stunned assembly, his voice resounding with authority, "The council seat goes to Orinceus, Brontes' brother. This meeting is adjourned." And with that proclamation, the matter was settled, the decision unequivocally accepted by every mermen there. After the confused and baffled Francosians departed, only the two mermen remained in the now quiet hall littered with overturned tables and broken pieces of furniture drifting through the water. As he slowly swam to the door, the Arbitrator turned one final time and caught Marius' eye. The king raised his hand with his palm facing his new friend. With a nod, Barretto indicated he understood—Marius would keep his secret.

The memory never failed to make Marius smile. Now as the marine life around him began to change and the waters became murky, Marius snapped out of his musings. He knew he was almost there—the abandoned settlement of Dionypoli. Even the marine life had left. As he entered through the decayed gates, he was reminded how primitive the town had been. Leave it to Barretto to choose a place like this, one completely desolate and uninhabited.

Arriving at the ancient remains of the settlement's temple, Marius swam up the nearly eroded steps and sat on the patio. He didn't wait there long. Carrying a large bag in one of his hands, Barretto emerged from the opposite side of the temple. He placed the bag on the patio beside him and bowed before his king.

"My king, I'm sorry I made you wait. Please forgive me, my lord."

Marius waved away his apology. "Rise, Friend. I just arrived. How have you been?"

Barretto sat down on the smooth stone beside Marius. "I have been busy. Disagreement and dissention seem more prevalent now than they did in our early tides."

Marius agreed completely, "Yes, there is an evil, deliberate attempt to disrupt the calm waters of our world. Just this morntide, Ettore and I were attacked by sharks. Even more disturbing is that Ettore was the target, not I. Needless to say, the sharks had been sent on a mission by some merman. They would have never attempted this on their own."

"Was Ettore harmed? Do you know who is behind the attack?" Though calm on the outside, Barretto was greatly enraged at the attack.

"No, he was unharmed. He doesn't know the sharks were after him. Massau, the Great White, revealed this to me after I coerced him to reveal his orders. He didn't know who had sent him, but I have a good idea." Marius raised his eyes and stared at his confidant. "Yes, Barretto, much dissent fills the waters."

Barretto continued, "There is one disagreement in particular that compelled me to meet with you this tide. Almost a forttide ago, I was summoned to settle a labor dispute at the Safety and Research Chamber. I surprised the director of the SARC by arriving three tides earlier than I had indicated. An immediate refusal from the director to conduct the arbitration that tide only raised my suspicion. Of course, I gave him no choice. Before the meeting started, he tried his best to shake me from his side. He made many excuses why he needed me to leave or why he needed to go, but I refused. I even voiced my distrust of his motives aloud. That admission caused him great distress, let me tell you." He stopped as something close to a smile lifted the corners of his mouth. From his waistbelt, he withdrew a kelp stick. He offered one to Marius, who without hesitation took it. Both sat chewing on the stick in companionable silence.

"Is Gregar still the director?" Marius knew he was, but the question allowed Barretto to elaborate.

He nodded. Then, Barretto continued his story. "Yes, he's been there many tides. Well, not long after my investigative team arrived, the meeting began. Among the claims made by one group of workers was the charge that some new weapons were being produced in mass quantity, yet who had designed them and who ordered them remained a mystery. It was as if once these mysterious weapons were made, they disappeared with no record or proof that they had ever been created. There were no purchase orders or records of outgoing orders. Of course, the opposing group of managers vehemently denied the allegation. They claimed the information about the weapons was confidential and refused to disclose the information to me. Naturally, I reminded them that my authority was constitutionally given; theirs was not. That seemed to silence them quite sufficiently. I ordered the weapon and the plans in dispute to be brought into the chamber immediately by one of the workers, not one of the managers."

Marius interrupted, "I've not heard a word nor given consent concerning any weapon development or production. This is disturbing news to me. Please continue." A frown creased Marius' brow as he listened intently to Barretto.

"Oh, I knew that even then. Needless to say, the managers were unable to produce the official order required by constitution law. The worker who filed the arbitration papers discovered plans for the weapon and had concealed one of the weapons his department had made in a drawer under a table. His fast thinking helped prove his case. Without the concealed weapon, there would have been no proof. All the other weapons that had been produced seemingly have disappeared. My inspectors found no trace of the weapon anywhere in the chamber. Someone covered this up very well."

"Tell me more about this weapon. How was it made? Why was it made? Who is behind this scheme?" Frustration and concern pitched Marius' voice higher.

"Instead of telling you, let me show you." Barretto leaned over and opened the bag that sat on the patio floor. He pulled out the etching that detailed the weapon's specifications and dimensions. Without hesitation, he passed it to Marius. Immediately, Marius studied the etching, stunned that something this dangerous and powerful had been deliberately kept from him. This was a conspiracy. Once more, Barretto plunged his hand into the bag and withdrew the newly developed weapon.

Marius gasped; disbelief turned to reality. He reached for the weapon and examined its construction. Its well-engineered design made the weapon, a cross between the humans' sword and whip, easy to balance and enabled its user to smoothly wield it through the water. The slender blade resembled the tail of a ray; its handle curved like a seahorse's tail. It was flawlessly designed to inflict damage. Powered by the force of motion through the water, it could cleanly slice its target. Impressed, Marius marveled at not only the design but also at the workmanship. With quiet intensity he asked, "How many were produced?"

With a solemn look, Barretto murmured, "According to the workers, almost twenty of them were made over the previous five tides. Unfortunately, this was the only one we recovered." Barretto swam over to the other side of the king. He resumed the account of the meeting, "When my inspectors found no trace of the weapons, I halted all activities at the SARC, locked down all production lines and departments, and charged its director with constitutional conspiracy. He was taken into custody without delay. I assigned two highly trusted AA inspectors to stand guard at the doors refusing any merman or merwomen entrance without your consent. That includes your brother, I might add."

At the insinuation, Marius nodded. "Good call, my friend. I suspect that with a little investigation, we will find his handiwork in this treachery. What is being done about the situation at the SARC right now?"

Smiling slightly, Barretto replied, "Nobody will enter that chamber without your consent. My investigators are poring through the files and records at the chamber. The director is in custody at the Chamber of Law. He refused to answer any questions or divulge any details about the weapon. I have ordered his detainment until he is released personally by you and no one else. Your majesty, we will find a resolution to this problem. I give you my word."

"Well done, my friend, well done. I have never doubted your ability or your integrity. Please keep me informed of any further developments. As for Gregar, tell him it will be three more tides until I return. Then I will interrogate him myself. Double his guards and allow him no visitors, especially not Calder. Hopefully by the time I return, he will be singing a different tune." Marius once again examined the ray weapon and the etched plans. He handed both to Barretto. "Keep these until I return. I trust you with them."

Barretto placed them back in the bag. "My lord, I will not be far from you in case you are in need of my services. As always, I am your servant." Marius extended his hand. Barretto placed his hand on top and bowed humbly before his king.

"Thank you, Barretto. Go in peace." Marius watched his friend swim west back to the capital. Sitting down on the steps once more, Marius deliberated his course of action for the situation. Unfortunately, there would be no easy solution or peaceful ending. Slowly rising from his seat, the king turned and swam toward Cecilia.

Chapter Thirty-five

Calder swam toward the Safety and Research Chamber for a meeting with the SARC director. Great excitement had filled the director's voice as he described to Calder just five tides ago the breakthrough on the new weapon's development. Since then, he had heard nothing more from Gregar. He decided to swim to the SARC personally to find out about the progress since then and let the director apprise him of any new developments.

As he swam past several of the capital chambers now empty and still, Calder's thoughts turned to Massau. No doubt, his defection hurt. Only a strong power could have dissuaded the aggressive shark to abandon his orders to harm Ettore. According to the other sharks, the king had imprisoned their leader. Calder had been careful not to reveal his identity to Massau; he communicated his plan by overpowering Massau's brain activity. Admittedly, Calder had underestimated his brother's powers, and begrudgingly, he had to admit his power of communication was not as strong as Marius'. Yet again, Calder didn't measure up to his older twin.

Only on rare occasions had Calder seen Marius display any of his Mystical Gifts. Their parents were unaware of which gifts, if any, Marius possessed until after their seventh birthtide. Calder still wondered if there were other Mystical Gifts Marius possessed other than Interpretation and Water Bending. Could it be true that he had more than two of the Mystical Gifts? From what the shiver of sharks described, Sand Stirring had been employed. So rare were the Mystical Gifts that most merpeople believed they were extinct. Healing and Prophecy had been noticeably absent from the kingdom's waters since his great-grandmere's death. So long had it been since some of the gifts had been exhibited that many merpeople believed they had never existed. Even though the Mystical Gifts were taught as fact to them as merchildren during everyone's formal schooling, many dismissed them as fantasy, mere legend. Had Calder not seen them exhibited, he too would have sided with that school of thought; however, he knew they were real and that their power could shift the balance of control to their possessors.

He tried to remember back to their childhood for a memory of Marius using his gifts, but most of those memories were as elusive as the gifts themselves. Marius had mastered Water Bending in his youth, much like his son Ettore who with a waterbow was unrivaled. From his taking control of Massau, Calder realized his twin's Language Communication greatly overpowered his own. However, at no time could Calder ever recall even a fragment of a memory of Marius using Sand Stirring. Perhaps the sharks had been mistaken. Still, the thought was unsettling. By Marius having yet another Mystical Gift, the scales became even more unbalanced in his favor.

Calder spotted the SARC a short distance ahead. As he approached the chamber, Calder felt a ripple of excitement. Talk about a shift in power! His new ray weapon would change things around here drastically. He swam excitedly toward the chamber, covering the last remaining distance there quickly. He arrived at the impressive structure as some of the workers were exiting. Engineers had designed the capital in a compact, two-sided reflection; the buildings facing each other were identical. Through the epicenter of the Capital Center, mermen and merwomen moved with deliberation and purpose. This was the heart of Atlantis. Here, all the important decisions concerning the kingdom were made. The SARC sat adjacent to the Capital Center's Government Complex. Marius seldom worked there other than attending council meetings. He preferred to work from his chamber, but the Government Complex housed a magnificent royal office. It was extravagant in its furnishings and contained many priceless relics from the past. Calder secretly coveted the space. *One tide*, he thought, *it will be mine.*

His brow wrinkled in confusion as he spotted two mermen treading at the door. *What are they doing here?* thought Calder. He decided the conciliatory approach might work best, so he smiled broadly as he approached the two guards wearing uniforms with AA emblazoned on their chests. The officers accompanied the arbitrator on official business. What brought the arbitrator here to the SARC? Surely Gregar could smooth out any trouble between his workers. Summoning the arbitrator seemed like such an extreme measure for a dispute involving government workers.

"Good morn', my friends. What brings the arbitrator here so early in the tide? I'm here to see the director about an important matter, official government business. Is everything all right this tide?" As he spoke, Calder smoothly tried to enter. The larger of the two guards halted his progress. He placed himself squarely in front of Calder, preventing him from going through the large doors.

The other, smaller guard spoke nervously, "I'm terribly sorry, sir, but we have been given explicit orders to prohibit anyone from entering the SARC, even you. Forgive me, sir, but these were our orders." The merman seemed ill at ease at enforcing the order. Calder sensed his fear and nervousness even though he tried to conceal it. Calder smiled at his weakness. The guard mistook the smile for Calder accepting the ban of entering the chamber diplomatically. He relaxed somewhat thinking a scene had been prevented. He couldn't have been more wrong.

Calder leaned toward the small merman and in a menacing voice whispered, "I will go through this door. I'm the Defense Director. Surely you do not seriously believe these orders apply to me. Call Gregar. He will clear this misunderstanding up immediately." Calder crossed his arms like he had all tide to wait.

The larger merman spoke. Confidence and something similar to a smirk accompanied his words, "Gregar is not here to clear up anything. He has been taken to the holding chamber at the Confinement Center for processing." He met Calder's angry eyes with a steady, calm gaze.

"Processing? What does that mean? Who's in charge here? I demand to speak with him at once. Preventing me from entering the very chamber under my domain of power is absurd. These people work for me!" Calder practically shouted.

As if on cue, the doors behind the guards slowly opened. Calder, feeling somewhat smug that his bullying had seemingly worked, crossed his arms and staring down the impudent guard, waited for their chief. Arrogance turned astonishment as the doors opened to reveal the Atlantic Arbitrator himself. Calder had never seen a merman this large. His presence filled the entire doorway as he fluidly and calmly swam up behind his guards. He towered over the large guard as an adult merman dwarfs a small merchild. Calder gawked with disbelief. Never having met him before, Calder had heard stories about Barretto, the reclusive arbitrator, but had believed they were wild exaggerations. Now, his eyes realized the stories had been greatly understated. Barretto was a giant.

"Ah, Calder I do believe it is. Hello, I'm Barretto, the Atlantic Arbitrator. I am a friend of your brother, the king. What can I do for you this morntide?" No small talk or banalities ensued. Without any pretense, Barretto cut straight to the matter. Calder was caught off guard at his bluntness.

Composing himself, Calder cleared his throat. "I have come to speak with Gregar. I demand to know why I am being banned from my own chamber. On whose authority have these orders been issued? I am the Director of Defense, after all. Only Marius' authority is greater than my own." Arrogance accentuated the last statement.

"On my authority, by my command has this chamber been closed indefinitely. There is no need to tell me your title or remind me of the hierarchy of command. I am quite versed in the constitutional law of Atlantis. It's called *my job*." Calder cringed at the subtle smile that flashed across the larger guard's face. Barretto sent the guard a withering look that immediately erased the smirk. Shifting his attention back to Calder, he continued placidly, "As for Gregar, he is indisposed and will be for quite a while. He is in the Confinement Center at the Chamber of Law until Marius returns to the capital. I've been informed by a reliable source that the king won't arrive here for at least two more tides." Pausing slightly, he finished, "Until I meet with Marius, there is nothing more to discuss. If you will excuse me, I must attend to my duties. Farewell and good tide." Barretto turned toward the opened chamber portals.

Fury surged through Calder's entire body at being treated with such disrespect for someone of his high position. "How dare you dismiss me like I'm some sort of plebian! You don't know who you are dealing with! I demand an explanation of what you are doing here and insist that you allow me to speak to Gregar. Surely this is some misunderstanding blown completely out of proportion."

Barretto rotated his tail ever so slightly. With the inconspicuous move, he floated around slowly to face Calder. Condescension dripped from his voice. "First, I care not who you think you are. Second, I heed only the demands or commands of Marius himself. The king's orders state no one—and that includes you—has permission to speak to Gregar. Finally, you are not entitled to know what my affair is here, so this discussion is over." With that, Barretto disappeared through the portal panels that closed behind him. The two guards resumed their position blocking entrance into the SARC. Stunned by the arbitrator's rejection, Calder realized he had summarily been dismissed.

Infuriated by the blatant disrespect shown to him, Calder swam straight to his chamber. He shut the portal behind him by hitting the button with an angry thrash of his tail. This was not over, not by a long shot. It was this current to take matters into his own hands. Moving a panel and reaching into a clear wall of his chamber, he grasped one of his messenger fish. The brightly colored fish stilled as Calder relayed the information he was to deliver. Calder once again pressed the button to open the portal. He released the fish, and watched it glide through the waters of Atlantis, back toward the Capital Center. Satisfied with his next move, Calder prepared for the assembly that would soon gather in his Capital Chamber.

Chapter Thirty-six

A new season warmed the cold currents of Atlantis. More sunshine brightened the waters bringing lightness not only to the ocean itself but to the merpeople dwelling there. Selale felt much better since the nausea and dizziness had passed. Sometimes she almost forgot she was pregnant as she went about her work at the Language Translation Chamber, but the baby was never far from her mind. Even while she translated documents, phrases would trigger a daydream of the baby: what he would look like, smell like, feel like and sound like. She would catch herself sitting for several currents of the tide lost in the daydream. Then, feeling guilty, she would double her efforts to finish each tide's work, so she could spend the remainder with Thad or Monica. Her routine had varied little since she had befriended Monica. She spent two tides each quarter cycle with Monica when Thad worked late at the university.

Marius was delighted that Selale had renewed her acquaintance with Monica, Giada's best friend. His daughter needed a maternal presence that she had lacked growing up as a merchild. The worry Marius had felt before his trip to Cecilia had disappeared because Selale now seemed so happy, so content the last cyclotide.

This morntide, Selale kissed her father on the top of his head as she prepared to leave for work. "I'm going to see Monica later this tide after work.

Do you need anything from her? Why, Papa, she has a remedy for almost any ailment! She is delightful. I understand why Mama loved her so. In the past few tides, she has become dear to me as well."

"You've needed a friend like Monica. I feel guilty for not taking you to her chamber to build your friendship before now. Tell Moni to send me some of that clam syrup. It was always a good remedy for managing an even temper. I'm going to need that syrup over the next several tides. Some tough decisions will need to be made soon." Marius let his thoughts drift to Gregar.

Selale stared at her father as he became lost in the worries of the tide. "I will make sure I bring you some. Who knows? Maybe you can spike the drink of everyone involved."

At that picture, Marius laughed. "I guess there are far worse things that they could drink. Good tide, Selale." Marius hugged his daughter tightly. Smiling at him affectionately, she departed.

After her shift at the Language Translation Chamber ended, Selale swam to Monica's chamber. Monica saw her long before she reached the portal and waited with arms open wide ready to embrace her new friend. Selale had become like the daughter she had never had. Monica knew deep in her heart that Giada would pour her blessings on the friendship. She hoped her advice provided Selale with wise guidance. She sensed there was something important, some secret Selale was afraid to divulge to her. While Monica did not have the gift of prophecy, her intuition understood Selale's hesitancy to confide in her meant she was struggling with something very difficult. Monica felt something almost like fear whenever she thought about Selale's situation. Without a husband, Selale faced many questions and definitely ridicule. Monica embraced the young merwoman and brought her into her chamber.

"What a tide it has been! I didn't think I would ever get here! Let me catch my breath." Taking a seat at the table, Selale put her hand on her stomach and declared, "He moved today, Monica! I felt him move. Fortunately, nobody was around when it first happened. It gave me quite a shock, let me tell you." A look of wonder on her face, Selale gazed down at her stomach. She murmured almost as if she was talking to the baby, "Things are only going to become more difficult the farther along we get, aren't they?" Raising her eyes, she met

Monica's serious gaze. To Selale's softly spoken question, Monica could only nod in answer.

"Will you help me figure out a plan, so I will be prepared before I face these problems? I'm scared. Soon I won't be able to conceal my pregnancy. There are far too many questions that I can't or won't be able to answer. Monica, I need your help, and I really want to confide in you. You are the only person whom I can trust, yet what I'm going to tell you is dangerous. By telling you this secret, I am putting you squarely in harm's current. You've become someone whom I love. I don't know what to do. I just don't know what to do."

Monica swam over to sit beside Selale. The older merwoman took her young friend's hands into her own and squeezed them gently. "My child, I have known for a forttide your struggle to confide in me. If my safety is what prevents you from telling me, let me ease your mind. No one cares about an old merwoman like me. I'm an afterthought in our society. Your secret will remain safe with me. Let's make some plans. Let me help you, my dear. I'm much tougher than I look." A twinkle gleamed in Monica's eyes as she tried to ease Selale's worries.

Smiling, Selale rose and went to the remedy wall. She took the clam syrup off the shelf and turned to Monica. "Papa wanted me to bring him some of this syrup. He's got something serious that he's dealing with as well." Pausing she traced the tins of ointment. "Do you have something to cure fear?" She didn't turn around, but continued to study the concoctions that filled the shelves covering the entire wall. Monica understood Selale was trying to find her nerve to reveal her secret. Straightening the line of bottles, Selale asked, "Monica, what do you know about the Hybrid King prophecy?" She turned to face her friend.

Monica admitted she knew the story almost word for word. Everyone who still believed the prophecy hoped they would live to see the Hybrid King. Generations of mermaids hope they would be the chosen one to birth the king. Confused by the shift in the conversation, she thought Selale once again was stalling to reveal her secret. Monica continued, "It's been so long since Marius' great-grandmere proclaimed that vision. I was a very small merchild. I don't remember her actually making the proclamation, but I do remember studying about it near the end of my formal schooling. Oh, I know the story by heart and hope the king will come. I know your father believes the prophecy with all his heart, soul, and mind. Why? Does this fear involve telling your father about your pregnancy?"

"Telling him I'm pregnant is the least of my fears." Selale swam over to once again sit beside Monica.

Monica was clearly mystified. "What then, if not telling your father, is it that you fear? Are you worried because by no longer being chaste you can't birth the Hybrid King? Your father will understand, especially if you love this merman."

Taking a deep breath and closing her eyes, Selale blurted her confession before she lost her nerve, "The father of my child is a human, not a merman." She kept her eyes closed as she waited to hear Monica's response. The chamber was filled with silence. Finally, Selale found the courage to open her eyes and raise them to meet Monica's. She saw no condemnation there in her friend's eyes, only shock, concern, and wonder.

"Oh, my child!" Monica put her arm around Selale and pulled her into her arms. The confession explained so much and now she understood the fear Selale felt. Fear threatened to consume Monica as well. Did this news mean what she thought it meant? She could hardly wrap her mind around the implication of Selale's news. The Hybrid King would soon be born! Could their meeting four cycles before have been more than mere coincidence? Fear, hope, concern, and joy all mingled together creating a blur of emotions. Monica sat speechless trying to get over the shock of the news. Perhaps destiny had ordained their friendship and orchestrated this reunion with Giada's daughter for precisely this time. Monica always believed she would live to see the Hybrid King come. Now the opportunity presented itself for her to be a part of his story, his legacy. She would do everything in her power to help Selale because by helping her, Monica, in essence, would be help the future king save the entire Mer race.

"Say something, Monica!" Selale implored.

"I-I'm shocked, but I feel humbled and so honored that you trusted me enough to tell me. Surely you understand the implications of this birth? This baby could be the king who was prophesied over a centennitide ago. Oh, Selale! Blessed are you! Don't you see? This child could be the savior of our people, the one destined to save us! Rejoice! Don't despair. You know how this story ends!" Monica clapped her hands together.

"But I'm so afraid, Moni! I'm paralyzed by the heartache that I know is to come. I just don't know about anything anymore. I'm terrified of what I don't know." Sobbing, Selale fell into Monica's arms.

Holding her and stroking her hair, Monica whispered, "I'm scared too. Scared for you and for the baby, but we can't worry about the unknown, about what we can't control. We must deal with the here and now and put our trust in knowing that everything will work for good. Though there is great danger between this present tide and the baby's birth, we must make preparations to ensure his future, not shrink away from our responsibilities because we are afraid. True courage is when we act in spite of our fear to save others and not ourselves."

Selale understood the truth in her wise friend's words. Pulling out of Monica's arms, she realized she would do anything to protect her baby. Though she had no idea what would be required of her in the tides that were ahead, right now she had to prepare for the baby's future. In a strong voice she asked, "Where do we begin?"

"That's my girl! First, you must tell Marius. He has to know so he can protect you both. How, when, and where you tell him will be up to you. My advice is to tell him soon. The sooner he knows the secret, the more tides he will have to help you plan for the king's birth."

Selale arose. She treaded beside Monica and softly murmured, "He will be so disappointed in me. I have brought shame upon our family."

"I have known him for many, many tides. Marius is a man of great integrity and grace. His reaction may surprise you, my friend. Give him time to adjust to the news, and I believe you will find his excitement will rival your own. Come; we too must be prepared. Let's map out the rest of your pregnancy, so we can prepare for any problems that may arise." Taking an etcher and stone from the table, the two outlined their plans. The Hybrid King would arrive in about four cyclotides. There was much to be done.

Chapter Thirty-seven

Two tides later, Marius entered the Confinement Center where Gregar had been detained for the past quarter cycle. Upon his return to the capital, Marius decided to take an entire tide before he visited the former SARC director. After having been in confinement for almost five tides, Marius concluded that two more tides would not matter. The longer Gregar was imprisoned, the more willing he may be to discuss the weapon. Freedom was a great motivator. Marius was determined to discover the answers to his questions. Gregar could do this the easy way or the hard way. The choice rested entirely in his hands. The empty Confinement Center could accommodate him as long as he remained silent and refused to cooperate. Marius definitely had the advantage.

Four AA guards had remained at the Confinement Center alternating morn and eventide shifts. Bowing before the king, the two on duty quickly pressed the portal release allowing Marius to enter the small prison chamber where Gregar sat. Noting the cramped, sparse accommodations, the king nodded his approval to the guards. This chamber was the smallest room in the Confinement Center. He swam to the middle of the chamber and faced the sullen merman who sat silent on the sleeping couch. Much to Marius' dismay, Gregar's angry and arrogant eyes challenged him.

In a strong voice laced with hostility, Gregar sneered, "Well, if it isn't the honorable king. To what do I owe this pleasure? Why, such courtesy have you extended to me, an innocent man. Have you come to release me? You have no reason to keep me confined."

Marius gazed at the former director and calmly replied, "I am the king. I need no reason to keep you here other than the charge of conspiracy to commit treason. You will stay here in confinement until you disclose the location of the manufactured ray weapons. Until then, you will be allowed no visitors. I shall not see you again until you tell the guards the weapons' location. When the site has been verified and the rays confiscated, then, and only then, will I visit you again. Think long and hard about it. The charge you face is treason. Need I remind you of the sentence?" Marius saw fear and the first sign of doubt shadow Gregar's face. Without another word, the portal opened and Marius left the small prison chamber. He turned to the guard and within ear-shot of the fallen director said, "Be sure to double the guards and allow absolutely no one in this area of the chamber—no family, no colleagues, no friends, and especially no one from the Atlantic Council or SARC. Summon me when he comes to his senses and decides to talk."

Marius swam away from the Chamber of Law back toward the Capital Center. Perhaps it was time he paid his brother a visit. It was time for a serious discussion on the division of power and what Calder was and was not allowed to do. Marius ultimately made the decision of how far his twin's authority reached. Calder needed to be reminded of that important detail.

Entering into the Capital Center, Marius took note of two interesting sights. First, two of Calder's closest allies, Gaillard and Rahwah, covertly made their way into the side portal of Calder's personal office chamber. Second, a guard had been posted beside the portal. Marius smiled as he swam toward the chamber portal. He did love crashing a party, especially when he had the element of surprise. He approached the portal casually, and without asking permission to enter, he reached to press the portal release.

I—I'm sorry, your Majesty, but I have been given orders to prevent any merman from disturbing Calder. Y—you must come again later if you wish to speak to him." Issuing orders to the king obviously made the guard nervous.

"Is that what you said to Gaillard and Rahwah? Well, they must have disregarded your orders as am I. Surely Calder did not mean I, his brother, your king, could not enter. You must have misunderstood. In the future, you need to be more attentive to his commands." To the guard's confused and questioning look, Marius smiled and added, "I will forgive this lapse of manners this time, but I expect you will attend your duties with more respect in the future." With a clear dismissal, Marius opened the portal and entered, leaving the bewildered guard outside the chamber.

Calder's office chamber was situated at the end of a long corridor lit by illuminating panels in deep gold, which cast a warm glow on the cold stone walls. Making his way silently down toward the Conference Chamber, Marius listened intently trying to determine if this secret meeting had begun. Far down at the corridor's end, Marius heard voices. He paused just outside the portal listening intently and trying to determine who was present. He could make out about five of the voices other than Calder's.

As he inched his way forward, he heard his brother's voice tell those present he was ready to begin. Marius realized this meeting had a clear agenda; unfortunately, he didn't know what the agenda was. Hopefully the reason these mermen were assembled here would soon be clear. Marius was prepared to listen outside the chamber for the entire tide if he could discover Calder's plans.

Suddenly, a hand covered the king's mouth, and strong arms grabbed his body around the shoulders, dragging him swiftly away from the chamber meeting into another small chamber on the opposite side of the corridor. Marius struggled to free himself from his captor's firm hold, but his strength was no match for the merman who held him. Pressing the portal release button, the merman's strong arms immediately released Marius upon the chamber being sealed. The king turned angrily around to face his captor. Anger turned to confusion as Marius stared into the concerned expression of Perimicles.

Placing a finger over his lips, the young merman listened to be sure no one was in the corridor. After he made sure no one was within earshot, he bowed to the king and said in a hushed voice, "Forgive me, my lord, for dragging you in here, but you could have placed yourself in grave danger. You know not why these men have been assembled. I do, and it definitely places you in harm's way if they were to discover your presence here. Please, sir, leave this place and let me inform you of the events later. These mermen have no clue I am an enemy to their plans. I, along with two others, have infiltrated their inner circle. They trust me and have confided their plans to me. They view me as an asset to their cause due to the nature of my job of being messenger for the Capital Center. Be patient, your Majesty. I will reveal all to you when the tide is right. Leave this place, I beg you, and let me do the job I was commissioned to complete."

Marius nodded his head and held out his hand. Perimicles touched the king's hand, his ruby ring visible to the king, and bowed. Pressing the portal release once more, the young merman swam out of the room and calmly into the chamber assembly. The chamber sealed behind him, silencing all the sound from the covert meeting. Marius retraced his path down the long golden corridor and out the side portal of the building. He encountered the guard again and sternly chastised him, "There was no meeting. Calder was nowhere to be found. Tell him I will see him later." At the guard's relieved look, Marius knew the guard would not mention his visit here. He turned and swam in the opposite direction toward his chamber.

Marius decided to keep the infiltration plot to himself for now. Telling Ettore or Sandoval could possibly endanger them. This espionage would require utmost trust in Perimicles in order to find out the plans of this secretly assembled group. Marius was overcome with a sense of foreboding. While he knew it wasn't part of Perimicles' job as messenger, Marius recognized that it was part of his sworn, secret duty. This young merman was risking his life to save his king. If his deception or involvement in this counterplot was somehow discovered, Perimicles' death was eminent. Marius would do everything in his power to protect him, but in the end, it may not be enough to save him or the others involved if their true identities were discovered.

Would it come to that? Marius wondered. *Would Calder commit murder to gain more control of the kingdom?* An alarming, terrible thought pushed its way into his mind: Calder wanted to be king. Marius stopped swimming abruptly and turned to gaze at the Capital Center, now a watery silhouette off in the distance. If Calder wanted to be king, Marius realized he, Ettore, and Selale had to be eliminated in order for that to happen. Acute fear for his children spread through Marius' entire body and pierced his heart. He would die trying to protect them. His fear turned to anger, and it propelled him to action. If Calder wanted a fight, he had better be prepared for the fight of his life. Marius shifted his body and swam hastily toward home. Plans had to be made now to thwart the evil that was coming. He would go to Beulah Cave. There things made sense. With enough time and planning, he did not doubt that he could devise a solution to this serious problem. As he was about to enter his chamber office, Ettore came through the portal.

"Hello, Papa!" Ettore beamed a broad smile. On his arm was his lovely friend Julette. "Are you terribly busy right now? Julette and I have some wonderful news." His eyes glanced down to look at the lovely mermaid.

Marius forgot his anger and flashed a genuine smile at his son and Julette. "I am never too busy to hear wonderful news! Come, let's sit at the table. Julette, after you, my dear." He led them to the table. Just as they were about to sit down, Selale entered the chamber closing the portal behind her. Taking stock of the situation, she caught her father's eyes which confirmed her speculation. Ettore and Julette were ready to share some good news.

"Selale! You arrived at the perfect tide! Come join us. One more makes the news even more joyful!" Ettore kissed his sister on the cheek and guided her to her usual place at the table. Smiling, Selale allowed herself to be taken there like a helpless merchild.

"Papa, Selale, Julette and I are in love. I want to spend the rest of my life with her, making her happy, making a life, making a family. If she will have me, I want her to be my mate." To his questioning look, the lovely mermaid nodded yes. Ettore whooped and took her in his arms.

The rest of the tide, a festive mood settled on them, allowing Marius to temporarily forget his earlier concerns about Calder. Now was a time of celebration. Finally, Ettore and Julette left to go share the news with her family. Marius and Selale remained in the chamber watching the happy couple leave swimming hand in hand.

Selale turned around and embraced her father tightly. "They are so happy and so in love. I'm glad they can be together." Sadness tinged her words as she continued to hug her father.

Marius pulled his daughter back to stare into her face. "Let's go to the cave. I need a peaceful place to think, and I can tell you've got something weighing on your mind as well." Too choked up to speak, Selale nodded at the invitation. Marius pressed the button and the secret tunnel that would take them there suddenly appeared. With his hand extended to his daughter, Marius had only a moment to wait until she took his hand firmly in her own. Together they made their way to Beulah Cave.

Surfacing in the cave, Selale saw a light left on the stone by Thad. Frantically she searched the cave with her eyes to see if he was there. At her father's amazed and frightened look at the lantern, she knew this was going to be much more difficult than what she and Monica had planned. Thankful that Thad was not around, she took a shuddering breath and quietly said, "Papa, I've got something that I must tell you. Before I lose my nerve, I need to say it all." Selale pulled herself up on the smooth rock and patted the space beside her for her father to join her. He sat down and took the lantern in his hand, examining it closely.

"Selale, what is this light? Where did you get it?" Without raising his eyes from the light, he waited for her explanation. Tearing his eyes from the light source, he realized Selale had remained silent. She began to cry. "What is going on? You know you can tell me anything. What is it, sweetheart?" Marius put the light down on the rock and grabbed his daughter's hand.

Sobs wracked her body before Marius could take her in his arms. "Talk to me. Tell me what is wrong. Is it Ettore's news? What has upset you so?"

Selale tried to regain her composure, but the tears continued to run down her cheeks. "I'm scared, but I am tired of keeping this to myself. Monica told me I should tell you, but I don't know how to begin. Everything is so complicated." Selale continued to cry.

"If Moni advised you to tell me, then this must be important. I will hold you until you find the strength to tell me. You know how much I love you, Selale." Those words helped her find the courage Monica had spoken of two tides earlier.

"Papa, I'm pregnant." If his daughter had told him she had sprouted wings and flew, he would not have been as surprised. He pulled her away from him and looked at her.

"What? H-how can this be? I mean, I know how, I—uh. How far along are you? Who is the father? Selale, I—I've seen you with no merman. Are you certain you are pregnant? I don't understand how this could happen to you. You've never shown any interest in any merman that I can recall." Her father looked absolutely confounded.

"Yes, I am pregnant, about six cycles along. There's no doubt. I won't be able to keep this pregnancy a secret much longer. I've been afraid of disappointing you that's why I didn't tell you sooner, but now I realize I must have your help."

Hugging his daughter even more tightly, Marius reassured her, "Oh, darling, you could never, ever disappoint me. Everything will be all right. I will help you in any way I can. Of course you're scared. While this isn't the way I would have planned it, being pregnant isn't the end of the world. We will plan for two weddings instead of one. It will all work out. Who is the father? Does he know? You have told him, haven't you?"

"No, Papa, it won't all work out and everything won't be all right. There won't and can't be a wedding. It's an impossible situation. I have dishonored our family. I'm sorry. I'm so sorry, but I do love him and—"

Marius interrupted, "Selale, why is marriage impossible then? You just stated you love him. Does he not love you back?"

Thad suddenly appeared, walking around from behind the adjacent cave wall. "Oh, yes, your Majesty. I love her back. And I love her more than life itself."

Marius jerked his head around, alarmed when his eyes locked with the eyes of a human.

Chapter Thirty-eight

Selale gasped, "Thad! I didn't know you were here."

The two men stared at one another. Marius couldn't believe what his eyes were telling him was true: his daughter was in love with a human. How could she have done something like this? How could she have brought him here to this personal, private place? She couldn't have been more accurate in her assessment of the situation. It was impossible.

Marius tore his eyes away from the human and said through clenched teeth to his daughter, "Somebody better start explaining this to me. Selale, what are you thinking? You know this breaks the commandment of our society! How could you have such blatant disregard for the law? Do you not understand the severe consequences of this choice if anyone were to find out?"

Turning to the human, Marius continued his inquisition. "And you? What is your motive here? You say you love her, but nothing good can come from this relationship. Why, you can't be together, you have nothing in common, and the penalty is death for you both if this relationship is discovered. So again, why are you here?" Marius' angry eyes pinned Thad down for an answer.

"I love her. That is why I am here. I can't, I won't live without her in my life. I don't care what obstacles we face. Destiny brought us together. You can't keep us apart." Thad approached the rock where both Marius and Selale sat.

"Thad, please sit down here beside me." Selale patted the stone. Thad sat down, but his eyes never wavered from the hostile stare of her father. He took Selale's other hand in his own. "Papa, I would like you to meet Thad Destin, my husband. Thad, this is my father, Marius, King of Atlantis." The two men sat staring at each other, neither willing to break the contact.

Marius scoffed, "Husband? What can that mean to you, Selale? End this right now, this tide. These are dangerous waters in which you tread. For his safety and your own, end this relationship. I can't protect you if you insist on destroying yourself. Please, Selale, please."

"Papa, did you not hear what I told you? I'm pregnant. This baby is the Hybrid King. Don't you understand? Our love was not by chance or merely by choice. I have accepted these events willed by a higher power. Why can't you? All my life, you have proclaimed an unshakable faith in this prophecy, and now that the events have begun to fulfill what was foretold so many tides ago, you refuse to open your eyes and see what is right before them! Papa, the Hybrid King will be born in less than four cycles. I didn't choose this! Fate chose me! This great responsibility scares me to death, but I know if you and Thad are by my side, love can overcome the heartache that is to come. You, Thad, and I are traveling down the prophecy's unchangeable course. Who am I or you to try to thwart destiny?" Selale's tears continued to run down her cheeks.

Without a word, Marius dove into the water. He surfaced on the opposite side of the cave near the prophecy wall. He pulled himself out of the water and lifted his hand to touch the delicate etching that covered the side of the cave. His eyes scanned the prophecy as if they were reading it for the first tide. Fear and hope warred inside him. Tearing his eyes from the wall, he stared at his beautiful daughter and the human she loved. It had begun. All these tides he had spent anticipating this event had not prepared him for the prophecy's reality and the dangers that were to come with the birth of this baby. Marius realized he faced an important decision this tide. Scanning the prophecy, he lowered himself into the water and swam to the rock ledge to once again sit at Selale's side.

He sat in silence for several moments trying to collect his swirling thoughts. Again, he stared at his daughter and the man she loved and realized she was right. Could this be the baby for whom he and the entire Mer race had waited for hundreds of annutides? Taking his hand, he tentatively placed it on his daughter's stomach. Suddenly, the pearl from around his neck radiated a blinding light that illuminated every niche of Beulah Cave. Light bounded of the walls, like a comet streaking through the heavens. Golden light bathed them in its warm glow. Selale gasped as the baby leaped inside her. Marius' looked at her with surprise and awe, unable to believe he felt the baby move. She rubbed her hands over her stomach and took in the beauty of the moment. Thad sat watching these events unfold as if he were watching a movie. It was just too much to take in at once. Wonder filled their faces as the pearl slowly dimmed.

Tears now coursed down the faces of all three. In the waning light, Marius coughed and murmured, "Well, now. I guess we need no further confirmation than that." Selale threw herself into her father's arms and laughed. She had never seen him at such a loss for words. Thad smiled at the King's succinct acceptance of the situation. He was going to like Marius, he could tell.

Suddenly animated, Marius turned to both Selale and Thad. "We need to plan for the events that are to come. Selale, you know the prophecy and understand the events that are to come, but do you?" He directed his question to Thad.

"Sir, Selale has read the entire prophecy to me. Events as other-worldly as what just happened here have already occurred. This only confirms what we know to be true about our child: he is the Hybrid King. I will do anything to protect him and Selale. There are parts of the prophecy which greatly disturb me, many things I cannot conceive or wrap my mind around how or why they must occur. However, in saying that, I am committed to protecting this child and Selale at any cost. As I told you before, I love them more than life itself."

Marius recognized the truth in his words. He knew Selale felt the same way. He could see it shining in her eyes. He nodded his approval. Selale tore her eyes away from Thad and spoke softly. "Papa, I won't be able to keep this pregnancy a secret much longer. Monica feels it is best that you assign me a position as ambassador in one of the far-northern regions of Francoso or Argonia, somewhere remote that will not raise suspicion. I will only be gone four months, for by then, the baby will have come. After that, I don't know what we will do about him."

Marius grew very serious. "This idea is a sound plan. Selale, you must stay here in the cave. We can't let anyone know our plan, not even Ettore. His knowing will only endanger him more. The child's safety is jeopardized by too many of us knowing. Since Monica knows, we can bring her here as the tide draws near for the birth. What is your role in this, young man?"

"Papa, his name is Thad! He has been a part of my life and has been coming here to this cave for many cycles. There are so many things that have happened of which you are unaware that involve him. You need to know these things, especially about the shell, the missing historical tome. Only Stedman knows about the shell. Even Monica is unaware of its existence. Tell him the story, Thad." Selale laid her head on Thad's shoulder.

Placing his arm around her, Thad drew her close. "Our story begins with the shell's discovery. My best friend found it on the beach, uncovered by a powerful storm. Almost simultaneously, I discovered Selale's existence. When I examined the shell, I touched it and saw a vision of the baby, the Hybrid King, long before he had been conceived, long before Selale brought me here to tell me of the prophecy. I have never been one to believe destiny commands absolute control of our lives, but who can argue with how these events have been so neatly mapped out? It can't be attributed to mere coincidence.

"As for my role, well, I am the Hybrid King's father. My role is to do what any father would do—be there, protect, love unconditionally. Aside from those things, I have no idea. This is all new to me."

Marius regarded Thad. He liked what he saw, at least from the waist up. This human seemed to be trustworthy, steady, and truly committed to the relationship. "Tell me about the shell. What does its history reveal about the genesis of our people? Does this not put our people in grave danger since humans have the shell?"

"Fortunately, no one has been able to decipher the language on the shell. Selale read it, and while it does recount the events that led to your people's beginnings, the exact formula that created the transformation from human to merman is not revealed on the shell, at least from what the pictures I took show. Are the photographs still here, Selale?" Thad's question was answered with a simple nod of her head.

"They are still in the box, hidden behind that rock ledge." Selale pointed to the location. Thad rose to retrieve the box. He opened it and handed the pictures to Marius.

Marius scanned the photographs, his eyes drinking in the words etched by his ancestors from millenitides before. "I want to study these closely, but it must wait." Thad handed him the box used to protect them from the water. "Put them back where they were hidden. I will read them later. As for now, here is what I suggest. Selale, you swim to Monica's later this tide and inform her of the details. I will issue an assignment that dispatches you to Francoso to work on translating some documents. Since Stedman is aware of the shell, do you think he will help validate this story? For his protection, he needs to know very little of the details, only that it involves the missing tome. Stop there on your way to the Language Translation Chamber and enlist his help. In the meantide, I will be in contact with Perimicles and have him fabricate a message from Francoso, just in case there is suspicion. He too can be trusted."

"Stedman will aid us in this endeavor; there is no doubt. Monica will be relieved that we have a plan regarding the birth of the baby, but what about after the baby is born? What will we do then? Keeping him here in this cave forever is not an option. What can we do to keep him safe?" Selale's worry was evident.

"That's where I come in," Thad interjected. "True, I know nothing about raising a baby, but he will be much safer with me on land than here in the waters of Atlantis." To Selale's cry, Thad held her close. "Selale, you know this must happen! We won't be too far away that you won't see him every tide if you must! It has to be this way!"

"He's right. Don't you remember that part of the prophecy, Selale? For his safety, he must be raised in the human world." Turning back to Thad he continued, "Thad, you make the preparations for his arrival in your world. I won't pretend I know what those are. If we each do our part and enlist the help of those whom we trust, the Hybrid King will be safe. Now I must leave to attend to these and other duties. Listen, both of you. These are dangerous tides; I've said that before." Squeezing both of their hands, Marius warned, "Caution is of the upmost importance. Don't become careless in your haste to see one another. The eyes of our enemies are watching us even now. Be strong in what you must do, in the decisions you must make. Love will give us strength to bring these events foretold so long ago to fruition. Good-bye, Thad. Until we meet again, take care." Marius reached out his hand. Thad, thinking that it meant shaking hands, grasped the king's hand firmly. Marius registered his surprise and with a smile, shrugged his shoulders to his daughter.

"Humans!" He laughed as he sank under the waters back toward the secret tunnel.

To Thad's befuddled question, "What did I do wrong?" Selale's laughter echoed off the walls and followed Marius out of the cave.

Chapter Thirty-nine

Michael loved the month of May for many reasons. First, the weather on the coast of the Mid-Atlantic was perfect—not too hot, not too humid, but just right. The sand was warm enough to stretch out on and soak up the bright golden rays. The water temperature heated quickly with the abundant sunshine allowing him to swim, surf, or simply wade in its salty current. Second, classes at the university came to an end, freeing up his and Charise's time to enjoy the outdoors. While students still poured into the restaurants, bars, and shops, they didn't demand his time or attention. He loved spending an hour of the morning beachcombing, looking for shells at low tide with only a bucket and a small shovel. Charise enjoyed gardening and often roped him into helping her. Secretly he didn't mind. There was something relaxing about digging and planting in the soil, watching something started from a tiny seed grow into a vibrant green vine bursting with fruits or vegetables. Michael liked it best when he and Charise worked side by side in silence. Her serenity at being in the garden washed over him like the gentle ebb and flow of the calm ocean. Often, she would catch him staring at her like they were teenagers in love. He did love May.

He and Charise had spent much of the morning finalizing the plans for their annual Memorial Day cookout. It was their kick-off to summer. This year they both agreed they needed to keep it simple. The guest list included mainly close friends and colleagues from the university. Every year he and Charise came up with a theme and centered everything—that included the food, the decorations, and the games—around it. The theme was what made the annual event so much fun. This year they decided to do a beach theme. While it was not the most imaginative of ideas, the theme lent itself toward great seafood, easy decorations, and some silly games. Michael couldn't wait. With just one day left before the big shindig, he had many little things he had to do to get everything ready for the party.

Thad had agreed to help him prepare a clam bake. He would buy the seafood and vegetables from the local market early that morning before the tourists were awake, that way it was sure to be fresh. Michael made him promise to bring at least one crazy game, but all he would agree to do was bring the beer so the guests would want to play the silly games. Michael realized he had a good point, so he settled for the offer.

Thad had been so incredibly happy for the entire winter and spring. Every time Michael was around him, he would end up feeling exhausted with his ebullience. Although Thad had still not confided completely in him about his and Selale's relationship, Michael realized he was happy, the happiest he could ever remember his best friend feeling. For the time being, that was enough.

Michael had called Thad right after lunch and told him he would pick him up around 12:00 to make sure he had been able to purchase everything at the market. That would give them a couple of hours to exchange the propane tank at the local grocery store, clean the grill and stock pot, and grab a couple of beers at Chaney's to assure they would stay out of Charise's way while she decorated. She tended to go a little crazy when it came to decorating for parties. He made a mental note to himself as a reminder to stay far away from the house tomorrow morning. The guests were set to arrive around 4:30. If he and Thad arrived back here around 2:00, the worst of the frenzy would have passed. He decided it was a good plan to avert being put to work by the decorating demon. After this party, both he and Charise would definitely need that upcoming vacation.

Michael had surprised Charise with a Caribbean cruise for her birthday. He had planned the trip itinerary with a seasoned travel agent who was a close friend of Michael's mother, so he had gotten many perks with minimal cost.

Charise had been delighted. Their ship was scheduled to disembark in less than three weeks. They would be back home near the end of June. He couldn't think of a better present for both of them.

Michael finished cleaning the chairs and tables that had been stored all winter in the shed. He set them in the back yard exactly where he was told to put them. Charise looked out the window and gave her nod of approval. She laughed at his silliness when he saluted to her.

He came into the kitchen where Charise was setting out the serving platters and bowls she would need for the food. Colorful plastic plates, cups, and plastic utensils filled a wire container. Michael came up behind her and wrapped his arms around her waist in a gentle hug.

"Is everything set up in the back yard?" Charise asked as she put a bright blue metal tub in the center of the countertop.

"Ay, ay, Captain!" Michael teased. He turned her around to face him. "I've swabbed the deck and hoisted the sails. We're set, milady." He dipped a surprised Charise down in a back-bending kiss, set her up on her feet again, and then sauntered jauntily out of the kitchen.

Smiling, Charise shook her head and muttered, "You aren't all there, Michael Moses."

The next day, Thad arrived back at his house early about eight in the morning. He had stopped by the local fish market and purchased the food for tonight's clam bake. Locals knew the market opened up early, so they arrived and purchased their seafood long before the languishing tourists started their day. Thad had spent the entire night in the cave with Selale. He had fallen in to a routine since the semester had ended at the university. He would take the boat to his designated spot early in the afternoon, put on his scuba gear, swim to the cave, and leave early the next morning. Since Selale no longer had to report to her job at the Language Translation Chamber, he could spend much of the day and night with her. Sometimes he came home only to eat, shower, and sleep for a few hours. Then he headed back to see Selale. Today though, he had changed his routine. Michael would be by to pick him up in about four hours. He put the seafood in the refrigerator. Thad realized he could sleep for a few hours before he showered for the party.

Living in two different worlds presented many challenges. He missed Selale when he was in the human world, and he was terrified at the thought of missing the baby's birth. When he was in the cave, he missed the comforts of a soft bed, good food, and the fellowship of sharing Selale with his friends. He knew Michael was concerned about his long absences, but true to his word, he had not pried into Thad's business.

He had to talk to Michael sometime soon about getting things ready for the baby. Unfortunately, he didn't know how to initiate the conversation. What could he say? *Um, Michael, I am going to have a son, and I need you to help me get him a birth certificate because he won't be born in a hospital. Oh, and by the way, his mother is a mermaid.* The entire conversation seemed absurd even to his ears. The reality of the situation was Thad desperately needed to enlist Michael's help if he was going to bring the baby home to live with him; however, informing his best friend with the small details like how he had a son and Michael had never met Thad's wife, why the baby's mother couldn't raise him herself, and why she didn't use a hospital or at least a midwife would send up a red flag to anyone with half a brain that there was something strange about this relationship. That was leaving out the most bizarre part: the baby was half human and half merman. The conversation would be surreal, but eventually, it would have to take place for the baby to live in the human world.

By now, Selale's abdomen had swollen so that there was no doubt she was pregnant, precisely why she had remained hidden in the cave now for the past two months. Marius had taken care of the numerous minor details of successfully dispatching his daughter as a temporary ambassador to a place they called Francoso. It seemed everything was falling right into place. Selale's brother Ettore had married Julette in a simple ceremony the day before Selale was scheduled to "depart" for Francoso. Ettore had offered to forego part of his honeymoon to accompany his sister safely there. Both Marius and Selale had adamantly refused. Marius insisted he would go with his daughter and take care of other minor duties while he was there. Both Ettore and Julette were relieved.

Now Thad had to do his part. Every time he mentioned anything related to the baby living with him, Selale cried. She couldn't bear the thought of being apart from him, but deep down, she understood why it was necessary.

Their child couldn't live his entire life stuck in Beulah Cave, and outside its walls, danger lurked everywhere. She would sacrifice her role as mother to secure his safety. The baby would arrive sometime at the end of July or the beginning of August, so he still had a little time to figure out the best way to deal with the minute, legal paperwork required now at the birth of every child. He would enlist the help of his best friend in due time. Until then, he would do some investigation himself about getting the documentation he needed to raise the baby as his son in the human world. Lying down on his bed, Thad fell into a dreamless sleep.

Later in the morning, Thad awakened with a little less than an hour to shower and get everything ready for the party. Right on time, Michael arrived just before 12:00. Thad had packed the seafood in ice and loaded a cooler into the back of Michael's SUV. This morning at the market he had also purchased the veggies and sausages for the clam bake. With only needing to exchange the propane tank, they planned to swing by Chaney's for a beer before arriving back at the house with just enough time to help with any last-minute preparations. Michael had cleaned the grill and stock pot this morning as a strategy for staying out of Charise's way. Careful planning by them both resulted in a couple hours to play pool and catch up. Neither had talked to the other since exam week a little over three weeks before, yet now both men fell into the familiar, comfortable routine of their usual good-humored banter.

"So, what did Charise make you do last night and this morning? There is no way you would have been on time if you hadn't been trying to escape. Let me see those dishpan hands. Do you have any battle wounds?" Thad reached over the table, pretending turned Michael's hand palm up. He laughed at his friend.

"Charise has been combing my shop, the home office, and every drawer looking for shells and little knick-knacks to decorate. She created some kind of swag-garland thing and ordered me to hang it above the back door leading to the deck. It looks hideous, something that only a woman would like. I told her this wasn't some sissy garden party, but she insisted that it stay there." Michael shook his head with disbelief. "Women sure go crazy when it comes to decorating for parties. It will be ten degrees hotter outside on the deck due to the hundreds of scented candles she has placed out there. Trying to be practical, I suggested we use citronella candles instead. I have some of those kinds of candles in metal buckets. Well, you would have thought I suggested burning the American flag. She was appalled at the suggestion." Michael shook his head and drank his beer. "So what has been occupying your time? I haven't seen you around in a few weeks. Has Selale had you under her spell and kept you as her love slave?"

Thad snickered. If Michael only knew how close to the truth that was, he would go crazy! "Maybe. Don't think I'll spill all my secrets to you, but I will tell you I spend every moment I can with her. She doesn't get a break from her job like I do."

"We professors do have it made. Charise and I are going on that cruise in less than a month. That is, if we don't kill each other first before this day is over." Michael suddenly grew serious. "I think it's about time I broach the subject of adoption with her. Up until now, I really don't believe she has been ready to think about another child. What do you think about our adopting a child? I know it is a long, expensive process that often requires years of waiting, but adopting may be the only chance we ever have to be parents." Michael held his beer and waited for Thad to respond.

"I think it is a great idea. You and Charise will be amazing parents. I just hope I can be half the father you will be." Thad trailed off, unaware of the implication his statement had conveyed.

Michael sat there gaping at Thad, unable to believe what he now knew to be true. He felt the strong, unmistakable emotion of protection and paternal love flowing through the entire being of his best friend. Placing his beer gently on the table, he stared at Thad. Very quietly he asked, "When is she due?"

Thad almost dropped his beer at Michael's on-target question. How his friend knew things about him both scared and awed Thad. He knew there was no way to evade the question or lie about it. He had to come clean. "She is due in less than two months. Sometime near the end of July, I will be a father, Michael. I'm going to have a son. I'm terrified and yet, I'm ready. I've never wanted anything more in my life than this baby."

Michael asked the questions Thad hoped he wouldn't. "What about Selale? Are you going to marry her or not? How is it that you are going to have a baby and I've never met Selale?" Thad dropped his eyes from Michael's intense stare. Unable and unwilling to answer the questions his friend wanted to know, Thad remained silent. When the silence stretched on, Michael's voice softened with resignation. He continued, "I know she isn't from here, so will you live with her? I'm being selfish, but I don't want you to move away. You're my best friend. I want to see your baby and be a part of his life too."

Thad raised his eyes to once more meet the brown eyes of his best friend, "Michael, I promise you will be a huge part of his life. I don't have a lot of answers I can give you right now, but soon, I will tell you everything. I'm going to need your help and advice on some very important legal matters. We don't have time today to talk about it, but when you get back from your cruise, let's have dinner at my house and discuss it. By then, I should have some answers. You are the only person I trust, but be patient for just a few more weeks, all right? Will you promise me you will help me and wait until then for me to answer those and any other questions? No more today, okay?" Thad held out his hand and waited for Michael's handshake.

Though he still had a million unanswered questions and the answers Thad had given him really weren't answers at all, Michael was convinced of one thing—there was something significant, perhaps even something dangerous about this relationship with Selale that Thad refused to disclose. Worry and uncertainty filled his best friend, and Michael could feel it in every cell of his body. He was concerned and yes, even frightened for his friend. Yet, in spite of all the mystery surrounding Selale, Michael realized he would give Thad his word for one over-riding reason: love. It overpowered all the other emotions and he realized that Thad would protect Selale and his son above anything else because he loved them more than anything else. Michael stretched out his hand and firmly squeezed that of his best friend. "I promise I will do anything and everything I can to help you."

With a succinct nod, Thad downed the rest of his beer and said, "Let's go to a party."

Chapter Forty

It had been over two cycles since Gregar had been imprisoned. Since then, he had been visited by no one other than Marius not long after his confinement. True to his word, Marius did not return to the Confinement Chamber. He waited patiently for Gregar to break his silence, knowing that eventually, he would break. AA guards still implemented alternating shifts, which prohibited visitors of any kind—no family, no counselor, no colleagues. Surprisingly, he had withstood the solitude much longer than Marius ever imagined. No doubt Gregar believed Calder would somehow rescue him from his imprisonment. But as the tides came and went, he must have realized Marius meant what he said: no visitors.

Acorius, the highest-ranking AA officer whose shift had just ended, summoned Marius early in the tide that Gregar was ready to talk. The AA guard, who had stationed himself outside the SARC for one cycle while Barretto audited the entire agency, was now placed in charge at the Confinement Center. He was Barretto's most trusted and capable officer, a no-nonsense kind of merman who attended his duties seriously. The other guards liked him immensely not only because he was unfailingly impartial, but also because he had a quirky sense of humor and enjoyed a good laugh. The guards under his command respected him and were obedient to his every command. Marius and Ettore were in the executive chamber at the Capital Center when Acorius arrived with the news.

"My liege," Acorius bowed, "it seems our infamous former SARC director has tired of his solitary confinement. He appears willing to disclose the location of the weapons, but once again, refuses to discuss this matter with anyone except you and Barretto. I felt disposed to alert you in this matter immediately. It may be the first sign of a crack in the polished Gregar. What would you have me do, your Majesty?"

Marius smiled at the imagery of Acorius' description of Gregar. "Ah, this is good news. Inform our guest that we will be there in two tides. Since he made no haste in making this decision, two more tides is of little consequence at this point. Either he knows where the weapons are located or he doesn't. That should be sufficient for Barretto to make his way to the Capital Center. Have you a man to spare to inform him of these developments or should I send someone else?"

Ettore spoke from across the room. "Papa, I will travel to Zephah to inform Barretto of the news. There is no need to relieve one of the AA guards of his duties. They have kept a constant, exhausting schedule at the Confinement Chamber guarding our stubbornly silent inmate, so sparing one will create an even greater hardship on their schedule. I will go. It is but a half tide swim there. Lodging will be easy to acquire. The Arbitrator and I will return early on the next tide. Gregar shall have his audience later that eventide."

Marius had to admit it was a logical idea. Of course, the dangerous events from two cycles before had not faded from his mind; Ettore could still be the target of a conspiracy. He was torn as to whether he should send his son alone. Competence in Ettore's ability was not the issue. He trusted his son could hold his own against any merman. However, it was the evil intentions of those who attacked him and who still intended him harm whom he distrusted. Marius realized he couldn't isolate his son forever. Ettore was adept at fighting and could take care of himself. Staring at his son with pride, Marius agreed, "It is a sound plan. I will send an official order with you. He will be expecting it." Turning his attention back to Acorius, Marius continued, "Tell Gregar this had better not be a deceptive trick. He will answer every question asked of him truthfully and forthcoming. I will not be foresworn. He will reveal every-thing he knows or he will never look upon freedom again. He will have his meeting in two tides. Thank you, Acorius." Marius extended his hand. The officer touched it, bowed and exited the chamber.

Ettore studied his father. "Do you think he knows where the weapons are? It has been over two cycles. Surely the traitor who possesses those weapons has moved them to an alternate location. His co-conspirators must realize at some point Gregar would negotiate his release."

"We won't find the weapons where Gregar thinks they are located. By dis-closing any information to us, he has made himself vulnerable. They will have moved the weapons. Gregar may have no idea where they are if he ever did. However, he and his information still may prove valuable to us. Names of those who were involved in developing this weapon may ultimately prove more valu-able. Gregar will be eliminated if those with whom he has conspired believe he betrayed their trust. I can't and won't protect him once he is released. Speaking of protection, make certain you take your waterbow with you to Ze-phah. The tentacles of the enemy are long, and we know not how far they reach. Use utmost caution as you travel, son." Marius swam and embraced his son. Releasing him, Marius smiled. "Go to your chamber and inform my lovely daughter-in-law Julette that you will return soon. You've wanted to meet Bar-retto for many cycles. Well, now you shall have your chance. I anticipate your return. Go in peace and protection." Ettore turned and swam through the por-tal and out of the chamber. The eyes that watched him go were more those of a concerned father than of a noble king.

As Ettore made his way to his chamber, he spotted Rahwah coming toward him. Ettore stopped and waited on Rahwah. Instead of a smile, he was greeted with a sneer. Not one to be deterred so easily, Ettore replied cordially, "Good tide, Rahwah. I haven't seen you in a while. Did you not receive the wedding invitation? I wish you could have made it to the celebration. It seemed some-what empty without my childhood best friend at my side."

Ettore's friendliness caught Rahwah off guard. His overt blindness to the animosity Rahwah felt only angered him more. "Those tides are a blur to me. Surely you don't consider me your best friend anymore. Wake up, golden boy!

I don't even like you. Why would I come to your celebration? We are no longer friends." Hostility flared in his eyes.

Ettore, hurt by his words, quietly murmured, "Those tides were some of my happiest childhood memories. I'm sorry you no longer consider me a friend. If I have offended, or harmed, or hurt you, please accept my apology. This hatred seems so intense, and yet, I am unaware of its reason. Why, Rahwah? Please tell me what I have done to deserve this hatred. I will try to make amends to rectify any transgression I have committed."

Rahwah laughed bitterly at the offer. "Done? You were born with a crown on your head. All of our lives, you've been first at everything. I am tired of being second, of swimming in your wake, of seeming invisible. Let's just say, I'm over it. I am surrounded by people now who see me for me, not for being your best friend. I matter." He all but spat the last word.

Ettore shook his head sadly. "You always mattered to me. Regardless if the feeling is reciprocated, I will always consider you my friend. I'm sorry you are bitter, and yes, you are right. You are far too talented and intelligent to be in the shadows. Good tide, Rahwah. I wish you well." Ettore turned and swam toward his chamber.

Confused and angry, Rahwah could only stare as he watched his former friend swim away. Frustration at coming across as petty and immature only fueled his raging emotions. His antsy fingers traced the top of the ray weapon he had concealed in his waist belt. Calder had trusted him enough to give one to him, cautioning him to exercise extreme patience in using it. Considering patience was not one of his virtues, Rahwah thought he had done well in keeping his possession a secret. He turned to report in at the SARC. Since the audit, all SCEROH members were now required to track their shifts and alternate duties each quarter cycle. No longer was one SCEROH member assigned the same duty tide after tide. The many annutides of service he had served thereby earning the coveted position of border patrol chief officer no longer carried any clout. All SCEROH officers were of equal rank; no one out-ranked anyone else. Again, he was no longer in a position of importance. The Atlantic Arbitrator rendered this decision regarding the SCEROH, and even Calder had been powerless to revoke or reverse it.

At the meeting in Calder's official chamber, that decision and many others caused great concern and anger. The assembled group agreed that Marius was the real culprit; he was the source of this decision to strip the SCEROH of its power. It was he who had alerted and summoned the Arbitrator to the Capital Center who had then shut down SARC. It was Marius who had sequestered Gregar in the Confinement Center. The consensus among the group was that the king had overstepped his bounds. In Rahwah's opinion, Marius' goal was to limit Calder's power. With some of these recent events, the balance of power had undoubtedly shifted. Marius had gained almost complete control of the kingdom, and Calder had been all but stripped of all of his. That, however, was about to change.

Plans were being made at this present tide that would propel Calder to power. Great excitement had filled the chamber when Calder unveiled his master plan. Granted, it would take many cycles just to set the events into motion, but the result would be worth the wait. Calder would eventually be king. Rahwah couldn't wait for the tide.

He entered the SARC and received his assignment for the next half tide. The new protocol demanded a strict compliance with the assignment given to each officer for the tide. No longer did patrols monitor various areas during their shifts. They were assigned one specific stretch of the kingdom. Yet another change designed to limit the SCEROH's authority. This tide he would be patrolling the southern border of the capital. Exiting the chamber, he resigned himself to the fact that it would be a long, monotonous shift. He set his sights toward the south and swam for the border.

•　　•　　•　　•　　•

Ettore had traveled almost to the southern-most point of the capital which bordered the regions of Cecilia and Zephah. Traveling along the Benthic Tunnels had slowed his progress quite significantly. For the past quarter tide, he had ventured away from the security of the populated tunnels and had made up the lost tide. Now with most of the journey behind him, he stopped to read the official order from his father to the Atlantic Arbitrator.

The etching was concise yet explicit. He stared at the royal seal his father had affixed to the bottom of the tablet. Its unique design left no doubt that the missive was from the king himself. Securing the tablet in his waist belt, Ettore pulled his waterbow from off his back and looped it around his shoulder. This stretch of Atlantis was unfamiliar territory. He had traveled through here on a couple of trips with his father and other groups, but never had he navigated these waters alone. Consulting his map, he realized he only had about a quarter tide left to travel before he would arrive in Zephah to meet Barretto.

Nervousness filled Ettore as he thought about the legendary Atlantic Arbitrator. Some stories told of his giant stature, towering over the most massive of mermen. Others told of his innate ability to discern truth and rule with wisdom so profound that it could only have been bestowed by divine means. While Ettore believed the truth lay somewhere in between the two extremes, he, nevertheless, couldn't wait to meet the man himself. He would make up his own mind about the mysterious Barretto.

Ettore had no doubt in his mind that he would like the merman immensely. His father spoke very highly of him. That he isolated himself from the rest of the hierarchy of command troubled Ettore somewhat. Leagues and leagues of water separated the Capital Center from the Arbitrator's Chamber in Zephah. Maybe he was a loner. For whatever reason, the Arbitrator chose to live in a remote area and preferred the solitude of the southern kingdom to the hustle and bustle of the Capital Center.

Off in the distance Ettore saw a border patrol. The officer's uniform left no doubt as to who it was; the blue vest, distinct in its color and design, was easily recognizable by every citizen of Atlantis. The patrol had seen him at almost precisely the same moment Ettore had seen the patrol. Knowing that this duty was not the most exciting in the waters, he decided to swim over to greet the officer and converse a while with him. As he made his way toward the guard, he noticed the officer had not acknowledged him. Ettore waved his hand, but the merman ignored the gesture and turned to swim in the opposite direction. Confused by the overt discourtesy, Ettore dismissed the rude officer with a shrug and turned back south toward Zephah.

Rahwah could not believe his good fortune. If he hadn't seen him with his own eyes, he would have never believed it: Ettore was in Zephah. Alone in Zephah. Why was he here? An insidious thought crept into Rahwah's mind. Looking around he realized there were no other mermen remotely close to the prince. Making a rash and precipitous decision, he headed away from the populated area of Zephah and doubled back to the remote border. There he could intercept Ettore. He thought of how frustrated Calder had been at the last botched attempt to eliminate the crown prince. He resolved to take matters into his own hands, implying to Calder that the other attempts had been poorly designed and implemented with ineptitude, and that he could accomplish the task. This opportunity was Rahwah's chance to prove his value. He alone would take care of Ettore, thereby making himself invaluable to Calder.

He moved stealthily through the waters and positioned himself behind a shelf of rock. He didn't have long to wait. Ettore moved mindlessly toward the region's populated center, unaware of the impending attack. The light-filled waters made the prince an easy target. Rahwah hastily removed the conspicuous vest and crammed it under a rock. He had the element of surprise, so it would take little effort to eliminate the prince. How easy it would be to make the attack appear to be accidental, merely an unfortunate or untimely attack by a wayward shark or orca.

He darted out from the concealed rock and seized Ettore around the neck. In a matter of a current, Rahwah had rendered him helpless. Ettore struggled to reach his waterbow, but his attacker had pinned his arms behind his back where he was unable to grab his weapon. Not one to surrender easily, Ettore slammed his head hard against his captor. Rahwah, stunned from the impact, loosened his grip momentarily, allowing Ettore to break free from his hold. Ettore turned and, with incredulity stared into the hate-filled eyes of his former friend. Momentarily stunned by the betrayal, Ettore had no current before Rahwah once again pounced for the attack. A blow to the temple temporarily disoriented Ettore and sent him sliding along the ocean floor. He landed with his head and shoulder lodged between two boulders. Shaking his head, he tried to prevent the next blow by scurrying behind the biggest boulder. He pulled his waterbow from off his shoulder and saw the quiver lying not far from where he was. Diving over the rock, he grabbed an arrow and prepared to go on the offensive. Before Ettore could grasp the arrow, Rahwah had pulled a strange sword-like shaft from his waistbelt and had split the arrow in half.

His mocking laugh drifted through the water. "Well, golden boy, it appears your luck has run out. What? Papa's not here to help you, is he? Your reign as heir apparent ends this tide. With you out of the way, it clears the way for a new regime, a new order: out with the old and in with the new. Of course, I will tell our subjects how bravely you fought in the face of an orca. Oh, such a sad ending to such a promising future they will say." Rahwah swam over to tread over Ettore. He held the ray weapon in his hand and rested its shaft in the palm of the other one. Suddenly the waters darkened significantly as if a storm had blown in above the waters, obscuring the sun. Light that moments before had suffused the water seemed to have diminished, and now shadows filled the waters. Both mermen noticed, but neither took his eyes off the other.

Ettore stared at his childhood friend. "Why? Is this fueled only by your jealousy? Do you hate me so much that you would now slaughter me, unarmed and helpless, just because you don't want to feel inferior? Well, if this is the last thing I ever say to you, I hope you remember it well. I forgive you. I am truly sorry I failed to make you feel important, but you always were. You were my best friend. There was no other person aside from my family whom I loved more. Forgive me for failing you as a friend. Now, do what you must, but I warn you, I'm not going down without a fight." Waving his hand through the water, Ettore sent the ocean abruptly roiling in a strong current that sent Rahwah tumbling backwards. Rolling immediately to his right, Ettore grabbed the arrow and sent the shaft flying toward his opponent. It sailed off the mark along the path of the water's current. Darkness continued to fill the waters making the use of his bow extremely difficult. Ettore's eyes wandered to the ray-like sword Rahwah held in his hand, and he realized his bow was no match for the sophisticated weapon.

Rahwah's scornful voice derided Ettore, "You will have to do better than that to beat me this time. Your waterbow and Mystical Gift of Waterbending are not enough to overpower me. You like my ray? It burns with the twist of my wrist. Your arrows are of no consequence to me. The ray will slice them in two." Rahwah flicked his wrist and the weapon glowed blue as it sliced easily through the water. Again, the waters darkened abruptly and markedly, startling and confusing both mermen.

Trying to peer through the darkness and make sense of it all, Ettore realized he needed to move to the other side of the shelf of rock. Rahwah, seemingly one step ahead of him, came out of his stupor and anticipated the move, streaking there to prevent Ettore's escape. He sliced through Ettore's chest with the weapon; the shock and searing pain caused him to fall down on the ocean floor. Blood mingled with the water creating a current of red. The wound was deep, but not deadly. It merely served as a precursor for the fatal blow to come.

Rahwah swam over Ettore, treading there. "Say good-bye, Prince." He took his wrist and wielded the ray back and forth through the water. The ray's blue light was suddenly extinguished. He tried again, but the shaft remained unlit and harmless.

Ettore, injured and in great pain, saw a shadow rise up from behind Rahwah. No longer were his eyes focused on his adversary. His eyes widened as he made out a hazy outline of someone or something towering well above Rahwah's head. Ettore rubbed his eyes to make sure he wasn't hallucinating. Everywhere darkness filled the waters as if it was nighttide. The only light that pierced the blackness was held in the creature's hands. Initially puzzled, Ettore saw the light compacted into a sphere, and it slowly dawned on him what was about to happen. His mouth dropped open in sheer awe.

Rahwah became acutely aware that he and Ettore were no longer alone. Watching Ettore's face transform in shock, he turned to get a glimpse of the largest merman he had ever laid eyes on. He too gaped in shock. The merman had gathered all the light and heat into the radiating sphere he now held between his hands. Light emitted from the illuminated globe cast an eerie glow transforming the partially concealed face into a menacing, disfigured countenance. Taking the sphere in between his huge hands, he suddenly and violently ripped it into two halves. Ettore knew what was about to happen. Though he had never witnessed this display personally, he had studied about the phenomenon many tides ago. With a determined effort, he dragged his badly injured body behind the shelf of rock for shelter. The mammoth merman nodded to Ettore, recognizing the prince was protected, just before a powerful light was hurled in their direction. The merman pushed a wall of energy through the water like a tsunami of heat and light. It moved swiftly, temporarily immobilizing an awestruck Rahwah. He realized too late what was happening. Right before the wall of light engulfed him, he managed to shield half his body. The blast of light seared one side of his face with volts of energy, wracking his body with excruciating pain and blinding him in his exposed eye. Rahwah fell writhing on the ocean floor, screaming in obvious pain.

The huge merman reached down and scooped up the stunned, injured prince in one effortless motion. With the other hand, he casually seized the ray weapon lying on the ocean floor. Placing the weapon in his belt, he swam hastily toward the south as he cradled Ettore like a little boy in his massive arms. The last thing Ettore remembered just before unconsciousness took him under was looking into his rescuer's eyes that were still ablaze with light.

Chapter Forty-one

Perimicles entered the Capital Center. He had to get a message to Marius to meet and discuss with him what he had learned at the meeting. Plans had to be made now to thwart Calder's insidious plan. When Calder revealed his master plan, it took everything in Perimicles not to react visibly to such an evil plot that included not only the plan to kill Ettore, but also Sandoval and Selale. Even Rahwah had vehemently objected to killing Selale, rationalizing his protest by saying it would incite the people to revolt, that her death would be too much for the people to accept. Of course, Perimicles understood Rahwah wanted Selale for himself.

Calder refused to be deterred from this course of action. He argued that she too must be eliminated because she could rule in place of Calder. Selale could possibly ascend to the throne ahead of Calder. This news stunned everyone there. A similar situation many centennitides ago set the precedent that Atlantis could be ruled by a queen if there were no direct male heirs of the previous king. Queen Tarah proved that merwomen could adeptly rule Atlantis just as well as mermen. She had been not only a powerful force during her tenure as queen, but had been a people-empowering one as well. She established many of the aspects of Atlantis' government, including the Atlantic Arbitrator and the Center City of Atlantis. Queen Tarah remained one of the most beloved and most effective rulers of Atlantis. In Calder's estimation, Selale posed just as great, if not even greater, threat to their plan than Ettore. This part of his master plan divided the assembly. Many left the meeting with a feeling of unease and with the same question on their minds: did this plan require such desperate, ruthless measures? This violence-laden part of the master plan alarmed many of Calder's most loyal allies.

Perimicles had volunteered to deliver a message to the Center City, so he could be in close proximity to the king without raising suspicion from the other members of Calder's inner circle. He knew he could get a message to Marius requesting a covert meeting. His actions here at the Center City would not seem suspicious. Rumors had spread throughout the capital that Gregar, the former SARC director, planned to implicate his accomplices in the next couple of tides. Speculation as to who was responsible for the mysterious weapons spread rapidly like a destructive, roaring wave. Perimicles no longer had reason to speculate; his own ears had heard confirmation of the identity of Gregar's accomplices. Both Calder and Rahwah boasted about the weapon to everyone in the inner circle. Though they had voiced only part of their plan to eliminate Gregar, most of the assembly dismissed it as wishful thinking. Gregar was under constant guard and had been for over two cycles. Security at the Confinement Center would be impossible to breach.

Perimicles entered the lobby of the executive chamber at the Capital Center. The portal to Marius' chamber was closed. Aristeus, the king's executive assistant, recognized the messenger and smiled. He had served Marius from the first tide he had inherited the throne. No merman or merwoman was allowed to speak to the king without Aristeus' consent. Not only was he unfailingly efficient and diplomatic, he also was a skilled fighter.

"Good tide, Perimicles. What matter brings you to the Capital Center?"

"Good tide, Aristeus. I have a missive for the king. Is he here this tide?"

The assistant shook his head. "No, he had a meeting with the engineers early but still has not returned. I expect him soon. Is this a missive I may deliver or is it classified?"

"I'm sorry to say it is a classified message. Only I can deliver it personally to the king. Do you mind if I wait? I am not scheduled to deliver any other missives the rest of the tide, so I am in no hurry. Is the southern Benthic tunnel still on schedule to be repaired? I haven't been there since the collapse."

"It is proceeding well. It should be completely repaired in less than one cycle, much faster than anyone believed possible. I attribute that to the sabotage. The people of Cecilia created quite a stir, and merpeople sympathetic to their cries rallied together to repair the damage. It is quite unlike anything I have ever witnessed before. It has restored my faith that goodness will prevail over evil every tide." Aristeus looked Perimicles right in the eye.

Perimicles understood he was being sized up. He stared unwaveringly back at the assistant. "I have never doubted it."

Aristeus smiled. He was pleased with the young messenger's answer. He murmured good-naturedly, "Oh, to be young and idealistic again…." Just then, Marius swam into the chamber. Aristeus rose and simultaneously, both he and Perimicles nodded their heads respectfully. Marius greeted them with a smile. Obviously, the meeting had gone well.

"Perimicles, what a pleasure it is to see you again! Do you bring important news?" Not waiting for the answer, he turned to his assistant and said, "Alert me when Barretto and Ettore get here, so we can proceed to the Confinement Center to question Gregar. They should arrive shortly, before the tide shifts. Until then, no one is to disturb Perimicles and me."

Nodding, Aristeus replied, "Yes, your Majesty."

Marius led Perimicles through the portal which opened then immediately closed behind them. The executive chamber was sparsely furnished and could easily have been mistaken for any ordinary office chamber. Unlike Calder's lavish office chamber, this one served one purpose: executive matters. Calder's office was decorated extravagantly to impress its visitors, its design and furnishings there for Calder's comfort. The two chambers were as different as the two brothers, yet the chambers' designs accurately reflected each brother's personality and priority.

"What news do you bring? You have not placed yourself in harm's way by being here, have you, my friend?" Marius' concern was genuine.

"My lord, I do have news, not a missive. I'm sorry for deceiving your assistant, but it was imperative that I speak to you personally regarding the developments at the assembly of Calder's inner circle. The news is grave, my lord. Calder revealed his master plan to the entire assembly. He will not stop until he has complete control. No one in your family is safe, especially Ettore and Selale. To Calder, they are merely minor obstacles to his ascension to the throne. His plan includes not only eliminating you, but murdering Ettore and Selale as well. I will say this part of his plan brought much dissension and discontent among those assembled. My lord, we must act quickly to counteract this violence. Calder has already set parts of his plan into motion, and understanding the disapproval of some of his loyal members, he has no doubt withheld some things he has planned from the assembly. He referred on several occasions to an army of some sort he had formed, and both he and Rahwah boasted about the ray weapon, even brazenly wielding one in the presence of the assembly. Your Majesty, Calder must be stopped. What shall we do to thwart his plans and how may I help?"

Marius sat on a bench beside Perimicles with his chin resting on one hand closed in a fist. So still was he that he resembled a statue. The only movement was the almost imperceptible waving of the tip of his tail. Finally he rose and swam around back behind his desk. He placed his hands on top of his desk and spoke calmly yet strongly. "We will force his hand. When Barretto and Ettore arrive, we will interrogate Gregar. The information, whether what he really reveals or what we chose to disclose he reveals, can be used as our bait to catch our fish. Calder and his minions won't get a chance to set this plan into action. We will—" An alert sounded and suddenly Aristeus swam through the portal.

"Forgive me, your Majesty, but there is an urgent message from Barretto. His personal messenger requests immediate entry."

Without hesitation, Marius nodded. "Send him in at once." To Aristeus' questioning glance toward Perimicles, Marius added, "Perimicles is trustworthy. He is to hear the news." Satisfied, the assistant exited the chamber and immediately returned with the messenger.

The messenger swam to the king's side and bowed humbly before him. "Your Majesty, my name is Ermaus. I am Barretto's personal messenger. Ettore has been injured badly in a rogue attack. Barretto is attending to his wounds. I was told to relay to you not to worry and that Ettore will recover completely, but it will take several tides. Barretto requests that you proceed to interview the suspect without him and come whenever you can to Zephah. He has other important news to share whenever you arrive."

The fear and alarm were evident on the king's face. "What happened? Do you know any of the details regarding the attack? When did it happen and where?"

"No, my lord, I know nothing of the attack other than what was relayed in the message. Barretto would not have sent his assurance if your son was not going to recover. Trust him when he tells you he himself is nursing your son back to health. There is no one more adept at healing remedies than the Arbitrator."

Somewhat comforted, Marius sat down behind his desk. "Ermaus, tell Barretto I am forever indebted to him for his help. The interview will proceed as planned, but I will take Sandoval instead of him and Ettore with me for the interrogation as we had originally planned. I will travel to Zephah as soon as my duties here are completed. Thank you for bringing this news. Until I can personally thank Barretto, relay my gratitude to him for his kindness and ministrations to my son." Marius rose and swam around to stand beside the messenger. He held out his hand and the messenger touched it with his hand and bowed humbly. Both Marius and Perimicles felt enormous relief when they saw the square-cut ruby ring on his finger. He withdrew his hand, and then swam out of the chamber.

Marius looked at Aristeus. "Send for Sandoval at once. Tell him to leave immediately for the Confinement Chamber. I will meet him there."

"Yes, my lord." The assistant quickly disappeared through the portal.

The king turned toward Perimicles. A sense of urgency deepened his voice, adding precision and emphasis to his words. "Meet me here in two tides. You will accompany me to Zephah." It was not a request. "By then, I should have the information from Gregar to set the plan into action to counteract this treason. Those responsible for this attack will regret the tide they ever thought about harming my family. Retribution will be rendered to every merman involved. Let me give you the official order to return. I want you to stay above suspicion. No one must know where your loyalties truly lie. Deliver this message now to Acorius, the chief guard at the Confinement Center, telling him that Sandoval and I will arrive soon to begin the interrogation. Inform him of the latest developments as to why the plans have changed." Marius etched the official order and handed it to his messenger. "Until then, be safe and go in peace." Perimicles touched the king's extended hand, his square-cut ruby ring, identical to the one worn by Ermaeus, was positioned prominently to the king. Marius nodded his approval.

"Thank you. my lord. Please use caution. Our enemies are desperate, and desperation causes men to do great evil. My life I pledge to you." Touching his forehead to the king's hand, Perimicles hastened out of the executive chamber to the Confinement Chamber to deliver the king's message.

He swam out of the two tall front portals of the Capital Center west toward the place where the former SARC director was incarcerated. The Confinement Chamber was a small part of the Chamber of Law and its building sat at the westernmost edge of the Capital Center. The engineer had designed its solitary structure distinctly different from all the other chambers in the capital, its austere walls a bleak gray instead of a smooth black. Perimicles saw the chamber in the distance and with a determined effort swam even more swiftly toward his destination. As he approached the chamber, Perimicles could not believe his eyes. In order not to be seen, he darted around the corner of a nearby building. He looked just in time to see Calder put something in his waistbelt before making his way clandestinely away from the chamber, his stealthy manner immediately raising Perimicles' suspicion. His presence here meant trouble. He was too close to the Confinement Chamber not to have a questionable and dishonorable motive, considering his close proximity to it.

Calder did not see the messenger as he turned and swam south out of the Capital City though Perimicles watched him until he was completely out of sight. Frustration at wanting to follow him warred with his duty to deliver the king's missive. His sense of duty won, and he swam the last several leagues toward the Confinement Chamber. Two AA guards stood outside the chamber. A sense of relief at the tight security outside the chamber doors alleviated the fear instilled by Calder's presence so close to the chamber. He approached the guards slowly and handed the etched message to them. After searching Perimicles, they motioned him inside after ascertaining the missive contained the king's official seal.

The inside of the chamber appeared even gloomier than the outside. Dim light filtered through the narrow halls obscuring Perimicles' vision. He followed one of the guards closely until he arrived in the processing center of the chamber. Acorius had positioned himself there. He took the missive from the guard and examined it carefully. He nodded, dismissing the guard back to his position and motioned Perimicles into the chamber.

"Why is the king bringing Sandoval instead of Barretto? Tell me what has happened to warrant this change." The steady eyes of the chief guard demanded an answer.

"Barretto sent a message with Ermaus, his personal assistant, telling the king his son Ettore had been attacked and injured. Barretto is attending to his injuries. He sent word for Marius to conduct the interview as planned, so Marius is meeting Sandoval here so together they can interrogate Gregar. They should arrive very soon. Marius and I will travel to Zephah after this matter with Gregar is finished."

"Gregar is anxious to talk to the king. This confinement is wearing on him. He can't take these cramped surroundings much longer. I have had to constantly reassure him since this morntide that he would speak with the king before the tide was over. He was a nervous wreck. He kept asking me how much longer it would be like he was terrified he wouldn't get to talk to the king. I just assured him a couple of currents ago that Marius and Barretto would arrive before the tide turned again. He seemed relieved. If you will excuse me, I will go inform him of his impending interview. Can you wait here until I return? I too have a message for you to deliver to Barretto. Perimicles nodded and took a seat on the bench in the corner of the office. A blaring alarm sounded through the chamber. Loud, agitated voices came from the holding chamber. Perimicles rose as foreboding filled his entire being, the memory of Calder fresh on his mind. Something terrible had happened.

Acorius entered the processing chamber, his face blotchy and white as he struggled to get the words out. Finally he whispered, "Gregar is dead."

Chapter Forty-two

Thad had spent the last two weeks finalizing everything for the birth of his son. He had taken a vial of Selale's blood and obtained verification of her pregnancy. Getting her blood screened and verified was, in and of itself, the most stressful part of the process for fear her results would not register like a human mother's blood hormone levels. Those fears had been allayed by the normal pregnancy label affixed to the affidavit. As for the two adult witnesses required, he would have Charise and Michael sign, and because Charise was a notary public, her signature and seal would take care of the final requirement for that part of the legal process. Finally, for the last legal hurdle, Thad had personally contacted a pediatrician to schedule an appointment for the baby's post-birth exam necessary to obtain the documentation to legally acquire the legal birth certificate. He still had to schedule an appointment at the local vital statistics office for a time shortly after the birth to complete registration with all the legal documents. Tomorrow he would call the office before he went to see Selale. He never realized how much paperwork was involved just to have a baby! He had taken a large manila envelope and placed all the documents inside. He had taken the time to write a letter to Michael just to practice saying what he was going to tell him regarding this baby and Selale. It was going to sound crazy regardless of how many times he practiced writing it or saying it aloud.

He read through what he had written. Shaking his head, he realized he had to tell him more than what was here on this piece of paper.

Selale was due any time now. He so wanted to spend every waking minute right by her side. She dominated his thoughts. As he was leaving the pediatrician's office, he had seen a glass paperweight in the store window next door to the doctor's office. Inside the glass globe were two flowers, one red and one yellow, and a delicate, multi-colored butterfly. For reasons still unknown to him, he had bought it on impulse because it reminded him of Selale. He would give it to her tonight. It was beautiful and bright. When he shook the glass, golden flecks showered down on the flowers and butterfly like the sunlight reflecting through Beulah Cave. It also contained a music box. When he turned the button on the bottom of the globe, it played "You Are My Sunshine." He knew she would love it.

Now that Thad had everything set for the baby's arrival, he could enjoy the time he spent with her without worrying about the details. Michael and Charise were not due back for another two days. He had plenty of time to talk to Michael about the situation. Selale would have the baby within the next two weeks. Thad was certain of it. Already the false labor pains had begun; the first ones had about scared him to death! Monica had assured him and Selale that they were a normal process leading up to the baby's birth, and that these false labor pains were nature's way of preparing Selale's body for the real event. Thad had remained skeptical until after several of the false pains had come and gone. Selale explained the real labor pains would last much longer and would be much more painful. She was ready for it nonetheless.

Once again, Thad thought of what specifically he could tell Michael and Charise. Maybe he should just go with the plain truth. Nothing else he realized would work. He so wanted Michael and Charise to meet Selale. How, he didn't know, but when he slept at night, he dreamed of the three of them meeting and liking each other immensely, the fact of her being a mermaid, an inconsequential detail none of them noticed. What did he have to lose by writing the entire truth down on paper? Michael would never read it. He could destroy it after the baby was born. The need to write the entire story of his and Selale's story down suddenly overwhelmed Thad. Why had he never thought of this before? He could save it for the baby, so he would know the story in his father's own words of his birth. Taking several sheets of paper and an ink pen, Thad sat down and started at the beginning, the very first time he saw Selale on the recording.

It took him two hours to recount the events on paper. A sense of satisfaction filled Thad. He took the written record of their story and put it in a sealed envelope and then in the manila envelope with the legal documents. He would take it out of the envelope of documents later and put it in the safe deposit box for his son to have when he was older. The phone rang just as he finished sealing the envelope.

"Hello?" Thad wondered who was calling at this time of night. It was already eleven o'clock. He was greeted by Michael's voice.

"Hey, buddy, how are things at home? Have you missed me?" Michael crooned.

"Things have been so much quieter in the neighborhood since you've been gone. Seriously man, I have been bored out of my mind. When are you coming home?"

Michael chuckled, "I've missed you too. The reason I'm calling is about when we are getting home; it will be delayed for several more days. We just got off the ship and received word that Gramma Winans fell this morning and broke her hip in two places. She is scheduled for surgery tomorrow afternoon. We are going to travel to Georgia for her surgery and help get her back home before we arrive back from the cruise. It may be another week or so before we get there. Will you go by and check on the house? I will contact the post office and have it continue holding our mail."

Thad could tell Michael was worried about Charise's grandmother. "Sure, don't worry about things here. I will take care of the house. Is there anything else you need for me to do? Just ask. No problem."

"No, there's nothing else. Just don't forget you and I have a man-date when I return. You aren't gonna weasel out on me, are you? You owe me a pizza and an explanation." In the background, Charise called for Michael to hurry. "I've got to go. Say hello to your Selale. Tell her I will meet her soon. Gotta go. Charise sends her love. See you in a week or two." Michael hung up before Thad could say good-bye. Thad laughed at how in love his friends were.

He looked at the clock. He should probably get a couple hours of sleep before he went to see Selale, but he wanted to see her more than he wanted sleep. Grabbing his keys and the glass globe, he headed out the door. He closed the door behind him, smiling as only a man in love could.

He arrived at the cave's entrance shortly after midnight. He had packed a lantern and the glass globe in a bag. Making his way to the cave through the dark ocean took longer than usual. The lack of light made it difficult to orient his position to that of the cave. Common sense told him to use the lantern, but instinct warned him not to. Thad found himself relying on instinct and his innate sense of direction. They had never failed him. Looking around through the dark waters, he couldn't help but feel someone or something was watching. Just to be certain he wasn't being followed, he circled around to the backside of the towering mountain of debris and hid behind a rock in a nook carved into the side of the outside wall. He waited for several minutes. With more stealth than he realized he possessed, he sneaked back around and entered the mouth of the cavern.

He found Selale asleep on the ledge of the rock. Pulling himself up out of the water, he stood beside her and simply stared at his beautiful wife. He unzipped his wet suit and laid it on the rock jutting out just above his head. Quietly he sat down beside her and gently caressed a strand of her dark hair between his fingers. Selale smiled before she ever opened her eyes. She turned to gaze at Thad, and pulling herself over to rest her head in his lap, she closed her eyes once again as his fingers lightly traced the features of her face.

"Obviously you are too sleepy to open a present I brought for you, so I will save it for later." Thad teased as he drew the delicate arch of her eyebrows with his finger.

Selale opened her eyes suddenly and laughed, "I am never too sleepy to open a gift!" She slowly raised herself to sit beside Thad, shoulder to shoulder.

Placing his arm around her slender shoulder, he pulled her over to him and kissed her tenderly on her temple. With his other hand, he reached inside the bag and pulled out the lantern. "Close your eyes and don't peek." He turned on the lantern. Immediately the cave was bathed in golden light.

"How can I open a gift when my eyes are closed?" Selale asked, but she had already closed her eyes.

"All right, here is the first surprise. Don't peek." He pulled the glass sphere from the bag and turned the button on the base. Music filled the cave as Thad sang the words to her:

> *You are my sunshine, my only sunshine.*
> *You make me happy when skies are gray.*
> *You'll never know, dear, how much I love you.*
> *Please don't take my sunshine away.*

Tears flowed out of the corners of Selale's closed eyes and rolled down her cheeks. Thad joked, "I knew my singing wasn't the greatest, but I didn't know it was that bad! Surprise! Open your eyes, Selale."

Still crying, Selale gasped as she stared at the object Thad held in his hand. Thad shook it and gold rained on the inside of the sphere. Selale whispered, "What is this? I've never seen anything so beautiful." She held out her hands like she was receiving a priceless treasure, a cherished heirloom. Thad turned the knob on the bottom and music continued to fill the cave.

"It is a glass globe. Sometimes they are called snow globes, but since this one contains flowers and a butterfly, I don't think snow is appropriate. When I saw it, I was reminded of you. Do you like it?"

Selale sat holding the globe. She leaned over and kissed Thad. "It's the most beautiful, most precious gift I have ever received. I will treasure it always. Every time I look at it or hear its music, I will remember how much you love me and how much I love you." Thad took her in his arms and held her. In the golden glow, they remained embraced in one another's arms, basking in the beauty of the moment. They lay down on the rock resting in each other's arms, enjoying the silence and joy of just being together.

Thad broke the silence. "Do you know what I did today? I wrote down the story of how we met and fell in love for our son. I have struggled with what to tell Michael, so I spent about two hours writing down the record of how we met, how we fell in love, so I could think about what to tell Michael when he returns from his trip. After I finished, I decided to save what I had written for our child, so when he gets older, he can know the entire story himself. It will be my gift to him."

Selale marveled at how tender and kind Thad was. He was so special. She kissed him passionately. "I love you so much. I feel so inadequate because I don't have a gift for you. The only thing I can give you is me and my love."

"That is all I ever want. Selale, you have made me the happiest man on land and in the waters. You are giving me a son. I can never compete with a gift like that!"

With a sleepy yawn, Selale whispered, "Tell me about flowers and butterflies from your world, Thad. I want to know all about them." As she drifted off to sleep, Selale dreamed of Thad and her son playing in a field of yellow and red flowers with butterflies fluttering in the air.

Chapter Forty-three

Barretto gazed down at the injured prince. Ettore seemed so young, so innocent. His wounds were not life-threatening, but they were quite severe. The
attacker had been intent on killing the unsuspecting prince. Barretto was not
idealistic enough to believe this would be the last attack on him or the other
members of the royal family. The perpetrators of this plot would not be so
easily deterred by this minor setback. He turned concerned eyes to inspect the
two ray weapons lying side by side on the stone table which dominated one
entire side of the Arbitrator's chamber. This new technology in weaponry
could potentially shift the balance of power. Much damage could be inflicted
by the possessor of such a weapon. The evidence was in Ettore's injuries. If he
had not arrived when he did, the prince would have been killed. Of that fact
the older merman was certain.

He sat down on the bench on the opposite side of the table so he could
keep an eye on Ettore if he happened to regain consciousness. Lifting one of
the two identical weapons off the table, he inspected the craftsmanship of the
weapon. No doubt it was impressive. He slashed the weapon smoothly through
the water which immediately illuminated the shaft. Its blade became an obelisk
of burning metal lit from the inside out. Somehow the motion of the blade
and the current of the water activated the ray's power source. When Marius

arrived, perhaps together they could figure out the complex mechanics of how the weapon functioned. With his other hand, Barretto easily gathered the weapon's light, extinguishing its power, and flicked the light energy into a shell which immediately glowed like a lantern. Placing the weapon on the table, he waited for Ettore to awake and Marius to arrive. He sat rather patiently gathering and flicking the small amount of light energy he always had on hand.

The first thing Ettore's eyes were able to discern was the largest merman he had ever seen sitting at a table throwing beads of light into a small cup. He shook his head to make sure he wasn't dreaming. It all seemed so surreal. As he tried to sit up, pain shot through his entire body from the top of his head to the tip of his tail. He moaned as its severity threatened to swallow him, sending him once again into the black sleep from which he had just emerged. The merman swam over to his side.

"Be still," he commanded. Ettore had no choice but to obey. Though he was mammoth in size, his hands were gentle as he replaced a poultice on the deep wound on Ettore's chest. Ettore winced waiting for the pain that never came. He looked at the merman towering over him. He had a good-natured smirk on his face. "This remedy won't cause any more pain. I think you have enough, don't you? You, my young prince, are one fortunate merman."

Confused at the merman knowing who he was, Ettore looked at him. "How do you know who I am? I don't believe I have ever met you before. No, I am certain of it. You are someone whom I would never forget meeting, if you will pardon my saying so. You are the largest merman I have ever seen. Who are you and how do you know me?"

"I am a friend of your father, Marius. My name is Barretto. I am the Atlantic Arbitrator whom you were sent to summon. Isn't that so?" He glided smoothly through the water to sit on the chair next to the couch where Ettore lay. "I have sent word with my personal assistant to your father explaining what happened. He should arrive later this tide. But now, tell me what you remember about the attack."

Ettore closed his eyes. In his mind's eye, he saw the entire scene replay: Rahwah preparing to kill him amidst the ever-darkening appearance of the waters; some strange weapon slicing through his chest searing his entire body with pain; his hiding behind the ledge of rock while this huge presence hurled a wall of light toward them; finally, watching Rahwah writhe in pain from the blast of light as he was whisked away by the Light Gatherer. Recognition dawned in his eyes as he stared at the Arbitrator. With awe, Ettore said simply, "You are a Light Gatherer."

With succinct affirmation, Barretto said, "I am."

The prince stared in amazement at his rescuer. He whispered, "I was always skeptical that the Mystical Gift of Light Gathering ever existed, I must tell you. As merchildren we were taught that this Gift had vanished, had become extinct. To not only know it exists, but to have seen it in action changes my entire view of many of the Mystical Gifts. Does my father know this about you?"

Barretto laughed. "Although it is my best kept secret, your father is one of only three merpeople who know this secret: my assistant, your father, and now, you are the only ones who know I am the last Light Gatherer left in the waters of Atlantis. Of course, your attacker now knows the secret as well, so that makes four. Possessing this gift brings not only great responsibility, but great danger as well. This gift brings enormous power, and if misused, it could bring much destruction. Your attacker found this truth out the hard way earlier this tide. Luckily for you, I am one of the good guys." Barretto flashed what might have been considered a smile in Ettore's direction if he weren't so menacing in appearance.

"Did you kill him?" The whispered question brought pain of a different sort to Ettore. That Rahwah had been intent on killing him caused him just as much pain, if not more, than what he had inflicted upon Ettore. The truth was evident: Rahwah wanted Ettore dead.

Barretto watched the myriad of emotions pass over the prince's face. "He was a friend of yours at one time." It was not a question. "No, he is not dead, but he will wish he was for many tides to come. The blast of the light I hurled at him will have left him permanently disfigured. I could have killed him, but long ago I learned to restrain and control the power I possess. You see, I recognized its lethal potential long before I was appointed to the position of Arbitrator. Your grandfather saw that as well. Perhaps that was the main reason he selected me for this position. He, like few others, had seen my power in action when as a young merman, I served as a Guardian. Do you know what that is?"

Ettore again found himself gaping in astonishment. "The Guardians? Are you serious? They don't really exist, do they? In my formal schooling, the Guardians were legendary. As youthful mermen, my friends and I dreamt of the opportunity to serve; it was what caused us to do our best and work our hardest. But as the tides came and went, no one in our tight circle of friends was ever called to join the Guardians, and none of us knew of any merman who had ever served, so naturally, we believed it to be fantasy, merely some honorable standard. I believed the entire "Duty, Honor, Loyalty" mantra instilled in us during defense and weaponry class simply was an ideal our teachers encouraged us to strive to obtain."

"Oh, the Guardians are real. Have you ever asked your father? Perhaps their secrecy is the reason they have been so effective all these centennitides. Their principles and purpose go hand in hand. Those selected for service are sworn to secrecy. Not even their own parents know of their service. It was during my tenure in the Guardians that I learned to harness the power of my Mystical Gift. Because I am the last known possessor of this gift, Nero saw the potential for good by my serving as the Arbitrator. He knew I could handle the pressure and the dangers associated with the job. I was appointed to this lifetime position before your father ever ascended the throne. Of course, with my appointment as Arbitrator, I had to relinquish my position in the Guardians. I think it was a good decision."

"Do the Guardians still exist, Barretto? If they do, why are they not more visible during these dark times in Atlantis? Aren't they bound by duty to protect the kingdom?" Ettore could not help but feel doubtful about the Guardians' effectiveness or their existence in light of recent events.

"The Guardians still exist and are vigilant about protecting Atlantis. However, the members will never be openly visible to us. Only the king himself knows who they are. There is a secret sign that only they know. That sign identifies them to each other and the king. No other merman would even recognize this sign. Being a Guardian is a lifetime appointment. I still consider myself a member of the force. When your father arrives, you must be strong enough to speak to him about the attack. For now, rest until he arrives. We can talk later this tide." Barretto handed Ettore an elixir. "Drink this. It will ease the pain and help you sleep." Ettore drank the thick pasty liquid. Within a few currents, sleep had dragged him to its black waters.

•　　•　　•　　•　　•

Perimicles met Marius and Sandoval in the Processing Center of the Confinement Chamber. They had arrived there shortly after Gregar's death, shocked when Acorius informed them that Gregar had been murdered in his chamber. Marius was furious. He demanded an explanation of how it had happened. The guards were at a loss. Nobody except the guards who had been on constant duty for the past two cycles had been in the chamber and even Marius himself recognized the impossibility of a merman breaching the security at the Chamber. Sandoval requested to examine the body. To the guards' questioning look, Marius replied, "Sandoval is skilled in anatomy. He may notice something we may overlook. Allow him to inspect his body." The guards led Sandoval, Marius, and Perimicles down the corridor to the chamber where Gregar's body still lay. While Sandoval inspected every inch of Gregar's corpse, both Perimicles and Marius examined the chamber itself where Gregar had been detained for the last two cycles. They found nothing. Suddenly, Sandoval gasped. Marius and Perimicles simultaneously swam to the body.

"Look here," Sandoval said, pointing to a place on Gregar's neck. A small barb had pierced Gregar's skin; its red, slightly swollen mark could have easily been attributed to an abrasion. "This looks like the sting of a miniature black stonefish. I thought the species was long gone from these waters. I haven't seen a case of its venom in almost forty annutides. These fish are small and often undetectable, one reason why they are so dangerous. What are the chances that one entered this chamber and killed Gregar? Too much of a coincidence, I am certain. What a painful and terrible way to die. The fish's venom renders its victim paralyzed almost immediately and then its fiery hot poison spreads rapidly shooting all over its victim's body. It's almost as if the victim is burned alive from the inside out in the water. What is really going on here? This can't be an accident or merely chance. Gregar has been murdered." Sandoval was clearly mystified by the circumstances surrounding the former SARC director's death.

Perimicles knew who was behind this attack. This fish was what Calder had placed in his waistbelt outside the chamber. He was absolutely certain of it. He turned toward Marius. "It's Calder, your Majesty. He was here near the Confinement Chamber as I arrived. He didn't see me, but I saw him put something in his waistbelt. His presence so close to the Confinement Chamber portended trouble, and I struggled with the decision to follow him or deliver your message to Acorius. The tight security here lulled me into thinking Gregar was safe, so I chose not to follow him. I am sorry I was wrong." Perimicles clenched his teeth in an effort to control his anger.

Marius turned to Acorius. "I want two guards posted at Calder's chamber immediately. Sandoval, you take care of signing the Order of Confinement. You accompany the two guards to issue the order. If he is not in his chamber, find him and escort him there. Don't let him out of your sight. He is to be confined there in his own chamber until I return from Zephah with Barretto and Ettore. If he tries to leave or becomes uncooperative, he is to be brought here to the exact same chamber that held Gregar the last two cycles. His treasonous behavior stops this tide. Make it so."

Acorius responded, "Yes, your Majesty. It will be my pleasure." Turning to the other guards, he barked out orders to put the command into action. Immediately, he dispatched two of his most trusted guards. They prepared to swim with Sandoval from the Confinement Center toward Calder's chamber on the southern end of the Capital Center as soon as the Order of Confinement was signed.

"Perimicles and I will swim to the Executive Chamber and have Aristeus take care of Gregar's arrangements: informing his family, preparing the legal documents, and properly disposing of his body from this place. Then, Perimicles will accompany me to Zephah. First, I must stop by my chamber and send word to Julette and Selale concerning Ettore's injuries. Selale is not due back until at least another cycle and Julette will be sick with worry if Ettore isn't back later this tide. Be vigilant, my old friend." Sandoval bowed and touched this oldest and dearest friend's hand. Marius swam out of the Confinement Center portals with Perimicles close behind him.

"Would you like me to send the missive to Selale with one of our messengers? I could dispatch the missive right now to someone." Perimicles was surprised the king refused the offer.

"No, I will take care of this missive myself. I will dispatch one of Selale's acquaintances who will deliver the information and provide her comfort and reassurance. I must stop by a friend's chamber before I go to my own. Perimicles, please swim to my Executive Chamber and inform Aristeus of these developments with Gregar. He will know what needs to be done in my absence. I will meet you there as soon as my affairs are complete."

Without hesitation, the young messenger swam back toward the Capital Center. Marius watched him go. He then turned and swam toward Monica's small chamber. She was inside her chamber putting some of her elixirs in a satchel. An alarmed look spread over her face as she saw Marius enter through the portal. "What is wrong? Is it Selale? The baby?" Fear almost strangled her words from being spoken.

"They are fine, Moni. It's Ettore. He has been attacked and injured. I must travel to Zephah this tide, and I don't know when I will return. The time draws near for the baby's birth. Selale must not be left alone. Will you go to the chamber to be with her? I will let her know you are coming, so she will be ready for you. Let yourself in through the portal and swim to my chamber in the back of the house. Selale will meet you there and take you where she has been staying. She will explain more than I can right now." Marius looked at the potions. "Can you send a healing balm with me? Ettore may need it."

Monica swam to the shelves and took a flat canister from a stack near the bottom of the shelf. She turned and placed it in Marius' hand. "This paste will heal his wounds faster than anything else. I will go to Selale. Don't worry, Marius; she still has a few tides before the baby comes. I will prepare to stay with her until you return. Godspeed and be safe, your Majesty."

Marius swam to his chamber. As late in the tide as it was, Selale was still in her own bedchamber. As quickly as he could, he relayed the events of the past tide. Selale burst into tears when he told her Ettore had been attacked and injured. Taking his daughter into his arms, he reassured her that her brother would be fine and informed her of Monica's impending arrival. She assured him that she would be all right and for him not to worry about her. Finally, he sent word to Julette about Ettore's injuries with a reassurance that he was recovering well and would arrive home in a few tides. He hoped she wouldn't worry too much. He would not tolerate his family being the target of Calder's pursuit of power. It ended this tide. Swimming toward the Capital Center, he came to a bold decision: the Atlantic Council would be temporarily disbanded and Calder would be stripped of his duties until further notice. As king, he had the power to implement both of these decrees.

As he arrived at the Executive Chamber, he informed Aristeus of his decision regarding the control of Atlantis. "Prepare the etched order. Until further notice, the Atlantic Council is disbanded. All decisions concerning the kingdom will be made solely by me. Calder has relinquished his right to help lead Atlantis. Until I return, he is not to enter the Capital Center. He is under chamber arrest until I return with Barretto and Ettore." Both Aristeus and Perimicles applauded the bold order. Marius issued the official edict and etched it into law. Finally, he affixed the royal seal. For the first tide in his reign as King of Atlantis, Marius wielded complete control. Satisfied with his decision, he and Perimicles swam toward Zephah.

They arrived in Zephah late in the tide. Ettore had made remarkable improvement. After inspecting his injuries, Marius smoothed the thick balm Monica had sent over his wound. Barretto inspected its contents and found himself impressed with its healing power. Marius sat on the bench beside his son. "Tell me what happened. Don't leave anything out."

Ettore looked at his father and simply said, "Rahwah attacked me. I was swimming toward Zephah, almost there, when he attacked. I saw the bright vest of a patrol guard, but I didn't recognize it was Rahwah. My wave to the patrol was ignored, so I swam on. He doubled around and ambushed me. He meant to kill me with the ray weapon he possessed. He would have succeeded if Barretto had not intervened. Before he could inflict the fatal blow with the weapon, Barretto defused its light properties and severely wounded Rahwah. I still don't understand what I did to him to make him hate me so. He was my best friend, but he tried to kill me." Hurt and confusion at Rahwah's betrayal laced Ettore's weak voice.

"Hate is a powerful and too often an all-consuming emotion. It can be fueled by many other things—greed, ambition, jealousy, and power. According to Perimicles, Rahwah is one of Calder's most eager followers. He will find out the hard way that his loyalty has been misplaced. Unfortunately for Gregar, he learned that lesson too late. He is dead, murdered in his cell before we could question him. I know he was ready to implicate Calder, but he waited too long. But as of this tide, Calder no longer has any power. I officially disbanded the Atlantic Council and stripped my brother of his power. He is being detained at his own chamber until we return, charged with treason."

A troubled look crossed Barretto's already stern face. "Who has been assigned the guard duty and how many were dispatched? Calder has numerous allies in positions of power, mermen who are wealthy, ruthless, and resourceful, and whose influence stretches far and all throughout the kingdom. You are within your right as King of Atlantis to issue this order, especially in light of his treasonous activities; however, you must prepare yourself for the almost certain probability that Calder will not easily and quietly submit to your order. He will fight this order that strips him of his power with all his resources."

Marius rose from the bench and swam over to the large table. He picked up one of the ray weapons and examined it. Without facing the mermen behind him, he said strongly, "Acorius has dispatched two of your AA guards to Calder's chamber and Sandoval is to accompany them with the Order of Confinement. But you are accurate in your assessment of the situation. Calder is a danger to anyone who stands in his way to control Atlantis. I am prepared for war if it means protecting the kingdom of Atlantis. It would be extremely irresponsible of me not to prepare for the inevitable conflict that is to come." He turned then with the ray still in his hand. He met the gaze of each merman assembled in the room. "It has been foretold, has it not? This impending war only confirms the truth of the events destined to happen. The prophecy has already begun to be fulfilled, my friends. We must be ready to fight the dark times that lie ahead in order to preserve our beloved Atlantis."

The silence of the room intensified his proclamation. Perimicles boldly stated, "The Guardians are with you, my lord. I will sound the call. We will be ready at a moment's notice. From our previous conversation, you know that I and two other Guardians infiltrated Calder's inner circle. We Guardians are aware of the plans Calder has devised and are one step ahead to avert them from being attained. What else would you have me do? I pledge my life to you."

"Thank you, my friend. Go now. Summon the force. I will be in touch with you soon." Perimicles placed his hand on the king's. After bowing humbly, he swiftly turned, and opening the portal, swam off into the waters.

A gaping Ettore, watching Perimicles leave, turned and caught Barretto's eye. "They are real. And I thought Perimicles was a messenger."

To Marius' confused look, Barretto laughed and then interjected, "Your son thought the Guardians were a myth, a legend, so to speak. He now knows the Guardians exist."

Marius looked at Barretto. "How soon will Ettore be ready to travel back to the Capital Center? I don't want to risk his recovery, but we must act quickly to ensure Calder's release is not procured through underhanded tactics for which he is renowned."

Barretto turned toward Ettore. "You are strong, but now you need to rest. Take this. It will help you sleep." He handed a kelp stick to Ettore that he had dipped in a thick green paste. Without question, Ettore put the stick in his mouth. Facing Marius, Barretto continued, "We will try to leave in one tide. That miracle balm you smoothed on his wound has already helped, but we may have to wait one tide more. Ettore is seriously injured, and he is still very weak. But, I agree with you about Calder. Our actions must be one step ahead of his. We must avert and thwart his devious plans long before his allies have time to organize. Let's strike first, my King. Let's take out his allies by arresting them before Calder has time to rally them to his cause."

Marius smiled. "It is a good plan. Send Ermaus with a missive to arrest every merman Perimicles can identify, every merman who attended Calder's meeting. Lock each one in a different cell in the Confinement Center. Acorius is to assign a guard to each cell. They are to be detained until either you or I release them and allowed no visitors, including family members. We should arrive within the tide after their arrests. Yes, my friend, it is a good plan. Come. Let's crack the code of this weapon. We can use it for our advantage."

Marius sat down at the table. Barretto joined him. Together they examined the plans and mechanical workings for the ray weapons. Before they retired for the eventide, they had not only figured out its complex design, but had altered the light source on both ray weapons to render any other ray weapons used against theirs useless.

Chapter Forty-four

Calder swam into the Infirmary Center to the small dimly lit chamber where Rahwah lay. Even though the chamber was equipped with only one small illuminating panel, the scars that so disfigured Rahwah's face were still prominent even in the wan light. It was difficult for Calder to look at him and not feel repulsion and pity. The young man would never be the same; he was barely recognizable. The SCEROH patrol had dispatched its rescue team when Rahwah failed to report back in from his duty in the southern region. It had taken most of the tide for the team to find him, so far away was he from his assigned area. He had been unresponsive and had yet to completely emerge from unconsciousness. Calder wanted to know what happened. Severe burns covered half of his face and body. His prognosis was grave. A cycle may pass before he gained consciousness, according to the physicians attending to him. How he could have been burned in the water mystified not only the physicians, but also Calder. It seemed impossible, yet Calder saw it with his own eyes. These scars were the result of a burn, and Rahwah was in the water when someone or something inflicted them.

Another mystery was the location of Rahwah's ray weapon. Even after Calder gave him one of the weapons, he had misgivings about the decision because Rahwah sometimes acted recklessly and often lacked patience. Calder requested permission to search through Rahwah's materials. As the director of the SCEROH, even though his powers had been restricted by the Atlantic Arbitrator, he was granted permission. The ray weapon was not in Rahwah's possessions. This missing weapon concerned Calder as much as the source of the burns. Two of the ray weapons were now missing. Something about this situation alarmed Calder.

Rahwah moaned and murmured a series of incoherent phrases. Calder moved closer to listen. "Light wall coming. Can't hide. Nowhere to hide!" Rahwah was delirious. His fever had spiked once again. The doctors debated about how long he should stay sedated. Obviously, he still needed more of the cycle to recover from his devastating injuries. Calder moved closer to examine the badly burned skin that covered half of Rahwah's body and to listen for any clues that the young man's incoherent mumblings might reveal; unfortunately, Rahwah had once again succumbed to the sleep of unconsciousness. Upon closer inspection, Calder saw that even his tail had been singed somewhat by whatever it was that caused the burns. Frustrated that he would find no answer this tide, Calder swam out of the chamber.

As he exited the Infirmary Center, he saw Gaillard, one of his assembly members, hastily heading in his direction. From the look on his face, Calder immediately realized something was wrong. As Gaillard approached, he grabbed Calder's arm and pulled him back inside the Infirmary Center. Looking around covertly, Gaillard led him into a small, secluded room at the back of the long corridor. He pressed the portal release behind them.

"We've got trouble, Calder. Real trouble. Three of our assembly members have been taken to the Confinement Center, charged with conspiracy to commit treason. Preslar, Montes, and Eurymele are in there. There are only five of us left. We must go into seclusion and plan our next course of action before they come for us. Perimicles needs to be notified of these developments. He can get word to the other members about when and where we will next meet. My power and influence extend far, but we must act quickly before we too are incarcerated. I own several properties where we can seek refuge, places where mermen will willingly harbor us from the Atlantic Arbitrator and his forces. It is he who seems to be the driving force behind these arrests."

Calder shook his head vehemently, "No, these orders come straight from Marius. Apart from the king, the Atlantic Arbitrator has no authority to issue an Order of Confinement. Something has happened in the last two tides to initiate these orders. Rahwah is still unresponsive, so I have been unable to find out what happened to him. No doubt his injuries and the events leading up to them have something to do with these orders. You're right. We need to leave immediately, within the tide. There is no reason for us to take any undue chances. I don't want to give Marius the satisfaction of placing me in the Confinement Center. He will rue the day he tries to confine me. Lead us where we need to go, and I will follow you. We can get word to Perimicles from there."

Gaillard pressed the portal release and cautiously swam into the deserted corridor. Calder joined him and together they made their way toward the exit of the Infirmary Center. As they approached the tall portals, two AA guards accompanied by Sandoval entered through them. They swam face to face with Calder and Gaillard. Calmly, Calder swam in front of Gaillard. He stopped their progress toward the portal and treading there, poised himself in the middle of the corridor. Crossing his arms, he casually waited for the mermen to broach their business.

Sandoval wasted no formalities or small talk. He pulled the Order of Confinement from his waist belt and looking Calder in the eye, read it to both Calder and Gaillard. "I hereby order you both to surrender your waist belts and come with us. You have been charged with conspiracy to commit treason. You will be held in the Confinement Center until the king returns to the Capital." Turning to the guards, he said, "Gentlemen, seize their waist belts."

Smirking at his old acquaintance, Calder raised his hand to stop them and asked, "On whose authority have these orders been issued? On what evidence has this decision been made? Surely you don't think I will go willingly with someone inferior to my rank, Sandoval." Fury blazed in Calder's eyes as he looked with contempt at his brother's closest advisor.

Sandoval clenched his teeth at the insult. "Oh, I clearly understand the power you think you have, but according to this Order, Marius has stripped you of all your duties and your power. The AA has approved the shift in the authority based on evidence of treason. I don't know what that evidence is, but Marius now has seized complete control of the kingdom. You and your friend Gaillard no longer have any power, so I guess that does make us equals after all. Seize them!"

A flash of light slashed through the water. Suddenly Sandoval could not breathe. The waters that floated through the corridor slowly turned red. Sandoval reached for his throat, but it was no use. He could not breathe. Darkness already had him in its grip as his surprised eyes looked into the eyes of his murderer. Before the guards knew what had happened, they too saw a flash and felt a burning slice across their throats. With all three mermen thrashing on the corridor floor, Calder leaned down beside the dying Sandoval and whispered, "You chose the wrong brother to support. Sadly, it has cost you your life, and it will eventually cost Marius his. I will be king. Good-bye, Sandoval." He ushered a shocked Gaillard through the crimson waters toward the portals, and immediately they disappeared into the waters of the Capital Center.

Without any conversation, Gaillard led Calder to the Olympus Complex. They entered through an inconspicuous portal concealed to the naked eye at the rear of the complex. Equipped with a special release code known only by Gaillard, the portal opened into a long tunnel-like hallway that had no interior portals. He led Calder down to the end of it and through a narrow archway that opened into a private office dominated by a large table situated in the center of the room. Calder swam to one of the chairs at the table and sat down. He looked at Gaillard who, treading beside the table, seemed hesitant to sit down.

"What's on your mind, Gaillard? Surely you aren't feeling remorse at doing what we had to do? This is not one of your games, a mock contest for entertainment with a predetermined winner. This is a fight to the finish, a fight to the death. The prize is the throne of Atlantis. There can be only one winner in this contest, and it is I. Those guards and especially Sandoval were expendable, necessary casualties in this war for control of Atlantis. They won't be the last victims. Are you still with me, or will you too abandon my vision for the kingdom so soon?" Calder's intense eyes pinned Gaillard for an answer.

With newfound reassurance, Gaillard confidently replied, "I am with you, Calder. I'm in to the very end." He moved to take the seat beside Calder.

"Excellent. Now have your assistant summon Perimicles to deliver a message to the others in the Inner Circle regarding when and where to reconvene to discuss our next move. We must meet covertly. Is this chamber a refuge for us or must we relocate to another place? Soon, Marius will return to the Capital Center and discover his closest advisor and even dearer friend has been murdered by one of us. There will be few places to hide and few mermen to trust if the bounty he issues for our capture is significant, and, believe me, it will be significant."

"This place is more secure than a fortress. No one knows about this back chamber of the Olympus Complex. It is not in the plans of the Complex, nor does anyone else have the code to the portal through which we entered. No one even knows it exists. We are safe here. Stay. I will go through the interior of the Complex and have my assistant contact Perimicles to meet us here. My assistant is extremely capable and trustworthy. I will find out from him what he knows about the arrests of any of the members of your inner circle. If any other guards come here, he won't reveal I have been here, and because he does not know this chamber exists, he knows nothing to divulge. When I return, I want to know more about that ray weapon. Very impressive it is." Gaillard swam down the long corridor then disappeared through a narrow portal.

Calder withdrew the weapon from his waist belt and activated it, its shaft now a beam of hot blue light. Yes, his weapon was impressive, much more lethal than the others manufactured at the SARC before the Arbitrator had arrived. Right now two of the ray weapons were missing: the one seized by the Arbitrator and the one lost by Rahwah. While the missing weapons did concern him, Calder smiled knowing that his weapon was much more powerful than the others designed using the same plan. His had been altered and improved using a different design that he had created himself. Though the other ray weapons could inflict great and possibly even fatal injury, his was specifically designed to inflict death. Sandoval and the guards were evidence of that fact; they never even realized what had hit them. Yes, his weapon was impressive indeed. He deactivated the weapon and replaced it in his waistbelt.

His thoughts turned now to the battle over control of Atlantis. Now that Gaillard had seen the weapon in action, Calder was certain his loyalty would not be swayed. If the other inner circle members joined him along with some of his other allies, Atlantis would be under his control in the next few tides. His primary objective at this tide was getting all of his allies assembled and battle ready for a synchronized, surprise attack against Marius and the Atlantic Arbitrator as they traveled back to the Capital Center. Ettore was an afterthought. Those three were no match versus Calder and his collaborative allies. He relished the thought of the impending battle. He had waited for this tide for so long, and now that its arrival was eminent, Calder could hardly contain his excitement.

Gaillard returned with the news that Calder's request for his assembly to secretly meet would occur later that tide. Gaillard's assistant had gotten in touch with Perimicles and was told he would arrive soon, but the news was not all good.

Gaillard seemed troubled by the news. "Three members of our Inner Circle have indeed been taken to the Confinement Chamber. Word has spread quickly regarding the death of two guards and Sandoval. According to my assistant, a suspect has not been named in the brutal attack. Two other AA guards visited my assistant earlier in the tide after the attack at the Infirmary Center. He informed them you and I were here when the attack happened. They had come with an Order of Confinement for me. Of course, my assistant told them I was no longer in the Capital, and he had no idea where I was or when I would return. We will be safe here. My assistant has been instructed how to get our other members here safely for the meeting."

"Which of our members have been detained?" Calder knew this was crucial to success of the attack later to come."

"Thankfully, Perimicles, Fideus, and Arnelles have avoided being apprehended. They by far are our best weapons with their youth, strength, and weaponry skills. Unfortunately, the loss of Rahwah really hurts. The three members in the Confinement Center would not have helped us much physically. They are older and their resources financially and politically are primarily what they brought to the group."

"This is mainly good news. Because there were no witnesses to implicate us at the Infirmary Center, you and I have now constructed a solid alibi. I can't imagine what evidence exists strong enough to issue an Order of Confinement as Sandoval suggested there was. Perhaps Marius is desperate enough to fabricate evidence, but knowing his strong sense of integrity, I must conclude that he has some concrete evidence to indict us on charges of conspiracy. I feel somehow this is connected to Rahwah and the injuries he suffered. Maybe more information will be forthcoming at our meeting. Surely Perimicles with his contacts and some of the other members will be able to give us more information regarding this Order of Confinement issued by Marius and the evidence used to support the order. Let's plan and prepare for the meeting. I want there to be no misunderstandings about our plan of attack: the specifics must be established, coordinated, and implemented cooperatively among all the groups involved. Contact the commander of the Defense League and have him ready them for the attack. I don't want him or anyone in the Defense League given any information prematurely. I will take care of alerting the sharks, so when the tide is right, all of my allies will be assembled and ready. My friend, in the next couple of tides, I will be King of Atlantis." A beaming Gaillard bowed before Calder as if he had already ascended to the throne. He then took his seat beside his future king, and together they finalized the plans.

Chapter Forty-five

Monica arrived later in the tide. She entered the home and found Selale in her own chamber room asleep on her couch. Monica took the opportunity to inventory the remedies she had brought with her. She had selected many different balms and elixirs from the many stored on her shelves, so she would be prepared for any and every problem that the birth might cause. She had also brought other personal items from home just in case she was here for more than two tides. Ettore's injuries could be greater than Marius realized or was told. It may take longer than one tide for him to recover enough to travel the distance back to the Capital. Hopefully the balm she had sent would help. Monica busied herself by reading through the remedy book she and Giada had written many tides before.

Almost a half tide later, Selale slowly opened her eyes and found Monica sitting on the bench beside her bed couch. She smiled at her gentle friend and said, "Sorry. I didn't know you had arrived. I have been so tired the past two tides. The baby will come soon. I can feel it." With a gentle caress, Selale ran her hands over her extended stomach.

Monica agreed. "Yes, it won't be long now. Hopefully he will wait until your father returns, but that is not the way nature works. This baby will come on his schedule and not on anyone else's. We must talk about the baby's birth and make some preparations. Where will you want to deliver him, here or in another chamber?"

"No, he will not be born here. I will take you where he will be born. Once we arrive, you will understand completely why I chose that place," Selale said mysteriously and then laughed at Monica's perplexed expression. "Let me get everything I will need and then we will—Oh!" A shocked, sharp cry came from Selale.

"What is it? What is the matter, Selale?" Monica had moved to Selale's side and concern etched her already wrinkled face more.

Selale lay still on the bed couch and looked at her friend with wonder and surprise. She whispered, "The baby is coming, Monica."

The older merwoman looked at Selale's stomach and then ran her hand over it, checking for the stiff contractions of labor. Nodding, she confirmed, "You are correct, my dear. However, this will not be a short process. It will take all of this tide and into the next before the baby makes his arrival. Come, we still have a while, but preparations need to be started right now." Monica extended her hand to Selale to help her up.

They gathered everything Monica had brought and other items and placed them in a satchel Monica placed around her head and shoulder. Looking at Selale, she said, "Take me to the chamber where you want to deliver this baby."

Selale grinned and said softly, "Follow me."

Together they swam out of her chamber into Marius' private office chamber. Monica became nervous at being in so private a place. "Should we be here? This is the king's office!"

Selale reassured her. "It's all right, Monica. He doesn't mind because this is the only entrance to where we are going." She swam over to the wall and depressed a hidden button. Suddenly a hidden portal opened revealing a long, dimly lit tunnel. Monica gasped. Smiling conspiratorially, Selale looped her arm through her friend's and led her down the illuminated tunnel. Monica looked back as the portal behind them closed automatically.

The swim to the cave was difficult for them both. Once, Selale's body was wracked by labor pains halting their progress right when they came to the edge of the tunnel. Monica had no idea where they were headed. The murky waters of the tunnel revealed no clue as to the destination where they were going, so she had to trust Selale to lead her there. As they exited the tunnel, the waters became dark. The eventide had come many currents ago, and Monica became disoriented in the darkness. Selale, however, kept her course fixed on their destination. Monica clutched Selale's hand and the satchel around her shoulder. She blindly let the younger mermaid lead her. Monica felt herself being guided up toward the surface. As her eyes adjusted to the darkness, she became aware that in the distance toward which they were swimming, the waters lightened.

"We are almost there, Moni," Selale said it as much to reassure herself as her friend.

Up they swam toward the light. When they broke the surface, Selale was exhausted. She struggled to slowly pull herself up on the shelf of rock. She switched on the lamp left by Thad and helped Monica up out of the water. Her eyes watched the wonder spread over Monica's face as she took in the magnificence of Beulah Cave.

Breathing hard, Selale murmured, "What do you think of the place where the baby is to be born? It seems an appropriate, really a perfect place to birth the Hybrid King, does it not? Your reaction to the cave was a mirror to my own the first tide I was brought here by my father. Take all its beauty in, Monica. It really is a special place."

"This place is ancient; I can tell it has been here many tides. How has it remained a secret? Where in the Kingdom are we?" Monica looked at the writing etched on the cave wall.

"We are in the condemned waters of Atlantis. My father used the toxicity decree to discourage our people from venturing into these waters so this place would remain undiscovered. His great-grandmere brought him here when he was ten annutides. She had been coming since she was a merchild. After she had the vision of the Hybrid King, she etched the entire prophecy on the wall, so my father and those with whom he shared this secret, special place would know the story. Since we have more than a tide before the baby will be born, read the prophecy while we wait. Some events have already come to pass and others are being set into motion this very tide. The baby's birth signals the beginning of the dark tides to come, I am afraid." Sadness tinged Selale's words. How ironic that her baby's birth was the beginning of such joy and yet such sorrow!

Monica took Selale's hand into her own. "Do not worry, my dear. Let's forget about the future for right now and concentrate on the present of your having this baby. What is this artificial light source and from where did it come?" Like Marius, Monica raised the light to examine it carefully. "I could use one of these in my chamber!" As she placed it back on the rock, her eyes caught a glimpse of the glass globe sitting on the back of the rock ledge. She reached over and picked it up. "What is this? How is it that I have lived to be nearly seventy annutides and I have never seen these kinds of things? Where did they come from? Are these things from the world of your human?"

Selale reached over and turned the knob on the bottom of the globe. Music filled the cave. She shook the globe and golden flecks floated through the water inside the sphere. She handed the globe to an amazed Monica who held it as if she were holding a treasure. Selale gasped as another labor pain ripped through her body. She breathed shallow breaths to help herself cope with the pain. Monica placed the glass globe far away as music continued to fill the chamber. She continued to hold Selale's hand while the pains subsided.

Once the contraction was over, Monica made an astute observation. "There must be some good in a world that makes such beauty. You must love each other very much." Just as Selale nodded, a bubbling fountain disturbed the waters. Startled, Monica gasped as a man surfaced in the cave.

Thad was as startled to see Monica as she was to see him. He looked at Selale and knew something was wrong. He immediately pulled himself and a bag he had with him out of the water and went to her side. He threw the bag on the back of the ledge and sat down beside Selale. "What's wrong? What's going on? Talk to me, Selale." Fear ripped through him as he took her in his strong arms.

She wrapped her arms listlessly around his neck and said softly, "Our son is on his way. There is nothing wrong. I am so glad you are here." She laid her head against his chest and shut her eyes as he pulled her closer in his arms.

He looked helplessly at the older merwoman staring at him. "Hello. My name is Thad. I am Selale's husband. Thank you for being here with her.

Will she be all right?" She sent a smile back to him, but made no reply to his question.

Selale laughed weakly. "This is my friend Monica whom I told you about. She doesn't understand English. I will have to translate for you and her." She turned and spoke to her friend in their strange yet beautiful language. The older merwoman conversed with Selale; then Monica looked at Thad and nodded. Selale translated for Thad. "She said I will be fine, and for you not to worry. Babies are born every tide."

Thad relaxed a little, but replied, "I can't help but worry. This is my first experience with having a baby. I'm a nervous wreck. What can I do?" He took Selale in his arms and held her.

"Just being here with me is all I need from you. The baby and I will do the rest. According to Monica, this will be no short process. If it is any consolation, it is all new to me as well." Another pain sliced through her body. Thad looked scared to death.

Monica addressed Selale. "It will help if you get into the water. It will lessen the intensity of the pain."

Selale looked at Thad and gasped, "Help me into the water. Monica says it will help the pain." Thad instantly lowered Selale into the water. He treaded beside her with his arm firmly supporting her under her arms. Finally, the pain passed, and he once again lifted her back onto the rock ledge. Over the course of the tide, this became the process. Once the pains would start, Thad would lower both of them in the water, and he would support her by holding her as he held her up. Each time the pain would subside, Thad would return them to the ledge. Selale would take the glass globe and turn the knob so that the soothing music would fill the chamber in between the pains which were coming closer and closer together.

The lamp had long ago been turned off. Light had filled the cave as the overhead sun that shone through the holes in the cave brightened the waters and reflected off the golden walls. Throughout the entire tide, the light coupled with the haunting music created a magical, mystical place. But now the light had begun to dim, deepening the cavern colors to a warmer hue. Eventide had come.

"They say that music soothes the soul. This song is such a small part of the volumes of music that fill my world. Doctors say babies can hear music while they are in the womb. Wonder what our baby thinks of this song?" Thad smiled and reached over to place his hand on Selale's stomach.

Monica whispered, "Music."

Selale nodded and then said, "He loves it and so I do." The next contraction ripped through her body. She screamed in pain.

Monica got in the water beside her. "The baby will arrive much sooner than we thought. The pains are much closer together. You must stay in the water until he is born, but also close enough to the surface just in case he can't breathe under water. I mean, I know the prophecy, but these are unchartered waters for all of us. Better to err on the side of caution. Tell Thad to be ready. The baby is coming soon. Push the baby out, Selale. Push hard the next time the pain comes. I will be there to catch the baby once he is in the water."

The next pain caused Selale to cry out. It felt as if her body were being torn apart. "He's coming, Thad. The baby is coming." A piercing scream split the silence of the cave as she held onto Thad's hand, almost crushing it as she birthed the baby. The baby slipped into the water into Monica's waiting hands.

Just as the baby hit Monica's hands, suddenly the walls of the cave and the water itself shook violently. Rocks dislodged from the beams and pelted the churning, wave-filled water. The items on the rock ledge rattled and shook noisily. The lantern tipped over, and the glass globe, lodged against the back of the rock shelf, shook so that its golden flecks floated through the liquid.

Thad treaded in the water as he held Selale; alarm and fear filled their expressions. In the midst of the chaos, Monica stayed calm and motioned for Thad to lift Selale, exhausted and listless, back onto the ledge. He gently laid her down and pulled himself out of the water. Monica swam over and placed the baby on Selale's chest. The baby's cries echoed off the cave walls. Thad lay down beside them and shielded them with his body to protect them from any rocks or debris that might fall. As quickly as the earthquake started, the shaking suddenly ceased, and the waters in the cave slowly calmed. The baby, nestled in Selale's arms, calmed too. He yawned as he gazed around the cave trying to get his blue eyes to focus. Both Thad and Selale lay marveling at their son, this child who was both human and merman. Thad clasped tiny fingers in one hand while the other hand traced a finger over the strangely-shaped birthmark on his son's shoulder. Selale gently caressed the baby's very human foot. Tears slowly rolled down their cheeks as they held the Hybrid King. Thad leaned over and kissed them both.

A startled cry caused them to look at the water where creatures rose from the depths and surrounded Monica, who still remained in the water. Fish of all sizes and species swam in circles around her and leapt into the air, their eyes focused on the strange trio in order to get a glimpse of the baby. Monica's tinkling laughter filled the cave. She called out, "Selale, the fish have come to celebrate the birth of their future king! Hold him high! They wish to see this strange new king!" Selale whispered the translated message from Monica to Thad.

Thad sat up and stared, amazed at the congregation of sea creatures. It resembled Sea World, but on steroids. The fish leaped and danced in frenzy, and Thad sat there, with mouth agape, taking it all in. He reached over and gently gathered his son in his arms and stood on the ledge with the baby facing the waters for all the admirers to see. They responded by clapping their fins and flippers together, jumping and splashing in the water around the elated Monica, and creating a kind of music of their own. Thad had never witnessed anything so beautiful in his life. Eventually the celebrations dissipated and quietness returned to the cave. Thad gathered his son and his wife in his arms as they both slipped into a peaceful sleep. He held them tightly unable to take his eyes off his beautiful wife and his tiny, newborn son. For several hours, occasional fish rose to the surface to peer at the king, only to reverently slip back into the depths after they had glimpsed his and his mother's slumber. Thad took in everything that had happened and tried to wrap his mind around the miracle of his son's birth. Nothing in his entire thirty-three years could have prepared him for the magic of this day. The details of the day were forever etched in his memory. Contentment and joy lulled him into a deep, peaceful sleep.

Monica had finished taking care of Selale and the baby and then slipped quietly into the back chamber of the cave where the prophecy was written.

She touched a withered hand to the ancient manuscript delicately etched on the wall. Closing her eyes, tears ran down her wrinkled cheeks as she rejoiced in the prophecy's fulfillment of her people's long-awaited king. With praise still on her lips, she glanced back across the cave to see mother, father, and son peacefully asleep in each other's arms.

Chapter Forty-six

Michael and Charise finally arrived home, both exhausted from the long trek driving from Gramma Winans' house. After being away from home for over three weeks, they had never been so happy to see their modest little house. They dropped their bags in the foyer and sluggishly made their way to the bedroom. The only light Michael switched on was in the dining room which lit the center of the house. Everything in the house was exactly as it had been the morning they had left for their cruise, the familiarity comforting in its mundane ordinariness.

It had been an exhausting three-week ordeal. The two-week cruise had been a wonderful diversion from reality, everything and more than Michael could have planned for Charise to get her mind off their lost child and rekindle their relationship. They arrived at their next to last destination when they received the news that Gramma Winans had fallen and broken her hip. She had been taken to surgery not long after being admitted to the hospital. Both Michael and Charise understood the danger and complications that could result from such an injury for someone her age. They immediately departed from that port and drove back to Charleston to get their car before making their way across the state to the mountains. They worried the entire way there about her recovery.

They found Gramma Winans barking orders at the interns and sharing old wives' tales with the nurses about the cure for everything from the common cold to a broken heart. She had the entire nursing and physical therapy staff eating out of her hand by the time they arrived. After making arrangements to install a ramp at her house and working out shifts to stay at her house, they prepared for her being discharged from the hospital. It was a tearful departure for the hospital nurses and care staff who were sad to see her go, but thrilled that she had recovered so quickly. Gramma Winans attributed it to good genes and a strong faith.

Michael and Charise stayed the first week with her. The progress she made in one week's time was nothing short of miraculous. Only seven days after coming out of surgery, Charlotte Winans made her way with her walker down to her mailbox and back unassisted. She declared herself well, and then demanded Charise and Michael return home. In her words, she could recover just as quickly with or without them there. After setting up an around-the-clock schedule with the rest of the family, they set out for the coast of North Carolina, an almost six-hour drive.

Charise had driven the first part of the trip while Michael caught up on some lost sleep. When it was his turn to drive while Charise slept, his thoughts kept returning to Thad and the long overdue conversation they were to have about his relationship with Selale. If Michael had calculated correctly, Selale was due any day now. Something about their relationship was strange, but he knew that Thad would be forthcoming and candid about it just as he had promised. Several different scenarios played through Michael's brain as to the mysterious nature of their relationship: everything from race, religion, politics, and finances to alien abduction. Nothing quite added up to an out of the ordinary factor to which Michael would object. Well, maybe the alien abduction was a little far-fetched, but still, he was open to any relationship that made Thad happy.

And Thad was happy. Michael could tell his best friend was elated as the birth of his son approached. To be honest, Michael was equally excited. He wanted the chaos and noise of a baby crying. A part of him could become jealous of his best friend if not for the fact that this baby would be a large part of his and Charise's life. That thought was what kept that dark emotion at bay: the baby would be a part of their family, just as Thad was. Michael couldn't help but smile. Throughout the remainder of the drive home, he tried to imagine what the baby would look like, sound like, smell like, and feel like. He could already picture that tow-headed baby in Thad's arms, in his arms, and in the arms of Charise. Those images and thoughts helped speed the last leg of the journey by quickly. They arrived home just after nine that evening.

Now as they made their way through the foyer and into their house, Charise yawned and said, "Let's just leave those bags there until the morning. I'm tired, and I have all day tomorrow to unpack." She walked to the dining room and stopping there, she turned and wrapped her arms around Michael's waist. "It was a wonderful cruise, a vacation I will never forget, but I am glad to be home." She kissed him and laid her head on his chest.

Suddenly the floor began to shake, and everything on the shelves and tables rattled, haphazardly falling on the floor. The light hanging over the dining room table swayed back and forth like a pendulum. Still holding hands, Michael and Charise grappled for the wall, for anything to brace themselves so they wouldn't fall. He pulled her over to door jamb that joined the dining room to their study so they could cling to something sturdy. In the study, drawers in the tall cabinet and in the mahogany desk slid open and out of their pockets, spilling their contents onto the floor. Everything on the massive mahogany desk slid to the floor as if someone swept it off with a broom. What seemed like minutes lasted only seconds. The shaking abruptly stilled causing both Michael and Charise to gasp and look at each other with stunned amazement, neither able to speak. The house resembled a crime scene: chairs and furniture were overturned, books and papers were strewn throughout the room, and decorative knickknacks and planters, some broken and some intact, littered the floor.

In the eerie silence, both held their breath waiting for the inevitable aftershocks. The power had been knocked out, so that the entire house was bathed in darkness except for the light streaming through the windows from the almost-full moon. The dining room light fixture still swung back and forth. Suddenly piercing the dark, a strange, unforeseen glow radiated from a dislodged, overturned drawer. Its pulsing, dim illumination cast a warm glow over the destruction. Without warning, light exploded from the drawer, bouncing and reflecting off the walls like fireworks in a July 4th night sky. With her hands covering her ears, Charise screamed and cowered down, crouching in the doorway that connected the dining room and the study. Michael gripped the door jamb tightly with both hands and gazed with fearful fascination at the mysterious light show on display in the room. Light beams bounced around the room like an arcade pinball machine. Finally, the strange incandescence from the drawer slowly dimmed into a small ball of light no larger than a pen-light; the study was bathed only in the small glow and the indirect light from the windows.

Michael still had an iron grip on the door jamb. He let go and ran to Charise's side, gathering her in his arms. She was trembling. "Shhh, it's all right. Everything's all right." He said it as much to reassure himself as her. His heart was racing, and his mind tried to make sense of what had just happened.

Charise whispered, "What just happened, Michael? This isn't California; this is the East Coast. Earthquakes don't happen here. And the light? I'm scared."

Michael arose and went to the drawer where the small beam of light re-mained. Charise's eyes followed his every move. He stooped down and to his amazement saw that the source of light was coming from the pearl which was still wrapped in the cloth bag he had placed it in many months before. It still glowed, but its faint light gradually grew dimmer. He tentatively reached his hand in the drawer and withdrew the cloth bag. He opened it and removed the light-filled pearl. It felt warm to the touch. He walked over and sat down beside Charise. Both sat staring at the pearl with a mixture of awe and fear. Slowly, like the setting sun, the light faded into the darkness. Michael closed his fist around the pearl. Charise placed her trembling hand over his. With his other arm he drew her close and with reverence he murmured, "I don't know what it means, but I do know it means something, and yes, probably something significant. Let's keep this part of the night a secret. Something tells me we won't understand all of this tonight, but I feel certain that in time, we will. The woman's voice told me the day I found this pearl to keep it safe and keep it secret. Until we can make sense of its power and significance, I think I should put the pearl back in the drawer." Charise nodded in agreement. He stood and pulled her to her feet. His shaking fingers rubbed over the still-warm, large pearl. Michael placed the mysterious orb back in the bag before he picked up the drawer and slid it in its empty slot the cabinet. He slid the bag back into the corner of the drawer before he closed it.

"Let's call Thad to check on him. There's no way he slept through this," Charise said. "I want to know that he is all right. While you call him, I'll go assess the mess in our bedroom to see if we can sleep in our bed."

"Good idea." Michael dialed the familiar number and let it ring until Thad's voicemail answered. He left a message for his friend, "Hey, bud, it's Michael. I'm just calling to check on you after the earthquake. Surely you didn't sleep through it. Call me so Charise and I will know you are all right. Hope Selale hasn't had the baby. Call me back as soon as you get this."

Charise came back into the room and sighed. "Thank goodness the bedroom isn't quite the mess the dining room and study are. Let's go to bed, Michael. I know it's not that late, but I'm exhausted, and you are too. We can clean this up tomorrow. What did Thad say?"

"He didn't say anything. He didn't answer his phone. Either he isn't home or he slept through the earthquake. Even if he was the world's deepest sleeper, I doubt he slept through it. He must be with Selale. Do you think she has had the baby? Could that be where he is?"

"Well, maybe. It's not like the baby was going to wait for us to get home. He's going to arrive on his schedule, not ours." Charise yawned. "Let's get ready for bed." She grabbed Michael's hand and led him to the bedroom. After they lay down, both kept visualizing the scene with the pearl and trying to make sense of what it meant. Neither could quiet their mind from the many speculations and theories. The last thought that crossed Michael's mind was that Thad's son might have been born on the night of the earthquake. As he pondered the coincidence, sleep finally took him under to its dark, dreamless ocean.

Chapter Forty-seven

Marius, Barretto, and Ettore were unable to leave until later in the tide. Ettore awoke with dark circles under his eyes, and the slightest swim across the room weakened him. Barretto concocted another restorative elixir for him to drink. After another few currents of rest, Ettore seemed stronger, and so they prepared for the swim back to the capital. As they embarked on their journey, the three swam slowly and prepared for many rests in between. Though it would take much longer than usual, they could still arrive late in the eventide. Marius knew Monica attended to Selale, so she was in good hands if the baby arrived before they returned to the capital.

As he swam, Marius' thoughts turned to the baby and the prophecy. He couldn't help but feel excitement, anticipation, and nervousness for his birth. When Selale had told him she was pregnant, in the deepest part of his soul, he had been skeptical and maybe even fearful that this baby was the promised king. He didn't pretend to understand all the implications and events that this child portended. They were too complex and numerous for his mortal mind to take in. What he did comprehend beyond all doubt was that with this baby came change and not all the changes would be good. He and the entire merman race had waited so long for this king, however, that change, no matter how difficult, was welcome. Change was when faith was tested. And now, Marius realized his faith had more questions than confidence. He hoped his faith in the prophecy would not be shaken. He had to trust that in the end, good would conquer evil just as the prophecy predicted.

Marius felt certain Perimicles and some of the Guardians were in the vicinity. Because Ettore was so vulnerable and they were so exposed, the Guardians would undoubtedly send some scouts to scope out the perimeter of their journey to avert any potential problems. This was part of the unofficial duties of the Guardians. They were there, yet no one knew they were there except Marius.

Even though Marius, Ettore, and Barretto made many stops, the tidal current was swift and helped drift them north toward the capital. They were approaching the newly constructed Benthic tunnel that had been almost destroyed from sabotage. Construction had progressed quickly and relatively few delays had allowed the tunnel to open nearly two cycles early. Marius had been pleased with the many improvements he and the engineers had made to not only the southern tunnel, but to all the others as well to make them safer and less vulnerable to attack. The walls of every tunnel had been reinforced, thickened, and strengthened, and illuminating panels and safe rooms had been installed at specific intervals. Security had also been heightened at every tunnel. Officers had been stationed at each entrance and their mere presence established a clear message—safety for all merpeople traveling through the Benthic tunnel system was top priority. It mattered little that the flow of people moved somewhat slower; no one seemed to mind the minor inconvenience. Marius decided to take a break here and rest in the officers' station. Though it was a small space, it would provide a sufficient place for Ettore to rest while he and Barretto mapped out the agenda for the tide once they arrived in the capital. The waters were darkening quickly; eventide was fast approaching and would arrive before they entered the Center City.

Ettore stretched out on the ottoman inside the officers' station. Almost instantly, his eyes closed as exhaustion from the slow but arduous swim settled upon him. Marius and Barretto swam to the table situated in the middle of the room. The officer-in-charge at the station had generously offered them a place to rest before they continued to the Capital City.

"We can't stay long, but maybe a short rest will enable Ettore to make it the final stretch to the capital. It will be long past eventide when we arrive. Hopefully by then, Sandoval will have everyone in custody. That will make our jobs much easier," Marius confided.

"Unfortunately, I'm afraid this won't be a quick or easy matter. Calder has many powerful allies. Few will likely implicate him. We witnessed that with Gregar. They will help him long before they will betray him. We need to be prepared for a lengthy, drawn out struggle, my lord." Barretto cast Marius a solemn look. Marius had a strange look on his face. "What is it that troubles you, your Majesty?"

"What if we're wrong, Barretto? What if Calder is not planning a coup, is not out to depose me, is not plotting the evil that we believe he is? Could we be wrong? We have very little proof of his treason." To Barretto's emphatic no, Marius continued, "I want to be wrong! I want to believe the best about him. After all, he is my twin; he is my flesh and blood. Everything is so…complicated."

Without warning, a flash exploded from the Atlantis pearl suspended from around Marius' neck. Its bright blast of light knocked them from their seats and temporarily blinded them. Both mermen simultaneously raised an arm to shield their eyes. Marius instinctively grasped the pearl with his right hand which obscured some of the light emanating from it. Heat radiated from the pearl and warmed Marius' clasped fingers. He and Barretto gazed transfixed at the glowing orb. By the pearl's pulsing light, both mermen tried to re-seat themselves. As they tried to sit, the table suddenly tilted, sending its top slowly floating down to the quaking chamber floor. The entire waters around them reverberated with the shaking of the ocean floor. Ettore, who had remained asleep through the blast of light, was abruptly awakened as the quaking ottoman dislodged him. Confusion was evident on his face as he took in the eerie glowing pearl and the quaking ocean floor. Emergency sirens blared in the officers' chamber and all throughout the Benthic tunnel. With the pearl's light to guide them, Marius, Barretto, and Ettore swam into action. They opened the chamber portal, and directed by the officer-in-charge, swiftly moved to the mouth of the tunnel. The glow of the pearl began to fade, but Marius refused to release the hand that clutched it. The earthquake continued for many currents, and officers assigned to the tunnel worked frantically to escort Marius, Barretto, and Ettore, along with all the merpeople moving through the passage, into the safe rooms built every so many lengths of the tunnel for just an occasion such as this.

Once the quaking subsided, stillness silenced the darkening waters surrounding the tunnel, but Marius' mind was reeling. He understood the implication of the earthquake and the pearl's explosion of light—the Hybrid King had been born! A mixture of joy and sadness warred inside him. This long-expected baby had finally come, yet he had missed his miraculous birth. Marius looked at his surroundings with a new awareness. Nothing had changed in the small room, and yet, now everything was different. The kingdom of Atlantis would never be the same. Marius felt excitement at the thought that the future savior of his kingdom had finally arrived!

In the currents following the confusion of the quake, illuminating panels dimly lit the safe room and cast a reassuring glow that enabled the inhabitants to see. Everyone inside waited motionlessly where they were for any subsequent aftershocks that frequently followed a major earthquake. Barretto never took his eyes from the pearl that hung around Marius' neck. Marius understood the giant merman's confusion and prepared himself for the many questions and discussion which were certain to happen once they were alone. When the safety siren sounded, a collective sigh of relief came from the assembled group. They were safe and uninjured. Shaken from his musings, Marius was personally congratulated by many of the officers and common mertravelers for the improvements he and his engineers had made to the Benthic tunnel system. The reinforced walls and safe rooms had saved their lives. The officers requested everyone stay inside the room until the tunnel was inspected. Marius insisted on accompanying them with the inspection. Though he had a million questions and was about to burst from curiosity, Barretto comprehended his role was to remain in the safe room while Ettore rested near the back wall. His questions could be asked later in the tide on the swim back to the capital.

Marius swam with the officers as they carefully inspected the tunnel. Satisfied that the structure was safe, Marius felt a sense of satisfaction at the redesigned workmanship of the tunnels. There was no structural damage, so the tunnel could immediately reopen. Everyone had left the safe room, and most had continued on their journey. Barretto and Ettore joined Marius, and together they continued north toward the capital. They still had several leagues to travel. No sooner had they swum away from the tunnel, Barretto asked the question that had weighed on his mind since the earthquake.

"What happened back there, Marius? From your reaction to these events, I recognize that this was no random earthquake. What do these events signify?" Barretto's manner was even more intense than usual. After hearing Barretto's description of the pearl's explosion of light while his father inspected the tunnels, Ettore listened intently to his father's explanation. He too wanted to hear what his father had to say.

Marius stopped swimming, and in a calm, confident voice succinctly pronounced, "The Hybrid King has been born."

Both Barretto and Ettore treaded in stunned silence. They looked at each other and then back at Marius. Doubt and confusion filled their faces as they searched Marius' face for confirmation of the truth. Finally, Barretto asked, "How do you know this? You have been with us for the past four tides."

"First, I know because these events—the earthquake, the pearl's exploding light—were foretold centennitides before. Moreover, I personally know this baby was due any tide now. This specific baby's father is a human; his mother is a mermaid. I had my doubts about this child, whether he would be the long-awaited Hybrid King. Many signs have erased these doubts over the last cycle. Other events have happened that can only be verified by the mother of this child and me. Trust me when I tell you that during this very tide, the prophecy has been fulfilled." Without any more discussion, Marius turned his gaze north toward the capital. "Come now; we must make haste. There are so many things to which we must attend upon our arrival." With that, he swam off giving both Ettore and Barretto the rest of the swim to the capital to work through and process the shocking news they just heard.

They swam silently for much of the remainder of the journey. The matter of the Hybrid King had not resurfaced. Marius wanted to give both Barretto and Ettore time to digest and adjust to the news. He knew this required a great amount of trust from his son and his close friend. He wanted them to believe wholeheartedly the truth of his confession. The three mermen were lost in their own thoughts as they started the last stretch of the journey. The capital city sat just a few leagues away.

Off in the distance through the murky waters about a league away, Marius made out the shadowy silhouette of an army of mermen. Lined up in ranks, hundreds of soldiers from an army whom he did not recognize appeared to be bracing for battle, their rigid posture tensed for battle. Both Barretto and Ettore saw the assembly as well. Alarm raced through Marius as he took stock of the situation: the three of them were in danger. He stopped abruptly and turned toward Barretto. "Take Ettore and turn back. We don't know who these fighters are. Find the Guardians if you can, but above all else, keep Ettore safe. I will hold them off as long as I can." Marius pulled the modified ray weapon from his waistbelt and turned to face the assembly.

Neither merman moved. Barretto grabbed Marius by the arm and came face to face with his king. "No, my lord, we will stay and fight. This is not a matter to be taken lightly. Please do not send me away. There is no way you alone can hold them off. Together, the three of us will do this until the Guardians arrive."

Ettore too voiced his protest, "No, father. You are my king, and regardless of the fact that I am your son, I have pledged my oath of fealty to you. My life I give to protect yours. Together we will fight. I will not flee to be protected. I would rather die fighting with honor protecting you than live fleeing with cowardice protecting myself."

Marius nodded as respect for both his son and his friend surged through him. "Together then we will fight. Men, ready your weapons. We won't go down without a fight! Atlantis is our kingdom! We have our Mystical Gifts should we need them. I shall summon help from the creatures of the deep." A shrill melody pierced the still and silent waters of the ocean, its familiar call rippled out like a tidal wave moving across the waters. From the depths, marine life of all shapes and sizes heard and answered the call. A company of twenty dolphins lined up in front, ready for battle. Fifty orcas encased at the rear of the army the various companies of other fish which included octopi, giant squid, and assorted marine life. Leading the marine army was Massau, the Great White. He swam toward Marius, and bowing before him, replied, "My troops are ready. They are here for your protection, my lord. You are our king. Signal us when you are ready." Massau returned to the front row of the assembled aquatic army, and facing their king, patiently awaited their orders. They too readied themselves for attack alongside the other sea creatures and next to their king, Barretto, and Ettore.

At Ettore's gaping stare, Marius observed, "Well, that evens the odds tremendously now." His eyes scanned the depths for the Guardians, but they were nowhere in sight. Telepathically, Marius turned his attention to the line he faced and demanded to speak to the assembled group's leader. "I am Marius, King of Atlantis. What are your demands? What are your intentions?" The opposing army remained obstinately still in their lines.

When no one made a move to come forward, Ettore volunteered to go as an emissary to determine the assembly's intentions. "Father, I will go. I will determine who is in charge of this treasonous assembly. It is my duty to protect you and the entire kingdom of Atlantis from this traitor. Give me your blessing and allow me this honor." Ettore bowed before his father. Marius held out his hand. Ettore touched it and bowed low before his father, the king. Barretto retrieved a glowing band from his waistbelt and placed it around his head. Marius nodded in approval. The immunity ring symbolized protection from capture and harm in all the waters of Atlantis. As Marius and his assembled army watched the young prince leave the safe waters behind and approach the front of the enemy line, they anxiously waited to see who would emerge as the leader of the other side.

Gaillard and the Defense League commander watched as an unarmed soldier approached the line. They had no idea it was Prince Ettore. Around his head was the immunity ring. The other sharks swam right behind the ranks of the DL battalion, and they hungrily eyed the lone messenger from the opposing side. Gaillard looked around for Calder and the three young members from the Inner Circle. The leaders of this army were nowhere to be found. Only Gaillard, the platoons of possibly two hundred Defense League soldiers, and the three sharks faced the opposing and intimidating army. Gaillard could not help but think of an analogy the humans sometimes used: a ship without a captain. That saying seemed quite appropriate because there was clearly no one in charge to guide the ship.

The only information given to the young and inexperienced DL commander was that the king had committed genocide. He had issued an order killing thousands of innocent merpeople in the southern province. Word had spread quickly that the next orders would be to terminate the members of the Defense League. Since he viewed them as a threat, Marius wanted them eliminated. Upon hearing this, the DL forces eagerly agreed to rebel against the king. Many of the young fighters were anxious and perhaps even zealous to test their mettle in a fight for Calder, their commander in chief. The plan had been for Calder to meet here with his allies and, as Marius traveled back to the capital, confront his brother face to face, giving Marius a chance to abdicate the throne in front of all these witnesses. Of course, this plan had failed to take into account the opposing army. Their appearance had not been factored into the equation. How they had been assembled so quickly, Gaillard did not know. Being a gambling man, he didn't like these odds. Clearly without the help of Calder, Perimicles and the others, he, the Defense League, and sharks were outnumbered and outmanned. An uneasy feeling filled Gaillard as he awaited the soldier's approach. He did not want to make any decision concerning an attack. That was Calder's call, not his. Desperately he scanned the ocean floor for the future king's presence.

Calder had lingered well behind his allies. The untimely earthquake earlier in the tide had almost destroyed their well-calculated plans. Fideus and Arnelles had met Calder at the outskirt of the capital. They conveyed to Calder how Perimicles planned to execute his part in the attack: his job was to take down the strongest soldier on the opposing side. Satisfied with the details of the battle plan, the two mermen convinced Calder that his presence at the battle was not crucial. On the contrary, they argued that his safety from harm was much more important because he would be king by the end of the tide, and a king must be protected at all cost, so they had concocted the plan to meet here at the shoal. Calder agreed with their logic and therefore tarried east of his troops, waiting for the bloodshed to be completed before his arrival. He could arrive after the battle was long over and play the part of the grieving brother and uncle well, pretending to be deeply saddened at the senseless tragedy of their deaths due to miscommunication and misunderstanding. His absence from the bloodshed would serve as an excellent alibi which would absolve him from suspicion of treason once all his brother's allies were eliminated.

With his distance goggles, Calder could see the scene unfold right before his eyes. He could see his brother and all his assembled forces, yet no one was aware of his presence except Fideus and Arnelles who treaded by his side. He had strategically placed himself on a sand shoal close enough to the action to make a grand entrance when the fighting ceased. Remnants of an ancient frigate that had run aground on the shoal in a storm helped obscure him from the soldiers assembled to the east. Perimicles had scoped out the area and had chosen their position well. Calder stared at Perimicles as he made his way toward them, intently gliding through the water toward the designated meeting place. The trio of his Inner Circle had obviously miscalculated some of Marius' resources. After seeing the assembly of force Marius had gathered, Calder decided he would wait for the battle to begin before he made any decisions concerning his next move. Again, he raised the goggles, and to his amazement, he saw his nephew swimming toward the enemy line. A sinister smile spread across Calder's face. He could not believe the good fortune that he was being granted!

Ettore approached the line of soldiers. Immediately he recognized Gaillard at the same time Gaillard realized that the soldier was wearing the immunity ring was the prince. Confused at his next move, Gaillard obstinately held his ground, refusing to acknowledge he recognized Ettore. Gaillard decided he would not be the first to make a move. As cowardly as it might appear, it was not his responsibility to lead this army. Surprisingly, it was the youthful Defense League commander who made the first move toward Ettore to receive the message from the king.

"Are you in charge of this group of soldiers? I am Prince Ettore, and as a representative of my father, he would like to know your intentions for bringing this group of soldiers to stand in treasonous rebellion against him. Who are you, who sent you, and why are you here?" Outrage at such audacious disrespect toward his father made his voice more brusque than normal; however, Ettore stared confidently into the eyes of the young commander.

"This force of soldiers is the Defense League, a specially trained youth army, and I am their commander, Lieutenant Colonel Martes. Our battalion of soldiers has been apprised of the orders your father, the King of Atlantis, issued to eradicate an entire village of innocent merpeople in the province of Cecilia simply because its councilman voted against him at an Atlantic Council meeting. We have been told the Defense League is the next target of his vengeance. We will not stand by and see our people and our fellow soldiers killed, regardless if King Marius issued the orders. We will fight to the death to defend our waters and each other." He stared straight into the prince's eyes.

Ettore could hear the contempt in the lieutenant colonel's voice and see the fury in his eyes. He swam closer to the commander. "When did this attack occur? My father has been in Cecilia for the past three tides, but there has been no attack. We have been with the Atlantic Arbitrator. Someone has misled you, Commander. The King of Atlantis has issued no attack. All is well in Cecilia. He doesn't even know about your army's existence, so how could he issue an order to eliminate you and your soldiers? Come with me and let's discuss this with the King. Let's resolve this conflict through diplomacy, not bloodshed."

The soldier looked very young and uncertain. Confusion filled his face. He turned to Gaillard for guidance. "Sir, you told us of this attack in Cecilia. Is it or is it not true?" As he searched the older merman's eyes, he realized the truth of the prince's assessment: the attack had never happened; the Defense League had been deceived to compel them to rebel against their king. He moved closer to Gaillard, and with anger and desperation, he fiercely demanded, "Why? What have you done to us?" He gripped Gaillard by the shoulders and turning to the line of soldiers behind, he ordered, "Seize this man!" In the chaos of the scene, two of the DL members mistakenly grabbed Ettore. He wrestled free from their grip and threw them violently to the ocean floor.

A shrill whistle pierced the waters. The three sharks broke through the ranks of the Defense League, toppling them aside as they swam to attack the prince. Ettore tore his eyes from the two stunned soldiers just in time to see the sharks torpedoing toward him. Deftly he reached for his waterbow. He let fly one arrow that sliced through the water hitting its intended target with lethal accuracy. The wounded shark writhed in pain. Undeterred, the other two sharks reached Ettore, and their sharp serrated jaws clamped down on his body. Blood from both man and shark colored the pristine waters a crimson red. Ettore thrashed his tail loosening one of the shark's strong jaws from his injured torso. With a second whip of his tail, he sent the shark through the water to bowl down several DL soldiers. The last shark still retained a tight grip on Ettore's body, inflicting deep gashes and shredding his tender flesh. Desperately, Ettore tried to reach for his waterbow, but weakened from the loss of blood and his previous injuries, Ettore could feel his strength ebbing and himself losing the fight. Taking his free arm, he pounded on his attacker's head striking a vicious blow at his nose, but the shark could sense his victory. With one powerful bite, he opened wide his razor-sharp jaws and latched down on the prince's upper torso, inflicting a mortal wound. With one final look toward his father and his beautiful wife Julette's name on his lips, Ettore slowly sank to the ocean floor face down, his lifeless body obscured by the blood-filled water. Screams of shock from both sides reverberated through the waters.

Calder and his Inner Circle trio watched the scene unfold with entirely different reactions. The trio of mermen with Calder watched with horror the death of Ettore. Calder, however, was exultant at the elimination of Ettore and decided to seize the opportunity to make his presence known. Now was the tide to rally the troops and finish this struggle once and for all. This would be Marius' last tide as king of Atlantis. Without any preface of his next move, Calder left the shoal and swam straight for his army. Still reeling from the violent death of the prince, the trio of Calder's Inner Circle followed, darting after him, the relentless pursuit of revenge uppermost in their minds.

Calder reached the stunned Defense League troops quickly. He faced the battalion of young soldiers he had personally chosen and trained and declared in a strong voice, "Prepare yourselves for battle! You have been trained for this tide your entire lives! Make me, your future king, proud. The valiant shall be rewarded! The victory is ours this tide!"

Perimicles, Fideus, and Arnelles surrounded Calder. Their left hands were poised at the black pouches that hung on the side of their waistbelt. Perimicles interrupted Calder abruptly, "Not this tide or any other shall you gain victory. Your reign of terror ends now!" Fideus and Arnelles reached for Calder. Withdrawing the ray weapon from his waistbelt, Calder sliced through the two mermen's throats as easily as slicing a small fish. Instantly their bodies floated through the bloody waters, their faces frozen in shocked horror. Through the water sailed a spiked star thrown by Perimicles. It sliced a gash in Calder's arm causing him to drop the ray weapon. Perimicles dove to the ocean floor to retrieve the weapon. Both mermen struggled rolling around trying to wield control of the ray to eliminate the other. Twice Perimicles was wounded by the ray, but Calder never gained complete control to inflict a lethal blow.

Stunned, both sides treaded the waters unable to take their gaze from the carnage, but were as powerless to save the two men as they had been the prince. A cry of despair and grief from Marius flooded the waters and spurred both sides to action. Protocol had been disregarded. Ettore's attack and subsequent death had been completely unprovoked. The sharks had drawn first blood; now the battle raged. Waiting no longer for the Guardians to arrive, Barretto and the other marine life charged across the expanse of water to avenge their fallen prince. Both sides crashed into chaotic battle just as Perimicles and Calder fell to the ocean floor.

Orcas and both large and small fish led by Massau the Great White attacked the rogue sharks. The sheer number of marine animals fighting with the king easily overpowered the sharks and quickly injured or killed the instigators of the battle. Massau's giant jaws snapped the neck of his traitorous counterpart. With a shake of his head, he discarded the carcass and swam to continue the fight.

Some of the Defense League soldiers raced toward the other sea creatures slashing their tentacles with the ray weapons they possessed. These creatures were no match against their newly forged weapons. Barretto, aware of the shift in the tide of control, refused to leave the king's side. As fast as he could, he gathered the light from each ray weapon rendering it useless. His worried eyes scanned the waters hoping for the Guardians' arrival. Marius' countenance reflected the same concern: without the Guardians, Calder's forces would be victorious. Undeterred, the two continued to fight and hold off the young soldiers' attack, but the orcas and sea life could not withstand the assault and injury inflicted by the ray weapons. Their numbers were being reduced with every passing current.

Suddenly from the south, an army burst into view like an octopus injecting ink into the water. The Guardians attired and armed in full battle gear slashed through the murky waters intent on saving their king. On the right side of their belt hung a massive whip that with one flick of the wrist could inflict pain and death. The other side of their waistbelt held a specially made pouch containing secret weapons that dated back to the original Atlantis, weapons forged of metal by smiths long extinct and whose skill and expertise had long vanished from both the ocean and land. Part of the Guardians' training involved skills known only by the Ancients, the mentors and keepers of the forgotten martial arts who trained the Guardians.

The Guardians quickly surrounded many of the young DL soldiers who were completely inept against their older, more skilled counterparts. Most crossed their arms as a symbol of surrender. Some, however, zealously supported Calder and chose to fight to the death to defend a phantom cause. Their paltry weapons were no match for the whips and other lethal weapons the Guardians possessed. Young soldiers were cut down like flimsy stalks of seaweed. The ocean floor was littered with almost one hundred of their corpses.

Lieutenant Colonel Martes floated in a state of shock and disillusionment. Right before his eyes, everything he had believed about life and Atlantis had been completely shattered. The Defense League's mission had been nothing more than a lie. As he treaded in the midst of the death and carnage, his eyes locked with those of Perimicles who still fought to keep the ray from killing him as it had his friends.

Calder realized he needed to escape soon. Perimicles was already injured, so it would be hard for him to pursue. While the chaos of the battle was at its height, Calder released the ray weapon and carelessly turned his back to swim north. As he looked back, his eyes locked with those of his twin. The tide stood still. At that moment, hatred was a tangible thing. Calder could feel it. Marius hated him with every fiber of his being. Never taking his eyes off his brother, Marius desperately fought his way toward Calder, but too many skirmishes and bodies made the distance impossible to cover; Calder was able to escape unscathed and undetected.

Martes made his way to Perimicles. He dragged him from the battle to safety, dodging the flying weapons, thrashing whips, and swinging fists being wielded by the elite Guardians soldiers. He laid Perimicles against a rock well away from the battle. From out of his own backpack, he pulled some balm and bandages to bind up and treat the injured merman's wounds. He opened a vial and, leaning Perimicles' head back against his chest, Martes poured some medicine into the soldier's mouth. Right before Perimicles lost consciousness, he stared into the young commander's eyes. Martes whispered, "I'm sorry." The limp Guardian soldier let the dark waters take him under.

Gaillard had fled before the battle had ever begun, but not before Barretto and some of the Guardians apprehended him as he cowardly tried to swim away. One of the Guardian officers had flicked his whip as the gambling entrepreneur swam away. The whip painfully wrapped around his tail, its barbs sinking into his fins. Instantly he was pulled back like a fish on a line with his hands bound with the same whip that captured him. Blood oozed from his forehead and the trace of a bruise was already darkening his cheek. This was one gamble where he had lost it all. He had bet on the wrong brother.

In the aftermath of the battle, all eyes turned to their king cradling the lifeless body of his only son, Prince Ettore. The grief was palpable; his sobs and despair audible. Heads bowed in sorrow as they too mourned the loss of the prince. As the last vestiges of light faded from the waters, Barretto's eyes scanned the battle field and mentally he assessed the casualties. The ocean floor was littered with the bodies of the dead. Ineffable sadness filled the giant merman. Most of the dead were young mermen who had been misled and manipulated into thinking Marius was the enemy. For many currents, Barretto treaded numbly, too upset to do anything but stare. The Guardians had captured and subdued the remaining Defense League soldiers who appeared overwhelmed and completely unable to comprehend the turn of events that left so many of their comrades slain. Slowly, Barretto swam to Marius' side and made the move to help the king rise with the prince's body still in his father's arms and escort the troops back to the capital. With heavy hearts, the entire group followed the king and made the long, slow procession back to the Center City.

Chapter Forty-eight

Thad awoke to the silence of the cave. In his arms were his beautiful wife and newborn son. The baby was awake and his eyes were fixed on Thad, like he was inspecting this strange new world. Smiling, Thad reached over and traced his tiny nose and lips with his finger. Automatically his mouth opened like a baby bird waiting for a worm from its mother; obviously, he was hungry. Thad laughed at how the baby kept opening his mouth when he ran his finger over his lip. He looked like a guppy. Slowly Selale opened her eyes. A tired smile spread over her face. Thad leaned over and kissed her softly.

"He's awake, and I believe he is hungry. Like father, like son I would say. I'm hungry too." Thad teased him again by touching his finger to the baby's lip. Again, his mouth opened looking for food. Thad whispered, "He's so tiny. Look at him, Selale. Look what we created together. We did great, didn't we? Hey, what are going to name him? I haven't even thought about that. In the human world, people make a big deal out of naming their baby. They buy books, trace their lineage, and even research the name's meaning. Have you thought of his name?"

Selale smiled. "In the Mer tradition, we wait three tides, days to you, to name the baby. I'm not exactly sure of all the reasons, but it has been the tradition for many generations. Let's wait, and while we do, you can buy a book, trace your lineage, and research several names' meanings. That way in three tides, we will fulfill the traditions of both worlds." Thad laughed at her quick mind.

Feigning a look of chagrin, Thad said, "I'm sorry I brought it up." He leaned over and kissed Selale and gently took their son from her arms.

Thad stared down at his son and whispered, "Hey, little man. We're going to teach you the best of both worlds. Why, when you're down here, you'll tell your mother about the birds, cats, and dogs, and then when you're with me, you will tell me all about the dolphins, octopi, and swordfish. You truly will be a Hybrid King!" Thad laughed and confided to Selale, "I can't wait to teach him to surf and ride a bicycle. Those are two things I still remember my father teaching me." He leaned down and kissed the baby's smooth forehead. He handed the baby back to Selale. The baby's loud cry ricocheted off the cave walls.

"I must go soon and take care of all the paper work for his birth. He will need to come to the surface with me sometime in the next week. A physician must examine him and sign his birth certificate. There is other important documentation that must be completed to legitimize his birth. But, here is the good news—I have the nursery finished. I will bring you pictures of it when I return. His room is blue like his other home, the ocean." Not making a move to leave, Thad lingered beside Selale. He wanted to stay here with her forever. Taking her into his arms, he embraced her with a desperation and intensity that alarmed Selale. Tears coursed down his face as he held her.

She pulled back and searched Thad's beautiful blue eyes. "What did I do to deserve such a powerful love as yours?" She touched his cheek with her finger and tenderly kissed away his tears. "What is wrong, Thad?"

He stretched out and lay down beside Selale and the baby. Turning on his side, he looked deep into Selale's eyes. "I don't want to leave, but I must go back to my world. How can I leave when my heart is here? It will remain with you always. You have my heart, Selale. I am merely a shell without you. A day apart from you and the baby will seem like an eternity."

The baby yawned and slowly closed his eyes in sleep. Selale smiled. "Go while he is sleeping. I am tired too. As we sleep, we both will dream of you while you are gone, and when you return, you can wake us with a kiss."

Lethargically, Thad rose and put on his wetsuit and tank. He lowered himself in the still water beside the ledge where Selale and the baby lay. Before he pulled down his visor, he first kissed Selale passionately and then gave his son a kiss on the head. "I love you both. I promise I will return later. Cross my heart. Dream of us, Selale." Then, Thad disappeared under the water.

Fear clutched her heart and foreboding filled the silent cave as Selale watched the last ripples from Thad's departure touch the sides of the cave. She whispered, "Hurry back to us."

He swam quickly down through the mountain of debris and out into the ever-lightening waters. Day would dawn about the time he reached the surface. A concerned furrow wrinkled his forehead as he drew nearer to the surface. His boat was not where he had left it. Breaking the surface of the water, he treaded water and straining his eyes, searched in every direction for his missing boat. Nothing but blue water could be seen horizon to horizon. The sun was peeking just over the horizon and angry orange streaks colored the southern sky. A storm was coming. He began to feel the first flicker of panic burning in his stomach. He did not have enough oxygen in the tank to return to the cave. If he did make it to the cave, he had no way to return to the surface. Thad faced a dangerous dilemma.

He turned toward the west and resigned himself to swim to shore. It was a little more than two miles. He had an emergency floatation device in his supply bag if he started tiring before he spotted land, but for now, he resigned himself to the arduous swim. It was the only way to the shore. *Swimming starts with a single stroke*, he remembered his father saying to him. Repeating the adage over and over in his head, he swam west with even, deliberate strokes, so he could conserve his strength.

•   •   •   •   •

Calder made his escape fast and headed straight to the capital. If he arrived well before the others, he had an opportunity to gather his documents and personal things and make it out of the capital long before anyone knew he had been there. He knew exactly where he would go. He had planned this alternative in case something went wrong. No one knew his hideout existed—not Gaillard, not his

Inner Circle. The betrayal of his most trusted advisors cut deep. Calder tried not to dwell on it right now when he had only a few currents to gather the necessary items and retreat into hiding. He would have plenty of tides to think about Perimicles then. He took from his office only what was essential. Exiting through the portal, he never once looked back as he swam southwest to safety.

Martes had remained behind at the battle field to tend to the Guardian officer's wounds and supervise the recovery of the fallen soldiers from both sides. He felt the weight of responsibility on his shoulders. The scene replayed over and over in his head, and he kept trying to somehow rewrite the conclusion. But every glance at the gruesome scene produced the same tragic ending. His friends and fellow soldiers were dead. Could he have done more to prevent the slaughter? Should he have known Gaillard and Calder's real intentions for the Defense League? He wondered how he could ever forgive himself for not being more discerning. His blind loyalty had cost nearly one hundred of his fellow soldiers their lives.

Perimicles stirred and slowly opened his eyes. It took him a little while to get oriented to his surroundings. He spotted the young DL officer who had dragged him from the battle. He sat on a rock and looked as if he was completely crushed. His young shoulders sagged from defeat and his head hung looking down at the ocean floor, staring at nothing but the sand. Perimicles examined his injured arm where the ray weapon had sliced through the skin in the scuffle with Calder. The wound wasn't long, but it was deep. Surprisingly, the ray weapon he and Calder had fought to obtain hung at his side secured in his waistbelt beside his weapon pouch. The young soldier saw Perimicles moving and swam over to his side.

Perimicles was the first to speak. "What is your name, soldier?" He stared straight into the young soldier's eyes. To his credit, the DL commander met Perimicles' eyes with a steady, respectful gaze.

"My name is Lieutenant Colonel Martes, sir. I am…was in charge of the Defense League, also known as Calder's minions. That is, what is left of us." Bitterness tinged the voice of Martes.

Perimicles felt compassion for the youthful commander. "Don't be too hard on yourself, Lieutenant. You weren't the only ones fooled by Calder's charms. Look around you. The ocean floor is littered with them. You were prudent enough to understand his ulterior motive before he rallied the troops to join in the fight. You tried to warn your fellow soldiers. You did everything in this situation that you could to protect them. I and the two slain Guardian officers infiltrated Calder's Inner Circle." Just mentioning his fallen friends brought pain and grief to Perimicles. He cleared his throat and continued, "We have been aware of his intentions for many tides, but when we first heard from his lips the traitorous plans he had for the kingdom, it shocked all of us. Calder can be very charming and convincing."

"Sir, we—"

"Call me Perimicles. You rescued me, so I believe that puts us on a first name basis. Forgive me for interrupting you. Please continue." Perimicles waited for Martes to regain his composure.

"We were told that King Marius had annihilated an entire village in the southern province because their councilman had disagreed with a decision the king had made. We were told he killed everyone, mermen, mermaids, and merchildren. Everything Calder told us we believed blindly. Not once did any of us question the legitimacy of these claims. Thinking on it now, I realize that I have been a fool. Marius has never given any of us a reason to believe this sort of lie. Why didn't I question it, Perimicles? It was my duty, and I—I failed."

Perimicles swam to sit beside the grief-stricken soldier. "Your duty was to do as ordered. The one to blame here is not you. It is Calder. These mermen died because of his ambition to be king, nothing less, nothing more. The way I see it, you have a choice. You can react or act. Reaction is to sit around help-lessly blaming yourself. What good can come from that? Action, however, is to bring Calder to justice for this atrocity. So, young Martes, which will it be?" Perimicles didn't have to wait long for an answer.

"You are right. Calder is to blame. Starting this tide, I want to make him pay for the death of my fellow soldiers, my friends." Again Martes' eyes trav-eled to the battlefield.

"Good decision. Now help me swim to my company to report that I sur-vived Calder's assault. Let's make a pact. Our mission is to bring Calder to justice. I will not rest until he pays with his life for the deaths of Prince Ettore, Fideus, and Arnelles. They never had a chance." His hand ran down the side of his tail to touch the ray weapon. Martes eyed the weapon and nodded.

"I believe you earned the right to carry that weapon. You won the fight fairly. When I dragged you from the battlefield, that weapon lay right beside you. Calder left without taking the time to retrieve it; he didn't have a current to spare. Marius almost caught up with him. Unfortunately, he did escape. I agree to this pact. I too will not rest until he faces the consequences of taking these young soldiers' lives." Perimicles extended his hand. Martes eagerly grabbed Perimicles' forearm to seal the pact.

Perimicles released Martes' arm. He pulled the ray weapon out from his waistbelt. "I want you to keep this weapon for me. I am already armed with weapons. Over the next several tides, you will be faced with opposition and quite possibly death threats. Protect this weapon; use it if you must, until I come find you to retrieve it. Without it, you are defenseless." Perimicles extended the weapon toward Martes. The DL officer saluted his superior.

"Sir, Perimicles, I will not let you down. You have my sworn word from one officer to another." Martes took the proffered weapon from Perimicles and examining it closely, finally nodded and slipped it into his waistbelt. Then, helping the wounded officer off the ocean floor, they swam toward the group of Guardians assembled near the battlefield.

· · · · ·

Thad had swum almost a mile. The shore, unfortunately, was still nowhere on the horizon. He stopped to rest for a few minutes and clung to the floatation device. He was glad he had it and secured it around his midriff. It very well could save his life. Again his eyes scanned the horizon looking for the *Sea Science*. He knew it was wishful thinking, but it was worth a try. Seeing nothing, he sighed and continued his swimming. He had so much to do when he returned home. So much of the legalities of the baby's birth had to be put into action in the next week. He thought of Selale and the baby sleeping in the cave. Fear knotted in his stomach. He must keep swimming. They were counting on him.

Suddenly off in the distance, he spotted someone break the surface of the water. Knowing there was no ship anywhere on the horizon, Thad realized it must be a merman. Staring intently at the distant figure, Thad recognized the distinct profile. It was Marius! Luck was on his side! He waved his arm high above his head excitedly as he tried to get the merman's attention. Yelling with all his might, Thad screamed, "Marius! Over here!" The merman's head turned slightly, and he veered toward Thad. As the figure swam closer, Thad slowly dropped his hand. The merman that approached was not Marius, though he resembled him. Turning quickly, Thad tried to swim away from the approaching figure, but he was easily outmatched in the water.

Calder swam toward the human swimming in the ocean and waving his hands in the air. Who did he expect to be out here? Maybe he was out here with others. Instantly on guard, Calder searched the water's surface, but no one was around, just this lone man. He saw it as an opportunity to rid the waters of one more human. Good riddance. Thoughts of Marius came to him. Yes, good old Marius would save this foolish human. That thought made Calder all the more determined to kill this intruder. As he approached, the man initially acted like he recognized him, but Calder knew that was impossible. Suddenly, the human yelled his brother's name. Outrage flooded Calder when he realized that this human knew his brother and by his first name. Like a torpedo, he made a straight line for his target. He smirked at the human thinking he could out-swim a merman. Turning, Calder thrashed his tail hard knocking the human back and sending him skidding over the water. Thad, temporarily dazed, floated on the water. Shaking his head, he frantically kicked his legs and tried to distance himself from the merman. Diving down, Calder swam underwater toward his enemy and suddenly grabbed the human's legs. The last thing that crossed Thad's mind was Selale and his son as he was dragged underwater.

Martes had left Perimicles and now made his way alone back to the capital. The rest of the Defense League troops had been detained by the Guardians and were to be escorted back. With the help of Perimicles, Martes was allowed to slip out of the area undetected. The long, solitary swim back to the Center City enabled him to analyze and ponder the events of the last tide. Resolutely, he decided he would never again blindly follow anyone. He would question everything. Gone was the naive young merman he had been. He had died today on the battle field along with many of his lifelong friends. He would spend the rest of his life trying to atone for that mistake. He didn't know if he could ever do enough to earn forgiveness, especially from himself.

Both sky and ocean had darkened, and the waters of Atlantis roiled making dark shadows appear that usually occurred much later in the tide. A storm would arrive in the morntide. Martes quickened his pace and swam up toward lighter waters. Up ahead in the distance, he spotted two figures, one dragging the other down into the depths. Confused, the young merman made his way toward the scene. As he approached, to his amazement he recognized the strong figure of Calder who was towing a human down through the murky waters. Anger made Martes' heart beat harder, faster. He couldn't believe his good fortune. Here was his chance to kill his sworn enemy and to bring justice to his slain friends.

As he neared Calder, he withdrew the ray weapon bestowed upon him by Perimicles. Upon activation, the ray's metal glowed in the dark waters creating a beam of hot blue light that cast an incandescent glow around Martes. With focused determination, he streaked his way toward Calder and the human.

So intent was Calder on killing the human, he failed to see the incoming merman until he and the beam of light in his hand were nearly upon him. Startled, Calder released the foot of the human and turned, surprised to see the familiar face of Martes, his Defense League commander. A relieved smile spread over Calder's face. Slowly it changed to alarm when he saw the intense hatred burning in the eyes of his once loyal commander. Martes' hand wielded the ray weapon he had left behind on the battlefield. Calder headed for the surface away from the human's unconscious, sinking body.

Chasing Calder to the surface, Martes' voice rang with bitterness as he spoke to his former mentor, "I have come to avenge the deaths of my fellow Defense League soldiers. Their blood is on your hands. Now you will pay with your own blood. To think that I once idolized you, wanted to be just like you. How foolish and naive I was! I want to be nothing like you. You are evil and selfish; you epitomize everything I now despise. It will give me great pleasure to rid the waters of Atlantis of you." Both broke the surface of the ocean and each faced the other. Just then the skies opened and rain poured over the water. Thunder and lightning crashed around both mermen. Martes swam straight toward Calder. The ray illuminated the dark waters creating a blue nimbus of light that reflected off the surface enveloping both mermen.

Calder was ready for the attack and swiftly dodged the slash of the weapon. Recognizing he was defenseless against so powerful a weapon as the ray, Calder turned to flee. While he was pulling away, he sent a few words back in reply to the young, vengeful merman, "Someone has brainwashed you, my young commander. I am not your enemy; Marius is. Remain loyal to me and when, not if, I control Atlantis, you will have great power. If you betray me, you like all the others will be executed. What do you say? Do we have an agreement? Think about this offer carefully. I won't extend it to you ever again." Calder had distanced himself from the young merman. Halting his escape, he turned to face Martes to hear his response.

"Not for all the power in these waters or the threat of death would I ever align myself with you. These promises won't circumvent my vengeance. I will die trying to make you atone for my friends' deaths. That is the one promise I will make to you. You may escape this tide, but know that my singular mission in life will be to pursue you until either you or I or both of us die. Nothing will thwart me from that goal. Flee, coward. There has been enough bloodshed for one tide. I will have my vengeance some other tide."

Without a glance back, Calder retreated south. Martes slid the ray in his waistbelt and dove down through the waters to rescue the human Calder had been drowning. He scooped up the lifeless body and hauled him back to the surface. By now, the rain had settled in and the brunt of the storm had moved east. Thunder gently rolled across the heavens reverberating off the waters like an echo. Martes recognized the breathing apparatus used by humans. He tried putting it in the man's mouth. A faint pulse beat in the man's chest. A huge bluish-purple bump grew ever larger on the man's temple. His injuries were life-threatening. Torn by his next course of action, Martes decided to take the human to the shore. It was risky. He could be seen if he ventured too close, but after all the death he had witnessed this tide, he just couldn't let the man perish. Sighing, he set his sight on the shore and traveled to the northwest. Martes knew the exact location where he would place the human.

As he approached the shoreline, Martes scanned the horizon for nearby humans. Satisfied that nobody was in sight, he swam into the cove. Here, the water was deep and several human-made structures lined the water's edge, which stretched from the shore far out into the cove. With all his strength, he lifted the man up onto the one farthest out.

The man stirred slightly and whispered with his last breath, "Marius? Tell Selale I love her." The human's eyes closed on his lifeless body, and once more he fell silent.

Alarmed, Martes could hardly believe his ears. He had understood two of the words. This human knew Marius and Selale. Of that, Martes was certain, but how, he did not know. A sound on the shore startled the young merman out of his musings, and without a current's delay, he swam back to the safety of the waters of Atlantis leaving the fate of the human in his own kind's hands. He had tried to save his life, but chances were this human would not make it. Calder had shed more blood. If nothing else, Martes would request to see the king and pass on the message. That was the only thing left he could do for the man. With his sight set on his destination, he swam toward the Center City.

Chapter Forty-nine

"Could there be a darker tide than this one?" Marius asked his friend Barretto. He gazed out the chamber panel toward the Center City where families of the slain Defense League members had gathered in an angry mob last eventide, demanding vengeance. As he peered out through the dark waters, all was still, yet a current of unease still flowed through the capital. "Has all of Atlantis gone crazy in the last three tides? My son is dead and my life-long friend and adviser Sandoval is gone. Calder has disappeared and now a riot is brewing in the capital center. It is Calder who has caused everyone's grief and sorrow. The families still won't meet with me?" It was more of a statement than a question he posed to the arbitrator.

Barretto solemnly shook his head. "No, my lord, their grief is still fresh. Give it a few more tides before you approach them again about a meeting."

"Don't they understand I lost a son as well?" Anger caused Marius' voice to rise. At Barretto's raised brows, Marius closed his eyes and slowly shook his head. "I'm sorry. My sorrow gives me no reason to raise my voice to you. Forgive me." He swam back to his seat behind his simple desk and once more gazed across the Center City of Atlantis. He had not been back to the capital one tide before the waters darkened with a storm of anger, hostility, and controversy. He had not even seen the baby! Sorrow prevailed over his joy robbing him of the opportunity to rejoice at the Hybrid King's birth. He had comprehended that with the baby's birth would come pain and suffering, but he had not realized it would be so soon or that he personally would pay so high a price. The scene of Ettore's death replayed over and over in his mind. He closed his eyes as the pain threatened to overwhelm him.

Barretto gazed at his friend, helpless to aid him with his grief. He too felt guilt and sorrow at the young prince's tragic demise. Ettore's death had happened so quickly so that not he, nor Marius, nor any of the Guardians could have saved him. Barretto watched the play of emotions on the king's face. He could not understand the depth of his grief at watching his only son die right in front of his eyes. Barretto knew it must be nearly unbearable. Marius was a strong person, no doubt; however, the death of a child affected merpeople differently than ordinary deaths. It was a loss felt in the depth of their beings. Compounding Marius' grief were also the death of his childhood friend Sandoval and the rioting parents of the slain Defense League. Barretto had made the decision without a moment's hesitation to stay in the capital near the king. He would do everything he could to alleviate the responsibilities and duties required of Marius during this difficult tide. He swam to the king's desk and sat down on the bench facing him.

"Ettore's funeral will be the next tide, my lord. What would you have me and my AA officers do? Our presence, along with the Guardians, will be everywhere, on every stretch of the funeral procession. Your safety and Selale's are our utmost concern. We will protect you from the crowds. I will not leave your side. If I could change this tragic turn of events I would, my friend. Have you told Selale?" Barretto leaned forward and rested his elbows on the desk as he stared at the king.

Marius put his face in his hands. All he could do was shake his head. Silence filled the king's office chamber. Dusky light filtered through the chamber panels and floated through the waters. Barretto took his hand and gently summoned more light into the somber office, gathering it slowly to dispel the darkness that seemed to penetrate and pervade the chamber. With each ray that touched his hand, the chamber glowed and warmed gradually. Marius raised his head, and a sad smile touched his lips.

"The night is nearly over; day dawns and comes on the tide, my king." Barretto offered the light he held in his hand to Marius. Marius tried to grasp the light as if it was a tangible thing, but it sifted through his fingers like sand. Rising, he inhaled the water deeply and exhaled it with one long, cleansing breath.

"Will you go with me to tell Selale about Ettore? It will give you a chance to welcome the Hybrid King and offer me some strength by your being there. I will need your light when I impart this dark news to my daughter about her brother. Telling her will be one of the most difficult things I have ever done. I don't think I can face it alone." Marius turned to his giant friend. Barretto nodded solemnly. Without waiting another current, Marius swam through the office portal setting his sights on his own chamber. Barretto swam right behind him.

Light had somewhat brightened the waters as the mermen arrived at Marius' chamber. It was still early in the tide. Few creatures moved and even fewer mermen. Only the patrols could be seen making their rounds. Their presence exuded security throughout the capital and sent the message that Marius still had firm control on the waters he ruled.

Marius opened the portal to his chamber and entered in. He stopped and turned toward Barretto. Placing his hand on his friend's mammoth arm, Marius said, "I trust you with what I am about to reveal. Aside from my daughter and Monica, you are about to see something that no other merman has seen. Prepare to be amazed. I will tell you more when we have less sorrow on our hearts. Follow me." Marius turned and left the perplexed arbitrator to follow. They entered the king's personal chamber, and Marius pressed the portal release that revealed the long corridor that led to Beulah Cave. Without looking back or explaining, Marius swam ahead knowing that Barretto followed closely behind.

Selale awakened to the quiet of the cave. Sitting up, she searched the cave for some sign of Thad's return, but he still had not returned. The baby stirred and was ready to be fed. Selale laughed at his groping mouth. Monica was still there. She had been waiting for Selale to wake up. She swam to Selale's side when she realized both she and the baby were awake.

"Has Thad not come back, Monica? He told me he would be gone less than one tide. He has been gone for quite a while, almost an entire tide. I wonder what has hindered his return." Worry creased Selale's brow. That uneasy feeling that she had felt upon Thad's departure resurfaced and caused her heart to beat fast and hard.

Monica tried to soothe Selale's worries. "I'm sure he will return soon. He was so excited about the baby. Humans measure time differently than we do, don't they? Most of them seem to be in such a hurry."

Selale's anxiety was not allayed. Foreboding pressed down upon her like something tangible and caused her chew her lip. The baby, sensing her tension, reached up and placed his tiny hand on her chest. Peace poured from his hand through her. She glanced down startled at what had just happened and stared with wonder at her newborn son. Stroking his small fuzzy head, she whispered, "Thank you." She kissed his forehead and tenderly rocked him side to side. "No matter what happens, I know this baby is destined for greatness. He is the future savior of our people. The naming ceremony won't happen for almost two more tides. Thad will be here, and we can discuss names. Hopefully we can agree on a name before the ceremony. It can't come soon enough! I want to call him by his name." She continued to smile at the baby and sang to him, mimicking the song played by the globe.

The sound of bubbles gurgling the water in the center of the cave disrupted the silence and alerted them that someone was coming. Selale's heart leapt thinking that Thad had finally returned. Smiling broadly, she sat up and held the baby close to her. Her excitement and smile faded somewhat when she saw her father and a gigantic merman surface in the water. The large merman's confused expression matched Selale's. Surprised at her father's arrival to the cave, she exclaimed, "Papa! Come welcome the baby! I am so glad to see you." Marius swam to his daughter's side and pulled himself out of the water to rest on the stone ledge beside Selale. She studied her father's face, but his eyes were on the sleeping baby in her arms.

Marius reached over and then paused. He looked at his beautiful daughter and reverently asked, "May I hold the Hybrid King?" When Selale nodded, he gathered the sleeping baby in his large arms and cradled him gently.

Barretto took in the scene. It was surreal, like something out of a dream for him. This baby was the long-expected savior of the merpeople. The child had legs like a human. Had he not seen the princess holding the baby, he would think it was a human baby. Tearing his eyes away from the three generations of the royal family, his eyes wandered to the cave itself. It was spectacular, all gold and shining. Off in an alcove of the cave, he spotted an older merwoman. She smiled and nodded in understanding. He swam over to her in order to give Marius more time alone with his daughter and the baby. As he drew nearer to the merwoman, recognition registered in both of their faces.

"Ah, Monica! We meet again! How long has it been?" Barretto extended his arm to embrace her.

Monica let the massive merman wrap her in his arms. Smiling she laughed, "Barretto! The cave is spectacular, isn't it? Aren't you a balm for these old eyes! It has been twenty annutides at least since we last met. Not that I am not happy to see you, but why has Marius brought you here? It must be important to share the secret of this magical place and to disclose the secret of the Hybrid King's birth. What is the meaning of your being here?" She grew serious, and her smiled faded when Barretto confirmed her speculation by nodding.

"Come sit with me on the ledge, Monica." The two moved to the rock ledge at the back of the alcove. There, Barretto confided to Monica, "Ettore has been murdered. The king wanted me here to help tell Selale. His death was sudden, brutal, and carried out right in front of Marius. We both were powerless to stop it. The king is devastated, Monica, absolutely devastated. Do you have a remedy for grief?" His eyes wondered back to Marius, the princess, and the baby. Sadness dropped Barretto's voice even lower.

Monica lowered her head and silently shook it back and forth willing the news not to be true, but knowing that this was only the beginning of the tragic events that the baby's birth ushered in. Monica whispered, "When? When did all this happen? Tell me, Barretto, what led to his death? While you are re-counting the events, I will concoct an elixir for Selale. She will need it when Marius imparts the news." Monica swam to her potions bag on the opposite ledge and began preparations to concoct a strong elixir while Barretto told her of the battle between the king's forces and those Calder had assembled.

In the center of Beulah Cave, Marius held his sleeping grandson in his arms. His thumb circled the sun-shaped mark on his left shoulder. He examined each finger and ran his hand down the baby's long slender legs. "Legs,"

Marius murmured softly and chuckled. Turning toward Selale, he said softly, "Such a strange word and concept for me to comprehend. It is almost too much for me to take in. All these events have already been set into motion. The earthquake, the pearl's beam of light, and...." Marius voice faded as he stared at the tiny Hybrid King. Tears welled up in his eyes as he stared at the baby. For several currents he sat holding the baby in silence and wonder. The baby stirred and turned himself in Marius' strong arms to snuggle closer. He held the baby tighter and a surge of love and fierce protection flooded his entire being. This baby was not only his grandson but also the Hybrid King, the long-awaited one prophesied to come so many centennitides before.

Selale looked at her father as he tenderly held her son. It felt right somehow that her father had an immediate bond with the baby. She whispered, "So you felt the earthquake too? Oh, Papa, it was a magical moment. Shortly after the baby was born, fish and other sea creatures came to honor the baby! They kept surfacing to see him, bowing their heads back into the water for most of the tide here in the cave. How did they know? There is so much I don't understand, but I know that these events confirm who my child is. He is the Hybrid King, Papa. Tell me about the pearl's beam of light. Was it like the last time here in the cave?"

Marius nodded. "It happened right before the earthquake and yes, it was similar except on a grander magnitude. The light was so bright that it knocked Barretto and me from our seats. We were at the Benthic tunnel that had been repaired. The light streaked from the pearl and bounced around the room like a nervous school of fish evading a predator! It was...awesome." Marius never took his eyes from the baby. He continued, "Where's Thad? I figured he would be here with you and the baby."

Worry once again filled Selale at the mention of Thad's name. She shook her head and pressed down the panic she felt deep inside. Sounding much calmer than she really felt, she said, "He left early yestertide, but he has yet to return. I know he had many things to which he had to attend regarding the baby's birth, but I do wish he would hurry back and set my anxious mind to rest. Oh, Papa, he was so overjoyed! We discussed names, but we agreed the baby won't be named for another tide. When Thad comes back, we will decide on his name." Once more a comfortable silence settled on them as they watched the baby sleep.

Movement on the other side of the cave caught Selale's attention. "Who is your friend? I need not ask if he can be trusted. He would not be here otherwise, but why bring him now?" As if on cue, the large merman and Monica swam toward the three of them.

"Barretto, I would like to introduce you to my daughter, Selale, and her baby, my grandson, our future king. Selale, this is one of my oldest and most trusted friends, Barretto." The incredibly large merman bowed his head in honor. Without waiting long, Marius continued, "Selale, I have brought Barretto here for me. I am afraid I have imposed upon his friendship, but I must impart some very difficult news to you." At that announcement, Selale drew in a terrified gasp and covered her mouth with a trembling hand.

"Wh—What news, Papa?" Selale stuttered.

Closing his eyes, Marius fought to maintain control of his emotions. He knew he had to be strong for Selale's sake as well as for the baby. His heart ached deep in his chest from the pain of his loss and for the pain his daughter soon would experience. He choked out the words, "It's Ettore. He was murdered yestertide by Calder's sharks. He's gone, Selale. He's gone." Marius took the arm not holding the baby and enfolded his daughter's body with it as if he were trying to shield her from the inevitable pain of grief the news would bring.

Selale sobbed and vehemently shook her head, "No, no, no! No, Papa, no! Not Ettore." Her wail of despair rang through the cave. Powerless to stop her grief, Marius held her and let her sobs mix with his own. They sat clinging to each other for comfort in their sorrow. The baby stirred and squirmed in Marius' arms. All Marius could do was draw his grandson closer to his chest. The baby stretched his hand up and this time placed it on Marius' chest. A sense of serenity emanated from his tiny hand through Marius' entire being, filling him with comfort. Selale too felt the power of the baby's touch flow through both of them. Though their hearts were still heavy with grief, the pain seemed somehow more bearable because they had each other and the baby. For several tides they sat huddled together in silence, offering comfort and strength to each other in their loss.

"It's true," Marius said with reverence. "He has the Gift of Healing." He turned to Monica and Barretto who treaded the waters on the other side of the cave's deep pool. "He has the Mystical Gift of Healing so absent from our waters since my great-grandmere's death. No doubt he has the other gifts as well." Leaning over, Marius kissed the baby's fuzzy head and faintly whispered, "Thank you, Tadpole."

Monica swam to Selale' side and offered her the restorative elixir. "Here, Selale, drink this. You need to rest and recover." Pointing to the squirming baby, Monica observed, "He's hungry, isn't he? Nurse the baby, and then this will help you rest. The three of us can take care of the baby while you sleep." Monica handed the thick, pasty liquid to Selale. She was too heavy with grief to argue. Marius handed the baby back to Selale. Then he and Barretto swam to the other side of the cave to give them some privacy.

Marius led Barretto to the wall containing the prophecy and rested his chin on the rock ledge with his tail still in the water. With his back to his friend, his eyes scanned the familiar words he had read at least a hundred times. "It's true, isn't it, Barretto? It's all coming true. I'd be a fool if I didn't admit that I am afraid. I'm afraid of what else his birth will cost me." Turning around to look at his large defender and friend, he asked, "Does that make me selfish or a terrible king?"

Barretto could see the pain in the king's face and could hear it in his voice. Grief and guilt were consuming Marius. Placing a consoling hand on the king's shoulder, Barretto offered his reassurance, "No, my lord. It makes you a merman. Tragedy has a way of leveling the ocean floor. Regardless of our status in society, eventually grief comes to call everyone's name. I'm just sorry I wasn't able to do more to stop its coming."

Marius turned back to the prophecy. "I couldn't protect my son. How can I protect Selale and the baby? She and the baby's father have decided to raise him as a human. Again, that fulfills the prophecy. But how can I let this child go? The human world is beyond the reach of my realm. I know his father will do everything in his power to guard the child, but I won't be able to protect him out of these waters." He once again placed his chin on his arms which rested on the ledge. He stared at the etching without reading it.

"My friend, may I offer the advice you once gave to me? Trust. It's about trust. We have to believe that in the end, good will be triumphant over evil. Isn't that what the prophecy eventually predicts?" Barretto swam over to the ledge, and he too stared up at the prophecy.

Marius nodded. "Good will win, but at what price? Must I lose everyone I love? Ettore, Sandoval. I can't lose Selale. She is all I have left. Somehow I will protect her and the baby." Just then Monica swam over with the baby right in front of her. His tiny legs looked awkward flailing in the water. Marius couldn't get used to not seeing a tail. The baby instinctively seemed to know how to swim and breathe underwater. A sigh of relief escaped from Marius. This child was both merman and human. His being able to breathe underwater fulfilled the definitive quality of the prophecy. They truly were in the presence of the kingdom's future king.

Both Marius and Barretto laughed at his tiny legs kicking in the water. They dove down in the water and played with him. In spite of the legs, the baby's innate movements were still fluid and propelled him easily from one merman to the other. He swam back and forth to each merman. Marius clutched the little boy and swam back to the surface. Holding the baby with one arm, Marius pulled himself back up onto the ledge. Barretto joined him. Perched on the other side of the alcove, Monica had watched the scene unfold. She laughed at the two mermen's actions.

Barretto smiled at the baby. He looked at Marius, "May I hold the child?"

"Of course you may." Turning to the baby, Marius said softly, "Go to Barretto, Tadpole." He handed the squirming baby to his friend.

"Tadpole, eh? Come here, child." Gently he lifted the baby high up into the air and brought him back down again to rest in his arm. Barretto's massive arm dwarfed the tiny body, but the baby nestled contentedly in the crook of his elbow and stared up into the large merman's smiling face. Barretto stretched out his other arm, and with his hand slowly summoned the light. Obediently, it came to his fingers where it swirled and gathered into marble-like orbs. The baby's eyes focused on the light. Barretto brought the small glowing globes of light close to the baby. The tiny fingers of the Hybrid King opened and closed instinctively gathering the light from out of Barretto's hand into his own. Light danced around his little fingers like they were ablaze with what the humans called fire. A hiccough from the baby dispelled the light like a bubble bursting. Barretto's joyful, deep laugh echoed through the cave.

Marius' laughter mingled with his friend's. The baby yawned and almost instantly he fell asleep. Monica swam over and took the baby from the mermen so he could rest. Marius turned to his long-time friend and confided, "I'm so glad you came here with me, Barretto. Thank you for your friendship and for bringing light during my dark time. My heart is still heavy over the loss of Ettore, but the joy this baby brings will help balm my soul to help me begin to heal and soothe my overbearing sorrow." Barretto nodded in understanding.

"It's amazing—isn't it?—that we already know he has at least two of the Mystical Gifts, and he is only two tides old! Just think if he possesses all six! The prophecy does mention he will be endowed with them all. How many centennitides has it been since all the Mystical Gifts were present in and used by the merpeople of Atlantis?"

"It stretches too far back to comprehend, your majesty. You know, I wish I could mentor the boy in the use of Light Gathering. I could teach him the skills in just a few tides that have taken me many annutides to master on my own. You say he will live with his father? Where is this human? Have you met him?" Barretto couldn't help but feel curiosity about the baby's father.

"I have met him, and I must say, he seems quite different from the way most humans are perceived by us merpeople. Maybe I am just being idealistic, but I sense good in him, Barretto. What he and Selale feel for one another is real. I'm not certain why he isn't here, but I know he would be here if he could. He had numerous tasks to which he had to attend to prepare for the baby's birth on land. I don't know how long he will wait to take the baby up there, but for Selale's sake, I hope it will be a while. She needs time with the baby. It will be difficult for her once the baby is gone with her human." Marius stared across the cave at the baby sleeping beside his daughter. He could only imagine how the baby's leaving would affect Selale. His own heart was grief-stricken over losing his son. He wondered if he would feel complete happiness ever again after losing Ettore. Would Selale feel the same way after the baby went to live on land?

The tide passed quickly, and soon another would arrive. Ettore's funeral would be at midtide. Marius and Barretto left the cave swimming back through the same route from which they had come. The events over the course of the last three tides had sealed their friendship for eternity. Barretto departed for the Center City to make the final arrangements for the heightened security that would be needed to protect Marius and Selale. Unrest floated through the waters of Atlantis like a toxic pollutant and threatened to destroy the safety of not only the royal family, but also the entire social structure of the society. His primary concern was protecting the king and princess during the solemn funeral procession as they paid their respect to the son and brother whom they had fiercely loved, and yet so tragically and suddenly lost. He arrived at the Center City and summoned all the AA officers into his makeshift office at the SARC.

Marius had detailed the plans for the procession and the subsequent funeral plans to Barretto the tide before, and now he outlined each officer's duty and assignment to his assembled forces. Perimicles had arrived, and after consulting with Barretto, readied the Guardians to be on high alert. Their presence would infiltrate the crowds that were expected to gather to honor the fallen prince and keep a watchful eye out for any subversive activity either from Calder's allies or the slain Defense League parents.

The current arrived for the royal procession to begin. Julette, Marius and Selale swam behind the large shell that held the remains of Ettore as it was being carried by four of his closest attendants. During the long funeral march, the waters remained muted in a cool, somber gray. A storm raged on the surface of the waters above, and its thick, turbulent clouds prohibited the sun's warmth and light from permeating the water. Citizens from all over the entire kingdom had thronged to the Center City to pay homage to the murdered prince, and now they lined the avenue that ran through the heart of Atlantis' capital. A mournful spirit subdued them, and the procession moved slowly by the almost silent crowd. Once the funeral procession had come to the edge of the capital's boundaries right outside the Center City, the final portion of the procession toward the Royal Catacombs, the final resting place reserved for the ruling families of Atlantis for millenitides, was made alone by the family.

As the catacomb guards pressed the portal release, each family member came to bid a personal and final farewell. First, Julette came and lay her head down on the ornate shell that housed her husband's body. With one final touch, she swam into the arms of Marius. Next, Selale swam to the shell. On top she placed a small stone figure of a dolphin that Ettore had carved out of a rock and had given her as a present when she was just a small merchild. She gave the shell one last caress and joined her father gathering Julette into her arms. Finally, Marius moved to the shell that encased his son's body. With both hands, he raised Ettore's golden waterbow high into the water and closed his eyes. Reverently he lowered the magnificent bow and positioned it on top of the shell. Nodding for the attendants to proceed, they entered the ancient catacombs carrying the shell to its final resting place.

Long after everyone had left, Marius remained at the catacombs. Selale and Julette, offering comfort to each other, had traveled arm in arm back to the Center City. Barretto had remained on the outskirts of the ancient burial site waiting for the king to make his way back to the capital. He would not permit the king to travel alone. Too many dangers lurked in the shadows, and in his grief, the king was vulnerable. Near eventide, Marius made the move to travel back to his chamber near the capital. Barretto signaled to the guards the king's intentions, setting them on high alert for any potential threat. Without incidence, Marius arrived back to the capital and turned his sight toward his chamber.

As he passed the edge of the capital building, a group of six mermen swam from out of the corner and grabbed Marius. He struggled to free himself and thrashed his tail to send two of the attackers sailing through the water. Without a current's delay, Barretto and four of his AA guards apprehended the assailants.

One of them spat out to Marius, "You murderer! We will never rest until you pay for our son's deaths. This tide or some other tide, perhaps many annutides may pass, but you will pay in blood for their lives. I hope you constantly look over your shoulder, you and Princess Selale. Eventually, one of us—and there are many—will avenge our sons just when you least expect it. You might have stopped the six of us, but we won't rest until we see you and your family destroyed completely." The others echoed his vow of revenge.

Fury swept through Marius' entire being. He roared, "You Fools! Don't you realize that Calder caused the death of your sons and mine? I share the grief you feel too! He attacked my forces and then compelled your sons to blindly follow him. My men had no idea whom we were fighting. Calder spilled the first drop of blood, not my forces. Why can't you understand that he is the culprit you should blame and not I?" As they were being taken away, the mermen were deaf to Marius' reasoning. The king, wracked with anger, confusion, hurt, and most of all, fear for his daughter and grandson, treaded where he was, staring at his attackers until they were out of sight. At last, he turned abruptly and swam to his chamber. Barretto followed the king until he was safely inside. Positioning two more AA guards outside the portal, he traveled back to the SARC chamber for the rest of the tide. He hoped that perhaps the dawn of a new tide would bring more tranquil waters, but somewhere in the back of his mind lurked the fearful thought that peace would not visit the waters of Atlantis for many tides.

Chapter Fifty

Michael and Charise awoke the next morning with the strange events of the night before still fresh on their minds. Although it was early, Michael willed himself to wait until after he had eaten breakfast to call Thad again. His best friend sure did have some explaining to do. He could feel Charise's worry as they sat side by side at the table. Reaching out his hand, he took her smaller one in his.

"It's all right. I will bring him here so you can see him, okay? I know you are worried about him. So am I. You can chastise him for making you worry so much. You know how much he hates to upset you." Michael smiled at her trying to reassure himself as much as her.

"I will let him have it! You tell me how I am supposed to concentrate at this meeting while I am worried about him." She leaned over and kissed her husband. Collecting the dishes, she put them in the sink. "I've got to go. I'm supposed to be there early to go over the notes for the presentation. We really need this grant for the library. Let me know when you hear from Thad. I will be in the meeting for a couple of hours. After that, I will be in my office. Love you!" With a final kiss, she grabbed her purse and left.

Michael called Thad once again, but still no one answered. The morning was passing quickly. Where was Thad? Trying to keep busy, he decided to unpack the suitcases and wash a load of clothes. Charise would appreciate that. She had other things on her mind besides the mundane tasks of unpacking suitcases and washing clothes. He poured himself into his work hoping that the phone would ring. Before he realized it, it was already noon and still there had been no call from Thad.

Michael started to call Charise, but abruptly changed his mind. He did not want to worry her any more. Making a quick decision, he decided he would ride over to Thad's house. Perhaps the phone service had been disrupted from the earthquake or maybe the baby had been born and he was spending time with his new family. Whatever the reason for his not calling, Michael felt like he would find more answers there than sitting around here at home waiting for his best friend to call.

Grabbing his keys, he jotted a note to Charise just in case she returned home before he arrived back. He left the house and drove the short trip across campus to Thad's house. School would be starting soon for the students at the university. Already the grounds crew was busy pruning hedges, planting flowers, and landscaping the lawns as he passed the main part of the campus before turning off onto Thad's road. Michael parked his car in the driveway and walked up to the front porch. Thad's car was not there, and the house was dark inside. He knocked loudly knowing all the time that his best friend was not at home. Standing on the front porch with his hands on his hips, he turned around and scanned the surrounding roads hoping to see Thad's car come into sight.

Finally, he returned to his car and drove back home. The thermometer in his car registered ninety-five degrees, and the humidity was so thick that it sent the heat index soaring into triple digits. Frustration and the heat set Michael on edge. As he unlocked his front door, he heard the phone ring. Relief washed over him as he ran to answer it.

"Hello? Thad?" Michael answered. The voice on the other end of the line that responded was not the familiar one of his best friend.

"Hello, is this Dr. Michael Moses?" a deep voice asked.

Fear clutched at Michael robbing him of his voice temporarily. When he did not respond, the voice asked again, "Is this the residence of Michael Moses?"

Finally, Michael answered, "Yes, I'm sorry, this is Michael Moses. I apologize. I was expecting you to be someone else. How may I help you?" His heart was pounding hard inside his chest, and his palms had grown sweaty in spite of the air conditioning that had run almost constantly all day.

"Dr. Moses, this is Officer Clay Janzten with the coast guard. We have found a boat registered to Dr. Thad Destin, but he was not aboard. Do you know how he can be reached? According to the records at the marina, Dr. Destin did take the boat out some time in the last few days, but the marina manager was certain the boat had never returned. This morning, his boat was found unmanned adrift out at sea about three miles north of the marina. We have tried to locate Dr. Destin, but he has not answered his phone. Have you spoken with him in the last few days?"

Michael sat down on the couch afraid his trembling legs would not support him. "No, I have been trying to reach him since last night. My wife and I just returned from a cruise, and we arrived home late last night. Then, the earthquake hit. After it stopped, I tried to call Thad, but he never answered. I just went over to his house. He's not there." The staticky silence roared in Michael's ears.

After a lengthy pause, the voice on the other end of the line continued tentatively, "Mr. Moses, we are not going to jump to conclusions, but for the sake of erring on the side of caution, we are going to send a search and rescue helicopter to search the surrounding area where his boat was found. Do you know where he may have been going in his boat or where he may have been returning from to give us some idea of the scope of the search?"

Michael sat up suddenly, his mind swirling with questions. What was Thad doing out in the middle of the ocean so close to Selale's due date? Thad had been going to his research site several times a week while the funding had been there, but Michael assumed he had abandoned his research. It seemed all Thad had talked about was Selale. Could Thad have been at the research site? It was possible, but why he would be there at this time made little sense to Michael.

"Thad had been doing some research off the coast for several months. I am sure I can find the coordinates at his house. Is there a number where I can reach you? I will drive back over to his house and search through his files. It shouldn't be too difficult to find. Give me thirty minutes." The officer agreed, and Michael quickly jotted down the number. He hung up and raced out the door back to Thad's house.

The drive back to his friend's house seemed to take forever. Michael couldn't make sense of why his best friend would be out on the water alone. If Selale had already had the baby, Michael assumed Thad would not leave her side. He knew Thad valued his research, but after the funds had been abruptly halted, Michael assumed the research had too. Why would he have gone back there? He climbed the steps up to the porch and pulled the spare key from out of its hiding place. Thad had shown him where he had hidden the spare key in case Michael ever needed to get inside.

As he entered the house, nothing seemed amiss. Thad's desk contained several neatly labeled files. Perusing the titles, Michael pulled the one containing the research. After just a few minutes, he found the coordinates of the research site. He grabbed Thad's phone and called the number the officer had given him. Much more calmly than he felt, he relayed the coordinates.

"Dr. Moses, I know you are worried. Right now there is very little you can do except to pray and wait by the phone. We will contact you when we have more information. If you think of anything else that might be helpful or if you hear from Dr. Destin, you have my number. Don't hesitate to call me," the voice of the officer said.

Michael hung up the phone and sat motionless on Thad's couch. He sat staring into space seeing nothing. He stood and moved back to the desk. Perhaps there was something else there to give him some clue as to where his best friend was. Maybe the boat had returned to the marina and the earthquake simply dislodged it from its mooring. Even as he thought it, Michael knew it was a shot in the dark. Thad was nowhere to be found and now his boat was discovered without a captain. Those two facts pointed to a conclusion Michael couldn't ignore. Thad was missing.

He spied a folder labeled "baby," and quickly he opened it hoping that it would solve the mystery of Thad's whereabouts. There were many notes about at-home birthing and the protocol for paperwork regarding that type of delivery. Thad had made a checklist of what he had to do once the baby was born, but as of this moment, none of those items had been checked off. Could that mean that Thad was with Selale right now? Possibly she could be in labor even as the coast guard sent out a search and rescue team.

Michael felt frustrated that he had so little information regarding Thad's—what?—fiancée, wife, girlfriend. He didn't even know what to call Selale. He decided to leave the file on the desk. This was not something the coast guard needed access to. He turned off the light, locked the door, and got in his car. Instead of driving to his house, he turned toward the ocean. Thad always parked his car at the same place near the marina. If his car was not there, then Michael would assume he was with Selale, wherever that may be. He drove in silence, recalling everything he could remember about the little bit of information Thad had shared about Selale. He and Thad were to have met today. Thad promised him he would tell him everything about his and Selale's relationship. Michael could sense there was some important secret Thad had been keeping regarding this woman whom he had fallen in love with so hard and so fast. A thousand theories had been thought of and discarded by Michael.

Now, with the turn of these events, Michael felt fear pooling in the pit of his stomach. If something had happened to Thad, Michael would never know what it was that Thad so desperately tried to conceal from him. This secret involved something important about Selale; Michael just knew it, but what he didn't know. Could his best friend's disappearance be tied to this secret as well? It seemed more than coincidence that Selale's due date coincided with Thad's disappearance. Michael vowed to himself that he would find some answers. He turned into the public access parking lot that bordered the marina. There in its usual spot sat Thad's car.

Michael pulled his car in an empty spot near Thad's car and got out. He walked over and peered in the window. He tried the door latch and was surprised to find the car unlocked. Getting inside, he opened the glove box and other smaller compartments looking for some clue as to where Thad may be. Inside the center console was a photograph. Michael sat staring at the picture of Thad and a woman whom he assumed was Selale. She was beautiful but very exotic looking. The close-up shot was filled with just their smiling faces. There was no clue as to where or when the picture had been taken. Michael took the photo and slipped it into his shirt pocket. Aside from the photograph, nothing else was in the car.

Locking the doors, Michael walked over to the dunes that sheltered the ocean. He walked up the wooden stairs that led onto the boardwalk. His eyes stared at the horizon where the dark blue ocean met the lighter blue sky. From one end of the horizon to the other, Michael stared for some clue that could perhaps point to Thad's whereabouts. Crowds of tourists sunning themselves in the summer heat lined every few feet of the sand, and the tropical smell of suntan lotion wafted on the sea breeze. Umbrellas billowed in the wind and created a shady shelter to those who were taking refuge from the sun. Soon after the Labor Day rush, the crowds would dwindle and the locals would once again have the beach to themselves. Michael didn't mind the visitors, but today, he would give anything to see Thad somewhere among the crowd.

He retreated back to his air-conditioned car and drove home in silence. A terrible realization thrust itself into his mind. The more time that elapsed, the greater chance Thad would never be found. Michael couldn't bear the thought. He pounded the steering wheel in frustration, angry that such a thought had even crossed his mind. As he arrived home, he spotted Charise's car in the garage. Maybe Thad had called while he had been gone. Trying to remain optimistic, Michael smoothed the worried look from his face and entered the house.

Charise stood in the kitchen over the sink washing some apples. Her eyes stared not at the fruit she was washing, but out the window. She heard Michael come in and turned with anxious eyes that asked the unspoken question. Did you find Thad? Michael only shook his head to her. He walked over to the sink and took her into his arms. They stood holding each other without speaking.

Finally, Charise asked the question Michael had posed to himself all day, "Where is he, Michael? It's like he just disappeared. This is not like Thad. He would have called us, don't you think? Could he be with Selale?" Her barrage of questions reflected the anxiety she felt.

Michael took her hand and led her to one of the bar stools. Gently he said, "Charise, the coast guard called this morning. They found the *Sea Science* drifting out at sea, but nobody was aboard."

Charise gasped, "What? That makes no sense, Michael!"

Michael agreed, "I know. I've gone to his house and searched through his files about the research site. I called the coast guard back and gave them the coordinates of the site so they could narrow the scope of the search, but why would he be there? The funding for his research was revoked several months ago. Why would he be there so close to the time his son was to be born? I just don't get it!" Michael stood up abruptly and placed his hands on the countertop. Turning back to Charise, he continued, "There's something else. I found Thad's car at the beach access where he always parks. This was in the center console." He pulled the photograph of Thad and Selale from his pocket.

Charise held the picture and simply stared. She raised her eyes to Michael. "Wow, she is gorgeous. Is this the mysterious Selale?"

Michael nodded. "It must be. I tried to figure out where the picture was taken, but there is nothing but blue sky and water in the background. It could have been taken anywhere." Taking the photograph from Charise, Michael stared at the smiling faces. "He loves her and she loves him. Look at their eyes. That depth of emotion can't be faked in a picture. Why the mystery about her, Charise? What has Thad not told us?" Raising his eyes to meet his wife's, he continued, "Do you think perhaps that she is married to someone else? What could it be that has led him to keep her so...isolated from us? Thad and I were supposed to meet today, and he promised he would tell me everything and answer all my questions. Could that be the reason he has vanished?"

Charise closed her eyes and simply shook her head. "I don't know, Michael. Did you try looking for some clues at his house? Maybe there is something that can give us some insight into who Selale is and where Thad has been." Just then, the phone rang. Both Michael and Charise jumped, startled at its sudden intrusion into their conversation.

Michael rose and answered it tentatively, "Hello?" He eyes never wavered from Charise's.

"Dr. Moses, this is Officer Janzten. We have searched a ten-mile radius of the coordinates you gave us this morning. I'm sorry, but we have found nothing. We will go back out in a couple of hours for one last search. Have you heard from Dr. Destin?"

"No, I haven't. His car is still parked at the beach access where he always parks when he goes to the marina to take his boat out. His fiancée is due any day now with the birth of their son, so I can't imagine why he would be out in his boat. Unfortunately, I know very little about her. I don't even know her last name. She is a bit of a mystery to my wife and me." Making a rash decision, he continued, "We are going back over to his house right now to see if we can find out any pertinent information that might solve the mystery of his disappearance. Please keep me informed from your end, and if I find anything helpful, I will call you immediately." After a few more words were exchanged, Michael hung up.

He and Charise traveled back to Thad's house. The day was rapidly coming to an end. By now, the sun had dipped low on the western horizon and caused long shadows from the large live oaks that fringed his property to cast some cooling shade on Thad's house. Michael opened the door and they walked in.

"I have already been through the file labeled 'research' and 'baby.' If nothing else, Thad keeps organized records. Let's go back through them together. Perhaps I missed something. Then we will go through the other files and papers on his desk. I just keep hoping he will walk through that door any minute, but...." Michael let his words trail off.

Patting her husband's arm, Charise said, "Let's do this."

After several hours of combing through the files and papers on Thad's desk, night had fallen and still they had discovered nothing that gave them any more answers to their questions than when they began. Michael grabbed the manila envelope labeled "Baby" from the desk. He and Charise had decided they wouldn't open it, but would take this folder home with them, since it was sealed. Michael turned off the light and closed the door. As they had gone through the papers, he and Charise had verbalized many theories about Selale and the baby, but nothing had been found to validate any of their ideas. Now as they drove home, reality about Thad's absence began to set in, but neither was willing to audibly voice the ever-growing evidence: Thad had simply vanished.

The coast guard abandoned the search the next day, and after nearly a week without a trace, the police had closed the case and labeled Thad's disappearance a drowning. They too wanted to know more about Selale, but there was nothing to point them in the right direction. She was merely a face on a photograph. Without that piece of evidence of her existence, Michael could have believed she was a product of Thad's imagination.

However, Michael knew she was real. Thad had spent too many nights away from his house and too many hours in conversation about her. He was not going to abandon the search for her just because he had only a picture and first name. Somehow, he would find her.

Several times Michael drove to the ocean. His toes dug into the warm sand as he stood patiently waiting for some emotional communication from his missing friend. He encountered the emotions of many people's spirits, sharing in the joy, sadness, hope, and despair they felt, but not Thad's. As many times as he had yearned for this gift to be taken away in the past, how ironic it was that now when he needed his Empath ability the most to connect with his best friend, it failed him.

After more than a week had elapsed, Michael decided he would take Thad's boat the *Sea Science* out to the research site and search for any potential clues it might hold. This was his last resort at solving the mystery of Thad's disappearance. He knew he was grasping at straws, but he wasn't ready to concede defeat. Packing his scuba gear and oxygen tank in the boat, he started the engine and set his course with the coordinates for the research site's location.

Chapter Fifty-one

Calder's mind drifted on the cusp of sleep. Being so far removed from Atlantis gave him little else to do besides think and sleep. For several tides something had bothered him about the encounter with that human. It teased his mind, hiding deep in the shadows, peeking out from the deep recesses of his brain for but a moment, but then eluding his mind's grasp of its meaning. He knew he was missing something significant, but for the life of him, his mind failed to make sense of it all. Even as he dreamed, his mind had replayed the scene with the human over and over. He could see the human waving his arm, smiling broadly, like he wasn't surprised to see a merman out on the water. He had heard the human shout his brother's name.

Suddenly Calder's eyes flew open and instantly awake, he sat straight up in his bedchamber. This human and Marius knew each other. Breathing the water hard, Calder remembered the earthquake. Could these events fulfill the prophecy foretold so long ago? He tried to remember some of the details he had been taught as a merchild. An earthquake supposedly would usher in the birth of this baby. And then there was the human part of the story. How did that human know the King of Atlantis? His lovely niece came to mind. And Selale, where had she been for the past four cyclotides, an ambassador to Franconia?

Calder arose from his couch and swam into the outer room of his chamber. Staring far out into the dark waters toward the capital's Center City, he was filled with an overwhelming sense of foreboding as he came to the undeniable conclusion—the Hybrid King had been born.

Chapter Fifty-two

Monica couldn't bear the thought of leaving Selale, but she knew eventually she must. She had stayed for almost a forttide before she returned to her own chamber. She was worried about how much heartache one young mermaid could withstand. Why her human had not returned no one knew. Monica did know that Selale was heartbroken. Ettore's death had brought her deep grief, but with his burial came closure. With the disappearance of the baby's father, there was no closure, only the oppressive void of his absence.

The baby was growing and doing very well. He was healthy, and he and Selale had bonded quickly. She never let him out of her sight for a moment. They swam to the bottom of the cave, back through the tunnel, and all around the base of the cave, but they had not ventured any further than the condemned waters. It was too risky.

The riots and violence continued in the capital. Marius was unable to procure an audience with the slain DL parents. Many whose loyalties were divided between the king and Calder joined the parents' cause creating an even more turbulent, dangerous current in the capital. Barretto had tried to be the liaison between Marius and the parents, but the parents were deaf to any concession that did not remove Marius from the throne. So, talks of resolution were now at an impasse.

Martes neared the capital boundaries. He had needed the time away from the capital to refocus on his next move. The Defense League had been his life for the past seven annutides. Without it, he was lost. His mentor had been a charlatan, an imposter, a deceiver, and Martes struggled with where he should go from here. Perimicles had visited him at his chamber in Cecilia after he had taken time to heal from his own wounds. A bond was forged between the two mermen on the battlefield, and after his visit, Martes had truly found a mentor worthy of his respect. Perimicles urged him to come back to the capital center and meet with Marius. He promised that he would personally deliver the missive requesting a meeting with the king and assured Martes that he would be by his side for support.

Now as Martes neared the capital, he felt nervous. Even though Perimicles had reassured there would be no ill will on the king's part, Martes couldn't help but feel skeptical. How could the king not harbor animosity towards someone who had fought for the side that had slain his son?

As he turned the corner toward the Center City, off in the distance he saw an angry mob protesting outside the capital building. As he swam nearer, he recognized many of the mermen in the crowd. They were the fathers of his slain comrades. Confused at why they were assembled outside the king's chamber, he swam closer. He stopped near the corner of the opposite building. A crushing sense of sorrow and grief helped him make the split decision to go speak to them. The easy path would be to avoid them. The honorable thing to do, however, would be to face them. For Martes, it was not a difficult choice. Even if they blamed him, he wanted to offer his condolences. Their sons had not only been his fellow soldiers, they had been his friends. As he swam into their midst, the fathers greeted him as if he was a hero. They hugged him and patted him on the back as if they were celebrating his triumphant return. Guilt threatened to overwhelm him. He deserved no hero's welcome. In the group of mermen he recognized his childhood friend Philoteus' father. The older merman named Lennox took Martes in his arms and hugged him like a son. Martes turned to him and said, "It's great to see you here, but why have you assembled in the Center City?"

Lennox kept his arm around Martes' shoulder and confided to him, "We are plotting to overthrow the king. He must go! He killed my boy Philoteus.

He murdered them all, all of our sons. How did you escape, Martes? Tell us what happened." By now, all the mermen were huddled around him, eager to hear his story. They were a captivated audience.

Martes couldn't believe his ears. Emphatically he started shaking his head, "No! No! No! You have it all wrong, Lennox. I was there. Marius did not instigate this fight. Calder did. Gaillard intentionally misled all of the Defense League troops with a fabricated story about a massacre in Cecilia. None of it was true. He admitted the truth to me right before the prince was murdered by Calder's sharks. I tried to stop the troops, but by then, Calder had arrived and rallied them into believing that Marius had come to destroy them. It was all a lie, Lennox! It was a lie! Your sons died not because of what the king did, but because of what Calder did. His goal was to kill not only the prince, but also the king. He used your sons as insignificant pawns in his quest for the throne. I can't swim among you without you knowing the truth. Your sons died for Calder's ambition. That is the truth, plain and simple."

A murmur drifted through the crowd. Many of the welcoming glances now became hostile. Even Lennox grabbed Martes by the shoulder. Staring in the young merman's eyes he asked, "Why should we trust you? You're alive and our sons are dead. How do we know you aren't in league with Marius? Why are you here in the capital? Where have you been the last quarter tide while we buried our sons, your comrades?" Grief had hardened many of their hearts to the truth, including Lennox. They all wanted someone to blame and now Martes was the target.

Martes shrugged Lennox's hand from his shoulder. "Calder cowardly turned to escape, leaving your sons to die. I rescued many of my fellow soldiers from the battlefield. Ask the survivors. They will tell you the same story. I understand your grief. I have lived with my friends' deaths every tide since it happened. I see their faces and hear their cries each time I close my eyes. I watched many of them die right before my eyes, and I won't forget that sight until my last tide has come. Your sons' deaths will be avenged by me, but not against Marius. Calder will bear the brunt of my revenge. When I find him, that tide will be his last." Martes turned his back to the group and without a glance back, entered the capital building.

Barretto and Perimicles waited just inside the portal. With a nod of approval, Barretto gestured to the young commander to follow Perimicles down the long corridor. As he returned to his post at the portal, his eyes swept over the mermen in the crowd. Some of the parents including Lennox slowly dispersed, but others remained refusing to be swayed by the young commander's story. The arbitrator positioned himself at the door and with a haughty glare, dared them to try to enter without permission.

Martes was still shaking from the confrontation with the angry mob, so Perimicles pulled him into one of the empty office chambers to let him compose himself. The young officer took a seat at the long conference table and placed his head in his hands. Perimicles stayed near the portal allowing his young friend an opportunity to work through his emotions. Finally, he swam to take the seat beside him and waited until he was ready to proceed to see the king. When he raised his head and solemnly nodded, Perimicles knew the young merman was ready to face Marius. Both rose and exited back into the long corridor that led to the royal office. With more confidence than he felt, Martes held his head high and followed Perimicles into the chamber.

Aristeus met the two mermen in the outer chamber of the royal office. He swam to greet them both. "Ah, Perimicles, how are you, my friend? Have you recovered from your injuries?"

Perimicles nodded and said, "I am well, sir. Aristeus, this is Officer Martes. This is the merman to whom I owe my very life. It was he who rescued me on the battlefield. It is with great honor that I introduce him to you as my friend." Swimming slightly back, Perimicles made way for the young merman to move forward.

Aristeus turned his attention to the youthful officer and immediately greeted him with an outstretched hand. "It is an honor, Officer Martes."

"Likewise, my lord," Martes grasped the extended hand in greeting.

Impressed by the Defense League officer's poise, Aristeus replied, "I will notify the king of your arrival. If you will excuse me, I will return shortly." He pressed the portal button, and then disappeared through the passage leading to the king's royal office.

Gazing across the chamber at Martes, Perimicles could sense his anxiety. "Relax. Everything will go well. This meeting will be easy compared to the one you just had with those angry parents. Remember, I will be by your side."

Satisfied, Martes let the some of the tension ebb from of his body, but he understood the message he had for the king would be difficult. This human whom he had tried to save had known Marius, and now he would be told of yet one more tragedy. Aristeus returned and escorted both mermen down the short corridor leading to Marius' office chamber. Once they had passed into the king's royal office, Aristeus exited, closing the portal behind him.

Martes looked around at the simple furnishings. There was no grandeur. Everything in the chamber was functional and not fancy. For some reason, that helped him relax even more. He turned and met the king's eyes. There was sadness in them, yet they beheld confidence. Martes bowed, "Your Majesty, thank you for giving me an audience this tide. First, let me offer my condolences on the loss of Prince Ettore. We admired him. He will be missed."

Marius summoned Martes to rise. "Rise, Officer Martes. May I offer my condolences to you as well on the loss of so many of your Defense League comrades? If I could have prevented the bloodshed of those innocent young mermen, I would have." The king closed his eyes and shook his head solemnly.

"My Lord, I hold you blameless in their deaths. Forgive me for saying this, but it is your brother Calder whom I blame. Their blood is on his hands. I have been wracked with guilt wondering how I could have prevented their deaths, but after many tides of soul-searching, I realize he used us, discarding the value of our lives. We were only a means to an end. Nothing I could have done would have prevented their deaths. Nothing or no one is sacred from harm in his quest to become king." Martes' voice rang with the bitterness he felt toward Calder.

"Thank you for that, Martes. Let's sit down." Marius motioned to the benches around his desk. "Perimicles told me you had a message for me. But before we get to that, what is it that you plan to do now that the Defense League has been disbanded? Have you thought about your future?"

Martes nodded, "I have, your Majesty. I would like to train to become a member of the Guardians. I know that it requires royal consent and recommendation. Sir, if it is my allegiance that you doubt, let me assure you, I am your loyal servant now and for eternity."

The king kept his eyes pinned on the young officer. "The Guardians? How do you know they even exist, that they aren't some legend?"

Martes' lips lifted into a sardonic smile. "Your Majesty, I saved one of them from the battle. I have seen them in action, so I know they are real." Here, Martes turned to gaze at his silent supporter.

Perimicles simply shrugged at the king's quizzical expression. "It is true, my Lord. Young Martes did rescue me from Calder. He saved my life."

Marius knitted his fingers together and rested his chin on his hands. "I see. So, would you recommend him to the Guardians, Perimicles? You know the high standards the post demands. What do you think about Officer Martes' idea for his future?"

Perimicles flashed a smile to both the king and his friend. "I think he would make a splendid addition. Of course, I don't make this decision, Martes. Only the king himself can commission a merman for service. So, my Lord, the real question is what do you think about Officer Martes' idea for his future?"

Marius rose from his seat and swam around to face the youthful officer. Scrutinizing the merman, Marius grew serious. He stared straight into Martes' eyes and solemnly asked, "Do you understand the risks that come with this position? It is not a position of honor, recognition, or grandeur because your identity is anonymous. No one will know you are in the Guardians except other members. Your allegiance to me must be unshakable and strong even when you are faced with death. Training is rigorous and can sometimes last several annutides. This is not a service to enter into lightly, Martes. It requires sacrifice on many levels. Do you understand?"

Martes confidently stared at the king. "I do, your Majesty. As for my allegiance, it is yours."

Satisfied, Marius continued, "We will discuss the details of this training later this tide. Now, let's discuss the reason for this meeting. Be seated. I understand you have a message you were to relay to me." Swimming back to his chair, Marius had wondered who would have given this merman a message for him. His curiosity had definitely been piqued.

Martes cleared his throat and leaned forward on the bench. "Your Majesty, I want to start at the beginning, so I will give you as much context and detail as possible." When the king nodded, he began recounting the story, "After the battle, I was confused. Perhaps I was disillusioned. In any case, I had stayed behind tending to Perimicles and never reported back to the battlefield. He left the ray weapon Calder had abandoned in my possession and made me vow I would take care of it until he came to retrieve it from me. I decided to swim back to my home. I knew there I could re-evaluate my life without the distractions that I would face in the capital. On my way there, off in the distance I spotted a human being attacked by a merman. As I swam closer, I recognized Calder. He was brutally attacking a human and trying to drown him. I saw my chance to kill this traitor whom I had so blindly trusted and whom I had idolized. He had betrayed all of us and it cost my fellow soldiers their lives. I admit I was furious and wanted him dead. When he realized who I was, he actually thought I was still loyal to him, until he saw the hatred in my eyes and the ray weapon in my hand. He cowardly swam off, leaving the human for dead. Even as he left, he offered me a place in his "kingdom" he still envisions he will have if I went with him. When I rejected him and his offer, he swam away. I knew I would never catch him. It almost killed me to let him get away." Martes stopped his story. He rose from the bench and swam to the side wall. There he stared out the gazing panel at the Center City. Marius and Perimicles patiently waited for him to regain his composure.

Finally, Martes returned to his seat. "Please forgive me, your Majesty." When Marius brushed his apology away, Martes resumed his story, "After Calder disappeared, I remembered the human. Calder had dragged him down under the water, so I dove after him and pulled him to the surface. I tried giving him some of the air from the cylindrical machine strapped to him, but he was unconscious. He was injured badly and his pulse was very weak. I made a quick decision to take his body to the shore even though I knew it was a dangerous risk. I couldn't just let him die there in the water." Perimicles nodded at the assessment of the situation.

By now, Marius had a strange look on his face, a mixture of shock and pain. Even before Martes concluded his story, Marius had already grasped the realization of its tragic outcome. The human was Selale's husband, Thad. Overcome with sadness, he bowed his head and covered his face with his hands.

Seeing the king's reaction to the story, Martes became unsure if he should continue. "My Lord, are you all right? Do you wish for me to continue?" Even though he was confused by the king's reaction to the story, Martes' concern was genuine.

Marius raised his head and whispered, "Yes, please continue."

Martes looked at Perimicles who, with a slight nod, encouraged him to resume his story. Martes lowered his voice, "I remembered a place I could take him where I knew someone would discover him, so I swam there. His body was lifeless, but he had some sort of floatation device that enabled me to keep his head above the water. Long wooden structures jut far out into the water at this beach. After making sure I was alone, I hoisted his body up onto one of those human structures. Sir, he said your name, Marius, and your daughter, Selale. What else he said, I know not, because I didn't know his language. I wish I could tell you what he said, but I do know your names were on his lips right before he closed his eyes and collapsed. A noise from one of the humans' homes alerted me that someone was coming, so I hastily swam away. That, my Lord, is the message I was to give you. I am truly sorry it has brought you more sorrow."

Marius replied, "Thank you, Martes. Thad was a friend and yes, his death brings even more grief. When will these sorrows end?" He didn't expect an answer.

Perimicles rose and went to the king's side. "Is there anything we can do for you, your Majesty?"

Marius shook his head, "No, your friendship is sufficient. Thank you both for imparting this difficult message. I know you both have questions, but right now, please excuse me. This news brings great sadness. Perimicles, set the process into motion to admit Martes into the Guardians. Aristeus will help you with the details."

Marius rose and extended his hand. Perimicles bowed and placing his hand atop the king's, vowed, "My eternal allegiance, my life, I pledge to you, my Lord. I offer my life, all that I am, to protect you and our great kingdom of

Atlantis." He rose and signaling to Martes, he urged his friend to recite the same promise.

Martes felt honored. He bowed his head and positioned his hand on the king's just like Perimicles had. Marius asked, "Do you swear an oath of fealty to your king?"

In a strong voice Martes proclaimed, "My eternal allegiance, my life, I pledge to you, my Lord. I offer my life, all that I am, to protect you and our great kingdom of Atlantis."

Marius motioned Martes to rise. He escorted both mermen to the portal, and as they turned to exit, Marius said, "Go in peace and protection."

In the empty office chamber, Marius swam to the gazing panel and he too stared out across the Center City of Atlantis. Thad was gone now too. How would he ever break the news to Selale? Without ever voicing their concerns aloud, both had known something was wrong. Thad would have never abandoned Selale and the baby. Now, he too had become another casualty of Calder. When would it end?

Marius knew the answer to the question—only when Calder was dead would the bloodshed end. With that realization, the king knew it would be no easy solution, nor would it be quick. The prophecy predicted the long battle for power. Calder had disappeared deep into the recesses of Atlantis and finding him would be almost impossible. Marius realized that the next move in this strategic game was Calder's and that no matter how many tides his brother waited to make his next move and attempt to gain the throne, Marius and all his allies would be ready.

Chapter Fifty-three

Marius left the Center City and slowly swam away from the capital buildings. He decided to go to Monica's first before going home and bring her to the cave. She would need to be there when he told Selale the news about Thad. The Naming Ceremony was this eventide. Selale had asked Monica to be the baby's honorary grandmere, so she was expecting Marius anyway to escort her there.

As he made his way to Monica's small chamber, Marius realized that Thad's death created many challenges for the baby. The Hybrid King could not live in Atlantis. If Calder learned of his existence, he would be killed within a forttide. Marius remembered the threats not only against him, but also those against Selale made by the rioting parents. These were dangerous tides for what remained of his family. For now, Selale and the baby were safe inside the protection of Beulah Cave. He also knew the baby could not live his entire life inside the cave. That would be like a prison cell. With Thad gone, the baby's only tie to the human world had disappeared. Marius had no idea how all the details would work out, but deep within his heart, he knew somehow that they would.

He arrived at Monica's, and as she opened the portal, she saw his face and knew something else had happened. "What is it, Marius?"

With a sorrowful expression, Marius murmured, "Thad is dead. There is much to decide before we tell Selale. Let's discuss it on the way." She closed the portal and swam beside Marius to his chamber.

It had been almost a forttide since Selale had held Thad in her arms. They ached for his body. She knew something was wrong. He was gone. Already she could fill the void his absence left in her life. Deep in her heart, she knew she would not see him again. That thought caused her heart to physically ache, and a pain-filled moan echoed through the cave. His leaving was her fault. He would have never left if she hadn't urged him to go. She lay on the rock ledge immobilized by her sorrow. The baby slept in the nearby recess. Tears rolled down her face as she thought about how wonderful a father he would have been to their baby.

Marius and Monica surfaced in the cave and found Selale in the throes of grief. Marius realized his daughter already knew something had happened to her husband. She had begun to grieve for him several tides before. His information only confirmed what she suspected.

He pulled himself up on the ledge and took his daughter in his arms as he had when she was a merchild. She looked at her father. As tenderly as he could, he whispered, "Thad is gone, Lale." Pulling her closer, he simply held her and let her cry.

Eventide came, and Selale asked her father to tell her what he knew. He relayed the story Martes had told him. Selale sat there listening. When Marius finished, she dove into the water and swam to the prophecy wall. Her eyes stared at the delicate etching. It was all coming true, every detail, every prediction. Fear clutched her heart. She turned to her father and whispered, "I'm afraid, Papa."

He swam to her side. "I am too. But Selale, we can't let fear win. It can't control us. Together, our love for each other and for this child is stronger than fear." He held out his hand. "Come! Let's name this king! Though our hearts are heavy, let's rejoice this tide." Arm in arm, they swam back to the ledge where Monica held the Hybrid King. Earlier in the tide, Barretto had arrived for the Naming Ceremony. Creatures from the deep had already begun to arrive. The news had spread quickly among them, and they filled the waters in the cave in anticipation of the ceremony to come.

344

The Naming Ceremony dated back to the genesis of Atlantis. For millennitides, the Merpeople followed the sacred tradition of blessing each child with a chosen name and then bestowing a Token carefully selected by the Enlightened Endower. His or her vision of prophecy concerning the child enabled the Endower to select the symbolic Token, which according to the vision represented something significant in the merchild's life. For a royal birth, the ceremony carried more significance. The king served as the Enlightened Endower. If he did not possess the Mystical Gift of Prophecy, often he would consult with the Royal Seer regarding the symbolic Token.

All those in Atlantis endowed with Mystical Gifts eagerly attended the Royal Naming Ceremonies. They too played a part in the Naming Ceremony of a future king. After the Symbolic Token was presented to the future king, each of the Gifted would lay a hand on his head and offer a blessing related to his or her specific Mystical Gift upon the royal merchild. In the tides of the past, the Enlightened Endower ended the ceremony by anointing the merchild with special oil. The Seer's vision revealed which Mystical Gifts the baby possessed. The merchild's Mystical Gift determined the composition of the oil because its special properties along with the Chant of Blessing activated the gift, empowering the merchild to use it. The words could be found in but one source, the Tome of Kings. Only when the king served as the Enlightened Endower could the Mystical Gifts' real power be unleashed for he alone had access to the chant.

With the extinction of most of the Mystical Gifts, especially the gift of prophecy, the ceremony had become almost obsolete. Some merparents chose not to have a formal ceremony but most still held to the tradition where only the immediate family attended. The Enlightened Endower was merely a representative from the Hall of Records who was given a stipend to attend.

This Royal Naming Ceremony, however, held special significance. This baby was the Hybrid King and possessed all of the Mystical Gifts. Only the merpeople gathered in Beulah Cave knew of his birth. Marius, Barretto, and Monica had worked together researching records to find the specific ingredients needed in the Anointing Oil for a merchild endowed with all the Gifts. Each had individually consulted various records and notes. Marius had read the entire history of the Naming Ceremony found in the Tome of Kings. He alone had access to this record of history dating back to beginnings of their society. Only the king himself knew of the book. Its existence had remained a secret for over two millennitides. Together the three of them had compiled the necessary information about the ingredients to activate all of the Hybrid King's Mystical Gifts. And now, they were ready to proceed with the Naming Ceremony.

Holding her child, Selale swam to the center of the water in Beulah Cave. The Hybrid King was adorned in the traditional dress. Golden strips covered his chest down to his waist. The only difference between this king and the hundreds named before him was that this baby had no tail. His tiny white legs kicked in the water.

Barretto and Monica treaded on each side of the king to assist him in his duties. Marius turned to face his daughter and grandchild as he began the formal service. "We have gathered here this tide to celebrate the birth of the Hybrid King. This is no ordinary ceremony. This is one which we the inhabitants of Atlantis have anticipated for centennitides." A shout of celebration erupted from the assembly of sea creatures.

When order was restored, Marius continued, "A name is a source of identity. It first defines who a merman is. Parents are urged to thoughtfully consider what the chosen name conveys about a child. In consideration of this, what is this child's chosen name?" Silence filled the cave.

Selale lifted the baby high above her head. In a strong voice, she proclaimed, "His name is Destin Ettore, for he is destined to be the savior of our people." Once again, the cave erupted in noisy, overwhelming approval. Barretto and Monica clapped joining the celebration of the strong, meaningful name. Marius smiled and nodded as he too gave his endorsement.

Taking the child from Selale, Marius drew his grandson close to his chest. A powerful wave of love and protection welled up in him, temporarily rendering him speechless. Once again, the cave was filled with silent reverence. Finally, he resumed the ceremony.

"The Mystical Gift of Prophecy has long been absent in Atlantis. Many tides before this generation, those who once possessed this gift foresaw each merchild's future and presented a Symbolic Token during this ceremony. It is the Enlightened Endower's responsibility to carefully select this Token before it is bestowed on the merchild. Though I am not a Prophet, I know this merchild's future—he will be king. He will lead our people. After much consideration and thought, I have chosen a whistle as Destin Ettore's Symbolic Token. It represents leadership." Marius retrieved the Token from his waistbelt. He placed the shell-shaped object at his lips and blew. The shell emitted light and then a high-pitched, strong note rent the air, the tone beautiful in its simplicity. Everyone in attendance again displayed their approval. Marius raised his hand to quiet the crowd.

"When he sounds the call, both merman and human will rise up to follow him. The mark of true leadership is understanding when to seek help and from whom to seek it. Leadership requires patience, restraint, prudence, and integrity. It is not self-serving. Destin Ettore, the Hybrid King, embodies the light, which he wears on his shoulder. The light of goodness is so desperately needed for effective leadership. So, upon him by the power vested in me as the Enlightened Endower, I present this Symbolic Token of Leadership." Around his grandson's neck Marius placed a golden cord that held the whistle. Marius raised the Hybrid King high in the air for all to see. Approval resounded through the waters and off the golden walls of the cave.

Marius lowered the baby and gently placed him in Monica's waiting arms. Marius continued, "The Blessing from the Gifted has long been a tradition in the Mer Kingdom. Each future king receives this Sacred Sanction from everyone endowed with a Mystical Gift. At this tide, the Blessing from the Gifted will proceed."

Barretto swam forward first and tenderly placed one of his enormous hands behind the head of the Hybrid King. With the other, he summoned the light to him, gathering it like a glowing ball which hovered over his hand. Slowing moving his light-filled hand above the baby's head, he closed his large hand into a fist around the glowing orb. Suddenly light showered down on the baby like sifting sand.

Barretto's voice boomed loudly even though he spoke to Destin alone, "You are blessed with Light. It will be drawn to you, will surround you, and forever will go with you, wherever you go. Your Light will dispel the dark. Embody the Light, my King!"

Selale turned to face her beautiful son. She gathered him in her arms and looked deeply in his eyes conveying how much she loved him. Understanding dawned in his eyes. His tiny hand reached up and touched her cheek. He loved her too. Nodding, she spoke to him in a soft voice. "You are blessed with Interpretation. Speaking and understanding languages and their many nuances will serve you so that you may serve others. Using elocution effectively will enable you to bring peace in the midst of misunderstanding. Understanding others yields compassion and the ability to examine motivation inside the heart. Communication will empower you to unite the two worlds. Interpret with clarity and compassion, my son!" She kissed his cheek and relinquished him to Monica.

Finally, Marius took the child from Monica. "You are blessed with control of the waters and control of the sand. These Gifts command a commission to protect, not destroy. Control of these two elements requires good judgment and discernment. Controlling both water and sand will empower you to protect yourself, your family and friends, your people, and your home. Use this control with wisdom, our future king!" Marius raised his hand. On one side of the cave, a wave formed and poised itself near the ledge. On the side near the prophecy wall, a whirlwind of sand spun. Lowering his hand slowly, Marius made both disappear as quickly as they had formed. Kissing his grandson on the top of his head, the king handed him back to Selale.

The Anointing was final part of the Royal Naming Ceremony. Marius addressed the assembly, "The Anointing for a Royal Merchild activates the Mystical Gift the future monarch possesses. The oil's properties are both symbolic and physical. Pouring the oil over the merchild's head symbolizes royalty being ordained with authority to one day lead his people. Physically the oil is composed of ingredients to release the power of his Mystical Gifts. This tide, Destin Ettore, I anoint you future King of all Merpeople. You are destined to save us. Because you are both fish and man, water, earth, and air will sustain you; therefore, both worlds—Atlantis and the Lands Above—will play a role in your future. Let goodness be your guide in all you do for both worlds." Marius took

348

the baby in his arms. Opening the flask, he chanted the encrypted rune, which had no meaning to those present, and slowly poured the oil over the baby's head. Beulah Cave erupted in resounding celebration. Fish of all shapes and sizes leapt into the air and splashed noisily back in the water to offer their applause. Dolphins shouted their approval. Marius released the squirming baby and together with the adults nearby, he joined the festivities. Every fish, dolphin and creature from the deep in the cave swam by to touch the Hybrid King, to offer their symbolic blessing on him as well before diving down to exit the cave.

After the Naming Ceremony ended, a tranquil silence filled the cave, now golden orange in the waning light. The baby slept in the crevice of the ledge beside the water. Aside from that small stretch of rock, there was no other place for him to sleep. Marius decided to broach the subject with Selale of where Destin would live. He, Monica, and Barretto had already considered the possibilities. The child was not safe outside the walls of Beulah Cave, but he could not spend his entire life here. His legs would require land on which he could run, jump, and play. This cave could not hold a child who needed both land and water a prisoner inside its walls. Marius knew Selale would not willingly give up her son to a stranger, but now that Thad was gone, what else could she do? He dreaded this discussion.

With her tail in the water and her head resting on her arms on the ledge, Selale gazed at her beautiful son. She raised her eyes and found her father's intense stare on her. Barretto and Monica sat on the opposite side of the cave, their heads bent together in a whispered conversation. Selale swam to sit beside her father. She had seen that look on his face often as a young mermaid and knew he had something on his mind he wanted to discuss with her. She pulled herself up beside him on the ledge close to Destin.

"What is it, Papa? What do you have on your mind?" Smiling, she took his hand. "It was a beautiful Naming Ceremony. Thank you for making it so special." She leaned over and kissed Marius on the cheek and then placed her head upon his shoulder.

He took his arm and drew her close. "Have I told you how proud of you I am? You amaze me with your poise, your bravery, your compassion for others.

You are a great mother, Selale. We have both experienced great loss over the last several tides, haven't we? My heart still longs for Ettore, and you, well, you've also lost Thad. There's a hole in our hearts left by their absence that won't ever be filled." He let the silence stretch between them.

"Have you considered what to do about raising Destin as a human? He can't stay here forever. Outside of these walls, he is a threat to the Dark Forces of Calder. He would never be safe from our enemies. If they find out the Hybrid King has been born, they will be relentless in their pursuit of him. They will not stop until they have killed him. They must not find out where he is. You do understand what I'm insinuating to you, don't you, Selale?" Marius could see the huge pearls of tears falling from her eyes. All she could do was nod. Barretto and Monica had turned their attention to the conversation taking place across the cave. Marius motioned for them to join them to help devise a plan to protect the Hybrid King.

"How can I let him go knowing that I may never see him again? He won't even remember me! He will believe I abandoned him." A moan of despair escaped from Selale. She leaned over and scooped up the sleeping child and cradled him in her arms. "Not yet, Papa. I can't let him go yet. It's too soon," Selale pleaded.

Barretto observed, "The longer he is here, the more danger there is of discovery, Selale. We must act quickly. Our top priority must be to protect the child, no matter how much pain it brings to us personally. His well-being should be our only concern."

Monica was filled with compassion for Selale. This would be the most difficult decision she ever made in her life. The older merwoman knew Selale's actions would be motivated by her love for her child. She didn't know how everything would work out, but she trusted that somehow it would.

"We can't just leave him on the shore. There's too much danger for him and for whoever takes him there," Marius concluded. He too wanted Selale to have more time with Destin, but understood that the longer they allowed the Hybrid King to remain in Atlantis, the more they jeopardized his safety. He continued, "Let's think about the options for the next two tides and then reconvene. We will consider everyone's ideas and collectively come up with a plan. While we all are in agreement that danger lurks in the waters, we must not be too hasty in our actions. After all, we know the story. Good will prevail!"

"Yours is a sound idea. In two tides, I will return here to Beulah Cave. Marius, will you escort me out? Selale, Monica, until then, adieu." Barretto held his giant arms out for the baby. Selale gently deposited the sleeping future king in his arms. "You, Little King, are blessed. Sleep in peace." He kissed the baby on the head and returned him to Selale. The baby never awakened.

Marius kissed his grandson and daughter before diving down to lead Barretto out of the cave and back to his chamber. In the stillness of the cave, only Monica remained with Selale and the baby. She swam over to sit on the ledge beside her friend who protectively held her son to her chest.

"Let's get some sleep, my dear. A new tide may help us look at the situation with a different perspective and come up with a solution. It breaks my heart to know you must surrender the baby to a stranger, a human." Monica stared at the baby and caressed his tiny head. She confided in a soft voice, "I don't know if I could do it if he were mine." She raised her eyes to Selale. "Giving Destin up to be raised as a human will be the hardest decision you will ever make. You must be brave, Selale. Our plan to save the Hybrid King requires much deliberation. It not only affects you and the baby, but the entire race of Merpeople. What we decide will have eternal consequences. Come, sleep will give us clarity. Here," Monica reached over and took a vial from the bag behind them. She handed it to Selale. "Drink this. It will help you rest. I will stay by your side until you fall asleep." Selale drank the liquid then lay down on the ledge beside the crevice where Destin had slept for the last several tides.

She dreamed of Thad. The three of them swam together outside the confines of Beulah Cave. Dolphins and fish accompanied them as they not only swam above water, but also below. The clear, blue water sparkled in the morning sun. It was the start of a new tide. The trio dove down into the depths, swimming free. Even Thad was unencumbered with the breathing apparatus. Like both Selale and the baby, he could breathe the water too. He had become one of the Merpeople. Joy filled her heart. Now they could be together as a family. With Destin in between them, they swam toward his research site, the place where he and Selale had first met and fallen in love. Thad swam with urgency. He wanted desperately to show her something. He turned around and motioned for her to hurry. She knew it was important. She struggled to keep up. Thad and Destin were leaving her behind. She tried calling out, telling them to wait, not to leave her, but soon they both swam out of sight. She was left all alone.

Selale awoke with a start, gasping for breath. She sat up and looked for Thad. Tears coursed down her cheeks when she realized she had been dreaming. She was in Beulah Cave. Wrapping her arms around her waist for comfort, she fought the urge to take Destin and leave, just go someplace where she could keep him safe, but Selale knew that in Atlantis, safety didn't exist for the Hybrid King.

By now morntide had begun to stream into the cave, turning the walls a brilliant gold. Light reflected off the prophecy wall. Both Monica and the baby still were sound asleep. Selale swam over to the side of the cave to where the ancient words had been etched. Her father had more faith than she did. Even as she read the words, doubt crept in. How could she say goodbye to her son, the last link to the man she loved? As she turned around to look at Destin, light glinted off the glass globe that rested in the corner beside her sleeping son. Remembering her dream, Selale made an impulsive decision to swim to the research site with Destin. Gathering the baby in her arms, they dived down to swim out of the cave. Together, they could tell Thad goodbye and bring some closure to her loss; then and only then, could she take the next step to tell her son goodbye.

Chapter Fifty-four

Semirah knew Calder would visit her this tide. She had seen the reason for his impending arrival in the vision. The Hybrid King had arrived. Yes, the vision would bring him to her portal by the tide's turn. Though she had been banished many tides before from Atlantis by Marius, Calder had befriended her long before her fall from favor. There had been an instant attraction, and finding they were kindred spirits who preferred the dark waters, they became friends, then companions. They understood one another and appreciated the other's ambition, so there was no pretense in their relationship. Calder had made certain he maintained their connection after her expulsion from the Mer society, so he had constructed a chamber for her close to the one where he himself had now been forced to hide.

Semirah prided herself on how well she had adapted to her new surroundings far removed from the Center City of Atlantis. She had hardly missed it. She passed the tide practicing the Dark Arts for which she had been banished, and perfecting her skills. When Calder ascended to the throne, she would be restored to her place in the royal chamber and with her unrivaled skills in the Dark Arts, together they would rule the waters of Atlantis. Of course, this baby now stood in their way. It had been difficult to read the vision. There had been too much light which prevented her from seeing everything she wanted to know. A ripple of fear shot through her as the truth dawned upon her. This king's power was stronger than the Dark Arts she practiced. Calder didn't need to know this fact just yet.

She peered out the gazing panel and saw him in the distance. Two sharks were at his side, but they stopped several lengths away from the portal, and waited, circling the waters nearby. Swimming to her portal, she opened it right as he arrived at her chamber. Without a word, he entered and turned to look at Semirah with an unspoken question. Closing her eyes, she simply nodded.

"When?" Calder asked impatiently.

"Within the last cycle, my friend. I have seen the vision. The Hybrid King has been born. Have you conferred with the sharks? Surely they can confirm his birth." Semirah calmly swam to the bench beside the table and motioned Calder to join her. "Come let's discuss what we know."

Calder glared at her. "What we know is he has been born, and he must be eliminated before he leaves the waters of Atlantis. Yes, the sharks confirmed the Hybrid King's birth although none witnessed it. According to their sources, he is still here in Atlantis although no one can tell me where. We must use haste. If he is relinquished to the humans, we will have no power over him there." He swam to the bench and sat down beside Semirah.

She picked up a fishbone lying near a talisman. "Summon the sharks. In my vision, they were pursuing him. Have them search every inch of the waters. Sound the call to your allies and offer a substantial reward to the one who finds and kills the Hybrid King."

Calder remained silent for a while. He rose and swam to the gazing panel and saw the sharks still pacing the waters. He then turned to face Semirah and with a serious demeanor asked, "Can the auguries of the prophecy be thwarted? Surely there is a way to alter the destiny of this Hybrid King. Consult the Dark, Semirah. Seek its counsel before we put a bounty on this child." Desperation laced his voice.

Semirah gazed at her friend. She shook her head slowly back and forth, "Calder, come sit down. You know as well as I that your great-grandmere's prophecies were never wrong and the destiny foretold in her visions cannot be changed. However, the prophecy of the Hybrid King is different. Its meaning is definitely open to interpretation. I will consult the Dark as a means to find and destroy the child before he embraces his destiny and ascends to the land of humans. There is only a small space of opportunity. If the child escapes to the human world, it will be many annutides before we have the chance to destroy him. We must act quickly." She grabbed Calder's arm and pulled him beside her at the table.

Taking the fishbone and a human bone in her hand, she poured sand over them and tying them together, placed a large, smooth black rock on the duo of bones. She began chanting a conjuring spell to summon the Dark. Slowly the rock became translucent and inside as its swirling smoke cleared, Semirah saw the child and his mother swimming together. She and Calder stared, fascinated by the child who was both merman and human. Something in the dark depths pursued them. The mermaid took the child in her arms and swam toward a boat. As they neared the surface, the mother turned to look back, and then desperately made one final push to reach the air. A sudden burst of light dispelled the vision in the rock.

"What happened?" Calder roared. He shot up from the bench frustrated that he couldn't see the end result. He angrily faced Semirah. "Why did the light interrupt what we saw? Tell me what happened." His hand swiped the table clean, sending the rock and bones floating through the water.

"It's the Light. This child's light is strong. His aura of protection already has formed. We must act quickly. The longer he remains in the water, the greater our chance of killing him. We didn't see the end of the vision. That could mean an opportunity still exists to terminate the child before he falls into human hands. Come, call the sharks. Let the pursuit begin." Semirah followed Calder to the portal.

He summoned the two sharks waiting in the waters nearby and sounded the call for all swimming in the waters within the range of his signal. From every direction they came and circled the waters above where Calder swam. Suddenly the sharks stilled and listened to their orders. With three simple words, he dismissed them to complete their task, "Kill the child."

Chapter Fifty-five

Michael arrived at the coordinates late in the afternoon. The sun had not yet set, but sat low in the western sky. Its strong rays brightened the waters and glistened off the whitecaps that had formed on the ocean. Another storm would arrive before morning. He dropped the anchor, and quickly putting on the scuba gear, prepared to go below. After going through Thad's research notes and finding the coordinates, he had decided to gather the equipment from below and bring everything back to the facility. Perhaps some clues could be found there. He had brought along a basket to put the materials in if necessary. He would swim to the site and then decide if he needed the basket. He may be able to haul everything to the surface without lugging the basket down to the ocean floor. He pulled the basket to the edge of the boat and then dove in.

He spotted the research site as he drew closer to the ocean floor. It sat undisturbed as if it too waited for Thad's return. He swam toward the equipment and examined it. Everything seemed to be in working order. Thad had loved his work. Michael had read through some of the research data and was impressed with the copious amount of notes Thad had taken regarding the results of the samples he had collected at the site. Michael sat down on the ocean floor as the warm waters of the Atlantic pressed around him and allowed himself to grieve once more for his lost friend.

Selale and the baby swam through the waters in tandem. It had taken Destin a while to wake up. Now he swam fluidly in front of her, his little legs kicking in the water. They were nearing the site. She grabbed him around the waist and pulled him and herself into her long-abandoned hiding place. She sat reminiscing, lost in the memory of her first encounter with Thad. She drew her child close and grieved for the father he would never know.

After her tears were spent, still holding Destin, she swam out from where they hid and sudden fear stabbed through her. Ahead through the salty water, Selale spied a dark silhouette, someone definitely human. Someone was at the research site. Quickly she moved them back to shelter. Selale surreptitiously gazed from behind her place of concealment to see the intruder.

Michael felt her presence even though he could not see her. Her intense grief mirrored his own and it caused him to feel a connection with her. He stood up and looked around. She was close. A new emotion drifted through him—fear. Why was she so afraid? He tried to convey to her that he meant her no harm.

He spoke to her with his thoughts. "I mean you no harm. I'm here to retrieve these materials. They belonged to my friend. I'm sorry if I scared you. Don't be afraid."

The reply was one word, "Thad." Selale didn't know how this human could communicate with her, but he could. Was he an Empath? They once lived in Atlantis, but had disappeared when the one surviving Empath left the ocean for the land. He had fallen in love with a female human.

The word startled Michael. "Yes, Thad was my best friend. Did you know him? Who are you? Where are you?" He continued to look around the waters searching for the woman whose voice he heard. He could feel her drifting away. He urged her, "Please don't go."

Selale knew what she had to do. This was Thad's friend Michael. Thad had loved him, trusted him, and now she must trust him too. She retreated from the research site and made her way slowly to the surface holding her child. Off in the distance, she spotted a large shiver of sharks flanked by two enormous stingrays. They steadily made their way in their direction. Alarm shot through her as she realized she and Destin were the targets of the predators. Their eyes were locked on her and the baby. Frantically she raced toward the boat floating above their heads on the water's surface.

The sharks had almost caught them when the dolphins intervened. From different directions they attacked the sharks giving Selale enough time to swim toward the boat. Suddenly, one of the rays streaked out of the skirmish toward Selale and the baby. Just as they reached the boat, the ray struck, its long, black tail lashed across the baby's shoulder as Selale raised him up. The baby's cry pierced the waters and a stream of red spread through the waters. Furiously and with all her strength, Selale launched the baby and herself over the side of the boat. Destin's cries rang out across the silence of the waters. She clutched him tightly to her breasts and consoled him by rocking him gently. Soon, the baby's cries stopped. She turned him over to inspect his injury. Already the wound was healing, a scar forming right over the birthmark on his shoulder. Hugging him again, grief seized her at the choice she was about to make.

She knew this was the right decision. The Hybrid King had to be raised by a human, and who better to raise this special child than his father's best friend. She held him close as the sorrow and anguish of leaving her child ripped through her. "I love you, Destin. Some tide, you and I will be reunited. Oh, my baby," she sobbed, as she placed the squirming child in a basket she found on the deck of the boat. Its size cradled the baby perfectly in its hull. She rubbed his tiny head and ran her hand over the shell whistle that hung around his neck. "Until we see one another again, may the light of protection enfold you," she whispered, and with a final kiss, Selale submerged herself under the water on the opposite side, leaving the Hybrid King safely protected in the boat.

The fight between the sharks and dolphins continued nearby. Several of the sharks had fled, but some kept up the fight. The disturbed waters rocked the boat, but not enough to capsize it. The baby was safe. Selale evaded the battle by diving down on the opposite side and then swiftly swam to the research site. She had to warn the human of the danger lurking above. She returned to the hiding place far enough from the site to remain out of his line of vision, but close enough to communicate with him.

Michael felt her return. Her grief tore through him, almost paralyzing him in its intensity. "Who are you? How did you know Thad?" he asked.

Selale had to warn him. "Beware. Sharks are in these waters. His name is Destin, Destin Ettore. Keep him safe. Keep him secret, Michael."

"How do you know my name? Who? Keep who safe? Thad is gone. Are you warning me or him about the sharks?" He couldn't understand what her warning meant, nor why she would not answer his questions. He felt her intense anguish.

Selale stayed hidden. She had to make him understand. "His name is Destin Ettore. Keep him safe. Keep him secret."

A feeling of déjà vu struck Michael. Those were the same words he was told about the pearl by the woman's voice on the beach. This time, however, this woman was not speaking about a pearl. She seemed to be referring to a person.

Selale gazed back to the surface of the water where the boat floated. Now all that circled the waters near the boat were dolphins. She felt relief and overwhelming gratitude that the dolphins had guarded them so fiercely, saving both her and the Hybrid King from the sharks. They had been after the baby. Peace settled over her even though her heart was filled with grief. She had made the right decision. Destin was safe.

Michael felt her withdraw, so even though precious minutes ticked by, he waited. He desperately wanted her to return, but darkness was fast approaching, and his oxygen tank was getting low, so Michael quickly gathered the rest of the research materials. When he realized he couldn't wait any longer, with his arms full, he slowly swam to the surface. As he put the equipment over the edge of the boat, he felt her presence once again. He pulled himself into the boat and took off his scuba mask. Just then a baby's cry split the quiet of the ocean. Dropping everything into the boat, he hesitantly moved to the basket. There inside the empty basket lay a baby boy. With shaking hands, Michael bent down and gathered the tiny baby in his arms.

"His name is Destin Ettore. Keep him safe. Keep him secret," the woman's anguished, desperate plea wafted across the waters, filling him with sadness.

He understood now. This was Thad's child. "Selale? Wait! Why? What...? Where's Thad?" He could feel her grief, but he felt confused why she would give up her child. Did she have something to do with Thad's disappearance?

Where was she? How did the baby get here? Questions too numerous to ask swirled through his mind.

"He's Thad's son. His name is Destin Ettore. Keep him safe. Keep him secret."

Darkness had settled on the water. He knew she was still there; he could feel her waiting. He would do as she asked, even if he couldn't see her or understand why she had given him the baby. He felt her love and her overwhelming sense of loss. Yes, he would do as she asked. "I promise I will keep him safe. I don't know what you mean about keeping him secret, but I will protect him from harm. I promise." He could sense her acceptance of his vow. Slowly he felt her presence withdraw until she was gone.

In the middle of the ocean, Michael Moses stood holding Thad's son. His eyes looked in every direction for a boat. The waters were completely devoid of any type of watercraft. The *Sea Science* floated alone on the dark ocean. He couldn't explain how the baby got in the boat or where he had come from. He gently put Thad's son, Destin Ettore, back in the basket and started the boat. Yes, he would keep his promise. He would keep him safe. And he would keep the details of his arrival a secret. Who, besides Charise, would believe him? He turned the boat in the opposite direction and made his way back to the shore.